BUTTERFLIES

IN

GLASS CASES

PAUL KINGSTON

Story Well Publishing
2637 Northgate Blvd
Fort Wayne, IN 46835
www.storywellpublishing.com

Publisher's Note: At Story Well we believe that every author deserves to have their voice heard, and by purchasing this book you have helped us continue to find new voices to bring to the world. Thank you for supporting us and our authors!

Butterflies in Glass Cases/ Paul Kingston. -- 1st ed.
ISBN 978-1-952876-10-3

To my lovely wife Leslie, my parents Sharon and John, and my siblings Blake and Tara:

Your endless support, ceaseless encouragement, unwavering dedication and undying love always have always, and will always be my light in the darkness, my guide through the storm, and the solid foundation upon which I know I can always rest my weary head in the deepest times of need. I will never be able to properly express my thankfulness and fortune for having been blessed enough to have you all in my life, but rest assured I would never have been able to survive this 'artist's life' were it not for you all constantly having my back. I love you all. xoxoxo

CONTENTS

Every Night Is The Same

Every night is the same...

We all sit around the breakfast table for Andy's traditional Birthday breakfast. Most families would go out for a nice dinner, or throw some kind of overly elaborate surprise party, but that's never been Andy's style.

Andy's always been the early-riser, celebrating the start of each day as though it were some sort of golden parcel filled with endless possibility. Hence why we've always celebrated with a Birthday breakfast. Truthfully, it's one of the few days of the year that Mom and Dad wake up before Andy does.

As for me, I'm the last to the kitchen table. Contrary to my brother, I've always been the night owl. Don't get me wrong, I'm not some sort of degenerate 'waste case', just a recent graduate from my Master's program who's trying to make up for lost time in college... admittedly, a little more so than usual, the previous night.

I can hear sirens approaching, blue and red lights flash all around me. I hear voices but I can't make out what they are saying. It sounds urgent. Panicked even. My head aches.

Despite my savage hangover, I force myself to smile and laugh through Andy's Birthday breakfast as he cracks his trademark cheesy jokes and blows out the candles on his giant stack of banana pancakes. I immediately wince in response to the sound of Mom and Dad's horrible attempt at harmonizing 'Happy Birthday' at full volume but still, I smile.

My mouth is filled with the taste of warm, wet copper. It's blood. I open my mouth to drool it out, but it runs up my face into my nose and eyes. I'm upside down. What blood isn't coming out of my mouth is rushing to my head, making my head pound more and more. It's excruciating, like the pain in my right shoulder.

Dad sees me wincing at the sound of their singing so he purposely moves closer to me as he shifts to scream-singing. He jokingly shakes me by the shoulders with each syllable as he tries to sound mockingly operatic. While my ears are ringing, I can't help but smile at his playful form of punishment in response to my current state.

I grit my teeth as I try to move, but I can't for some reason. Blinded by my own blood, I move my left hand towards my right shoulder to find a metal post sticking through it, warm, wet, soaked in more of my blood. I try to look at it, but my eyes are still unable to open due to the sting of blood sneaking through my eyelids, rendering me temporarily blind.

It's now nighttime and I'm taking Andy out to celebrate his twenty-first birthday right. He doesn't know that I've invited my girls, partly for fun, but mostly to make Andy blush. As the girls pile into the car, Trish leans over and kisses Andy on the cheek, wishing him a Happy Birthday in a teasingly seductive tone. Andy turns his head away bashfully, but I can see his reflection in the window, with a smile from ear-to-ear. He's always had a thing for her. He's never said anything, but the way he always shuts down when she's around is evidence enough for Trish and myself and anyone with eyes to be able to spot it.

I turn my head towards the driver's seat, using my left hand to wipe the blood out of my eyes. As my vision clears, I see that there's no one there, it's just me, alone, upside down in the passenger seat. My head continues to thrum under the presence of so much blood and the swirling sounds of sirens and the voices of the emergency personnel surrounding the vehicle as they discuss their options.

Deafening music plays at the bars and clubs we go to. Andy doesn't drink, but the girls more than make up for it. Soon my friends have surrounded Andy on the dance floor as they make a show of grinding up on him while he rigidly dances like the adorable nerd he is. I turn my head and I lock eyes with a cute stranger who offers to buy me a drink. I think to myself, 'No harm in just one', so I walk over and say, "Hi."

I call out Andy's name. My head is pounding now. The pain is spiking with each scream that I release, but still, I call out my brother's name, forcing myself to face the pain until I can find him. With each scream, I find myself getting more and more dizzy.

I have one or two more drinks, at the next few bars that we pop into, but suddenly I start to feel the alcohol digging in its claws, giving me more of a buzz than I had anticipated. Seeing Andy still distracted by the girls, I disappear to the bathroom to sober myself up with a quick bump.

I start sniveling at the fact that Andy isn't responding to my screams. The blood in my eyes is now mixing with the bitterness of my tears, stinging even more. I keep screaming through the sobs, but he still won't answer. Why won't he just answer? I start trying to crane my neck to see if I can find any signs of him.

I poke my head out of the bathroom and see Andy still dancing with the girls, so I pop back into the stall and do another quick bump, just to keep me on my toes. I feel a sudden wave of fictional control washing over me as I confidently exit the bathroom and gather the crew to move on.

I hear the emergency crews gathering around the car, their voices closer now as their tone and tempo insinuate a sudden sense of urgency. My nostrils clear momentarily and are immediately invaded by the smell of thick smoke.

As we drive to the final bar, Trish sparks up a joint. Andy passes, so the girls close the windows and hotbox the car. Andy moves his hand to roll down his window, but Trish leans forward, gently grabbing his chin and steering his face within inches of hers. His eyes widen as she gently blows a plume of smoke into his mouth as though she were an ethereal being breathing life into him, sealing it with a soft kiss. Shortly after, Andy coughs out a cloud of second-hand smoke, and it dances across the windshield of the car towards me as he violently coughs.

I start coughing as the smoke continues to thicken and fill my lungs. I can hear the crackle of flames nearby as the urgency in the voices around me continues to grow and I hear a large mechanized tool prying the passenger door open.

I slowly open the driver's side window, a plume of marijuana smoke pouring out in the face of the parking attendant. She gives me a judgmental look, but I hold back from saying anything in response.

Finally, someone responds to my screams as I feel their hands pulling on my seatbelt, making my weight rest on the metal post that's been driven through my right shoulder. Somehow, the emergency officials are able to dislodge the post from behind me before cutting my seatbelt. Despite their best efforts, gravity takes hold and I fall, slamming my head on the roof of the car below me. I can feel the broken glass in my hair pressing against my scalp.

I'm running my fingers through my damp, sweaty hair as Andy and I are dancing furiously to the last song of the night. It's a cheesy old song from when we were kids, but I specially requested it to be dedicated to him on his 21st birthday. Most of my friends have either hooked up with someone or gone home by this point, so as the bar closes, Andy and I make our way to the car, just the two of us.

I feel two men pulling me out of the car, supporting my spine as more hands soon join in. Soon, I'm clear of the car and loaded onto a stretcher. I try to ask the people around me where Andy is, but no one will answer me. I scream at them, but they still won't respond, so I just keep screaming at them until someone does.

I'm scream-singing our song as we walk towards the car. Andy sees me stumble and tells me that I'm too wasted to drive. I tell him he's an asshole before perfectly negating my argument by vomiting on myself. Like the good brother he is, he catches me as my knees give out and holds my hair until I'm finished.

Andy hands me the rest of his bottle of water to wash out my mouth before gently loading me into the passenger seat of my car. I hear him fishing the keys out of my purse, and starting the car as my eyes start to drift closed. Soon, I feel my body echoing the movements of the car as Andy drives us home.

I feel my body echoing the movements of the stretcher as its steered towards the ambulance. Someone places a neck brace around my throat as other hands attempt to tend to my wounds. My head is immobilized so all I can see are the toes of my bare feet at the base of my peripheral view.

As the stretcher continues rolling me further away, I see a single tire resting against the concrete medium of the highway with a familiar hubcap.

I open my eyes to see the hubcap of a car on our right come closer to my window as Andy changes lanes. I suddenly feel the urge to vomit again. While I have the instinct to aim for the window, I also have a momentary lapse in judgment that makes me forget that I'm in the passenger seat of my own car.

I proceed to turn to my left and vomit into Andy's lap, causing him to swerve the car, nearly swiping a vehicle on the left of us. The jarring motion of the swerve causes me to vomit a second time, staining Andy's new chinos.

I feel the jarring motion of the stretcher being loaded into the ambulance, the bouncing causing my head to thump and my stomach to turn. As the top half of the stretcher is loaded into the ambulance, I'm tilted in a way that I can see a stretch of highway covered in broken glass and streaked blood.

In the middle of it, my car is upside down and on fire. My eyes scan back and forth frantically until they finally land on something in the center of my perspective.

Andy swerves the car back and forth, until he is finally able to regain control of the car putting it back in the center of the lane. The car on our left honks angrily before pulling ahead of us for its own safety, as Andy gives an apologetic wave. I'm so impressed by his defensive driving that I pat him on the arm to thank him for his vigilance, but the alcohol and drugs have affected my dexterity and I grip his elbow a little too hard and a little too suddenly.

Suddenly, a group of men in uniform who are standing in a circle twelve feet from the wreckage part, revealing a single white sheet laying on the ground, with a large red spot in the middle of it. The sheet lies there like a hastily crafted Japanese flag as the breeze picks up, lifting the corner of the sheet just enough that I can see what's underneath it, prompting me to scream.

All I hear is Andy screaming as tires screech from all angles as we swerve directly into the path of the transport truck beside us. Taking us under its tires, almost immediately as everything moved so fast it became a blur.

My eyes blur with stinging tears as I see what's left of Andy's lifeless body lying in the middle of the highway. There are so many pieces of glass embedded in his flesh that his corpse glitters like a disco ball in the flashing red and blue lights of the emergency vehicles.

I suddenly shoot awake, sitting upright in my bed and gasping for air.

My body and sheets are both soaked in sweat. I can actually hear my back peeling off of the fitted sheet as I roll to my right to check my phone and realize I've only been asleep for half an hour.

Even after two years of intense physiotherapy following the accident, it still hurts to rest my weight on my right shoulder. The doctors told me that I'd only ever get sixty percent mobility back in that arm. In my opinion, I don't even deserve five.

I sigh with derision as I flop back over onto my back, staring at my moonlit ceiling. Some might see the dim evening lighting as serene, but the beauty of the moment is tainted by my guilt-ridden sub-conscious as much as my sheets and t-shirt are soiled with my panicked perspiration.

Regardless of how uncomfortable it feels I force myself to lie there and bathe in the physical and emotional suffering. I force myself, because I hate myself. I force myself, because this is what I deserve. I force myself, because all of it is my fault.

While others sleep, refreshing themselves so they may start anew with the rising sun, I am trapped within the prison that is my mind, tortured with my thoughts, pinned down by the chains of guilt and force-fed memories of only pain and loss.

I lie here, waiting for the start of another day of a contemptuously silent home, fueled by vindictive silence and muted hatred.

I lie here, waiting until the nightmare returns or the sun rises, only to be reminded, either way, of both mistakes and what it has ultimately cost our family.

I lie here, reminding myself of all of the stupid decisions I've made in my life, including that night.

I lie here, and I think of all of the reasons I don't deserve to live.

I lie here, hour after hour, punishing myself and hating myself, each and every single night.

Every night is the same...

CHAPTER ONE

Day After Day

I watch as the light from the sunrise peeks through my curtains, revealing itself on my wall. The orange glow slowly creeps down the wall and across the floor before finding the side of my bed. From my vantage point, it almost feels as though the daylight is scanning my room, in search of me, so that it may switch places with my subconscious and instead, torture me with the reality of another day of my life.

One floor below, I hear the familiar beep of the coffee maker, signifying a fresh pot of coffee has been prepared, courtesy of the automatic setting. The caffeinated fumes slowly spread upwards through the house, summoning my parents to the kitchen.

Despite the smell triggering my undeniable craving, I remain lying here, staring at the ceiling until I hear the traipsing footsteps from my parents' morning commotion move downstairs. Only then do I slowly emerge from my prison, throw on a hoodie, and make my way to the bathroom to brush my teeth, readying myself for whatever form today's emotional abuse may come in.

Sure enough, my entrance to the kitchen is met with tension-filled silence. Dad briefly looks up from the newspaper to acknowledge my presence, yet says nothing as he turns his eyes back to the financial pages. I can't tell if he's actually reading the paper, or merely utilizing it as a prop to justify his lack of engagement. Either way, I quietly sigh to myself and make my way to the coffee maker, pouring myself a mug of black, bitter sludge.

Before I even finish filling my mug, Mom pipes up coldly, "Make sure you leave some for me to take to work." I want to point out that there's still six cups left in the pot, but before I can, she quickly follows up, "I have a meeting this morning, and God knows we can't afford to go to Starbucks anymore."

Just like that, the first shot of the morning has been fired.

Ever since the accident, Mom loves to remind me of my culpability towards the current state of our family's finances. After my stack of medical bills, the settlement with both the truck driver and the transport company, and the cost of Andy's funeral, we've fully sunk below the poverty line, even as a dual-income household.

What can I say? Not everyone can claim that they've singlehandedly bankrupted their family with one horrible mistake.

Mom cuts the silence once more, not even bothering to lift her head from her phone as she begins her diatribe, "You know, your father and I worked our asses off for *decades* to provide this kind of life for you; and now we're forced to continue to do so day, after day. It's not easy, Patty..."

Even though I know better than to respond, somehow I can't resist against the urge to blurt out, "I know Mom. I'm trying to find work, but no one is hir-"

She cuts me off, scoffing at my response, "So it's just another item on the long list of things that are everyone else's fault but yours, huh? Jesus, Patty! You know, sooner or later, you are going to have to take accountability for your actions and do something about it!"

Dad looks up from his paper, raising his eyebrows in order to silently plead for Mom to disengage, but the boulder's already been pushed and it's gaining speed as it rolls downhill. All three of us already know where this is going, before it's even begun. While the steps may vary from day to day, it's still the same dance, set to the same horrible music.

Mom puts down her phone and pivots in her chair to face me, "See, that's the problem with your generation! None of you understand how to take ownership of your situation and *adapt*! You think the world *owes* you something, but the reality is that you have to *work* to get ahead in this world!"

I feel my fists and jaw simultaneously clenching with frustration as I coldly speak through my teeth, "I know that Mom, I just-
"

Mom's back straightens at my perceived challenge, "-Just what, Patty? You're twenty-six years old and still living at home! You don't have a job! You don't contribute towards the household! All you do is sit around and feel sorry for yourself, as if the world is going to fix the things that YOU did! But guess what? Self pity doesn't fix *anything!*"

The tears of frustration start to well up in my eyes, I do my best to suppress them but my lower lip betrays me and starts quivering as if to announce that I'm breaking.

Mom sees the moment of vulnerability and pounces on it with ferocious contemptuousness, "Great! Here comes the waterworks! Right on cue! Poor little Patty!"

Dad finally puts his paper down, quietly interjecting, "Cynthia..." He thinks the use of her name is going to give Mom pause so she can think about her current course of action, but it's about as effective as trying to stop a freight train with a lace doily.

Dad's feeble attempt at diplomacy remains disregarded as Mom continues her attack; "You know, if you would just put *half* of the effort towards working that you put into feeling sorry for yourself, you might actually achieve something! 'Effort equals Results' *that's* what your brother used to say!"

Quietly shaking his head, Dad knows that the line is about to be crossed even before Mom takes a breath, slowing herself, before quietly adding, "I just don't understand why you can't be more like-"

The rage takes me over like a tidal wave before she can even finish her thought, and I erupt, "-*What*, Mom!? Why can't I be more like what!? ANDY!? Look, I'm sorry I'm not your 'golden child' but guess what? Andy is *dead*, and he's never coming back!"

I can't tell if she's going to start crying or throw the breakfast table at me. Either way, her face fills with sorrow towards Andy's death and hatred towards my mention of it as she venomously spits, "I know he's dead!! I also know who we have to thank for that!"

Dad makes another feeble attempt at interjecting, "Cynthia! She is your *daughter!*"

Mom keeps her scornful eyes trained on me as she finally responds to Dad, saying, "Oh, I'm well aware of that, Todd. I'm unfortunately reminded of that *every single day*, but you don't see me lazing about and talking about how unfair it is, do you?"

Abruptly standing, Mom pushes in her chair and throws her linen napkin onto what's left of her breakfast before making her way towards the coffee maker, snatching her 'to-go' cup and filling it with coffee in the same way she's filled the moment with contempt.

I feel my back straighten under Mom's proximity as she pauses directly behind me and quietly imparts her final blow, inches from my ear, "It should have been you."

My head dips, I can't look at her for fear of exposing how successful she's been at hurting me. Even though I can't see her face, I know she's finding joy in my pain as she saunters out of the kitchen, humming to herself while she moves into the living room and starts to gather her things.

As Mom leaves the room, the retention wire that's holding my emotions at bay finally snaps and I quietly start to bawl in the middle of the kitchen.

I can't tell what hurts more, the fact that Mom would have said that to me with such conviction or the fact that Dad remains at the table, saying nothing to contend her opinion as he finishes his breakfast and stares at that fucking newspaper. Either way, I run back up to my room to cry in seclusion until they've left for the day.

Fifteen minutes later, I hear Mom and Dad making their way towards the front door. They have a brief heated discussion in regards to our morning exchange, but within a matter of moments the tone shifts back to conversational, exhibiting how little my emotional welfare means to either of them.

Soon after, I hear them leave the house, get into the car and set off for the day, set to the soundtrack of the local 'oldies' station.

I take a cleansing breath. The house is now empty, save for me, and my self-loathing. Still, I wait a full hour before I even open my bedroom door again.

Taking a deep breath, I descend the stairs for my day of self-induced punishment while Mom's morning sentiments haunt me, echoing through my mind. Soon, her voice will fade and her words will be added to the pile of other hurtful comments she's made in the two years since the accident.

Not long after that, they will take on my voice as part of my torturous character assassinating mantra that I will repeat to myself as a reminder of what I've done and how horrible I am for it.

As I reach the main floor, I see a small stack of mail being pushed through the slot in the front door. They cease their wiggling as the post-office worker gives them one last shove and gravity takes hold, pulling the pile of letters to the floor.

Hitting the ground, the collection of mail cascades outwards to reveal a collection of envelopes with 'Past Due' stamped on them as though they're the feathers of a Peacock of encumbrance; spreading its plumage of burden so as to remind me of the consequences of my wrongdoing.

I let out a habitual sigh as I collect the mail from the floor, collapsing the collection of envelopes back into a stack before I filter out anything addressed to me. Of the sixteen letters in my hands, three are labeled with the name, 'Miss Patricia Woodall'.

The first is a bill for the outstanding amount still owed to my Physiotherapist's office, so I don't even bother opening it. The second piece of mail is a colorful package promoting a telecommunications company's promise to 'make life simpler'. I scoff at the idea of it being so easy and toss it to the side to be recycled later.

Looking down at the third envelope, I see the return address in the top left corner that says, 'Whittaker Children's Hospital', prompting me to sigh contemptuously.

I slowly open the letter with reluctance, already predicting its contents based on the thinness of the envelope's contents. Sure enough, as I unfold the single piece of paper within, and read the opening paragraph, the only sentence that matters, pops off the page:

'*We are unable to offer you a position at this time.*'

The letter blathers on for another six paragraphs of semantic bullshit, but no matter how many diplomatic phrases they use, I know the true reasoning behind the decision.

Had the accident been on any other road, it most likely would have gone unnoticed by the general public, save for a few elderly people and potheads that watch 24-hour news channels at 4am.

But because the accident resulted in the shutdown of a major highway for upwards of six hours, thus affecting the morning commute, most people were eating breakfast while learning of my severe negligence.

Soon after that, every little detail of the accident and those involved became public knowledge... including the results of my *supposedly* confidential blood-alcohol tests. With one twist of the facts for the sake of ratings, both Andy and I were then publicly mislabeled as, 'reckless millennials driving under the influence of multiple banned substances'.

Not long after that, Andy and I became household names by way of cautionary tales used by parents, footnotes for the media's cycle, and platforms for politicians as they disgraced our family name with each promotion of their 'safe-driving' campaigns.

Despite my attempts during the trial to vehemently explain that Andy hadn't consumed anything that night, the shipping company's silver-tongued lawyer was able to twist my words against me, making it sound like I was just trying to save my brother's reputation in the hopes of a lower settlement.

Soon after, the courtroom transcript was leaked and I was publicly labeled as an enabler towards my brother's fictional addictions and falsified recklessness. A couple million social media posts later, and my professional career was in ruins as a result.

Nowadays, one quick Google search of my name by a potential employer would direct them to countless editorials about the accident, painting the picture of reckless substance abuse and negligence. Not once mentioning my Masters Degree (with Honors) in Child Psychology, or any of my scholastic/professional achievements that I had accrued over countless years of study both in and out of school.

In a fit of frustration, I crumple the rejection letter, making sure to ball it up tightly and bury it deep within the trash so as to avoid giving Mom any more ammo than she already has. As I pull my arm back out of the trashcan, I turn on the kitchen faucet to wash the coffee grounds and other trash residue off of my hand and forearm.

As I'm scrubbing away, I pause for a moment to stare at the self-induced lateral scars located just above my wrists, running parallel up my forearm like the notches on a thermometer.

Amidst the fallout of the accident I went through a period of cutting myself, not with any lethal intentions, just as a punishment for myself any time I felt any semblance of happiness or joy.

Though the scars might suggest otherwise, I'm still terrified by the entire concept of death, despite how close I may have come to experiencing it first-hand by way of the accident.

Even though I know that my Mom wishes death upon me daily, if even only in the subtext of her silence, I still hide the scars from both her and Dad for fear of having to talk about them.

Part of me fears that they would be viewed as 'yet another failure'. Another part of me fears that upon seeing them, Mom might encourage me to 'finish the job'. But what scares me the most is the thought that she might end up successful in convincing me to do so.

I suddenly break out of my trance, pulling my sleeve back down and shaking away my thoughts, before resuming my daily routine of 'busy work' to distract myself from my guilt and pain as the day passes.

First, I wash the dishes from breakfast, nibbling on what scraps are left in the process. After putting everything away, I spend a couple of hours repeatedly checking my inbox, even though I know it'll be empty before it loads, save for a few automated notifications of job postings from the sites I'm subscribed to.

By the time I get fed up with checking for responses from employers that will never come, or messages of condolence from friends that have long since stopped talking to me, I masochistically send out countless applications to various Children's Hospitals, Child Care Facilities and Schools around the country.

As I send off each application, I already know they will only result in more rejections, if I get any response at all. Still, I go through the motions so that I can at least *say* that I've tried.

As of a year ago, I even started submitting to various job postings below both my pay grade and qualifications, applying for positions as a Nanny, Au Pair, even as a Dog Sitter. While it required me swallowing my pride in the face of unemployment, it only hurt me further to not even hear back from those positions.

Finally reaching the end of the new listings that have appeared in the last 24 hours, I start cleaning the house to a borderline neurotic level. When it's all said and done, I'm left with a few hours around sunset to catch up on news stories from the day, all of which seem to suggest the impending 'end of the world'. I should be so lucky.

Soon, the sun has set and I hear Mom and Dad's car pulling into the driveway to the sound of some poppy 80's song blaring out of the speakers before it's abruptly cut off and replaced with the jingling of keys.

I quietly ascend the stairs before I even hear the keys inserted into the front door.

Remaining in my room, I actively avoid another bout with Mom until I hear both her and Dad go to bed hours later. Only then, do I sneak downstairs for a snack before I submit to the physical and emotional exhaustion of the day and return to my room.

As I lay in my bed, I rub my sore shoulder, awaiting the pending onset of my returning nightmares. Soon, they will steal my restful sleep for yet another night of subconsciously driven torture, but at least it won't be reality.

The Letter

My nightmares have successfully haunted me for yet another night, continuing my endless cycle into a new day as though life were merely a skipping needle on a warped record.

As the sunlight slowly creeps back into my room it, once again, moves down my wall, across my floor and onto the edge of my bed as though it is scanning for any signs of life.

I remain lying in my bed, waiting to hear the familiar beep of the coffee maker that will eventually summon my parents downstairs. It's gotten to the point that I can almost count down to the exact moment of its pronouncement, starting the day.

Listening to their traipsing footsteps, I wait for my parents to make their way downstairs before I depart from the seclusion of my self-induced prison and enter into what's sure to be another combative morning.

As I enter the kitchen, I am once again greeted with the awkward tension-filled silence that I've come to know so well. Much to my surprise, Mom has opted to maintain her non-verbal state this morning, as opposed to breaking the silence with her typical cutting remarks.

I can't tell if she regrets how far yesterday's fight went, or if she has simply become as emotionally exhausted as I am at this point. Either way, it doesn't really matter. The likelihood of Mom's and my relationship being 'fixed' dissipated long ago. Her choice to not speak this morning is the closest thing to a peace offering that she's presented in months, yet somehow, her lack of engagement still hurts deeply, all the same.

After Mom and Dad have left, I resume my daily routine, save for a *few* less tears than yesterday. I'm halfway through washing the dishes from breakfast when I hear the mail slot sound out its familiar 'clink', signifying the arrival of a new stack of bills and rejection letters.

I dry my hands before making my way to the front vestibule to collect them, but before I even stoop to pick up the letters, my eyes narrow in on one envelope in particular.

While its dimensions are somewhat standardized, the envelope itself appears withered with age, slightly yellow in color with browning edges, as though it has been passed through a real-life sepia filter. As I pick up the collection of mail, I marvel at the distressed roughness of the envelope's fibers, especially in comparison to the smoothness of its bleach-white colleagues.

As I stand back up, I mindlessly stack the other pieces of mail under the object of my obsession as I find myself lost in the flawless penmanship with which the name and address have been written. I'm so mesmerized in the artistry of the lettering that it takes a full minute for me to realize that it's addressed with my name.

I place the stack of mail on the kitchen counter to be sorted later before realizing that this odd envelope has no return address written upon it, let alone other markings or stamps that would signify it had gone through the federal mail system.

It's almost as though this specific letter has somehow stowed away with our other mail, going unnoticed by the Postal Workers Union, yet arriving at its destination just the same.

My brow furrows with intrigue as I slowly hook my index finger between the sealed layers on the back before gently prying apart the dried adhesive that keeps the envelope sealed.

Inside is a hand-written letter on paper that looks twice as old as the envelope it came in. Upon the paper, is an extensive letter with the same flawless, cursive penmanship that was used to address the piece of mail.

The simple sight of the page is overwhelming, prompting me to realize that I haven't even *seen* a handwritten letter since back when I was at summer camp, twelve years ago. I had become so used to typed rejection letters and submission emails that even picturing someone taking the time to sit down and handwrite *anything* feels foreign.

Nevertheless, I begin reading:

Attention: Ms. Patricia Woodall,
I was once told that a letter must open with well wishes to the
Recipient, so that being said, I hope this letter finds you well.

I can't help but smirk at the transparent insincerity of the opening line, however I get the distinct feeling that its humor is unintentional.

Customary pleasantries aside, I shall get straight to the point.
The purpose for my writing, is to present you with an offer of
employment.

I feel my eyes pop open as the previous sentence is translated in my mind. I've received so many rejections over the past while that I literally need to take a moment to comprehend what has been written, before I can move on.

The position, upon your acceptance, would be to serve as an
assistant to the matriarch of the Morgan household, with the
intent of helping to maintain the home, thus lightening the
workload.

Admittedly, the initial description of the position lacks any form of prominence. The combination of the mention of house-work and an archaic title of, '*matriarch of the household*' and I find myself wondering how deeply 'old world patriarchy' runs in the Morgan family home. Nevertheless, a job is a job, so I continue reading.

Your duties will include: cleaning, running errands, and
occasional supervision of the Morgan children (assigned at
the discretion of the Matriarch of the home).

Despite the duties of the household sounding somewhat mundane, they have peaked my interest by mentioning the prospect of working with children again, even if it's as a glorified maid.

*You will be compensated fairly in addition to receiving
complimentary lodging for the duration of your stay.*

I feel my back straightening, not only at the mention of 'fair compensation', but at the mention of lodging as well that would allow me some time away from this toxic household. Something that I'm sure my parents would appreciate as much as I would.

*While there are concerns about the disappointingly sparse
nature of your previous employment history, your educational
background appears adequate enough to compensate for your
shortcomings.*

While I'm more than a little offended by my Masters degree being described as 'adequate enough', I'm still impressed at the level of research they have clearly put into me, not to mention their assumed willingness to look past my publicized transgressions to see the value of my qualifications.

*I am confident that you will accept this position, all things
considered. Based on that assumption, your travel
arrangements have already been attended to and have been
listed on the detailed itinerary included with this letter. Please
plan accordingly, as this offer is somewhat time-sensitive.*

Part of me cynically wonders why a 'time-sensitive offer' would be sent by standardized mail, but the thought quickly leaves my mind as the information sets in and I find myself practically salivating at the idea of employment after all of this time.

While pre-arranging travel plans is rather presumptuous on their end, I can't help but concede to the fact that they're not wrong in assuming I'll accept the position. In my mind, I've already accepted the job, packed my bags and made my way out the door.

I do my best to mute my excitement, so as to contain myself as I read the final paragraph, fearful that this is where they will reveal that it was all an elaborate ruse.

*I will be expecting your arrival at the Morgan Estate this
<u>Friday, the Nineteenth of June</u> at precisely <u>Three O'Clock</u> in the
afternoon. Should you fail to arrive by that time, I shall perceive
this offer as forfeit, and will move on to the next candidate.
Sincerely,
Ms. Rosalie Pierre*

Despite the cold rigidity of the letter's closing, I'm smiling for
the first time in a long while. Whether the smile is coming from
the little victory of sudden employment, or the idea of finally escaping this cyclical existence is, frankly, immaterial.

But sure enough, self-doubt kicks in and I start to worry that
I've misread something, somehow misinterpreted this letter
through a subconscious veil of desperation.

I quickly read the letter again, and then a third time, frantically
searching for the part that would reveal that this was, in actual
fact, just another rejection letter. Much to my surprise, it remains
the same.

I even have a sincere moment of questioning as to when I had
applied for this position, but quickly brush the inquiry aside as I
accept the fact that I lost track of the countless applications I've
sent out, months ago.

I'm so lost in the confusion surrounding the mysterious letter
that it takes me a full ten minutes to move on to the itinerary card
that is still in the envelope. As I remove the card and read it, I
realize that a car service has been scheduled to pick me up at 5am,
tomorrow morning.

I immediately run upstairs to start packing, not knowing if I'm
packing for a week, or a year. Three hours later, my suitcase is
bursting at the seams, as I drag it down the stairs towards the
front door.

As I'm descending the stairs, the wheels of my suitcase rhythmically thump on each step so hard that it almost sounds like a
slowly building rally drum at a sporting event, acting as the
soundtrack to my sudden growing sense of worth. I can feel my
heart beginning to race and find myself wondering if this is how
Andy felt every morning, when he was alive.

I fly through the rest of the day, tidying up the house, including my long-neglected bedroom, and even whip up some Chicken Parmesan as a peace offering for dinner, after all, it's Mom's favorite.

Hearing my parents' car pull into the driveway, I take a seat at the kitchen table and, for the first time in years, I await their presence, as opposed to evading it.

As I wait for them to enter the house, I notice that I'm still smiling from this sudden life-changing shift. What's more, for the first time in years I don't feel the compulsion to punish myself for being happy.

Perhaps it's the prospect of change to this endless routine, perhaps it's the sudden sense of self-worth derived from employment, either way I'd forgotten how nice it felt to embrace a sense of levity as opposed to hiding from it.

Soon after the front door opens, my parents enter the kitchen. They are initially shocked at not only the smell of dinner, but also the fact that I am waiting to greet them, as opposed to hiding in my room.

Dad almost immediately comments on how good the food smells whereas Mom remains warily silent. I can tell that she's wondering what my true intentions are, so I save her the stress of her suspicious curiosity and break the news to them.

While Dad is supportive, I feel as though he's more excited about the prospect of not having to sit through any more endless screaming matches as opposed to my achievement. Mom, on the other hand, remains surprisingly quiet.

For someone who had wished me out of this world only yesterday, I would have thought she would be happier about my departure. Part of me wants her silence to be her way of saying she doesn't want me to leave, but deep down, I know it's not the case. I may be leaving, but Andy's still not coming back.

I serve up dinner and the three of us eat our way through a relatively silent meal before I offer to do the dishes. Soon after, I make my way up to my room for one last night before my travels begin.

As I lie in bed, my mind continues spinning with possibilities, imagining a house I've never seen, a family I've never met, along with countless ways that my life will be better, simply by avoiding the grating memories of my past. It's as though it's New Years Eve and I'm the drunk teenage girl that thinks the changing of the date will magically birth a 'new me', erasing all the nagging reminders of my jaded past.

The foolish hypotheticals dance around in my mind for hours, almost making me forget to sleep. Soon though, my eyelids decide to take action on my body's behalf and increase their heaviness as I slowly drift from consciousness.

The smile on my face dissipates as I transfer into a subconscious state and my levity is shattered.

With sleep, comes the reminder of the one part of me that I won't be able to leave behind, as my nightmares return like clockwork, set to the orchestra of screeching tires, twisting metal and breaking glass.

CHAPTER THREE

Travels

My nervous excitement combined with my nightmares prevent me from clocking any more than one full hour of sleep, but for the first time in years I kind of don't mind.

I spend the hours leading up to sunrise double-checking my packing list before showering and getting dressed. I attempt to head out the door without disturbing my parents' slumber but, before I even reach the first step I pause.

Much to my surprise, Dad is already standing in the vestibule in his old, ratty, navy blue bathrobe, waiting to see me off. Mom, on the other hand, is nowhere to be seen.

As I descend the last few steps, I see a single tear starting to form in his eye. I hadn't considered that my departure would affect him like this, until I suddenly realize that he's now being forced to say goodbye to his second child.

Dad remains in place for a moment as he searches to find the right words, "Patty... your mother. She, uh- She-"

Watching his struggle begins to tug at my heart, so I save him the effort, "-I know. It's okay, Dad."

He gives me a gentle smile as he pulls me in for a brief, yet tender hug, during which he simply says, "Travel safe, Patty Cake."

I smile and try to hold back the tears that begin to surface in response to the nickname he hasn't used since I was seven years old. I remember the only reason he stopped calling me that was because I had stubbornly protested that 'big girls don't have nicknames'. I didn't realize, until this moment, how much I missed it.

I grab my suitcase and exit the house, walking down the concrete path towards the old, beat-up black car that has parked at the curb and left its engine idling.

The car is covered in mud splatter, and the two wheels I can see have no hubcaps. I almost begin to assume that the driver has just returned from some sort of off-road joyride, until I see him step out of the car.

After slowly rising from the open driver's side door on the opposite side of the car, a grumpy-looking, elderly man shuffles his way around the vehicle, revealing his dated chauffeur's uniform that's about two sizes too big for his frail frame.

While he has put the effort into getting into uniform, it's clear that he considers it a mere formality, based on the fact that his top button is undone, his tie is slackened and his shirt is only half tucked.

As I approach the curb, the driver pops the trunk open before turning to begrudgingly stare at the strained zippers on the large suitcase I'm rolling behind me. I offer to save him the trouble of loading my bag, but he curtly ignores me and seizes the suitcase by the handle. Grunting ferociously, he lifts it into the car in one smooth motion and slams the trunk shut with the fervor of a man half his age.

Despite his insistence to go through the motions of loading my bag for me, the formalities cease there. The driver then pivots sharply and shuffles back to the driver's side door, echoing his previous grunt as he bends at the knees to get in.

I slowly open the door to the backseat on the passenger side, giving one last wave to Dad who's now standing in the open front door's frame. I can't help but think of how many times the sight of my father standing outside in his old robe embarrassed me. In this moment though, it's a symbol of love that I haven't felt in some time.

My eyes quickly scan the upstairs windows of the house in the hopes that Mom cares enough to at least glance out at my departure. While I see no silhouettes against the sheer curtains, I choose to tell myself that she's watching, so as to enjoy the moment as opposed to reverting back to the familiar feeling of pain.

I finally get in the car, waving goodbye to Dad as he slowly reenters the house. No sooner do I have the door closed than the driver pulls away from the curb, and begins moving down the street.

The motion of the car alone is enough to make me suddenly begin to sweat. Reflexively, I scramble to do up my seatbelt before he makes his first turn, trying to keep myself as calm as I can, despite having not been in a car since the accident.

Soon, we have left my childhood street and departed the neighborhood that I grew up in. Shortly after that, we reach the edge of town, driving westbound. My fears begin to subside as I start to reflect on the fact that I can't even remember the last time I actually travelled outside of the city limits.

Amidst my quiet contemplative silence, I lean slightly forward in an attempt to engage the driver by asking, "So... where, exactly is it that we're going?"

I see the driver's eyes glance at me via the rearview mirror, but he says nothing. Something about his gaze tells me that he understood my question, but he is consciously choosing not to respond. I take it as a not-so-subtle hint that this is information that I should already know. That, and it's clearly his preference to not engage in small talk.

As the car continues to navigate the streets at the edge of the city, I suddenly realize that we are taking a right turn, towards the onramp to the Highway and my terror resurfaces with the force of a hurricane.

Even now, sitting in the security of the back seat with a, presumably, professional driver at the wheel, I can't help but firmly grip the door handle until my knuckles turn white as I try to ignore the memories that are flashing through my head.

I feel the sweat on my forehead beginning to converge into large drops that trickle down the sides of my face as we merge into the fast-moving traffic. With each lane change, my mouth feels increasingly devoid of saliva. Soon, I start to have trouble controlling my breathing, and then start to panic because my breaths are getting shorter and shallower which, of course, only intensifies the symptoms further.

I catch the driver glancing at me once more via the rearview mirror. Though he can see my clear state of anxiety, he still says nothing as he turns his attention back to the road with a not-so-subtle disapproving shake of the head.

Realizing that the driver has likely interpreted my panic attack as my questioning of his ability to operate a vehicle, I quietly use as many calming methods as I can remember as I try to suppress my panic and overcome the anxiety attack on my own.

I stare at a fixed point on the floor and try to rid my mind of all thought as I force myself to breathe rhythmically. As I do so, I imagine the incoming air as positive particles that glow with white light and the outgoing air as the dark, black matter of negative feelings.

While admittedly a hokey method derived from a self-help 'guru', I feel my symptoms slowly beginning to subside. I continue to attempt grounding myself until I feel my breathing return to normal and my lungs filling with air, only then do I attempt to distract my mind by turning my head to the right and watching the scenery in the distance go by.

For a moment, I find myself watching the flight of a bird of prey as it gracefully circles over a distant farm field, but just as the serenity of the moment starts to find me, a large transport truck passes mere feet from my window, causing me to audibly gasp as I direct my attention back towards the floor.

I revert back to my breathing routine, trying to quell the nattering voices of my memories, but my attempts at cheating my mind are proving feeble against, what feels like, the monumental speeds we're traveling at.

I try closing my eyes tighter, but that only causes a myriad of images to flash through my mind. Images of broken glass, fire, and Andy's body dance through my head like a sadistic slideshow set on high speed.

Nevertheless, I remain stubborn and continue forcing myself to focus on my breathing, reminding myself that the feeling will pass with time. With each passing moment, I start to feel the spell of anxiety incrementally subsiding.

Quietly, I fish out my phone and attempt to unburden my mind from my surroundings by loading up a brainless, slow-paced game. Thankfully, it's enough of a distraction that I'm able to pass the better part of an hour before I can feel my phone starting to get hot, prompting me to put it back in my pocket.

By the time I look up again, we have pulled off the main

causeway, and onto a more rural version of the highway with two lanes on either side of a solid line. In place of the smooth asphalt of the highway, this road is roughly paved with a cheap combination of tar and gravel.

Despite the shift in road conditions, the driver maintains the same speed as before, causing the entirety of the car to start vibrating as it navigates the coarse terrain. While most might feel the onset of carsickness as a result of the steady vibrations, I find a strange sense of comfort in it, the tires on the rough road acting as a reassurance of the presence of traction.

I feel the muscles in my body ache as they disengage from their sustained level of strained tension. While I have focused primarily on my psychological state for the better part of the journey, I have practically ignored my overwrought physical state until we exited the highway.

Taking a moment to flex and un-flex my right hand that has been feverishly gripping the door handle, I use my left to massage the sore spot in my right shoulder, tilting my head back and forth a couple of times to stretch out my neck.

The ache all over my body slowly begins to subside. With the absence of other cars on the road, I find my attention drifting out the window once more, but this time, less afraid to acknowledge the speed with which the scenery is passing us by.

Before I know it, the sun is in the middle of the sky and we are down to a single lane road, surrounded by nothingness. No buildings, no construction and, most importantly, no transport trucks... just pure, untouched Nature.

Whether it's the sudden relaxation of the tension in my body, the lack of sleep, or the gentle rocking of the car, I suddenly notice the scenery around me going fuzzy as my eyelids start to get heavy.

Despite trying to fight it, my body relaxes against my better judgment, as it slowly gives in to sleep's siren song.

Mom, Andy and I are sitting around the breakfast table as Dad brings over a stack of banana pancakes with candles in the top.

Andy makes a wish and, with a smile on his face, blows out the candles as Mom and Dad launch into their off-key rendition of "Happy Birthday".

I'm suspended upside down. I can hear sirens and see flashing lights. Panicked voices surround me and I can smell fire, but I don't know where I am.

Dad sings a little louder as he shakes me by the shoulders to subtly make fun of me for being so hung over. I smile through the headache and even laugh at the gesture.

Blood runs into my eyes and I feel something in my right shoulder. I desperately struggle to get free, but I can't move. I wipe the blood out of my eyes, and turn towards the driver's seat, but Andy's not there.

Andy and I are getting into the car for his 'big night out'. As we pick up the girls, I can see him smiling. Trish gets in and kisses him on the cheek, causing him to blush with equal parts excitement and bashfulness.

I call out Andy's name, but he won't answer. Why won't he answer? I feel the mixture of tears and blood stinging my eyes, when hands start to reach into the car, trying to cut my seatbelt and get me out before the flames spread.

We hit the bars, I drink too much, do a couple of bumps and vomit on myself. Andy takes my keys and gets into the driver's seat. He patiently drives us home. When I vomit into his lap, he carefully avoids a near collision with the car on our left, waving an apology to them as they honk and pull ahead of us.

I'm pulled from the car, and loaded onto a stretcher, but something feels off. Something about this dream feels different. Paramedics swarm the stretcher I'm strapped to, throwing verbal commands back and forth between them. I keep calling for Andy, but he's still not answering.

I try to pat Andy's arm in thanks, but accidentally grip his elbow too hard and too suddenly, swerving us to the right and into the path of an oncoming transport truck.

As the stretcher is lifted into the back of the ambulance, I suddenly find myself standing over the white sheet with the red spot in the middle of it. I look down to my wrists and see that my scars have broken open, spilling my blood onto the ground where it mixes with Andy's.

The deafening sound of twisting metal, screeching tires and breaking glass surrounds me. Everything I see is a blur of motion making me feel dizzy and nauseous.

The wind picks up and lifts the sheet. Where, normally, I would expect to see Andy's twisted and torn body beneath the sheet, I instead see a large crow emerge, flying towards me with intent as malicious as its speed is immeasurable.

I awake with a start, to find myself still sitting in the backseat of the black car. The elderly driver glances into the rearview mirror before rolling his eyes with derision towards yet another bout of audible panic from the 'snowflake' in the back seat.

Taking a moment to reacquaint myself with reality, I turn my gaze to my surroundings and see that we are now on a dirt road in the middle of nowhere.

I pivot in my seat, scanning the forests on either side of the road, trying to find my bearings. The plentiful nature of the oak trees on either side forbids me from seeing much further than the crudely dug ditches that act as a hastily drawn barrier between the road and the wilderness.

Rubbing my arms in an attempt to calm my lizard brain's residual sense of panic from the dream, I once again reach over and grab the handle on the car's door for stability as the driver takes a sharp turn. As the car careens to the right, I see that the only thing marking the hidden driveway are odd carvings on the trunks of the trees at either side of the entrance.

With the shift in direction, so too shifts the terrain on which we travel. The parallel tire tracks we now follow, wind through the woods as though they were carved by a giant snake who chose to adorn its path with occasional puddles of mud to accent the imperfections of the ground beneath it.

The driver traverses the uneven trail with a consistent speed, while my grip on the door handle continues to tighten. I place my other hand against the ceiling of the car's interior to protect my head as I violently bounce in my seat, echoing the movements of the back half of the vehicle.

Only now, do I learn why the car was so filthy upon arrival and why it had no hubcaps on its wheels... we must be getting close to the destination.

Soon, we pull into a small clearing, barely big enough for a three-point turn, and the driver pulls the car to a halt, putting it into park but leaving the engine idling as he exits the vehicle. With confusion, I open the door beside me to mirror his movements and get out of the car as well.

The mid-afternoon sun is as blinding as the sound of the cicadas is deafening. I look around the small clearing only seeing oak trees. No signs of a house, or any other signs of civilization for that matter. I start to wonder if the driver is confused... Then I start to worry that he's not.

My sadistic imagination suddenly kicks in, instantly envision a handful of ways that this man will attempt to kill me as I turn to see him walking around the car, scowling at me.

I take a defensive step back to maintain my distance from the driver's approach as a look of derision washes over his face in response to my retreat, showing that he couldn't be less interested in attacking me, let alone quelling my fears by clarifying his intent.

Instead, the driver silently opens the trunk and drags my suitcase out, letting it fall to the ground with a 'splat' as it lands in a substantial mud puddle. Glancing at me once more with an unimpressed look, the driver pivots and makes his way back towards the driver's side door.

Before he gets back in to the vehicle, I call out, "Wait! Where am I supposed to go?"

The driver pauses at the open door with one leg already in the car. With a contemptuous sigh, he extends a crooked finger towards a large oak tree behind me. I turn to see that the tree has a similar odd carving on its trunk, like the ones at the entrance to the hidden driveway.

Before I can even turn back around to thank him, I hear the driver's door slam shut and the car pulls out of the clearing, spinning its tires on the soft ground and showering my suitcase with even more mud.

I quietly mutter, "Thanks!" but it comes out sounding more sarcastic than even I had intended to let on. Thankfully, I'm the only one around to hear it.

Slowly, I tilt my suitcase upright, trying to wipe off what mud I can in the process. I extend the telescopic handle and attempt to drag it by its wheels, but within ten paces, I realize the ground is too soft for the miniature rubber wheels to render themselves functional.

I silently curse myself for over-packing as I use both hands to drag the behemoth bag towards the tree with the carving to figure out where it will supposedly lead me.

As I approach the tree I take a moment to examine the carving on the trunk. It looks like a pinwheel with three separate extensions that take the form of legs below the knee; in the center of the symbol, a perfect triangle.

I take a moment to admire the detail with which the symbol has been carved, before realizing that there is a path behind the tree that leads off into the woods, over countless hills and roots.

Begrudgingly, I pick up my suitcase with both arms and begin to traverse the uneven path, already tripping and falling not even three steps in.

Within an hour, my arms, legs and back ache, and there are still no signs of the Morgan Home, outside of the occasional tree with the tri-foot symbol that marks the trail while simultaneously mocking me as though it were signifying an endless path.

I let my suitcase fall to the ground and opt to sit upon it, taking a moment to catch my breath while rubbing my right shoulder if even for an ounce of relief from the searing pain. Amidst the sounds of the breeze amongst the oak leaves, I begin to wonder if all of this was just Mom's clever ploy to exile me from the city.

Taking a deep breath as I push the thought from my mind, I suddenly realize that the sun has already crested the middle of the sky and begun the latter half of its journey. I fish my phone out of my pocket to find that it's already a quarter to three.

I think back to the details of the mysterious letter, remembering the stern mention that if I don't arrive by three pm, sharp, 'the offer will be perceived as forfeit'. Thus, this entire laborious commute would be rendered as moot and even worse... I would have to go home and face Mom's judgment at my inability to hold the one job I had.

Pulling up my contact list with the intent to call the Morgan home and let them know I'm on my way, I quickly realize that there wasn't a phone number provided. Even if there were, it wouldn't matter anyway as I then notice that my phone has no signal, and my battery is at seven percent.

With no other options, I quickly collect myself as best as I can. I force my aching body to stand and grab my suitcase once more, double-timing it over the rough terrain for another ten minutes until I see the tip of a pointed brown roof in the distance, peaking out over a somewhat substantial hill.

The angle of the roof is sharp and its shingles are coated in a thick layer of dried oak leaves that have fallen upon it; likely from the single giant oak tree at the back of the house that looks as though it's grown through the home, at this angle.

Just when my sense of relief begins to kick in at the sight of my destination, the alarm on my phone sounds off, signifying that it is now three o' clock, and I'm still staring at the bottom of this monumental hill before me, facing termination from my position before the job has even begun.

CHAPTER FOUR

MS. PIERRE

I reach the crest of the hill, gasping for air as a result of the grading being far steeper in actuality than I had initially perceived from the hill's base.

Lugging my suitcase up the tail end of the embankment, I turn and see a small clearing before me with the Morgan home situated at the other side, laid out in all its immensity.

Even from this distance, the home seems gargantuan. The sheer grandeur of the sprawling estate, when set against the backdrop of the undisturbed oak forest is, in a word, breathtaking.

While the presence of a massive oak tree sprouting out of the back half of the property should theoretically dwarf the sight of the house by comparison, it only seems to compliment the grandeur of the entire estate as a whole.

Similar to the large canopy of the oak tree, the graded roof of the Morgan home extends twice as far as I had initially perceived. The distance with which the roof reaches out towards the forest on either side makes it almost look as if the house is performing some sort of structural curtsy, welcoming any and all visitors to the remote, and uniquely designed property.

The architectural style of the house is somehow a combination of both Victorian and Colonial styles. The prominent frame of the home is comprised of dark wood, almost black, seemingly naturally so as I realize with my closing proximity that it's not painted. Between each sturdy, dark beam of the house's frame are thin planks of grey wood, presumably gathered from the clearing that was made to erect this gargantuan structure.

While the planks look as though they are intended to be a stylistic grey, there is a certain aged nature to them, gently warping wherever water has gathered over the years.

As I continue to approach the home, one thing suddenly catches my eye. Despite the failing integrity of the grey planks from a combination of water damage and age, there is not a single sign of vines, moss, or mold anywhere on the house's facade. It's almost as if the aged home has been dropped into the middle of the forest prior to my arrival.

In front of the house, leading up to the door, is a pleasant winding path of circular stepping-stones that have been as carefully embedded into the earth, as they have been rounded, smoothed and polished before being placed there.

My eyes follow the stone path towards the large, charcoal grey, front door of the home. Standing in front of the door is an elderly woman, wearing a black lace dress, staring at something in her hand while tapping her foot impatiently.

I struggle to bring my suitcase across the remainder of the small clearing between us as I call out to her, "Hello? I'm here! I'm so sorry, I had some trouble with my bag on the path!"

The elderly woman looks up from what I can now see is her pocket watch. Her face shows that she is unimpressed, even from this distance. As she scowls towards my tardiness, she purses her lips in frustration, accenting the wrinkles around her mouth, making it abundantly clear that smiling is not one of her favored past times.

The woman's tightened lips part in the middle as she forgoes any formal greeting and lashes out in a stern Irish lilt, "I believe the letter *distinctly* stated three o'clock. Were my instructions not clear, Miss Woodall?"

I pause for a moment, taken aback by her abrupt, cold greeting. Despite feeling instinctually defensive, I remind myself that this is the only job offer I've received in years and opt to politely concede, "No, no. Your instructions were great; flawless even. It was entirely my fault. I didn't account for the walk. Kind of overpacked too, I guess."

The woman shifts her weight to one side to peer around me at my mud-covered suitcase, pursing her lips once more; she raises a single eyebrow as she rhetorically states, "Perhaps your *bag* would be better left outside until you have had a moment to clean it?"

I do my best to contain my growing frustration, letting go of the suitcase so it hits the ground hard enough to make my point for me while still seeming incidental. I step forward, barely touching the first of the three steps leading up to the front door when the elderly woman puts a single crooked index finger up in front of my face, adding, "Ah, ah! Your shoes as well, Miss Woodall."

I look down to my mud-covered sneakers, then look back up to see a single raised eyebrow of impatience staring back at me with the utmost sincerity.

Slowly crouching down, I say, "Of course," as I begrudgingly oblige her request, untying my laces and kicking each shoe towards my suitcase. Once I've kicked off my second shoe, I follow up the action by somewhat cynically stating, "We wouldn't want to mark up the floors."

For the first time in our short exchange, I see the elderly woman's face relax slightly in response to my retort. Only once we're inside, standing on flawlessly buffed mahogany floorboards do I realize the release of her tense expression was based on the false assumption that my statement carried some semblance of literality.

The moment I close the door, the elderly matron begins her, clearly rehearsed, half-hearted spiel as the intro to her tour, "*Welcome* to the Morgan Estate, Miss Woodall. I am the matriarch of the household, *Ms.* Rosalie Pierre."

I extend my dirty hand to shake hers as I say, "Nice to meet you, Miss Pierre."

Her eyebrow rises once more as she corrects me, "It's *MS.*" She then turns her scowl towards the mud caked onto my extended hand, responding to my offer with a disgusted glare as she not so subtly suggests, "Why don't we begin our tour in the powder room?"

I take the not-so-subtle hint and feign admiration towards the small bathroom off the vestibule before using the sink to thoroughly wash the mud off of my hands. As I do so, I make sure to keep my back turned to *Ms.* Pierre so she can't see the scars on my forearms while my sleeves are rolled up.

Once my hands are dried and my sleeves return to my wrists, concealing my dark secrets, I exit the powder room to find Ms. Pierre looking at her pocket watch once more.

Without a word, she quickly pivots and continues her tour, leading me towards the kitchen as she launches into her precision-driven diatribe, "As stated in the letter, your purpose within these walls will be to assist me in all matters of the Morgan household. Duties will include, cleaning, running errands on my behalf, and occasional supervision of the Morgan children... but *only* when I deem it to be necessary."

While I feel the impulse to cynically remark at the odd nature of the last portion of her statement, I suddenly find myself speechless as I walk through the door to the kitchen. Not only is it one of the biggest kitchens I've ever seen, it's one of the biggest *rooms* I've ever seen. I'm immediately intimidated by the grandeur of its design.

Directly in front of me is a large kitchen island with a sink reaching as wide as it is cavernously deep. Mirroring the shape of the kitchen island is a wrap-around countertop with a carefully polished grey stone backsplash that's almost reflective with its level of cleanliness.

To my left is a large dining table that has enough space to accommodate at least ten people, yet around the table are only four high-backed chairs, two of which are set side by side, the other two positioned at either end of the lengthy table.

While the room is brightened by the small amount of natural light that's able to sneak through the canopy of the immense oak outside, I assume the moments of natural illumination are minimal from day to day, as made evident by the lack of any plants, herbs or other forms of natural life one might expect to find in the kitchen of a remote home such as this.

The complete absence of greenery throughout the kitchen almost gives the room a cold, emotionless feeling that echoes both the predominantly grey and black motif as well as the general demeanor of the tour guide who is leading me through it.

As she cruises around the room with expediency, Ms. Pierre makes a point of directing my attention towards the pantry, and the various contents of each cupboard and drawer.

I try to take note of everything she mentions, as best as I can, when she finally summarizes this leg of the tour by saying, "Of course, *I* will be cooking the majority of the meals as the children have *very* particular tastes. You needn't worry yourself with memorizing the layout just yet."

As Ms. Pierre turns her back to me and leads me through another door, I secretly roll my eyes at the fact that the sizable portion of information that I was feebly struggling to track has now been rendered utterly moot.

Next, Ms. Pierre takes me into the living room, or 'salon', as she calls it. The room is painted dark green, which flows flawlessly with the mahogany bookshelves. Upon the shelves is a collection of leather bound, antique books that act as the perfect accent to the dark green leather chairs and couch set around the immense stone fireplace.

In the middle of the seating area is a large, polished, wooden table with a sublimely, beautiful sculpture of a leafless oak tree set in the center. At the top of the sculpture are winding, bald, iron branches sprouting out in a lateral fashion, mirroring the patterns of its exposed spindly, iron roots at the bottom that connect the sculpture with the block of granite at its base.

While the small, yet wide, sculpture covers most of the center of the table, I can see the edges of a beautifully crafted coat of arms embedded into the table's surface peeking out from underneath the block of granite.

Most of the crest is hidden from view, but I can still see the base of a shield, and the letters 'M' and 'N' on either side. I quietly wonder to myself why such a patiently crafted and polished family crest would be purposely hidden beneath such a sculpture, but I quickly opt not to inquire or comment on it, for fear of coming across as invasively curious on my first day.

Ms. Pierre takes position in the center of the room and I can't help but notice how much her surroundings seem to age her. Standing amidst the archaic books and old leather furniture, she almost looks like the subject of a photograph stolen from time.

The black lace dress that Ms. Pierre is donning only seems to add to the dark intrigue of the image before me, making her look as though she's a grieving widow, trapped in a moment of eternally silent contemplation.

I continue scanning the room, noticing a small sunroom

beyond the 'salon' that looks out onto the back half of the property. While I can only see a small sliver of the area beyond the windows, it's enough to see that the entire area is overgrown with roots and littered with fallen branches. It becomes abundantly clear that this portion of the property has been long neglected, likely the reason why it has been excluded from the tour.

Ms. Pierre abruptly clears her throat, seizing my attention once more and directing it towards an oil painting that's hanging above the fireplace's mantle on the opposite side of the room.

Upon the large canvas is a depiction of an archaic tall ship fighting a losing battle with a violent storm as it smashes into the jagged, rocky shore; the bodies of the ship's crew splayed upon the angry rocks and littering the turbulent waters. To say the imagery is graphic and dark in nature would be an understatement, to say the least.

My eyes naturally narrow in contemplation of the idea of such a violent painting being hung in a home with small children. Ms. Pierre presumably interprets my look of contemplation as one of intrigue, as she suddenly launches into the story of the image with deeply rooted passion.

"Centuries ago, a ship departed from Europe with intentions of sailing to the 'New World'. Some say, the ship was cursed by Death before they had even launched from the European shoreline. According to the crew manifest that was found decades after the fact, one third of the crew had already perished by the time the ship had gotten only halfway across the Atlantic."

As Ms. Pierre's story builds, I can't help but smirk a bit at how her Irish accent becomes more noticeable with each detail, making her sound like a retired pirate downing a glass of mead as she recalls the dark, nautical tale.

"Plagued by infection, disease and countless deaths the travelers had found no signs of land. The New World quickly became less of a goal for the Captain, and more so an *obsession*. For fourteen weeks, they sailed across that Ocean, despite the Gods doing everything in their power to stop them. All the while, the Captain's obsession continuing to grow, escalating into a vindictive rebellion against the forces of nature themselves as he commanded his skeleton crew to keep sailing forward, no matter the cost."

Ms. Pierre turns towards me, adding dramatic intrigue to the moment with an intense stare. In the momentary silence, I realize that I'm hanging off of her every word.

"One night, nearing the end of their journey the ship was broadsided by a tempest squall sent from the Devil himself. Waves crashed over the deck of the ship, washing countless crewmembers into the waters of the Atlantic, cracking the ship's hull in the process. Yet still, the Captain ordered his crew to stay the course, leaving his own men behind, to be swallowed by the angry black waters of the Atlantic."

Ms. Pierre pauses for a moment, as though she is dedicating a brief silence to the memory of the fallen crewmembers, before she turns her eyes back towards the painting with sorrow for what's to come.

"Those who were lucky enough to survive the storm would soon learn that they were anything but. As the remnants of the ship's crew feverishly attempted to repair their ship while tending to their own wounds, they continued sailing forward in the blinding darkness of night. It wasn't long after that, that the Captain and his crew found the New World... rather, *it* found *them*."

I suddenly turn my eyes towards the painting; now realizing the context of the collision with the rocky shore as my mouth instinctively opens in silent shock.

Ms. Pierre gently crosses her hands at her waist as she turns towards me for the finale of the painting's tale with a sorrowful, yet intense look upon her face.

"The history books will tell you that no one survived that crash, that every member of the crew perished that night. In doing so, they would only be *half* correct. While everyone who was listed in the ship's manifest did, in fact, have their lives claimed by the Gods of the sea that night, there *was* one man who walked away. An Irish stowaway escaping European persecution had hidden in the hull of the ship amongst the bodies of the deceased. As luck would have it, the bodies of the dead were what cushioned him from the impact of the ship running aground, allowing him to be the sole survivor. Whether it was the Gods of the Sea, or the

Angel of Death itself, *something* chose to save the life of that lowly stowaway that night."

Ms. Pierre turns back towards the painting one last time as she ties it all together with a metaphorical bow, "The name of that stowaway? Pater Morgan."

In response to the finale of Ms. Pierre's tale, I release an embarrassingly uneducated sounding, "Whaaat?"

Unimpressed by my cretin's response, Ms. Pierre opts not to acknowledge it as she moves back to the middle of the room, launching into the next chapter of the family's history.

"Pater proceeded to travel inland for fear of being discovered by other ships that were sure to follow. For months on end, he travelled the land on foot, bringing him here, to this property, where he worked tirelessly to build the home that you are standing in now."

Suddenly, the weight of the statement hits me as I do the math in my head, "Hold on, you're saying that this house is over *four hundred* years old?"

Unimpressed by my poor attempt at historical math, Ms. Pierre corrects me, "*Five* hundred."

Once again, my eyes pop open in shock to the maintenance that must have been required to keep this structure standing, let alone functional, for such an extensive period of time.

Strolling out of the 'salon', Ms. Pierre speaks to me over her shoulder as if to beckon me to follow, "Since the days of Pater, the Morgan bloodline has always resided within these walls. Generation, after generation, have been born, raised and educated within this home. To say that they are strong believers in tradition would be an understatement."

I continue scanning each room Ms. Pierre leads me through, my focus dancing back and forth as though my head is on a pivot. Soon, I begin to notice the complete absence of photographs in each of the rooms we wander, a subtle detail, but odd nonetheless for a home with such a supposedly rich history.

I wait for a break in Ms. Pierre's casual historical notes, before I inquire, "Where are all the photographs?" I can tell she's confused by the inquiry based on her sudden pause, so I clarify, "I mean, if countless generations of family have lived in this home, and the Morgan family is so rooted in tradition, you would assume there would be at least *one* or *two* photos of their ancestors kicking around. I haven't seen *any*."

There's a momentary silence that hangs in the air as Ms. Pierre contemplates her response, "The Morgan family have never been the kind of people to keep photographs. I guess vanity is simply not one of their core beliefs."

Despite her explanation, I can't help but still find it odd that there would be no signs of family history aside from a painting of a crashing ship, and a coat of arms hidden beneath a sculpture, but I also hear the thinly veiled frustration in Ms. Pierre's responses, so I opt to drop my inquiry for the time being.

Ms. Pierre then leads me around another corner, finishing our circle of the main floor and reaching the front vestibule, where we had initially begun our tour.

There is a brief moment where we linger at the base of the staircase before Ms. Pierre turns to me and says, "Should you have any questions or concerns, now would be the time to voice them."

With nothing coming to mind other than the lack of pictures, I shrug as I say, "Nope. I think I'm good."

I notice Ms. Pierre raising a single eyebrow in an almost judgmental manner towards my response, before her demeanor shifts back to 'tour guide mode' and she says, "Very well. This way, Miss Woodall... It's time for you to meet the children."

Macha and Nemain

Ms. Pierre leads me up the stairs to the second floor of the Morgan home. As she does so, I can't help but notice that she is gripping the banister with enough force that her knuckles are turning white.

Naturally, I assume that she must have lost her balance one too many times in her old age, so I choose not to comment on her vice-like grip on the railing. Still, I can't help but notice that she glances over her shoulder a few times, as though she's trying to keep tabs on me for the duration of our ascension.

Finally, we reach the top of the stairs and turn right. I now find myself staring down a hallway that's so long, its perspective makes it appear to narrow with distance.

As we traverse the length of the hallway I find my eyes dancing back and forth between the staggered sconces that have been mounted on either side, dimly lighting our way with small, gas-lit flames. Were it not for having just entered from outside, I wouldn't be able to tell it was daytime, based on the complete absence of natural light throughout the corridor.

After what feels like an endless distance, especially just having traversed the walking trail with my giant suitcase, we eventually stop at a heavy-looking, wooden door on the right side of the hall.

The door is about nine feet tall, and made out of the same wood that has been used in the floorboards and the paneling on the walls. In the middle of the large door is the symbol of what, at first, looks like an artistic interpretation of a three-petaled flower.

I stand there looking at the intricate design of the symbol, noticing that it consists of a single line that weaves around itself three times before returning to where it began. Around the woven image is a perfectly symmetrical circle.

The flawless curves of the design clearly demonstrate the skill of whoever it was that embossed it during the door's creation. Even now, some five hundred years into the history of the home, the polished edges of the symbol seamlessly glow in the faint, flickering lamplight that has been cast upon it from either side.

As Ms. Pierre gently opens the large door, the soft sound of 'Für Elise' being played by a music box, trickles into the hallway as though it had been cued up in preparation for the reveal.

Entering the room, I am immediately taken aback by the sheer immensity of it. I suddenly realize that despite the length of hallway we had walked to get to the door, we've only reached the *middle* of the room. It quickly becomes evident that the Morgan children have been given the entire front half of the second floor.

As though the sheer grandeur of the room wasn't enough, I look up to see that the ceiling stretches upwards one and a half stories at its highest point, then slants downwards as it crosses the room with the same grading of the sprawling rooftop I had admired whilst crossing the small clearing.

Lining the far wall and mirroring the tapered affect of the ceiling are large stained glass windows with colorful abstract patterns. Each little pane of colored glass tints the light of day to its own shade, yet when the rays of light are combined, they give the room an almost pinkish glow.

Between each of the immense windows, and in each of the corners of the room are large, white pillars, embedded into the walls. The top and bottom of each pillar is complimented with gold detailing, and each base is embossed with the same symbol of a three-petaled flower that is so prominently displayed on the door.

At the far end of the room, centered with precision, are two identical children's beds set side-by-side. Each are perfectly made with crisp, military folds in the sheets that would suggest a borderline-neurotic attention to detail.

Were it not for the presence of the beds, one could naturally assume that this room was a private wing of the Vatican, as opposed to the bedroom of two young children.

My focus suddenly shatters when Ms. Pierre claps her hands

twice, as crisply as it is authoritative. The soft tune of 'Für Elise' suddenly goes silent under the weight of the music box's lid being slammed shut. The momentary silence is then replaced by the scurrying sound of four small feet approaching on the hardwood floor.

I have been so lost in the sheer immensity of the room that I haven't even clocked the two little girls to my right until they are already standing dutifully in front of Ms. Pierre.

I can't help but be mildly impressed at the response elicited from a simple clap of the hands, as the children stand side-by-side with their backs painfully straight. It is abundantly clear that these girls are no strangers to Ms. Pierre's routine.

As I marvel at their attentive stances, I suddenly feel my own back straightening for fear that my lacking posture will make me look like a bad influence on the first day of my employment.

Ms. Pierre proceeds to introduce me to the children in her cold, formal nature, "Nemain. Macha. This is Miss Woodall. She is the one that I spoke with you about. I trust you will ensure her stay with us is a *pleasant* one."

Both of the girls curtly nod, without saying a word. The younger of the two looks up at me with a smile on her face that is filled with equal parts excitement and mischief. She seems happy to have someone new in the home to play with.

This is more than can be said about the older of the two girls as I shift my attention and find her scowling at me warily, assessing her new sworn enemy with lament towards me for simply daring to be here.

Ms. Pierre cuts the tension short by turning and reciprocating the introduction on the children's behalf, "Miss Woodall. These are the Morgan girls. Nemain and Macha."

The smile on Macha's face suddenly fades as her older sister, Nemain, suddenly turns her scowl towards Ms. Pierre and launches into a protest on her sister's behalf, "She doesn't like to be called that! She wants to be called Em!"

Something about the explosiveness of the fire in Nemain's eyes combined with the intensity of her Irish accent gives me a start, but to Ms. Pierre's credit, she holds strong and simply says, "Macha is her *name*. That is what I shall call her."

Nemain straightens her arms in response, making little fists in anger towards the resistance from her elderly matron. Her eyes fill with venom as she stares into Ms. Pierre's eyes as Nemain's face shifts into a mischievously dark, unwavering grin.

Ms. Pierre inexplicably yells, "NO!" before containing her sudden wave of inexplicably furious discipline. She takes a moment to calm herself before adding, "Remember your *manners*, Nemain."

Despite the over-the-top eruption from her elderly Matron, Nemain doesn't flinch. Still she stands her ground, defiant in the face of authority. Suddenly, Ms. Pierre grabs Nemain forcefully by her upper arm, leading her a few steps away for a hushed, yet disciplinary discussion in regards to her behavior.

Seeing the tightness of Ms. Pierre's grip and her seemingly unwarranted use of verbal aggression in response to a simple tantrum, my instinct is to interject, separating the two for fear of the situation escalating.

I am quick to remind myself of how much I need this job. While my instincts are pure, I am feeling the impulse to act on mere supposition. I am not nearly familiar enough with Ms. Pierre or Nemain, let alone their relationship with each other to potentially jeopardize my employment over a brief flare up of anger.

As Nemain and Ms. Pierre continue holding their tense aside, I turn towards a still-pouting Macha and crouch down to eye level with her as I say, "You know, I've met a lot of people in my life, but I've never met anyone named Macha before. That means your name is one of a kind. If you ask me, that makes it pretty darn special."

Macha says nothing in return, but slowly lifts her head at the mention of being special, revealing a smile slowly breaking through her pout.

A moment later, Ms. Pierre and Nemain suddenly cease their aside, and turn to see Macha and I smiling with one another.

The sudden silence pulls my focus, and I turn my head to see Ms. Pierre raising an inquisitive eyebrow, towards me finding an alternative solution in the moment.

Nemain also appears to be somewhat impressed by my

diplomatic approach, as her scowl towards me softens slightly.

Moving towards Macha, Nemain stares into her sister's eyes for a moment, before taking a sigh of derision, and turning to me to begrudgingly say, "*Macha* wants me to tell you that she likes you."

I smile in response to the compliment and say, "Well, thank you. I like both of you too."

Despite the momentary kindness, Nemain is quick to correct me, "I said *she* likes you. I didn't say *I* did."

I patiently take the hit. While most would perceive the comment as rude or insulting, I have studied this type of behavior extensively, even writing an essay in the first year of my master's program on 'the congruency between a child's age and their simultaneous increasing resistance to sudden change'.

Smiling directly at Nemain, I calculate my crafted response, "That's okay. Take all the time you need. In the meantime though, I'm still going to like *you*."

Nemain gives pause for a moment, unsure of how to respond. She looks at me with deep perplexity, like I'm some sort of trickster or mentalist. While she's trying to act unimpressed, I can see the wheels turning as she desperately searches for a scathing retort, yet comes up with nothing.

As I stand back up, Ms. Pierre directs me towards the door, "Come, Miss Woodall. I will show you to your room."

Ms. Pierre opens the door to the children's room to escort me out. Before I leave, I turn to wave goodbye to the children. I get a smile from Macha in return, whereas Nemain, on the other hand, continues her scowl of annoyance and frustration.

I know that Nemain will still require more time to adjust her disposition towards me as we build trust between us. Truthfully, I'm okay with her naturally standoffish nature. While most would see a personality trait like that as the quality of a 'problem child', I see it for the sign of a budding, strong personality that will blossom into a sense of independence some day.

Ms. Pierre closes the door behind us, soft enough to not sound like she's slamming it, but hard enough to make a final point of who's in charge. She then quickly pivots and starts briskly leading me down the hallway, identifying the next two doors on the left as her bedroom, and then the linen closet.

We suddenly stop at the third door on the left as Ms. Pierre plainly states, "This will be your bedroom" there is a brief moment before she oddly adds, "that is, for as long as you choose to stay."

When the door is opened, I'm shown into a lavish room, smelling of lavender and rose petals, draped with as much natural sunlight as there are silks and fabrics.

Before Ms. Pierre can even tell me anything about the room, I've made my way into the center of it, and find myself leaning against one of the eight-foot bedposts that suspend the silk canopy above the queen sized mattress.

Just looking around the room, I can't help but feel like I'm in one of those movies where the humble protagonist has suddenly learned that they are the sole heir to a forgotten kingdom.

Naturally, I'm drawn to the light coming through the sheer curtains over the windows, and I promptly throw them open to see the lush branches of the large oak tree at the back of the house reaching out far enough to tickle the panes of glass before me.

While the back portion of the property that I had caught a glimpse of through the windows of the sunroom is directly below me, I can barely see it through the thick canopy of oak leaves.

I hear Ms. Pierre clear her throat from the doorway, as she purposely pops the bubble of the moment by reminding me, "Miss Woodall? Perhaps you should tend to your bag before it gets dark out?"

Snapping back to the current moment, I find myself immediately humbled by the sudden shift from a daydream inspired by the lavish surroundings, to the reality of scrubbing mud off of my suitcase.

I chuckle to myself as I think, 'this is what Cinderella must have felt like at the stroke of midnight', but quickly suppress the thought and smile politely towards Ms. Pierre as I turn to see the cold sincerity in her face.

The distaste in her glare causes my shoulders to sag slightly, with humility, as my smile fades and I say, "I'll get right on it."

I make my way down the lengthy hallway towards the top of

the stairs, when I hear Ms. Pierre call out once more from behind me, "Oh, Miss Woodall? Do mind the stairs with your bag, will you? The bannister was just recently polished."

I politely nod, before making my way outside and starting to scrub the mud off both my suitcase and my sneakers, occasionally mumbling mocking impersonations of Ms. Pierre's requests under my breath.

Thirty minutes later, there's not a single trace of mud on my suitcase or shoes. I use every ounce of strength I have left to carry my bag upstairs without having to put it down, making sure not to graze the bannister or walls in the process.

As I finally return to my designated room, my face fills with joy, once more, to find it just as luxurious and impressive as the first time I had seen it.

For the better part of two years, I had sub-consciously transitioned my bedroom at my parents' home to embody my feeling of self-loathing and imprisonment; door always closed, curtains always drawn, the general feeling of it being lifeless, drab and dark. I had completely forgotten that a bedroom could also be a form of sanctuary, inspiring feelings of comfort and serenity.

I proceed to unpack my suitcase and put my clothes away, marveling at how many drawers and cabinets there are for just one room. Halfway through the process, I quickly estimate that it would take at least seven suitcases packed to capacity to even come close to filling all of the available storage options within the room.

In the process of putting away my personal effects, I open an armoire by the window to hang up some shirts, only to find that its rack is already full of various black and grey clothes, their age clearly evident from the smell of mothballs and dust emanating off of them. Based on the similarities to the dress Ms. Pierre was wearing earlier, I naturally assume that they must belong to her and I leave them untouched.

However, given the overpowering smell permeating from the armoire, even while closed, I opt to leave the doors open to allow it to air out, moving to a smaller cabinet in the corner of the room and hanging my things there instead. Before I even know it, a few hours have passed, the sun has set, and there's a sudden, stern knock at my door.

I cross the room as an equally sharp, and somewhat impatient second round of rapping is laid upon my door, mere seconds after the first one. Ms. Pierre then calls out from the other side, "Miss Woodall? It is time for supper!"

I realize I'm still wearing my travel clothes, reeking of sweat and dirt. I sheepishly answer the door, saying, "So sorry, I completely lost track of the time. I just need a few minutes to get changed into someth-"

Ms. Pierre cuts me off by shoving a tray towards me with a silver cloche in the middle of it. I initially hesitate, thrown off by the abruptness of the gesture. It almost feels like a prison guard passing a meal to an inmate through solid steel bars.

Thrusting the tray towards me once more, Ms. Pierre impatiently commands, "Go on. Take it."

I take the tray in my hands, still wary of the coldness of Ms. Pierre's offering.

With her hands now free, Ms. Pierre then instructs, "Once you have finished your meal, leave the dishes outside of your room and they will be collected in the morning."

With the heavy tray in my hands, I can't help but ask, "What about the girls?"

Ms. Pierre looks as confused as she is annoyed by the question, as she responds with her own inquiry, "What about them?"

I try to maintain a certain level of tenderness in my voice, as I rhetorically inquire, "Shouldn't we all eat together?"

Ms. Pierre furrows her brow in response. Her facial reaction comes across as both horrified and defensive, as though I've accused her of something, "Why would we do that?"

I feel ridiculous doing it, but I explain as pleasantly as I can without sounding patronizing, "You know, to get to know each another? Share in each others' company? Communicate over a meal?"

Ms. Pierre coldly crosses her hands at her waist, taking a deep, contemptuous breath to show me it's not up for discussion before saying, "Miss Woodall... I understand you're new here, so naturally your impulse is to question everything. *However,* we have a specific way of doing things here. A *routine*. When we adhere to this routine, the household runs inherently smooth. When we disrupt said routine, things can become... *difficult*. If you don't believe that you will be able to abide such a request, then I would suggest that you pack your belongings and promptly return home."

Part of me wants to lash out in response to the insinuated threat, but I feel my arms beginning to shake under the weight of the tray, so I relent and contain my anger as I say, "I understand."

Ms. Pierre curtly purses her lips at my compliance as her eyebrow rises with confidence, "Should you choose to stay, I will begin to educate you on our daily routine tomorrow morning. A word of caution though, it will require some *adjustments* on your part. Try to remind yourself that what the children require, above all else, is *consistency*."

As she concludes her cold statement, Ms. Pierre looks past me and sees the open cabinet near the window, "Ah, you've discovered your uniforms. Good. Should you require any alterations, you can notify me in the morning, unless you would prefer to sew them yourself, of course."

Quickly turning away from my baffled facial expression, Ms. Pierre marches her way down the hall towards her room. I desperately want to get further clarification on everything from the mention of 'uniforms' to this 'routine' she speaks of, but the silver tray is quickly becoming unbearably heavy. I feel my already exhausted arms shaking and my right shoulder screaming at me, as the searing pain from within steadily increases under the weight of my meal.

I retreat back into my room and place the tray on a nearby table before pulling over a wooden desk chair and sitting down to eat, alone. Even though I haven't eaten anything since the single piece of toast this morning, I've been so taken aback by my new surroundings that I hadn't noticed how hungry I actually was, until this moment.

With heightened anticipation, I wrap my hand around the top of the cloche's handle, quickly lifting it into the air and releasing a plume of steam that acts as a temporary fog, my meal slowly revealing itself as though it were the finale to a magic trick.

As the cloud of steam dissipates, my shoulders sink and my face drains of excitement as I find myself staring at a heaping pile of lumpy mashed potatoes with two grey sausages that have been over-boiled to the point that there's a visible amount of water trapped within their casings.

On the right side of the plate, is a small pile of what initially appears to be boiled spinach. Moments later I realize it's actually fresh spinach leaves that have been drowned in the small collection of incidental sausage water. The mixture results in a pool of soupy, olive green liquid that has collected around the edge of the plate and is slowly being absorbed by the bottom layer of the lumpy potatoes.

Despite the initial reveal of the messy meal, and even after the rancid smell of the dish hits my nose, I still can't deny that my stomach is empty and screaming for anything I could put in it, so against my better judgment, I start eating.

The first few bites of the potatoes are the hardest, both literally and figuratively. I force myself to chew everything into a fine paste, mainly just to ensure that the lumps in the potatoes are *actually* made of potato and not some kind of unconventional addition to the dish.

My stomach begins to turn as I continue breaking down the potato lumps, so I decide to move on, bypassing the wet spinach and foolishly cutting into the sausages.

A small typhoon of brownish grey water suddenly pours out and intermingles with the olive-colored soup that was already filling the base of the dish. Soon, there is enough liquid on the plate that it starts to dribble over the edges, onto the tray.

As disgusted as I may be, there is a silver lining to the absolutely nauseating sight. The liquid that was contained within the sausage casings did successfully keep the meat quite moist... it's completely flavorless mind you, but nonetheless moist.

I fight my way through the two bland, damp sausages before I submit to my better judgment and move the plates to the hallway outside my door, only spilling a bit of brownish-green liquid onto the floor in the process.

Somewhat satiated, and encumbered by the residual aches and

pains of the last leg of my long day of travel, I start to prepare myself for bed, pulling out my phone charger with the intent of plugging in my device before I go to sleep.

Scanning the walls of the room I soon find that there is not a single electrical outlet in the entire room. Thinking back to my tour of the house, I don't remember seeing a single electrical appliance either.

My mind flashes back to the propane lamps in the hallway as the memory of Ms. Pierre informing me of the home's age suddenly plays through my mind. I quickly come to terms with the fact that this archaic home has no electricity, and I place my charger on the bedside table, along with my lifeless phone.

I climb onto the immense, queen-sized bed and lie on my back, like a starfish. I stare upwards for a moment, entranced by the silk canopy above me as it dances amidst a gentle draft coming from somewhere in the room. The waves of the canopy's movements are perfectly accented by highlights from the dim light of the moon, making it look like the Aurora Borealis is putting on a private show, just for me.

With a smile on my face, I let my eyes softly close as my consciousness slowly fades away. The mattress is so soft, that I feel as though I'm floating on a cloud. I'm sure I would feel like I was in Heaven, were it not for the residual smell of the over-boiled sausage and spinach water lingering in the air.

As I drift further and further from the waking world, I feel the smile on my face beginning to fade. The feeling of weightlessness is soon replaced by a wave of subconscious guilt slowly pouring forward from the back of my mind.

I feel my recurring nightmare rearing its ugly head, and I curse it for ruining the serenity of the moment. Yet still, it returns with the intent of stealing my sleep once more, reminding me that some things... are inescapable.

CHAPTER SIX

The First Night

I'm sitting back at the breakfast table in my parents' home. Mom and Andy are in the chairs across from me as Dad brings over a stack of banana pancakes with lit candles in the top, placing them in front of Andy who closes his eyes to make a silent wish, before blowing them out.

As the candles are extinguished, the entire setting falls into the darkness of night. My eyes dance around the room in confusion, only to come back to the table to find the red wax from the candles pouring over the edges of the stack of pancakes in thick, slow-moving streams, making them look as though they are bleeding.

I shift my attention towards my parents and Andy to see if they're witnessing the same thing, but they all stare back at me with blank expressions on their faces. I try to speak, only to find that I have no voice.

In response to my sudden panic, Andy tries to offer a comforting smile, but as his lips part, blood begins to pour out of his mouth and down the front of his shirt. I bolt upright, knocking my chair backwards in the process. I frantically look towards Mom and Dad for help, but soon find that, they too, have blood pouring from their mouths.

I am lucidly aware that I am trapped in a nightmare, but it doesn't stop the panic from washing over me as though all of this were real. While my subconscious has occasionally permutated the standard pattern of my recurring nightmare, it has never taken this much liberty towards change.

Soon I find myself almost wishing that the dream would jump forward to the scene of the accident, as the familiar images of the crash would pale in comparison to the sights I'm currently being subjected to.

It's then that I start to hear a soft rapping on my parents' kitchen window, pulling my attention away from my bleeding family.

As I strain my eyes to look through the darkened pane of glass, I see a large crow perched on the outer sill. I immediately identify it as the crow that had viciously flown towards me from underneath the white sheet in my previous nightmare.

Frozen in my tracks at the sight of the bird, it simultaneously ceases its tapping on the pane of glass and stares directly into my eyes with a piercing gaze from its faint amber eyes, catching the light of the moon like two shining gemstones on a black velvet cloth.

Instinctually, I back away slowly in an attempt to distance myself from the creature, but soon I feel the backs of my knees bump into the overturned kitchen chair, compromising my balance, sending me sprawling backwards, tumbling towards the floor. I close my eyes in anticipation of the impact yet somehow, I never make contact with the ground.

Slowly opening my eyes, I find myself now suspended in the air, upside down, in the wreckage of my car from the accident. Blue and red lights flash all around me, and I hear the voices of the paramedics and fire fighters in the distance, urgently calculating the safest way to remove me from the car.

I scan my surroundings and see countless pieces of broken glass splayed out on the concrete surrounding the crinkled roof upon which the vehicle is resting. I smell the smoke and the fire that is coming from the car, but this time, no one reaches in to pull me out to safety.

I try calling for help, but still find that I have no voice, as blood pours from my mouth and into my eyes.

Soon, the voices of my would-be rescuers fall eerily silent. I frantically turn my head back and forth, trying to see where they have gone, but with all of the blood and tears washing through my eyes, I can barely even see my own hand in front of my face.

My right arm unable to move, I use my left hand to wipe away the stinging mixture of fluids so I can see again. I turn my head towards the driver's seat, expecting to find it devoid of my brother as I have in past nightmares, but soon find that I am not alone in the wreckage.

Perched, upside down in defiance towards gravity, is the large crow. Despite the change in location, it continues to stare at me with the same level of intensity as it had from my parents' kitchen window.

Unable to move, I keep my eyes trained on its unrelenting amber gaze, terrified of what inevitably comes next.

It only takes a few seconds before I see the crow's beak gently open and it suddenly calls out with a deafening chorus of screeching tires, twisting metal and breaking glass as it flies directly at me with immeasurable speed and vindictive intent.

I shoot awake, sitting upright in my bed in the Morgan home. I'm as drenched in my own sweat as I am disoriented by my surroundings, forgetting for a moment where I am, and why.

My eyes dance around the room, scanning the slivers of moonlight that are sneaking in through the window, creating glowing shapes on the floor. Slowly, my head begins to clear and the answers come back to me in a flood of recognition.

I try to catch my breath as I instinctually reach to my phone on the bedside table to check the time. As I pick up the device, I am reminded that the battery is dead and there's no way to charge it in a home devoid of electricity.

Putting the phone back down, I pivot back to the center of the bed and start to remove some blankets that are draped over me in an attempt to cool myself off.

It's then that I hear the sound of faint, yet audible, crying coming from the hallway.

I slowly get out of bed, approaching my door to attempt to listen through the thick layer of wood and make sure that I'm not just imagining the sound. Sure enough, the closer I get to the door, the louder the crying becomes. Almost as if whomever it is that's the source of the noise, is directly on the other side of the door.

I grab my long-sleeved robe and wrap it around me, not only to cover my sweat-soaked pajamas, but also to hide my scars from whomever I may find sobbing at my door, be it Ms. Pierre or one of the children.

Ensuring that my scars are not visible, I quietly turn the knob and pull the door inwards, feeling a rush of cool air from the hallway flowing into my room, intermingling with the muggy air that I have just awoken in.

Much to my surprise, there is no one standing on the other side of my door.

Even more unsettling, is the fact that I can still hear the sound of the crying, only now it seems to be coming from further away.

I step into the hallway, and hold my breath in the hopes of pinpointing the source of the noise. Within seconds, I hear it coming from somewhere at the far end of the hallway, near the top of the stairs.

Tightening the belt on my robe, I slowly tiptoe down the long hallway towards the source of the sorrowful sound, but as I reach the top of the stairs, I notice that the noise has moved once more.

I can now hear the crying coming from somewhere in the downstairs portion of the house. At first, I'm reluctant to wander this new home in the darkness of night, for fear of seeming nosey, or invasive, but my curiosity soon gets the better of me.

Glancing over my shoulder to see the hallway behind me devoid of anyone else, I slowly begin to make my way downstairs, softening my footfalls as much as I am able so as to not make any noise in the process.

Once I've reached the main floor, the sound of the soft weeping pulls me through the 'salon', towards the small sunroom that looks out onto the overgrown garden in the back portion of the Morgan property.

As I enter the room, I peer through the multiple panes of glass into the darkness on the other side. Straining to make sense of the dark recesses of shadow, I shield my eyes from the soft glow of the moonlight sneaking through the canopy of the large oak tree.

Scanning the gnarled roots of the towering oak, my eyes soon find their focus to see the faint outline of the shadowy figure of a woman kneeling at the base of the tree's trunk. I move closer to the panes of glass, shielding my eyes with both hands as I try to train my sight solely on her, in the hopes of getting a better look.

From what I can see, the woman is wearing a hooded cloak from which long, stringy, grey hair hangs from her downcast head. Her hands are covering her face, but I can see her shoulders shake with each audible whimper, signifying that she is the source of the sound I've been following.

I stand there for a moment, unsure of how to approach the situation. Part of me wants to walk out into the garden to see if this woman is okay, but another part of me is concerned by the presence of an emotional stranger on the property in the middle of the night.

Slowly inching towards the glass that stands between us, I see the figure's hands suddenly move away from her face, as I watch her hood move and she slowly raises her head to look back at me.

As I feel my eyes popping open in response to being spotted by the cloaked woman, I suddenly feel a cold hand gripping my right shoulder, sending a shot of searing pain down my arm. Before I know it, I'm being whipped around with surprising force.

Frozen with fear, I now find myself standing mere inches from the cloaked woman, inside the house. I feel the urge to jump back at the shock of her sudden proximity, but I am unable to move, not only as a result of my own paralyzing emotional state, but also under the unrelenting grip of her cold, talon-like hand on my ailing shoulder.

While the cloaked woman's face remains hidden amidst the shadows of her hood, I see two familiar amber eyes softly beginning to glow from within the darkness where her face should be.

Soon, a chorus of screeching tires, twisting metal and breaking glass, pours out of the woman's hood, deafening me in the process, as the large crow emerges from the woman's hood, flying directly at me with immeasurable speed and vicious intent.

I shoot awake once more, sitting upright in my bed in the Morgan home, soaked in my own sweat and gasping for air.

I immediately curse my subconscious for its heightened level of creativity tonight, morphing its nightly tortures to something upsettingly unfamiliar and deeply disturbing.

Feeling the instinct to reach over towards my phone, I stop myself, remembering that it has no charge.

Turning back towards the center of the bed, I remove some blankets in the hopes of cooling myself off, before flopping back down onto the sweat-soaked sheets. As I lay there, I let out a contemptuous sigh towards this new form of meta-torture in the shape of a nightmare within a nightmare, and lament the fact that even amidst a luxurious setting such as this, my ability to sleep has only gotten worse.

I roll back and forth for the better part of an hour, unable to make myself comfortable as I am haunted by the images of the cloaked woman and that Goddamned crow.

Just as my eyes start to get heavy once more, I hear a soft knock at my door. I lift my head to make sure I'm not imagining it, and sure enough, another soft knock sounds out mere moments later.

I quickly jump off the bed, pulling the covers up to hide the sweat-soaked sheets and wrapping my long-sleeved robe around me, making sure to pull down the cuffs to cover my scars before reaching for the doorknob.

As I turn the knob and slowly open the door, I feel a rush of cool air enter from the hallway. I look down to find Macha standing at my door in her nightgown. I can already tell from her face that something is wrong.

Kneeling down to eye-level, I softly ask, "Are you okay, Macha?"

She dips her head a bit, seemingly embarrassed as she admits in a faint whisper, "I had a bad dream."

I smile at her, "You know what? I did too. You wanna come in and talk about it?"

She smiles at the offer and immediately runs into my room, jumping up onto the bed and sitting cross-legged in the center of the mattress.

I softly chuckle in response to her excited fervor as I close the door quietly, and grab a seat on the edge of the bed to help dispel her fears as a result of her nightmare.

At this point of the night, the least I can do is try to help *one* of us get some sleep.

CHAPTER SEVEN

The Next Morning

I wake up suddenly, to find that the sun has already fully risen.

As I sit up, I realize that I'm lying on top of the blankets, still wearing my robe that I had put on in the middle of the night when Macha had knocked on my door, yet when I scan the room, I find no signs of her.

Naturally, I assume that sleep had inevitably found me before her, leading to the onset of juvenile boredom resulting in Macha returning to her own room at some point during the night.

I reach over to habitually check the time on my phone only to remember once more that it has no charge. Not like it matters. It's not like I have any friends looking for me, or parents that are worried if I got here safely.

Getting off the immense bed, I dress myself in a pair of old sweatpants and my hoodie with the thumbholes I've cut into the cuffs (to make sure the sleeves stay down). I yawn while stretching out my back and can't help but notice how well rested I feel.

Somehow, despite the horrific nightmares I was having prior to Macha's late-night visit, I feel more rejuvenated from a couple of hours of sleep than I have in years.

Slowly navigating my way downstairs towards the immense kitchen, my nose suddenly fills with the scent of burnt toast combined with some kind of bitter, earthy smell. Before I've even entered the kitchen, I can hear the shuffling of Ms. Pierre as she whips up some kind of mysterious, nauseating cuisine that I'm sure she refers to as 'breakfast'.

The moment I walk through the kitchen door, Ms. Pierre turns towards me with a cold comment on my timing, "Miss Woodall! I was starting to assume that you had fled in the middle of the night."

From anyone else, this might be seen as a mildly humorous

comment, but as she sees my clothes, her face shifts to one of disgust, only amplifying the bitterness that was intended with the initial statement.

Ms. Pierre pauses for a moment before saying, "The uniforms in the armoire are not there for decoration, Miss Woodall. They have the intention of being worn."

Despite feeling the impulse to respond as coldly as I've been greeted, I opt to maintain a pleasant tone, "I'm just letting them air out a bit longer. The smell of mothballs is still a bit overpowering."

Clearly frustrated with my insolence, Ms. Pierre turns back towards a large pot on the stove, pursing her lips to contain herself as she continues putting considerable effort into stirring whatever thick mixture it is that she's 'cooking'.

I softly approach, trying to extend an olive branch, "Could I give you a hand with anything?"

She is quick to block my path towards the stove, "This is for the children. There's toast for you on the counter, and coffee in the pot."

Despite how 'off' her defensive body language seems to be, I turn towards the stack of blackened bread that's been drying out on the counter for an unknown amount of time and promptly walk past it, toward the coffee maker and pour myself a cup.

As I blow on the steaming, hot beverage, letting its aroma come back towards my nose, I move towards the breakfast table where Nemain and Macha both sit rigidly silent as they await their morning meal.

I slowly pull out a chair to join them, prompting Nemain to immediately respond by making a production of inching her chair away from me in disgust. Macha, on the other hand, remains still. Her drooping face and sagging shoulders are clear signs of her level of exhaustion resulting from her lack of sleep. I begin to wonder if she even slept at all, the poor thing.

I address both children with a pleasant, and energetic, "So, how is everyone this morning?"

Nemain visibly rolls her eyes at my attempted greeting, whereas Macha barely even acknowledges the existence of consciousness. I curl both hands around my coffee cup, feeling its warmth against my palms as I lean towards Macha with a supportive, "Nightmares can be scary at first, but I promise, they get easier with time."

Suddenly defensive, Nemain chimes in sourly, "What are you talking about?"

I try not to betray Macha's confidence by mentioning her late-night visit, so I twist the truth slightly, "Your sister looks tired, so I assumed she didn't sleep well. Most often, people don't sleep well because of nightmares."

Despite my half-truth, Nemain fires back with arrogance, "Macha slept through the night. I know. I was there."

I kindly exercise my patience before responding; "So then *you* must not have slept? You know... since you were up all night to make sure that she was there."

I see the frustration bring a reddish hue to Nemain's face as she quietly mutters, "That's *not* what's wrong with her."

I patiently blow on my coffee as I attempt sarcastic humor that's beyond Nemain's years, "So then what's the prognosis, Dr. Morgan?"

The casual jeer comes out harsher than I had intended as made evident by Nemain's look of anger and Ms. Pierre's suddenly straightening back on the other side of the room.

I carefully alter course as a follow up, "Maybe we should just ask Macha herself, and then *she* can tell us why she's not feeling well?"

Nemain looks at me like she's about to laugh in my face, "Go ahead, ask her. She's not going to answer."

I feel my brow furrow with confusion towards Nemain's comment as my focus drifts towards an unresponsive Macha, then back towards Nemain.

Flagrantly rolling her eyes, Nemain explains, "Macha can't talk."

At first, I'm slightly put off by the response, knowing the false nature of the statement. Soon though, logic kicks in and I naturally assume that this is some form of sibling bullying taking the shape of a punishment-based game, so I instinctually counter, "Now, Nemain, your sister should be allowed to speak whenever she wants."

Nemain's face remains shocked at my ignorance, yet somehow becomes even more disdainful towards my inability to understand such a simple concept. I can't help but wonder if this is what Ms. Pierre looked like as a child.

As I try to suppress my smirk towards my realization, Nemain proceeds to explain in the most patronizing tone she can muster, "Macha *never* talks. She's *muted*."

Suddenly, Ms. Pierre pipes up from the kitchen, "She's *a mute*, Nemain. The clinical term in noun form is, a *mute*. Looks like someone will be spending today revisiting her grammar lessons."

I see Nemain's shoulders dip a bit, creating a crack of vulnerability in her judgmental shell. I feel a sudden pang of defensiveness towards Nemain, wanting to provide some support for her by saying something along the lines of, 'we all make mistakes', but I'm too distracted by my confusion towards the seemingly uniform belief that Macha is mute, when I know for a fact that it's not true.

Lifting my mug towards my face to hide my perplexity, I secretly glance towards Macha, wondering if her late night visit had just been another dream, but if that had been the case, how did I end up on top of my sheets wearing my robe that I had put on before I answered the door? Also, if she hadn't been up all night, then why does she look so tired that she could fall over any minute now?

I continue to puzzle over this as I take a sip of my coffee, my mouth quickly filling with warm bitter liquid and about a tablespoon of coffee grinds. I gag at their sudden presence, prompting me to not so casually spit the contents of my mouth back into the mug.

As I get up to hastily make my way to the kitchen sink and pour out the mug's backwashed contents, I can hear Nemain snickering vindictively behind me.

Ms. Pierre keeps her back turned towards me as she redundantly inquires, "Is something wrong, Miss Woodall?"

Rinsing my mouth out with water from the faucet, I clear out the remnants of coffee grounds between my teeth, as I say, "I think you forgot the coffee filter."

Ms. Pierre remains unaffected by the news, barely able to hold back the insincerity in her voice as she says, "Hm. Personally, I'm a tea drinker, so it's been a while since I've brewed that vile substance. Must have been an oversight on my part."

I force a polite smile, despite my mouth being filled with bitterness as I say, "It's okay. I'll just put on a fresh pot."

As I proceed to empty the coffee pot and rinse out the sludge at the bottom, where the grounds have settled, I watch as the children are brought two bowls of whatever rancid substance has been cooking on the stove. From what I can see, it looks like a lumpy, maroon mash and it smells like putrid rotted earth.

Ms. Pierre sees my nose turned up in the air as she places the bowls in front of the children, so she makes a point of proudly announcing, "Two bowls of beet porridge."

I can barely contain my gag reflex at the thought of such a dish, let alone how the recipe came to be. Much to my surprise though, both children dive in with such fervor that it seems as though two bowls of ice cream have been placed in front of them.

As Ms. Pierre returns to the kitchen stove, she casually, yet confidently mentions, "An acquired taste, but their favorite nonetheless."

I politely nod as I use my tongue to fish out another grain of coffee that's stuck between my molars.

As Ms. Pierre places the lid on top of the pot, I take the opportunity to have a quick aside with her while the children are distracted with their meal. I quietly ask her, "Has Macha *always* been mute? Or did she develop this condition?"

I can see Ms. Pierre's back stiffen a bit at the inquiry, though I'm unsure if it's because of the invasiveness of my whisper or the clinical nature of my inquiry. Either way, Ms. Pierre quietly responds, with her back turned to the children, "Since birth."

I furrow my brow as I watch Macha shovel beet porridge into her mouth. Based on my knowledge through my degrees, I know that children will typically develop mutism through one of two ways: one, a birth defect resulting in a life-long condition; or two, through severe trauma resulting in a sub-conscious shut-down as a defense mechanism.

But seeing as I had just chatted with Macha the night before I can't accept the idea that she has been mute since birth, the numbers just don't add up, so I continue pressing, "So she's *never* spoken? Not *once* in your entire time with the family?"

Ms. Pierre quickly grows exasperated by my line of questioning, turning towards me as the resting look of derision returns to her face, "Not once. That *is* what 'mute' means, Miss Woodall."

She can see I'm still struggling with this new information, more than I should, even as I watch Macha eat from across the room.

Ms. Pierre then uses the opportunity of the temporary silence to tee up her own inquiry, "Why, exactly, are you so interested in Macha's condition, Miss Woodall? Having second thoughts?"

Suddenly becoming aware of my facial expressions and the fact that the interrogation has flipped, I stumble through my response, "Oh, no. I've just- I've never worked directly with a child who has this kind of condition before. That's all."

Ms. Pierre is quick to jump on my response, "You needn't worry yourself with it, Miss Woodall. I will handle the majority of the childcare duties, so you will have plenty of time to adjust. Why don't you go get into uniform so we may commence the daily routine?"

I quietly nod and exit the kitchen, returning to my room with my mind still racing. Once there, I open the doors to the armoire by the window and become instantly dizzied by the smell of dust and mothballs that has accumulated within, showing that my attempts to air out the cabinet the previous night have been futile at best.

As I flick the garments from right-to-left, I scan the various drab shades of grey and black. Soon I have put together an outfit with full-length sleeves and some semblance of comfort... in a relative sense, that is.

With each piece of clothing, I put on, I can actually *hear* the fabrics audibly creaking as they move for the first time in however long they've lived in this cupboard. I start to wonder if the clothes might be as old as the house itself.

While I am dressing myself in the dated, woolen and lace

clothing, my mind keeps trying to think back to the previous night, spinning in circles as it tries to make sense of not only my own nightmares, but also whether or not Macha had actually visited my room.

When I had awoken this morning, I was *certain* that Macha and I had had a lengthy discussion about her nightmare. Even though both Nemain and Ms. Pierre seemed adamant that Macha's mutism is a reality, something inside of me refuses to let go of the counter argument of my supposed experience.

It's then that I attempt to think back to what it was, specifically, that Macha and I had discussed at length. I can remember that she was terrified of her nightmare, but for the life of me, I can't remember a single detail of what the nightmare *was*.

What's worse is that every time I try to recall any of the information from our conversation, my mind is suddenly flooded with images of the cloaked woman and the crow from my own nightmares.

I feel the guilt wash over me as I come to the realization that I have been gifted with Macha's trust in the form of her confiding in me, but in return I have seemingly developed the audacity to forget every single detail she had entrusted me with.

This isn't like me.

Usually, I have a great memory; too good, in fact, as made evident by my own vivid recurring nightmares of the accident that have haunted me for the better part of two years. But now, as I tie the strings on my grey smock, I find myself searching the depths of my mind in an attempt to find even one tiny shred of a detail from Macha's nightmare, yet none come.

Patting down the incidental pleats on my smock from the undetermined amount of time it has been folded, I look at myself in the full-length mirror and feel my thoughts continuing to drift.

Before I even know it, my mind is spinning in an obsessive tornado towards Macha's supposed mutism, and my own inexplicably wiped memory from the night before.

However, even when combining the perplexing nature of both internalized debates, the feelings of confusion pale in comparison to the feeling of fear and insecurity that keeps rising within me as a result of my memories being replaced by images of that damned crow and the mysterious cloaked woman, crying under the oak tree.

CHAPTER EIGHT

The Routine

The cold sound of Ms. Pierre's firm knocking on my door snaps me out of my trance-like state. Before answering, I quickly check to make sure that all my buttons are fastened and that my sleeves are hiding my scars, giving one last pat down to the creases in my smock.

As I turn towards the door, I hear Ms. Pierre impatiently knocking again, prompting me to scurry across the room to answer before she feels compelled to knock a third time.

Much to my surprise when I open the door, I see a mildly satisfied look on Ms. Pierre's face, likely in response to my willingness to conform to the system of the household.

In response to her seemingly pleasant demeanor, I playfully curtsy which, in turn, successfully drains any tiny fragments of momentary levity from her face as she sharply pivots and begins striding down the hallway while saying, "Come along, Miss Woodall. We have many things to discuss and we're already running behind schedule."

I hurry to catch up to her as she leads me down the stairs and into the kitchen, towards the breakfast table, where she has strewn out a series of hand-written lists across the table's surface.

Before I'm even seated, Ms. Pierre is handing me the first of many pages, and launching into her detailed dissection of each task, "The house is to be dusted, first thing, every morning. You will start at the top of each room, and work down to the bottom using *lateral* flicks. Understood?" despite the simplicity of the instruction, she repeats it slowly while patronizingly physicalizing the instructions, "*Top...* to *bottom* with *Lateral* flicks. Otherwise your efforts will be rendered futile and you will have to start over again."

I smile and try not to crack a joke, despite every fiber of my being wanting to make a cynical comment towards the obsessive-compulsive nature of her training methods.

Ms. Pierre proceeds down the list, "After you have finished dusting the second floor, each window must be cleaned. First, wipe them Horizontally... *then* Vertically, otherwise they will streak and you will have to start over again. After you have finished the upstairs, you will move down to the main floor where you will start by dusting each room, *top* to-"

For the sake of my own sanity, I quickly cut her off, "-bottom with *lateral* flicks, before washing the main floor windows horizontally, *then* vertically to avoid streaking."

I watch as Ms. Pierre's lips momentarily purse at my interjection into what feels like an over-rehearsed training regime, "...Once you have finished with the windows on the main floor, you will tidy the kitchen from breakfast, including both washing *and* drying the dishes, wiping *and* drying the counters and then taking a quick inventory of the pantry, refrigerator and cellar."

I can't help but give in to my instincts and cynically state, "Sounds easy enough."

Ms. Pierre gives a momentary pause as if to silently ask if I'm finished with my attempts at humor before she shifts gears, "Tell me, what is your preferred method of education?"

I hesitate in response to the question, unsure of the answer she's looking for, so I answer with ignorant sincerity, "Well... schools usually do a pretty good job."

Before I'm even finished speaking, I can tell by Ms. Pierre's face that this is the wrong answer. She promptly crosses her hands in front of her waist as she thinly veils her contempt towards me, "The Morgan Children have been home-schooled for countless generations, utilizing the family's extensive library and a customized curriculum both created and conducted by matriarchs such as myself."

I feel my face scrunching in response to both her stubbornness and the act of labeling herself as a 'matriarch'. I try to break the tension by jokingly inquiring, "The books in the family library, they aren't five hundred years old too, are they?"

Pursing her lips even tighter, I can tell that Ms. Pierre has taken this as a sincere criticism as she turns to me coldly, "You will find that the family's collection of texts is more than adequate for the purpose they serve."

I find myself shocked by the sudden realization that my joke seems to have actually been proven to be the truth of the situation and soon find myself filling with defensiveness towards the children as I consider the potential outdated information they are being forced to learn.

My defensiveness suddenly, and unjustifiably turns to a wave of anger as I coldly state, "I think it's far more important that the books are *current* than *adequate*, don't you?"

Ms. Pierre stares at me with a cold, blank expression, signifying that she doesn't care for the reasoning behind my inquiry, let alone its insolence.

Nevertheless, my anger compels me to clarify, pointing out the potential injustice towards the children as I do so, "The information available for subjects like Science or Mathematics alone have gone through massive modernizations in the past decade. Not only has their standardized methodology been modified, but their basic root understandings have changed as well. If Macha and Nemain are learning outdated material, you're already setting them up for failure."

I realize I've gone too far, even before Ms. Pierre's facial expression shifts from unimpressed to one of pure offense. It suddenly becomes clear what she meant when she told me that the 'routine would require some *adjustments* on my part'. I haven't even been here a full day and I've already accused her of sabotaging the children she cares for.

Swallowing my frustration, I begrudgingly back off, silently leaning back in my chair and putting my hands up in digression as I say, "I'm sure whatever system you have in place is fine."

Suddenly, Ms. Pierre picks up another piece of paper with meticulous notes written upon it, as she says, "Here is the daily schedule. Learn it. Know it. Live it. You will be solely responsible for the cleaning duties at first. Once I have become satisfied with your ability to consistently complete the housework in a reasonable timeframe, we will discuss the potential of adding to your responsibilities, including occasional educational duties and supervision of the children."

I silently take the paper from her, making sure to suppress my inner commentary as I begin reading:

5:30am - *Wake. Prepare breakfast. Begin cleaning.*
6:00am - *Wake, bathe and clothe children.*
6:15am - *Morning readings.*
6:45am - *Children report to kitchen for breakfast.*
7:00am - *Finish breakfast, children return to room for lessons.*
7:15am - *Morning lessons begin.*
12:00pm - *Tea. Light, in-class lunch.*
12:30pm - *Thirty minutes of outdoor time (weather permitting).*
1:00pm - *Afternoon lessons begin.*
5:00pm - *Daily lessons conclude.*
5:10pm - *Twenty minutes of indoor play time.*
5:30pm - *Warm supper brought to children.*
6:00pm - *Brush teeth. Prepare children for bed.*
6:30pm - *Evening readings.*
7:30pm - *Lights out.*

My eyebrows raise, impressed by the level of scheduling that Ms. Pierre has imposed on the children. Despite my every effort, I give in to my instincts and try to illicit a smile from Ms. Pierre by saying, "I'm surprised you haven't scheduled their bathroom breaks as well."

In response, Ms. Pierre stares at me with a look of disgust at the mention of such an act. I awkwardly turn my attention back to the page and it's then that a small portion at the bottom of the schedule catches my attention.

N.B. – Saturday lessons (morning and afternoon) will be replaced with equally scheduled time dedicated to assigned self-improvement studies.

I can't help but inquire, "What's an 'assigned self-improvement study'?"

Ms. Pierre gently folds her hands at her waist, "I once read that hobbies can help to round out a child's personality and develop their character, so I have taken the liberty of assigning a hobby to each child in the areas which I feel they are lacking."

I smirk at the fact that Ms. Pierre thinks something so grand can be achieved so simply, so I explain as clinically, yet diplomatically as I can, "You know, professionally speaking, children should really select their own hobbies. That way, they can explore things that they enjoy and find their own form of emotional outlet."

Ms. Pierre scoffs at my suggestion, "Surely, you can't be serious! If we were to allow children just do whatever they please there would be countless little boys running around, raping and murdering every living thing they see!"

I'm taken aback by the sudden leap of logic that she has made, but something about her demeanor suggests that this comes from more of a place of personal experience, than a logical one, so I soften my approach, "Obviously adult supervision is important, but if a child is permitted to choose their own hobby they can also gain insight into their specific learning style, be it creative, logistical, or physical."

Ms. Pierre knows I'm right. After all, I've got the credentials to back up my words. However, she remains unwavering in defense of her position.

Despite standing rigidly before me, Ms. Pierre's shaking hands betray her composure, telling me that she is secretly fuming with anger towards my continued insolence, "Miss Woodall, I have lived here for some time now. You haven't even been here for twenty-four hours. When it comes to the Morgan children, I know them *much* better than you do! Therefore, I *assure* you that I know what's best for their development."

Seeing this fire in her makes me realize that I should pump the proverbial brakes before it turns into a full screaming match. I tactfully concede with only a little spite in my voice, "I'm sure whatever hobbies you have selected for them are more than *adequate*, Ms. Pierre."

Despite my less-than-subtle use of the word 'adequate', Ms. Pierre takes a moment to calm herself before confidently affirming my statement, "They most certainly are. Nemain is learning harpsichord to improve the precision of her dexterity, whereas Macha is strengthening her problem solving skills by reading up on historical battle strategies."

I feel my eyes pop open in response to this. Truthfully, I'm blown away that these children have even been exposed to such advanced material at such a young age. Thinking back, I didn't even know what a harpsichord *was* until I was in grade eight, let alone understanding the concept of a historical battle strategy, or even the understanding there were differences between them.

Ms. Pierre catches the look of momentary intimidation in my eyes, so she leans in to mockingly remind me who has the upper hand, "Don't worry, Miss Woodall, I will provide the lessons in those fields. Unless, of course, you feel you're more familiar with the eight observable flaws of a Hoplite Phalanx?" she waits a few seconds for an answer she knows isn't coming, "I didn't think so."

There's nothing that I want more than to stand up and defend myself, utilizing my heightened level of education in other fields to lord over her like she has attempted to do with me. Instead, I fold my hands in my lap, desperately trying to contain my anger as I remind myself how badly I need this job. As I sit quietly, I feel my teeth gritting together while I attempt to maintain some sense of decorum.

Right on cue, Ms. Pierre then grabs another piece of paper as she moves on to yet another task, "In regards to the inventory of the kitchen, here is a list of ideal par levels that must be met. Should we be short on anything, add it to the posted shopping list on the refrigerator. Once I deem it necessary, I will permit you to drive into town to fetch any required supplies."

My back immediately straightens at the mention of driving as I feel both of my palms simultaneously fall into a flop sweat. I haven't sat behind the wheel since the night of the accident, and judging by the anxiety generated by the car ride here, I probably shouldn't be doing it any time soon either.

Ms. Pierre sees the concern on my face, prompting her to rhetorically inquire, "Is this going to be a problem, Miss Woodall?"

"No," I quickly lie, "just been a while since I've gotten behind the wheel."

Ms. Pierre coldly feigns reassurance with a dash of patronization, "It's a simple straight shot up the road. A shaved primate could successfully make the trip by accident. Surely it won't be a problem for someone like you."

I can see that Ms. Pierre is dissecting my sudden tension in regards to the mention of driving. Something about her eyes tells me that she already knows about the accident.

Given the detail with which she had seemingly researched me, prior to sending the letter that offered employment, I would find it shocking if she didn't know about it. However, the absence of electricity in the home, signifying no internet and no cable news, ignites a small spark of hope, that she might, very well, have no idea it ever happened.

Ms. Pierre grabs yet another piece of paper and hands it to me, explaining, "Here is a list of the specific vendors that carry the items we will require. Though town is west of here, the vendors are intentionally listed west-to-east so that you begin shopping at the far end of town making sure to pick up any items requiring refrigeration last."

I quietly nod and stare blankly at the page, using it as a prop to hide the lingering fear in me that has been incited by the mention of having to get behind the wheel again.

After a momentary pause under the belief that I'm actually reading the list of stores, the tone in Ms. Pierre's voice suddenly shifts to a much more cautionary one, "I must warn you about the people who live in this area. To put it mildly, they are not the most 'welcoming' of people. You would be ill-advised to linger in town any longer than required."

I look up at Ms. Pierre, expecting to see her standardized cold stare, but instead I see a look of reflective, fearful sincerity.

As she looks me in the eyes, she adds, "I cannot stress this enough, Miss Woodall. These people are horribly and unjustifiably prejudiced towards this Family. Be prompt. Be discreet. Most importantly, try not engage with anyone outside of this list of vendors."

Quietly nodding to signify my heeding of Ms. Pierre's warning, I can't help but find myself wondering if the locals are sincerely as horrible as she's making them sound, or if they're just unreceptive to Ms. Pierre's form of 'frigid charm'. Either way, I feel my whole body beginning to sweat profusely as my mind keeps circling back to the idea of having to drive against my will.

As much as I want to tell her that I refuse to get behind the wheel, I have grown wary of showing any potential weakness to Ms. Pierre through our tense exchange. I opt to heed to my pride and remain silent until she is satisfied that I have absorbed the information and will abide by the routine.

Ms. Pierre then sharply pivots to make her way upstairs, but before leaving, she points towards a bucket in the corner of the kitchen with a rag, rubber gloves and a feather duster resting on the edge as she says, "I've already cleaned the upstairs portion of the home while you slept in. I would appreciate you cleaning the main floor as I attend to the remainder of the children's morning lessons."

I nod in silent agreement as Ms. Pierre exits the kitchen and makes her way up the stairs humming to herself pleasantly. The sound of her jovial tune feels like salt being rubbed into the wound of my suppressed yet ever-present fear.

I begrudgingly glance at the collection of lists before me, still wondering if Ms. Pierre actually knows about the accident. If not, then she certainly stumbled across one of my biggest vulnerabilities on the first day of my employment. If she *is* aware, then this could all be a tactful attempt to try to break me for some reason.

Considering the sheer amount of information she's thrown at me this morning, along with the heightened tension towards my very existence, I feel like it must be the latter, but still, I have no way of knowing for sure.

I take a cleansing breath as I get up from my chair, slowly moving towards the bucket in the corner to collect the cleaning supplies. As I do so, I find myself silently cursing Ms. Pierre for testing both my intellectual and emotional strength. Not long after that, I find myself linking certain behaviors of Ms. Pierre to those of my Mom.

Similar to how my Mom would purposely try to break me emotionally as a way of dealing with her inability to accept Andy's death, I feel as though Ms. Pierre is also projecting some kind of unacknowledged painful experience on me.

It's then that I realize that the anger and frustration inside of me is the exact reaction that Ms. Pierre is looking for. She wants to upset me. She wants me to feel inadequate. She wants to retain control over her own pain, which I now personify in her mind. She wants me to fail to prove that she can overcome something that has nothing to do with me personally.

With this new perspective on the situation, I quickly make my way around the main floor, fulfilling my duties to the letter and in a timely fashion, purely driven by spite. I make sure to dust each room top to bottom with lateral flicks, and then wash each of the windows horizontally, then vertically, to avoid streaking.

All the while, I keep circling through the conversation with Ms. Pierre over and over again, dreaming of all of the things that I should have said in my responses. I fantasize over all the ways that I could have put her in her place, had I only had the presence of mind in the moment to do so.

I'm so distracted by the monotonous labor mixed with my own vindictive thoughts that I don't even register how much progress I've made until I feel the searing ache in my right shoulder, forcing me to take a break.

As I look up from my bucket, I suddenly realize that I'm halfway through washing the windows of the sunroom, standing in the exact spot from my nightmare where I had seen the cloaked woman crying under the oak tree.

As the soapy water drips down the panes of glass in front of me I find myself mesmerized by the gnarled roots of the gargantuan oak tree that have grown up out of the ground, taking over the landscape and shattering any archaic patio stones that attempted to block their paths.

While there's nothing overly spectacular about the roots themselves, I keep staring at them, unable to turn away, my instincts screaming at me for some indecipherable reason as I feel the hairs on the back of my neck standing on end.

My focus slowly moves from the twisted roots of the tree, up it's immense trunk towards the canopy of plumage above. Suddenly, I catch a glimpse of a dark shape moving amongst the branches that sends a shiver up my spine.

Leaning closer to the window, I furrow my brow as I try to make sense of the obscured figure's erratic movements amidst the branches and large leaves that block my line of sight.

Within moments, the dark figure moves to the left and reveals itself to me, causing my entire body to freeze in fear as I find myself gazing into the unrelenting, menacing stare of a large crow.

CHAPTER NINE

The Ache

I finish my day of chores, and begin to make my way to my room. Even though my duties were limited to '*only*' the main floor today, I quickly came to realize, mid-day, that one floor of the Morgan home equals about two times the total square footage of my parents' house.

As I ascend the stairs to the second floor, I feel my body ache with each step. My feet are swollen, having been on them all day, and my forearms are pulsing with pain from the repetitive strain of *flicks* and *wipes* for hours on end.

On top of the physical strain from the housework, the mental exhaustion has taken its toll as well. Between my endlessly looped negative thoughts towards Ms. Pierre and my Mom, combined with the residual fear from sighting the crow in the branches of the large oak tree, there's enough tension in my shoulders that it feels like they have been surgically grafted to my earlobes.

When I had initially seen the crow from my position in the sunroom, I had frozen in fear, immediately tying it to the crow I had seen in my nightmares. Even though this crow had only held my gaze for a moment before flying away, the haunting nature of its presence made it feel like a lifetime. No matter how many times I tried to shake the thought of it over the rest of my day, my mind just kept coming back to that damned bird.

By the time I reach the second floor, my knees are screaming for release. I turn and stare down the long hallway, cursing the distance to my room. The sheer thought of having to traverse it makes me want to curl up and sleep on the floor right where I am.

It's then that I realize I'll have to cover the same distance after even *more* work tomorrow, and then the day after that, and the day after that. I hang my head in derision as I mindlessly drag my feet down the lengthy corridor for what feels like an eternity, until I finally reach my door and enter my room.

I close the door behind me so quickly that I clip my own shoulder in the process. Rubbing the point of impact, I sit down on the edge of the mattress, still wearing my uncomfortable, aged uniform that smells of mothballs and dust.

As I rub my shoulder, I'm unable to tell if I'm hearing the creaks of the archaic fabrics of my uniform, or the sounds of my own aching joints. For a moment I contemplate changing out of these clothes, but before I even reach for the first button, I realize how much work it will entail and flop down onto the mattress behind me. As I lie in a starfish position, I stare up at the silk canopy and watch it gently billow above me as relaxation finally washes over my body.

Just as I begin to feel my eyelids getting heavy, I hear Ms. Pierre's sternly knocking at my door. Rolling my eyes with annoyance, I purposely wait for her impatient second round of knocking before I force myself to get off the bed to receive my 'dinner'.

By the time I reach the door, Ms. Pierre has begun knocking a third time. I twist the knob and pull the door open quickly, to see her gnarled fist, still raised, her sharp knuckles tilted towards me at eye level.

Having no energy left, I take the silver tray from her and politely say, "Thanks."

I desperately try to hide the sudden wave of nausea that takes over when images of sausage water, wet spinach and clumpy potatoes flood back into my mind, leading to a quick progression of morbid imaginings of what might await me tonight.

I can tell from Ms. Pierre's face that she wants to make some sort of comment about my ragged state, but she contains herself with a purse of her lips and only a slight smirk, almost signifying that she wants me to know that she's deriving pleasure from my physical suffering.

My instincts scream at me to say something, to stick up for myself and not set a precedence of weakness, but I barely have enough energy to continue holding the tray, so I turn from her and gently close the door behind me, placing my dinner on the small table in the process.

Even though I feel I might vomit at the sight of whatever is under tonight's silver cloche, morbid curiosity gets the better of me and I lift the dome quickly, leaning away so as to not be invaded by the smell of whatever rancid steam hides underneath.

As the plume dissipates, I look down to the plate to see a generous serving of over-boiled green cabbage, drenched in some sort of chunky cream sauce. Sitting on top of the cabbage and sauce is, what appears to be, a somewhat decently seared pork chop.

Despite the splatters of sauce around the edge of the plate suggesting the meat was more *thrown* than *placed* there; it makes the dish look somewhat inviting so, against my better judgment, I surrender to my grumbling stomach and start eating.

As I place the first forkful of sauce-covered cabbage in my mouth, I quickly come to learn that the sauce isn't chunky by design; it's curdled. The realization makes me begin to violently wretch so I quickly grab the linen napkin from the tray and spit out the contents of my mouth.

Immediately after doing so, my empty stomach screams once more causing me to move my hand to my belly in response to the sharp acidic pain that comes with its cries for sustenance.

Unable to deny my body's needs, I begrudgingly move on to the pork chop. As I begin to cut into it, I quickly realize that it is not pork at all, but in fact a squished chicken breast.

By pressing down on it while it cooked, Ms. Pierre has not only flattened the meat, giving it dark sear marks on either side, but she has also successfully squeezed every ounce of moisture out of it as well.

I spend the next hour chiseling away at the rock-hard poultry puck, making sure to scrape away any traces of sauce from each bite. I then fight to gather enough saliva to be able to chew and swallow as many pieces as I am physically able to.

By the time I'm halfway through the chicken, my jaw is sore from chewing, the pulsing aches in my forearms have returned from trying to saw through my meal, and my hunger shifts to a vicious spike of nausea.

I quickly give up on the food and push myself away from the

small table to take some cleansing breaths in an attempt to quell my sudden compulsion to vomit, but with each breath, my nostrils are invaded by the rancid scent of the cabbage and curdled cream.

In an attempt to flush the smell out of my room I place the majority of my dinner in the hallway to signify I'm done with it. Closing the door behind me, I lean against the wall as I continue to take deep, cleansing breaths.

A few moments later, the nausea begins to subside, so I take advantage of what little energy I have left by changing out of my uniform, and getting into bed.

Mere seconds after my head hits the pillow, my eyelids begin to close...

🐦 🐦 🐦

I'm sitting at the breakfast table with my family as Andy blows out the candles atop his stack of banana pancakes. As the candles extinguish, the room suddenly flips to night and I am voiceless.

The wax from the red candles pours down the sides of the stack, mirroring the blood that pours out of the mouths of my family members as they stare at me with blank expressions upon their faces.

Despite having seen this horrific sight before, I reflexively stand up in shock, knocking my chair back as I distance myself from the morbidity.

I hear the tapping of the large crow at the kitchen window off to my right. Slowly turning to face the creature, I notice that behind the bird is an impenetrable wall of thick oak trees in place of my parents' backyard. It is as though the house has been suddenly quarantined by nature, creating an airtight prison for my nightmares.

The crow ceases tapping, and stares at me from the other side of the glass with a surgical gaze. I remain frozen in place as the bird cocks its head from side to side, keeping its faintly glowing, orange eyes trained on me.

I feel a sudden pulsing ache in my forearms, spreading down

towards my wrists, as my hands start to feel warm, and wet. Looking down, I see that my scars have been opened as though they are fresh wounds.

Blood pours out of my arms like an open faucet, quickly pooling on the kitchen floor around my feet and merging with the growing pool of my family's blood as it spreads from beneath the kitchen table.

Entranced and horrified by the sight, I continue moving away until I feel the backs of my legs make contact with my overturned chair and I fall, summersaulting backwards until I am suspended upside down in the wreckage of my car, in the middle of the highway.

While the flashing blue and red lights around me signify the presence of emergency response vehicles, I hear no movement of their personnel.

Though I can smell the smoke from the car fire I'm trapped in, I hear no panicked voices in response to it, and I see no hands reaching towards me, trying to remove me from my twisted metal coffin.

I turn towards the driver's seat, wiping the blood and tears out of my eyes and see the large crow, perched upside down beside me, staring at me with ferocious intent.

The crow cocks its head back and forth, calculating its inevitable attack, but I lucidly seize control of the moment. Forcing myself to fight through the pain as I pull the metal post from my shoulder and undo my seatbelt, I immediately fall to the ceiling of the car and feel shards of glass and fragmented metal pierce my scalp on impact.

With my vision blurred, I slowly crawl out of the passenger side window, and start running away from the burning car before the fire grows any further, or the crow decides to pursue me.

Still running, I glance over my shoulder at the flaming wreckage behind me one last time before I feel myself run, full tilt, into something solid.

Rebounding off of the object before me, I fall backwards and hit the ground, dizzied by the impact. While I still feel the asphalt of the highway beneath me, my vision begins to clear and I find myself in a small, circular clearing, surrounded by a thick forest of oak trees, creating an impenetrable wall with their trunks.

I scan my surroundings, noticing that each of the trees have the same symbol carved into them; a pinwheel with three separate extensions that take the form of legs below the knee; in the middle of each carving, a perfect triangle.

I slowly stand up, turning away from the trees to face the middle of the clearing. As I do, my eyes fall upon something in the center of the circle... a white sheet with a large red spot in the middle... the sheet that's covering Andy's corpse.

Approaching the fabric as it gently billows in the soft breeze, I am reminded of the relaxing sight of the silk canopy, gently dancing over my bed in the Morgan home. Despite the similarity in movements, this image brings me no peace.

Even though I already know the horrors that hide beneath it, I continue to stare at the slowly opening gaps beneath the sheet's edges with each gust of the breeze, as though it's trying to tease me in advance of the eventual reveal.

Sure enough, the wind picks up and yanks the sheet away with sudden force as though it were a magician revealing the gruesome finale of their final trick in the form of my brother's mangled body.

The first thing I see is Andy's face, it is turned towards me and is almost torn up beyond recognition. I recoil at the sight of it, yet despite every fiber of my being wanting to avert my eyes, my subconscious state takes over and forces me to face the gruesome images.

My eyes dance back and forth, taking in every injury that Andy has suffered during the crash as the details from the Coroner in the courtroom flood through my mind.

"As you can see, Andrew is missing the majority of his lower half, severed at the mid-pelvic region. The sheer force of the impact was so severe that his seatbelt acted as more of a <u>blade</u> than a restraint...

...The separation of his right arm at the elbow and subsequent compound fractures to the upper portion of the arm is consistent with injuries from similar victims who have attempted to hang on to something, or someone, during a crash. In this case, the catalyst for this

result is his sister, Patricia, holding his arm in place at the time of the impact...

...The majority of the skin on the left side of his body is worn away with severe abrasions, suggesting that the victim either slid, or was dragged for a considerable distance upon the asphalt..."

I feel tears beginning to well up as I stare at the large pieces of glass that are embedded deep into what's left of Andy's flesh. I curse how they glow in the faint moonlight, making him look like some sort of morbid jewelry display.

However, despite all of the horrible injuries to his body, the one part that I can't stop staring at is his torso. Somehow, despite all the other damage to his body, this portion has barely been harmed by the accident.

I stare at his chest in confusion, when it suddenly begins to darken and thin wisps of smoke start to rise from it. I stand there, watching in horror, as a symbol is slowly branded onto Andy's chest from inside his body.

The swollen image reveals itself as the three-petaled flower I had seen on the door to the Children's room, consisting of one continuous line weaving around itself three times before leading back to its origin; around it, a perfect circle.

Tears begin to stream from my eyes in response to the mutilation of Andy's body. Every single part of me is trying to will myself to look away, but my subconscious still forces me to watch.

Suddenly, Andy's body starts to move.

At first, I'm foolish enough to believe that he might have somehow survived his injuries in this version of my nightmare, possibly returning to provide me with some semblance of closure, if even in a subconscious state.

I kneel down beside what's left of his body, voicelessly willing him back to life as I continue to watch his sporadic, twitching movements. It's moments later that I realize it's not Andy who's moving, but rather something *inside* of him.

The center of the three-petaled flower soon begins to rise and fall as though something is trying to push its way out. I back away, dreading what I already know is emerging, when something pierces Andy's skin from the inside.

The large crow forces its way through the breach, headfirst, tearing open Andy's chest cavity as it climbs free. Covered with remnants of organs and flesh, the crow proceeds to stand atop my brother's dead body and pick itself clean.

Still inching away, I feel my back slam into the trunk of an oak tree at the perimeter of the clearing. With nowhere to go, I freeze in place as the crow turns towards me, cocking its head from side to side, its piercing, glowing gaze trained upon me.

The crow's beak slowly parts as it screams the deafening song of screeching tires and breaking glass and flies with immeasurable speed towards me.

🐦   🐦   🐦

I awake with a start in a pool of my own sweat and immediately hear the faint sound of crying. Similar to last night, I move towards my door to figure out the source of the noise only to discover that the sound is coming from the *other* side of my room.

Moving towards the window, I pull back the curtains to look down on the back half of the property. Through the branches and leaves of the giant oak tree that obscure my view, I see a portion of a woman in a hooded cloak kneeling amidst the gnarled roots of the large oak tree, softly crying in the night.

I promptly move towards my bedroom door, grabbing my long-sleeved robe, and exit into the hallway, before tiptoeing my way downstairs, through the salon and out towards the sunroom.

Sure enough, as I enter the room, I see the cloaked woman in full, kneeling at the base of the tree, still covering her face in a failed attempt to mute her sobbing.

Despite my instincts screaming at me to run away and ignore her, some part of me feels compelled to face this woman once more, and I soon find myself exiting the back door of the sunroom and making my way over the uneven and cracked patio stones in my bare feet.

As I reach the perimeter of the aboveground roots, I quietly inquire, "Excuse me? Are you alright?"

The mysterious woman's crying softens, but she continues to keep her face obscured with the shadows cast by the hood of her cloak and the stringy, long grey hair, surrounding her hands.

I take a step closer, attempting to elicit a response once more, "Excuse me, Miss? Is there anything I can do to help?"

Slowly, the woman removes her hands from her face, keeping her head downcast as her hood gently lilts towards me and she whispers, "... *save them.*"

Her words are barely audible, so I take a step forward, carefully navigating the roots beneath my feet as I respond, "I'm sorry, I don't understand. Save who?"

The closer I get, the more her hood lifts towards me, her face still hidden in shadows. Slightly louder, yet still quietly, she repeats herself, "*Save them.*"

I take another step towards her as I await some semblance of context to her words. I'm moments away from asking her to clarify again, when I suddenly feel my left foot slip off one of the roots and promptly wedge my ankle in place.

Reaching down towards my foot to try to twist it free, I feel a sudden tightness around my right ankle. It's then that I realize that the roots of the tree are growing upwards, wrapping themselves around my legs, crawling towards my knees in spiral patterns.

Unable to escape, I turn towards the cloaked woman for help, only to see her reaching forward with her gnarled fingers and seizing me by the shoulders as she screams a deafening shriek, "*SAVE THEM!!!*"

I'm frozen in fear as I feel the roots continuing to tighten around my legs, now halfway up my thighs. Within the woman's hood, I see faintly glowing orange eyes emerging from the shadows.

I hear the deafening sound of screeching tires and broken glass emanating from the woman as a large crow flies out of her hood towards me, with menacing speed.

🜲   🜲   🜲

I awake with a start, soaked in sweat. I feel my heart racing and my hands shaking as I grab the sheets and throw them off of me to cool down. When I do, I freeze at the realization that I'm wearing my robe.

Sitting upright, I frantically tear it off of me and throw it across the room. As I do so, my foot shifts and I feel my heart skip a beat as something brushes against my heel.

I push the blankets all the way off the bed and freeze in horror as I find pieces of bark lying on the mattress around my ankles.

Triquetra

Nearly a week has passed since I woke up to find tiny pieces of bark around my ankles.

Shockingly, each night since then has consisted of dreamless sleep, suggesting that my subconscious might have exhausted itself in the twisted evolution of my nightmares.

However, in the process of finding peace at night, my waking hours have become just as haunting as my dreams used to be, resulting in blurred lines of reality and a tortured conscious mind.

I feel disorientated, questioning the validity of every moment as to whether it's reality or if it's some sort of altered perception of it; terrified by the idea that a large crow with glowing, amber eyes may be lying in wait around every dark corner.

With every passing moment, I hear the words of the cloaked woman echoing throughout my mind, begging me to, '*Save them.*'

While I have come no closer to figuring out the meaning of her words over the past few days, my instincts tell me that it must have something to do with the children. As to what I'm meant to save them *from* though, I have no idea.

Day after day, I mindlessly coast through the housework that Ms. Pierre has assigned to me, less focused on the physical strain, more worried that I've finally begun to reach my mental breaking point.

After the trauma of the accident, and the years of self-imposed psychological punishment that followed, it's entirely possible that my experiences within the Morgan home over the past week have spun the fibers of a final straw, resulting in a paranoid breakdown.

I'm almost to the point that I wish the nightmares would return so as to provide some semblance of contextual traction from which I can regain my bearings and collect my spiraling thoughts before it's too late and I slip over the edge of sanity.

I'm so lost in the confusion of every waking moment that I barely even register the fact that I've been able to successfully complete my housework in less time each day, my distracted mind somehow creating a process of streamlined efficiency.

By the time the smell of Ms. Pierre's rancid beet porridge reaches the second floor, I've already dusted halfway down the hallway. I begin my next set of lateral flicks at the top of the doorway to the children's bedroom, slowly descending towards the image of the three-petaled flower in the middle of the door.

The sight of the embossed symbol comprised of one smooth, continuous line has haunted me each day; every passing glance of it taking me back to my most recent nightmare, when I saw the very same symbol branded into Andy's chest.

While I realize it's entirely possible that my mind has simply projected the image into my subconscious by association, I still can't help but feel that it must possess a deeper meaning that I don't yet understand.

Despite the haunting nature of the symbol, I soon find myself lost in the intricacy of its design, curious towards its significance and why it would appear in my dreams in such a gruesome manner.

My eyes trace the image, following its never-ending, continuous path, when I hear Ms. Pierre suddenly clear her throat, a foot to my right.

I snap out of my trance to find her staring at me coldly, her arms crossed, with a single eyebrow of disapproval raised.

Feebly trying to excuse my zombified state, I stutter out, "S-sorry, I zoned out. I- uh- I haven't been sleeping well."

Ms. Pierre remains still, saying nothing as she continues to scrutinize me with her eyes.

In the hopes of cutting through the tension while simultaneously satiating my curiosity, I break the awkward silence and inquire, "...What's with the flower?"

Scrunching her face in annoyed confusion, Ms. Pierre asks, "What 'flower'?"

I point to the symbol embossed on the door as I say, "I noticed it's also on each of the pillars in the children's room."

Rolling her eyes at my ignorance, Ms. Pierre explains, "That's not a flower, Miss Woodall. That is a *Triquetra*," noticing my blank stare, she audibly sighs and dumbs it down even further, "a Celtic Knot?"

I softly nod, recognizing the term from conversations I had overheard at College between various tattooed douchebags. Though, admittedly, I have as little understanding of the symbol's meaning as said douchebags did.

Ms. Pierre picks up on my ignorance and proceeds to explain in a patronizing voice, "Celtic mythology believes strongly in threes. So too, they believe there is great power in the Triquetra."

Furrowing my brow ever so slightly, I push further, "But what does it *symbolize* though?"

Ms. Pierre gently crosses her hands at her waist as she explains; "There is debate over the *specific* meaning. Some believe it represents the Past, Present, and Future, others believe it symbolizes the Body, Mind and Spirit. Either way, it suggests a continuousness existence; one beginning, with no discernible end."

I find my eyes tracing over the symbol once more as I ask, "What about the circle around it?"

Ms. Pierre sighs contemptuously before saying, "Much like any culture, Miss Woodall, circles symbolize protection."

I suddenly hear the cloaked woman's words echo through my mind once more, '*Save them*' and can't help but ask, "Protection from what?"

Ms. Pierre's face tightens as fast as her back straightens, "It could be any number of things, Miss Woodall. It's a silly superstition, like throwing salt over your shoulder to ward off the Devil, or touching wood to wish away bad thoughts."

I turn my gaze back towards the symbol of the Triquetra, barely even registering Ms. Pierre's growing impatience until she suggestively clears her throat once more.

Snapping back into focus, I turn towards Ms. Pierre once more as she dismissively says, "If you'll excuse me, I'm already late to wake the children."

I gently step back as she practically pushes me out of her way and enters the children's room. Even as the door is curtly slammed in my face, I still hover in front of the symbol for a moment before going back to dusting the upstairs corridor.

Minutes later, I have reached the end of the hallway, across from the far end of the children's room. I am now standing in front of a door that had caught my attention a week ago, when I had first cleaned the upstairs portion of the house.

I had finished dusting the doorframe of this room and instinctually had reached for the doorknob so as to enter to continue dusting and wash the windows. However, when I turned the knob, I came to discover that the room was locked.

Later that day, I had asked Ms. Pierre about the mysterious locked room, in passing. I remember that she seemed oddly quick to dismiss my inquiry, telling me, '*You needn't worry about cleaning in there. It's merely a storage area, filled with old, family heirlooms that should have been thrown out ages ago.*'

Even now, days after Ms. Pierre's suspiciously curt response, I remain perplexed as I stand outside of the sealed room.

Whether it's my refusal to believe Ms. Pierre's explanation of the room's contents, or my paranoid theories taking over as a result of my sustained mental break, I feel an overwhelming compulsion to find out what lies beyond the door.

I glance down the hallway to check that I am alone before I drop to one knee and slowly lean towards the keyhole in an attempt to gain a glimpse of what lies beyond the barrier.

As I begin to close one eye to narrow my focus, I hear the sound of the children's bedroom door opening and I spring back up into a standing position, resuming my dusting before Ms. Pierre is able to spot anything that might raise suspicion.

As Ms. Pierre and the children make their way downstairs, I finish dusting the end of the hallway, wash the windows in the children's room and then move on to the main floor, putting aside the mystery of the locked room and adding it to the growing pile of unanswered questions that are accumulating within my mind.

Even as the children are eating their breakfast, I opt to forgo my own morning meal and continue with the housework while my brain continues doing backflips in the hopes of finding any semblance of answers, but only creating more questions in the process.

First, there's the unsettling echo of the cloaked woman's voice, persistently begging me to, '*Save them.*' While I have no proof to support my theory that this is in regards to Macha and Nemain, something in my gut keeps telling me that it *must* be the case.

If it is, in fact, the children that I'm meant to save, what am I meant to save them from, and how? Are they in immediate danger? Is that why the cloaked woman was crying at the base of the oak tree? Is that why the image of the Triquetra is embossed upon their door, as some sort of symbol of protection?

While Ms. Pierre had dismissed the symbol of the Triquetra as mere superstition, the presence of the image throughout the children's room, combined with its appearance in my nightmares signifies that it *must* be more than that, doesn't it?

Had I just projected this mysterious symbol into my subconscious state? Or is the image of the Triquetra in my dreams intended as a message from the mysterious cloaked woman? If it *were* intended as a message, why would it manifest in such a grotesque manner so as to present itself on Andy's chest by burning his flesh from the inside?

As I think back to the image of the Triquetra branded upon my brother's lifeless body, my memory naturally progresses to the horror of what emerged from within his torso... that damned crow.

I soon find myself asking why the creature keeps coming back in my nightmares? Is it intended to be a personification of my self-imposed guilt? If so, it would explain why its intent is so clearly malicious towards me. It would also explain the bird's deafening call of screeching tires and broken glass.

But even if the crow with glowing amber eyes *were* emblematic of my suppressed emotions, what would be the significance of it taking that specific form? I have no emotional connection to such a creature outside of my nightmares, so why would my guilt manifest in such a form, when there are so many other ways it could torture me? It's not like there's any shortage of suffering given the unspeakable things I've gone through.

As the word, 'unspeakable' passes through my mind, my thoughts shift towards Macha and the unresolved debate of whether or not she is in fact mute.

During my time in school, we had discussed multiple cognitive conditions seen in foster children, Mutism being one of them. I remember that during that discussion, the condition was attributed as the result of one of two possible scenarios.

Scenario A) the child is born mute as a result of a form of cranial damage whilst in utero. Scenario B) the child is *selectively* mute as a result of experiencing severe trauma.

I think back to my exchanges with Macha over the past week. While her visit to my room on the first night remains questionable in regards to whether or not it really happened, I've still had enough casual exchanges with her during waking hours to have a clear litmus test of her personality, thus allowing me to make some educated deductions.

The fact that a girl of Macha's age would exhibit such superior cognitive capabilities so as to be able to not only study, but supposedly *understand* an advanced topic like historical battle strategies would typically suggest a case of Savantism.

However, Macha's physical and emotional responsiveness to verbal engagement, combined with her ability to lock and maintain eye contact during said exchanges would seem to negate that diagnosis. It would also suggest no symptoms of Autism or most common brain injuries.

This forces me to consider the possibility of trauma being the root cause of her condition, and with that acknowledgement, I feel a rage growing within me on Macha's behalf.

Given my borderline obsessive work on case studies while achieving my Master's degree, I naturally assume the worst whenever it comes to children in potentially traumatic surroundings.

Despite the *supposedly* impartial stance of the judicial system when it comes to cases involving assaults of any kind, it's always better to believe the victim prior to investigation as opposed to giving the alleged aggressor the benefit of the doubt.

Sure, some would say that was a form of vilifying the accused before the facts are present, but tell that to a child with a fractured skull from the blunt force trauma of a grown man's fist.

By the time I'm halfway through washing the windows in the sunroom, I realize that I'm seething with anger towards an, admittedly, fictional narrative of how horrible Ms. Pierre is to the children behind closed doors.

My heart begins racing as the tide of my suppositions continues to rise, becoming increasingly darker with each moment. I soon find myself clenching my jaw at the idea of Ms. Pierre attempting to justify physical and psychological abuse as a *'traditional form of child rearing, by way of a firm hand.'*

My fury towards Ms. Pierre reaches an apex as I throw my soapy rag into the bucket with vengeful intent. I take some cleansing breaths as I attempt to find some semblance of calm and remind myself that I'm getting carried away with mere hypotheticals that have no basis in reality.

I continue to try to slow my heart rate, closing my eyes and breathing as slowly as I am deeply. I focus on the fact that I can't afford to lose this job as a result of a false accusation and remind myself that no matter how difficult Ms. Pierre may seem to be, going back to my parents' place in the face of failure would be a far worse situation.

I exhale as I slowly open my eyes and they travel along the gnarled roots of the giant oak tree. Whenever I've entered this room over the past few days I can't help but think back to my nightmare and how the roots had come alive, seizing me in their grasp, cutting into my ankles before I shot awake in my bed to find pieces of bark near my feet.

I feel my back straightening with residual fear as I scan the branches above me for any signs of a crow, when suddenly, I hear movement behind me as the children leave the kitchen and make their way upstairs for their morning readings.

Making my way through the kitchen door, I find Ms. Pierre moving the children's bowls from the kitchen table to the counter. I remove my rubber gloves and place my bucket in the sink before announcing, somewhat proudly, that I've successfully completed the dusting and window washing before the children's morning lessons have even begun.

Ms. Pierre silently nods in response, not impressed by any

means, but merely accepting of the information that my duties have been preformed with more efficiency than I had initially been given credit for.

Amidst the silence, I feel an overwhelming urge to try to find at least some semblance of information towards the thoughts that have plagued me for the majority of the past week.

Without thinking, I blurt out, "Ms. Pierre, do you mind if I ask you something?"

Keeping her back to me, Ms. Pierre responds, "Judging by your tone, I assume my opinion on the matter is irrelevant."

I tilt my head to the side briefly, signifying that she's not wrong in her assumption, before I proceed, vaguely at first, "What can you tell me about Mr. and Mrs. Morgan?"

This causes Ms. Pierre's back to straighten ever so slightly as she hesitates, "That's... a fairly broad question, Miss Woodall. Could you be more specific?"

I quickly cloak my inquiry with pretenses, "I guess I just want to know what kind of people they were. I'm trying to get a better sense of the children's respective personalities and you can discover a lot about a child by learning about who raised them."

Ms. Pierre quickly responds, "Well, then you should be asking more about me, Miss Woodall. I have raised Macha and Nemain since birth."

I feel my brow furrow a bit at this information; "Yes, but surely their mother had a hand in it as well?"

Finally turning to face me, Ms. Pierre explains solemnly, "Mrs. Morgan... was not long for this world."

My head bows at the mention of her passing, yet I can't let it go, "If you don't mind me asking, how did she die?"

Ms. Pierre pauses, "... I don't see the need to discuss such a morbid topic, Miss Woodall. These are private matters."

Sensing her avoidance, I switch gears, "What about Mr. Morgan?"

Suddenly, Ms. Pierre becomes even more rigid than she already was as she says, "Mr. Morgan is... no longer with us."

I perk up, "He died too?" Ms. Pierre hesitates as she cocks her head, so I continue prying for information, "Wait, he's alive?

Where is he then?"

With a curious look in her eye, Ms. Pierre calculates her response; "He has not been present for some time. To be honest, I would be surprised if the children even remember him."

Feeling the information starting to come out of Ms. Pierre more freely, I proceed to fire off more questions, "When did he leave? Why would he just abandon his children? Did it have something to do with Mrs. Morgan's passing?"

Ms. Pierre is quick to close the valve of information, cutting me off before I can continue my line of questioning, "Miss Woodall, while I understand you are merely trying to acquaint yourself with this home and this family, I feel as though your time would be better served attending to the rest of your duties for the day."

I gently concede to her not-so-subtle demand, "Alright. I guess I'll get started on the inventory then."

Ms. Pierre's shoulders slightly relax at my concession as she resumes stacking dishes for me to wash later. While my questions have ceased for now, I can still sense that I've stumbled upon an extremely sensitive subject.

As I grab the inventory paper and a pencil and move into the pantry just off to the side of the kitchen the quiet tension permeating from Ms. Pierre remains clearly palpable.

It's clear that Ms. Pierre senses the residual tension as well, as she suddenly changes the trajectory of the conversation with a calculated distraction, "Since you are taking such a proactive interest in the children, perhaps you should begin to spend more time with them."

I feel a smile come to my face at the idea of returning to duties that I actually went to school for, as opposed to continuing to serve my term as a glorified maid.

Before I can respond to her suggestion, Ms. Pierre adds, "We will begin with one hour per week, starting Monday. During that time you will conduct a lesson of my choosing. All under my supervision, of course."

Secretly rolling my eyes at her addendum, I respond with as positive of a tone as I can, "Of course."

There is an elongated silence, during which I'm expecting to hear more details, yet none come.

I suddenly see a new window of opportunity from which to gather some answers, so I somewhat casually say, "You mentioned that there was a family library that you use for your lesson plans. I'd love to get a look at some of the books in there, you know, to prepare myself to the *Morgan Family standard.*"

Even though I can't see her face, I can tell that Ms. Pierre is seeing right through my feigned over-enthusiasm, as she says, "You will require no such materials, Miss Woodall. Your first lesson will be in Arts and Crafts. Only after I have approved of your teaching methods will we discuss any further subjects you may inherit. Even then... it will be on a conditional basis."

I desperately try to veil my frustration as I ask, "... Any specific material that you would like me to teach them?"

Ms. Pierre audibly scoffs as she says, "It's Arts and Crafts, Miss Woodall. The subject matter is irrelevant. However, I *do* request that you avoid any sharp edges or flammable objects. They are children after all."

Despite the patronizing nature of Ms. Pierre's statement, I retain the positivity in my voice as I say, "Of course. Safety first." I pause for a moment before I take the opportunity to extend an olive branch, "... and thank you for this opportunity. I really am looking forward to it."

I can hear disgust in Ms. Pierre's voice as she flatly responds, "I'm sure you are." She then pauses for a moment before adding, "You are welcome to shop for whatever supplies you require for your lesson when you are in town tomorrow."

Thankfully, my position in the pantry doesn't allow Ms. Pierre to see all of the emotion suddenly drain from my face at the mention of having to drive again. Though I say nothing in response, I know my silence speaks volumes.

Ms. Pierre plainly adds, "See to the inventory and create a shopping list so that I may approve it before lending you the keys to the truck."

I know I should respond, say anything to show that I've acknowledged the request, but I remain frozen as the palms of my hands become clammy with flop sweat.

I can tell that Ms. Pierre is enjoying my sudden wave of apparent tension because I can actually *hear* the smile in her voice as she says, "This won't be a problem, will it Miss Woodall?"

While there is nothing I would love more than to avoid inevitably facing my biggest fear a bit longer, I worry about exposing my vulnerability to Ms. Pierre even more, concerned that she will flick the exposed nerve at will.

I quietly clear my throat as I unconvincingly say, "N- No problem at all."

As Ms. Pierre exits the kitchen, she casually mentions, "I'm going to tend to the children's morning lessons. See that you don't forget to do the dishes after you've finished the shopping list."

I listen to each of Ms. Pierre's cold, sharp footsteps as she makes her way up the stairs. Only once I'm sure she's reached the second floor hallway, do I let the tears that are forming in my eyes begin to fall.

My drops of sorrow fall onto the inventory list, marking the page with warped, circular stains, causing the paper to bend and expand as it absorbs the moisture of my vulnerability.

I quickly grab a new inventory sheet and transfer the information over, as I try my best to suppress my wave of mixed emotions.

The last thing I want is for Ms. Pierre to have even the slightest clue of how much her seemingly simple request has already broken me at my core.

CHAPTER ELEVEN

Nauseating Fear

By the time I get to my room to turn in for the night, my agitation towards the idea of driving in the morning is filling me with anxiety beyond anything I've experienced during my time in the Morgan home.

I pace back and forth in my bedroom, endlessly wandering in the hopes that the continuous movement will help to calm my nerves. However, with each passing moment, my heart races more and more as it fills with anger, hate and fear.

I keep going over Ms. Pierre's words in my mind, curious towards the timing and motivation behind the request. Does she really *need* me to go into town? Or is this some sort of punishment for asking too many questions? If it's the latter, does she know how deeply she has cut me with this seemingly simple request?

When I had initially received the letter about this job, it was clear that Ms. Pierre had done her homework on me, but how deep did her research go?

Without the presence of phones, television or Internet in the Morgan Home, it's entirely possible that Ms. Pierre doesn't know about the accident at all. But without those tools, how was she able to obtain such detailed information about my education, my desperation for employment or even my mailing address, for that matter?

Perhaps it's all just a horrible coincidence that I'm misinterpreting through the veil of my own growing paranoia. After all, similar to an addict at an intervention, it's not uncommon to instinctually project culpability onto an outside catalyst as a defensive measure against facing one's own vulnerabilities.

But what if it's not just a misread coincidence? What if Ms. Pierre knows all of this, and is purposely using the information against me in a deliberate attempt to break my spirit? After all,

I've felt the tension emanating from her since my arrival. It's abundantly clear that she doesn't want me here, despite being the one who hired me, but would she really go so far as to purposely incite an emotional breakdown?

My body feels like a volcano, shaking with increasing tension as it brims with anxious rage. With each passing moment, I can feel myself edging towards my inevitable eruption, though I have no idea what form it will take.

By the time I hear Ms. Pierre knocking on my door to deliver my nightly slop, I can feel sweat beading on my forehead and my hands aching from the tight fists I've been clenching for the better part of an hour.

I quickly wipe my brow with the crusty lace sleeve of my uniform and hear my knuckles crack as I spread out my fingers to release the tension in my hands. Taking a deep breath, I force a smile before I answer the door.

As she has every night prior, Ms. Pierre thrusts the tray with the silver cloche in my direction as I simultaneously reach out to receive it with a polite nod. Our nightly routine that has become as rehearsed as a formal waltz, only this time I notice that she lingers for a moment.

I raise my eyebrows expectantly, surprising myself with the level of coldness that my tone carries as I ask, "Is there something else?"

Ms. Pierre raises a disapproving eyebrow as she scans me up and down with derision. I see a dark intent flood her eyes as she asks, "Is everything alright, Miss Woodall? You seem a little... on edge."

As her question reaches its conclusion, a slight smirk reveals itself at the edges of Ms. Pierre's pursed lips. Just the sight of it confirms my suspicions and sparks the rage inside of me, forcing me to fight every instinct to throw the tray at her.

Successfully suppressing her malicious grin moments later, Ms. Pierre then inquires, "This wouldn't have anything to do with your trip into town tomorrow, would it? If such a rudimentary task is going to be a problem for you, then I would suggest you tell me now, so I may begin finding your replacement."

I grit my teeth so hard I can hear them squeak. Whether it's because of my desperation to keep this job, or pure spite-fueled resistance towards Ms. Pierre, I stand my ground as I reply through my clenched jaw, "No. I'm fine."

Gently clasping her hands at waist level, Ms. Pierre scans me up and down once more, clearly gaining enjoyment from my muted suffering, "... Good."

Ms. Pierre turns to walk away, allowing me to shoot a scowl in her direction before turning to close my door.

Before I'm able to even reach the handle though, Ms. Pierre calls back from the hallway with an addendum, "Oh, Miss Woodall?"

I begrudgingly roll my eyes before poking my head back into the hallway to hear her out.

Standing a handful of feet down the hall, Ms. Pierre says, "When you *do* go into town tomorrow, I suggest you wear something other than your uniform, so as to avoid being identified as a member of this household. As I've said before, the locals do not look kindly upon the Morgans."

I stand firmly, and respond flatly, "Noted."

Ms. Pierre then raises an eyebrow as she quickly adds, "And do try to keep your wardrobe choices modest, will you? A woman of your age should be wary of the message her clothing might communicate to others."

Suppressing every instinct to fire back at her, I simply mumble, "Mmm hmm."

Awkwardly facing one another in a tension-filled silence, Ms. Pierre finally breaks first, as she curtly nods and pivots to continue making her way to her own room. Even as she saunters away, I stare at her with venom in my eyes until I hear her door close.

I go back into my room, kicking my door closed behind me and slamming the tray onto the table. I continue grinding my teeth in fury, as I place my hand on the silver cloche.

My anxiety combined with my hatred towards Ms. Pierre has already silenced any form of hunger that I may have had, replacing it with summersaulting nausea, yet I still remove the cloche as if to continue fueling my hatred by seeing what horrors await me on the concealed plate.

As the steam clears to reveal the 'meal' within, I find a pile of noodles dusted with what appears to be grated Parmesan cheese. Part of me is surprised at the fact that a remotely edible dish has been brought to me for the first time since I've arrived. I suddenly start to wonder if this is some sort of silent apology from Ms. Pierre for her cold nature and venomous intent towards me with every waking moment.

I feel my nausea slightly subside as I grab my fork and move the noodles back and forth. Based on the way they break apart on contact, I can tell that they are quite overcooked, but compared to past meals that have been delivered to my room this one flaw is a small price to pay by comparison.

I proceed to insert my fork into the middle of the pile of pasta and attempt to gently twirl the noodles onto the utensil with moderate success. As I move the fork to my mouth and take my first bite, I quickly realize that what I thought was grated Parmesan cheese is in fact, raw garlic.

Dry heaving at the overwhelmingly pungent flavor, I spit the noodles out onto my plate, dismissing any delusions I may have had of Ms. Pierre doing something nice for a change.

I start to imagine Ms. Pierre sitting in her room, smiling to herself at the thought of the food I'm forcing myself to eat, knowing that she has succeeded in yet another form of malicious, yet subtle torture.

Seething with anger, I pick up the plate and throw it across the room, shattering it on the door and spilling the overcooked pasta onto the floor.

I take a moment to calm myself before I load the broken pieces of the plate and the partially disintegrated food onto the tray and nudge it outside of my door with my foot. I slam my door closed in frustration in the hopes that Ms. Pierre hears it and fears, if even for a moment, that I'm coming for her. Though, I'm well aware that's probably not the case.

I practically rip off my uniform, taking out a sizable chunk of my hatred on the inanimate fabrics as I ball them up to throw them at the corner as though they were rocks and Ms. Pierre were standing there to receive them.

The tears start to pour out of my eyes as I flop onto the bed, so I bury my face in the pillows and scream as loud as I can. As I run out of air, I take a moment to inhale in the hopes of calming myself, but even with freshly filled lungs I follow my instinct and go right back to screaming. It's the only thing I can do to relieve myself of the anger and hatred that fills every fiber of my being.

While I know my emotions are merely being amplified by my anxieties towards getting behind the wheel tomorrow, I can't help but continue screaming bloody murder into the pillows for the better part of five minutes until my throat starts to ache and the tears begin to slow.

Despite the momentary dip in my tantrum, I still feel all of the negative emotions swirling within me. My hatred towards Ms. Pierre, my frustration towards all of my unanswered questions about this house and this family, my fear of the cloaked woman and her crow, my anxiety towards getting behind the wheel, my self-loathing for being so dependent upon this toxic job, my paranoia from questioning my own perceptions of reality and then of course, my exhaustion from experiencing all of these feelings at once.

Above all else though, what hits me most in this moment is my loneliness. I have no shoulders to cry on, no one to act as a source of support. My Mom has all but disowned me; my Dad might be there if I needed him, but he would surely flake the moment Mom figured out whom he was talking to; as for my friends, well, their loyalty proved to be paper thin in the wake of the accident.

Whether it was their own feelings of guilt towards how the night had played out or the fact that they bought into the publicized narrative of my 'battle with addictions' no one would talk to me in the aftermath. During my extended stay in the hospital, there were no flowers, no cards, not even text messages of moral support in the form of emojis.

After I was discharged and sent home, I tried sending a couple of texts and even left a few voicemails, but sure enough, not a single message was returned. In all honesty, I can't really say that I blame them for abandoning me amidst everything that was going on, but it still hurt nonetheless.

While the loneliness at that point in my life was tough at first, I got used to it over time. Especially since the cold nature of the silence from my parents acted as a perfect daily training ground to grow accustomed to a life of seclusion.

As I lay here now though, face down on the mattress, I feel that pain all over again as I come to realize that even if I *did* have people that I could turn to in a moment like this, I would have no way to contact them. My phone has been dead for a week, and there are no landlines in the Morgan home or other ways of reaching the outside world.

I roll onto my back and stare up at the silk canopy above my bed, feeling the last of the tears rolling from the outside edges of my eyes and across the base of each of my temples, as I take deep, calming breaths.

Before I even know it, the emotional exhaustion reaches its apex and I start to feel my eyelids becoming heavy. I instinctually curl up into a fetal position to embrace the oncoming sleep as I feel myself fading from consciousness.

As I drift from the waking world, I find myself having the passing thought of how much I would embrace the return of the cloaked woman and her crow, if even for a moment of distraction from this awful life.

But with the world around me fading to darkness, I suddenly feel myself being transported back to the familiar surroundings of the breakfast table in my parent's kitchen.

It's then that I immediately regret even entertaining such a thought as to welcome my nightmares back.

CHAPTER TWELVE

A Gift

The stack of banana pancakes is gently placed on the kitchen table, set to the playful chorus of 'Happy Birthday' as being sung by my parents. Andy makes his wish before blowing out the candles, and as the flames are extinguished, the room suddenly shifts to darkness.

My eyes dance between the blank stares of each of my family members as blood trickles from their open mouths and pools on the floor around their feet.

I stand up at the sight of it, knocking my chair backwards. It's then that I hear the familiar tapping of the large crow at the kitchen window. Entranced by the bird's menacing amber gaze, I soon feel the pain in my wrists return, prompting me to look down to see a pool of my own blood gathering at my feet, spreading outwards and merging with the blood of my family.

I instinctually back away and, similar to the other times this scenario has played out, I tumble backwards over the toppled kitchen chair I had been sitting in moments before. As my body falls backwards, I close my eyes in anticipation of an impact that never comes.

Slowly opening my eyes again, I now find myself suspended upside down in the wreckage of my car, in the middle of the highway. The large crow is perched upside down, beside me, in the driver's seat. As it cocks its head and calculates its attack, I fight to get myself free of the car before it can part its beak and release its horrible cries of screeching tires, twisting metal and breaking glass.

Painfully removing the metal post through my right shoulder and struggling to undo my seatbelt, I suddenly fall to the crumpled roof of the car below me and feel the shards of glass and jagged pieces of metal piercing my scalp on impact.

Dizzied with pain, I crawl through the broken passenger side window and run free of the flaming wreckage, glancing behind me to make sure the crow isn't pursuing. Before I can shift my focus back to what's in front of me, I run full speed into a solid object, bouncing off of it and falling backwards.

As my vision clears, I find myself in a circular clearing, surrounded by an impenetrable wall of oak trees. Each tree bares the same symbol, carved with expert precision into their trunks, a three-armed pinwheel with legs at each of its extremities.

Already knowing what is waiting behind me before I look, I slowly turn and move towards the white sheet in the center of the clearing. As I approach I stare at the red spot in the middle that marks where Andy's bloody corpse lies.

The sheet playfully billows in the wind before a sudden gust whips it away, revealing the horrific state of Andy's body beneath it. Despite all of the horrible injuries, I only stare at his chest, already knowing what comes next.

Slowly, the symbol of the Triquetra is branded into my brother's torso from the inside. I back away in anticipation of the large crow's emergence from Andy's sternum but this time there seems to be no movement from within. Regardless, I continue slowly retreating until I feel the solid trunk of an oak tree against my back.

Turning away from the gruesome images before me, I frantically search for a way out of this circular torture chamber before my tormentor with wings can return. Finding no spaces between the trees, I start slamming my fists against their trunks, when suddenly I hear the soft sound of a woman crying behind me.

Cautiously pivoting to face Andy's body, I see the cloaked woman from under the oak tree, hunched over my brother's corpse as though she is mourning him on my behalf. While my instincts scream at me to stay as far away from her as possible, my feet betray me and slowly approach the woman with the downcast head as she continues to weep in the night.

Despite my inability to control the physical movements of this subconscious manifestation of my body, I still retain lucidity within my mind. As my feet carry me closer to the cloaked woman, I try to remind myself that this is just a dream in the hopes that it will calm my nerves.

I am mere feet from the cloaked woman when the sound of her crying dips in volume and I see a sudden jerk of her head as though she has sensed my presence.

My feet cease their approach in response to the cloaked woman's heightened awareness, fearful that she will summon the roots of the surrounding oak trees to seize me by the legs as she has before, yet as I stand here, the ground remains still and nothing happens.

I continue to apprehensively linger for a moment longer, realizing how eerily silent my surroundings have become. The complete lack of noise creates an odd sense of security, despite my current surroundings and company.

There are no cries from the cloaked woman echoing through the night, no tapping of the crow's beak against a window, no deafening calls of screeching tires, twisting metal and breaking glass, no panicked voices of emergency personnel, not even the sound of a breeze. It is as if this is some sort of temporary void, populated with the cloaked woman and I, side by side, sharing in a somber moment as we stare at what remains of my brother's body.

Whether it's the sight of my brother, the shared moment of sorrow or the sudden sense of security that's washing over me amidst the silence, tears begin to well up in my eyes.

As though she senses them coming, the cloaked woman reaches out with her gnarled fingers to offer a comforting touch, while lifting her head towards me. I embarrassingly flinch in response to her sudden movement, causing her to pull back her offer of consolation almost immediately, yet I can't take my eyes away from her hood.

While her face is still obscured by the shadows within, the wisps of stringy, silver hair must come from somewhere. I strain my eyes to see if I can make out anything within the darkness, a chin, a cheekbone, but it is as though the cloaked woman and light of the moon are working in tandem to keep her identity concealed.

Slowly, she reaches her left hand into the depths of her cloak before producing an old book from within. The cloaked woman lifts it towards me, offering me the object with both of her spindly hands as though it were a gift that she had been waiting to bestow upon me for centuries.

I reach out to receive the item, looking to her in the expectation that there will be some sort of explanation in regards to the purpose of the item, but instead, the cloaked woman turns her attention back towards Andy's body and says nothing.

As I hold the book in my hands, I feel raised portions beneath my palm. Slowly sliding my hand downwards, wiping away the thick layer of dust on the leather surface, I see the symbol of the Triquetra revealed beneath, embossed in the center of the book's cover, with a perfect circle around it.

I glance back towards the cloaked woman to see her still kneeling over my brother's body, unresponsive to my discovery, so I turn my attention back to the book, opening it so as to read what's inside.

As I lay my eyes on the first page, I see that it is filled with flawless, handwritten, calligraphy, but before I can read anything that's been written, the words begin to dissipate as though the ink is being washed off the page by an invisible wave of water. I quickly turn to the next page, hoping to catch at least the first few words, but before I can narrow my focus, they too evaporate into nothingness.

Turning to the cloaked woman in confusion, I try to ask her what's wrong with the book, but no words come out. I continue to look at her, expecting that sooner or later she'll turn to offer assistance, but she pays no mind to my struggles and continues staring down at Andy's body with unrelenting patience.

Shifting my focus back to the book, I continue flipping page-to-page, the words disappearing before I'm able to read anything. Amidst my frustrations, my lucid thoughts suddenly remind me that I am in a dream state that is controlled by the right side of my brain, thus preventing left brain functions... like the ability to read.

It's then that it hits me. This gift is merely a subconscious projection of a deeper message. It has nothing to do with what's written within the book, so much as the book itself. As for what it's meant to communicate though, I have no clue.

It's then that I hear the cloaked woman quietly whisper, "*Save them.*"

I feel a wave of frustration mount in response to the cloaked woman's request. I know this book she has given me is intended to provide some semblance of context towards her request, but with my current level of understanding, the book remains as meaningless as the request itself.

While I stand there, desperately trying to find some kind of answer, the cloaked woman repeats her request with more urgent insistence in her tone, "*Save them.*"

Whether it's the force of my heightened emotions, or a sudden wave of lucidity within my subconscious state, I suddenly find that my voice has returned as I yell at the cloaked woman in response, "I don't understand what you want me to do! Save who!?! How!?!"

Before the cloaked woman even has a chance to react to my insolence, I begin backing away in fear of the consequences I may have triggered. My outburst would have crossed a line in any conversation, let alone one with whatever ethereal deity I'm currently in the presence of.

The cloaked woman says nothing at first, but trains her gaze upon me as I continue backing away. I see the faint glow of orange eyes slowly growing in intensity within the recesses of her hood as she suddenly screams, "*SAVE THEM!!!*"

The sheer volume of her scream is deafening, forcing me to hunch over and cover my ears as they ring with resonance. By the time I lift my gaze once more, I feel myself fill with dread at the sight of the crow emerging from the cloaked woman's hood.

As it has countless times before, the large crow trains its amber gaze upon me before mounting its attack with malicious intent and immeasurable speed.

I bolt upright in my bed, coated in my own sweat. As I struggle to catch my breath, I hear someone softly knocking on my bedroom door.

Getting off the mattress, I quickly pull the covers up to hide the sweat-covered sheets and move towards the source of the knocking. Before I reach for the doorknob, I make sure to put on my long-sleeved robe, pulling down the sleeves to cover my scars and taking a moment to verify that they are not split open as they had been in my dreams, moments ago.

When I open the door, I find Macha standing on the other side, in the dim light of the hallway's propane lamps. While her presence is completely harmless, it immediately sends a shiver up my spine nevertheless.

My mind begins to race as I frantically try to figure out if this is actually happening or if it's merely another subconscious projection whilst in a dream state. Either way, I quickly become aware of how long I've been standing in silence, my wild eyes dancing back and forth as Macha looks up expectantly for some form of verbal acknowledgement.

I try to contain my wave of neurotic energy as I softly ask, "Did you have another nightmare?"

Silently, Macha nods her head. She seems ashamed of her fear, as though she's well aware that her nightmares aren't real, but still can't fight the feeling of vulnerability that they create. I immediately feel empathy towards her, especially seeing as I, myself, still can't tell if I'm still dreaming or not.

Opening my door further, I say, "Do you want to come in and talk about it?"

Just like her previous visit, Macha gives a quick nod and a smile before she runs into the room and jumps up onto the bed, sitting in a cross-legged position in the center of the mattress.

I make a point of trying to scan the room for anything out of the ordinary that might suggest that I'm still dreaming, but everything appears to be real. The lingering smell of raw garlic, the coolness of the air against my skin, the imperfect angles that the moonlight is shining into the room, all of it seems too natural to be a subconscious projection.

As I approach the bed, I suddenly think back to the book that the cloaked woman had given me, and how the words had seemingly washed off the page due to my dream state.

I quickly pick up a small paperback that's on the bedside table and flip it open to a random page. After a quick scan of the first sentence, I put the book down, *certain* that this is the conscious world. With this newfound certainty comes a wave of compulsion to finally figure out the truth surrounding Macha's supposed mutism, so I turn to engage with her.

I begin by asking, "Was it the same nightmare as last time?" to which she quietly nods. I then ask, "Do you want to talk about it?" but she only responds with an idle shrug.

It's clear that Macha is apprehensive towards reliving the details of the dreams that haunt her. However, despite my instincts to respect her fragile state, I continue pressing for a verbal response of any kind. With one word I can prove that she's not mute. With one sentence I might even be able to rekindle my failing memory in regards to the details of her dream.

Still only receiving silent, physical responses, I try a new tactic by offering a potential source of relief from the fear, "You know, sometimes the only way to defeat scary things is to talk about them rationally, going over every detail."

Macha looks up at me with confused fear in her eyes. I can see she is still tentative to relive the details, not to mention upset that I'm asking her to do so for a second time.

I quickly justify my prompt, trying to ease her tension in the process, "When you look at fear from the outside, it lets you see all the silly little things that make it less scary," the residual look of confusion in her eyes compels me to continue with a more playful tone, "like spiders, for instance. Lots of people are scared of spiders. But when you think about it, behind all of those creepy legs and those scary-looking eyes... their webs come out of their *butts*."

Macha covers her mouth as she smiles at my use of the word 'butt'. I can tell from her reaction that this is considered a taboo word in the Morgan home, thus making it all the more fun and rebellious in the eyes of a child Macha's age.

Taking advantage of the momentary levity, I push once more, "So tell me about your dream. Who or what could have scared you so bad? Maybe we can figure out what comes out of *its* butt."

Despite my attempt to get another positive response, Macha's face becomes solemn once more as her eyes look down to the mattress and her shoulders sink.

I start to realize that she's not even budging her lips in an attempt to answer my inquiry and soon find myself wondering if she really is mute after all, meaning that I had imagined our entire previous conversation.

After a solid bout of silence, I surrender my expectations, realizing that whether its mutism or fear, Macha is not going to provide any verbal details tonight.

I slowly turn away from Macha, letting her off the hook by saying, "It's okay. We don't have to talk about it if you don't want to. How about we do some drawings instead?"

I get off the bed to start digging through one of the drawers for scrap paper and some pencils, lamenting the fact that I didn't pack a box of crayons or markers. Foolishly, I had assumed that Ms. Pierre would already have things like art supplies for the children. How wrong I was.

As I'm digging through the drawer, I suddenly hear a frail voice behind me quietly say, "She... She came back."

I bolt upright so fast that I actually have to wait for the blood to come back to my brain before I can turn around and face Macha. By the time I turn towards her, Macha has lifted her gaze towards me.

I softly approach the bed, putting down the papers and the pencils as I gently sit and ask, "Who? Who came back?"

Macha's eyes quickly fill with tears prompting a sudden chill to shoot up my back as she parts her lips and quietly says, "The woman...the one who cries under the oak tree."

CHAPTER THIRTEEN

Departure

I awake in the morning to find myself sleeping on top of my blankets while still wearing my robe from the night before. Lifting up my head, I scan the room for any signs of Macha, but once again, she is nowhere to be found.

Laying my head back down on my pillow, I put my hands on my forehead as I, once again, find my memory devoid of the specifics that Macha had shared in regards to her nightmare. However, in the back of my mind, one detail keeps repeating over, and over again in the echo of her tiny, terrified voice, *'the woman who cries under the oak tree'*.

The fact that Macha claims to have seen the same woman that has haunted my own nightmares chills me to the core, but the lack of context as a result of my failing memory cuts the potential for any other commonalities short, leaving me in yet another growing state of frustrated confusion.

I start to wonder if my brain is purposely blocking out my memories due to some inability to comprehend such an anomalous occurrence. Perhaps it's suppressing the details to protect me from overloading my brain with more paranoid hypotheticals. Either way, it has only contributed to the whirling tornado of thoughts that are circling in my head, making my brain ache ever so slightly.

In a fit of frustration, I let my arms flop down on either side of me, but as my hands find the mattress, I feel my right palm land on something.

Quickly propping myself up, I look down to see a collection of pieces of paper splayed out on the bed with a few worn down pencils lying in their midst. Suddenly remembering that I had gathered these items before Macha had finally spoken, I assume this is the place where she and I had drawn pictures late into the night.

I sit upright and grab the nearest drawing. I scan the paper in the hope that it might provide further clues towards the details we had discussed, but as my eyes fall upon the page, I see that it is merely a collection of nonsensical scribbles.

While I see no sense of form in the pictures, I still carefully gather the remainder of Macha's drawings and fold them in thirds, before getting out of bed to place them on the small table at the side of the room.

As I turn towards the cupboards, I catch a glimpse of my reflection in the standing mirror by the window. The sight of my physical state draws me closer to my reflection, and the closer I get, the more I notice how overwrought with exhaustion I appear to be.

Days ago I had noticed that the, once small, bags under my eyes had consistently grown since my arrival at the Morgan home. At the time, it was something I had merely dismissed as the signs of restless sleep combined with days filled with anger, frustration and tireless physical labor. As I stand here now though, I begin to notice that the rest of my visage seems to be following suit.

At some point, I seem to have developed frown lines on either side of my nostrils, leading down to the edges of my lips. While they are faint, they are pronounced enough that my entire face appears to be sagging, creating an unintentional look of concession to the life I've been handed.

As if to add insult to injury, it's then that I notice a single grey hair coming out of the top of my head and draping down the side of my face.

I scrunch my nose in annoyance as I carefully pinch the single hair between my thumb and index finger before abruptly plucking its root from my scalp, leaving only a slight stinging sensation in its place.

As the hair hangs loosely from my hand, I pinch the other half and extend it out in front of me, twisting the dry, stringy follicle as I shake my head in disbelief.

I can't help but scoff at the fact that I'm now staring at physical evidence of how toxic this environment is. While I realize that I've been under a load of stress as of late (admittedly *somewhat* self-perpetuated), I never assumed it would manifest in such obvious physical forms. Yet even with this proof that I should cut my losses and leave this place for my own mental and physical health, my mind keeps looping back to Macha and Nemain.

I think back to the cloaked woman's instructions to, '*save them*' and can't help but wonder what the consequences would be if I were to ignore her request. What would happen to those poor children? Would Ms. Pierre take out her frustration on them in my stead? Would she go so far as to hurt them? If those poor girls were to be harmed, I would *never* be able to forgive myself.

As my mind cycles through the various hypothetical scenarios, I feel the whisper of my small headache beginning to intensify, mounting its counterattack against my incessantly looping thoughts.

Soon, my small headache is joined by a tiny wave of nausea. I quickly attribute it to the minimal amount of 'dinner' I had consumed the night before, combined with my anxieties towards getting behind the wheel for the first time since the accident.

I try to shake off my physical ailments and distract my mind by focusing on the task at hand as I make my way to the cupboards and get dressed in my own clothes for the first time since I've arrived at the Morgan home.

First, I pull on my favorite pair of old jeans with small rips above the knees. As I slip my legs into them, I feel a wave of familiarity wash over me, as though these pants are a part of my identity I had almost forgotten.

I then grab an old, long-sleeved, V-neck T-shirt with the image of a feminine bumblebee with pouty red lips and librarian glasses hovering under the words, 'Bee Serious'. While I never found the quote to be particularly funny, the shirt itself is easily the comfiest piece of clothing I own. As I pull it down over me, I feel as though it's an old friend hugging me, making up for all the time we had spent apart.

Before I leave my room, I return to the mirror and scan my outfit with scrutiny. While it is conservative by my standards, I realize that no matter what I wear, Ms. Pierre will likely find something wrong with it. In the hopes of minimizing conflict, I throw on a zip-up hoodie for good measure, but I still make sure to leave it unzipped for fear of excess heat amplifying my growing headache and waves of nausea.

Satisfied with my choices, I start to gather the last of my things, habitually pocketing my phone in the process, and then proceeding to grab my sneakers. For the sake of the floors that Ms. Pierre loves *so* much, I carry my shoes in my hand as I quietly open my bedroom door and exit into the hallway.

Gently traveling the length of the corridor so as not to prematurely wake the children, I pause at the top of the stairs to take another cleansing breath before I have to face Ms. Pierre and her inevitable criticisms.

Before I'm even halfway downstairs, my nostrils are inundated by the rancid scent of fresh beet porridge. Even though I have grown accustomed to this smell being a constant at the start of each day, it still hasn't made the experience any less offensive to my senses or my already churning stomach.

After depositing my sneakers at the front door, I walk into the kitchen, where Ms. Pierre immediately turns to see me in my 'civilian clothes'. Predictably, she raises a disapproving eyebrow as she stares at the V-neck of my T-shirt and the small rips in my jeans.

I say nothing in response, knowing that's it's just a matter of time before she launches into her judgmental commentary, so I move to the coffee maker instead, forcing myself to gnaw on a piece of dry, burnt toast en route in the hopes that it will soothe my stomach pains by providing some form of sustenance.

Sure enough, as I finish pouring myself a mug of coffee, Ms. Pierre quietly comments under her breath, "I suggested dressing casually, not disguising yourself as a common trollop."

I fight to swallow the mouthful of toast as much as I fight to swallow my anger towards the comment. I almost choke as I try to suppress sixteen combative responses at once, finally settling on the most passive-aggressive option: putting down my coffee mug, loudly zipping up the front of my hoodie, then moving to the kitchen table to sit in silence.

Ms. Pierre suddenly stops stirring her rancid mixture and turns to me, utterly serious, as she says, "Miss Woodall, I mean no personal offence. I know that your generation enjoys gaining attention in any form that you are able to get it. But *please*, believe me when I say that despite your intentions, exposed skin will only invite the dark intentions of men."

I look up towards Ms. Pierre, ready to fire back with a liberating comment in regards to the culpability of sexual predators having *nothing* to do with a woman's clothing choices. Before I can though, I notice the sincerity of the fear in Ms. Pierre's eyes. It's then that I realize this is the second time that she has mentioned something in regards to the violent tendencies of men.

The deep sense of conviction in Ms. Pierre's body language tells me that there is validity in her statement rooted in *personal* experience. While she is naturally a rigid woman, the straightness of her back and the unwavering nature of her stare, makes me legitimately feel a wave of sorrow for her, and even some concern for myself.

Instead of fighting back, I give an affirming nod to Ms. Pierre, "I understand. Thank you for your concern. I promise I will be safe, and keep an eye out for anyone who may appear to be a threat."

Even after my response, Ms. Pierre continues to look at me with unrelenting concern in her eyes. It is as though she has suddenly grown a conscience overnight and it is trying to make up for all of the horrible ways she's treated me with one foul swoop of maternal instinct.

A wave of empathy washes over me, making me feel compelled to stay and hear further details about Ms. Pierre's experience, if even to just delay the drive a little longer. However, I know that the likelihood of her sharing anything further is slim at best, and sure enough, she says nothing.

Equally out of awkwardness towards the unnerving nature of her unrelenting stare, and obligation towards my duties, I take one more sip of coffee before I start to make my way towards the front door and force myself to face my fear.

Only once I attempt to tie the laces on my sneakers, do I notice how much my hands are both shaking and sweating. I take a moment to repeatedly clench my fists and then widen my fingers but it brings no relief, nor does it sooth the growing anxieties within me.

I finally find success by way of tying my shoes on the third attempt, when Ms. Pierre appears beside me, handing me a ring with a collection of keys on it. As I look up, I see that her eyes are still filled with deep concern.

I stand to receive the keys, as Ms. Pierre hands me a shopping list with notations written beside each item in flawless penmanship. As I take the list from her, she explains the methodology behind the route, "I have listed the locations west-to-east so that you drive all the way to the far side of town, and then backtrack. That way, the items that may spoil will be the last ones you pick up."

I nod in accordance, "Sounds like a plan."

The level of sincerity in Ms. Pierre's voice then grows further, "I must caution you once more, Miss Woodall. Do *not* spend any more time in that place than you need to. Those people are *not* the kind you want to be in the company of for any longer than required."

Forcing a smile, I try to bring some levity to the moment, "Well, there goes my plans to get drunk at 8am with a bunch of strangers."

Unimpressed, I watch Ms. Pierre's eyebrow rise and her lips purse, as if to silently curse me for not taking her seriously. Instead of saying anything, she quickly moves to the front door and opens it to usher me outside.

Naturally, I begin to follow the stone path in front of the house, towards the trail that I had used to get here on my first day, but before I'm even ten steps away Ms. Pierre calls out from behind me, "Miss Woodall? The truck is that way."

I turn to see her pointing a crooked finger towards the east side of the house, prompting me to adjust course accordingly. Were it not for my anxieties towards my impending journey dominating my every thought, I would likely feel embarrassed right now.

As Ms. Pierre closes the door, I see her shaking her head as she mutters, something to herself about '*lists*' and '*actually reading them*'. I pretend not to hear anything as I continue walking with purpose.

I travel about five hundred yards on foot before I finally come across a small, warped shed with an old, rusty, brown pick-up truck parked underneath its tilted awning.

It's then that I start to wonder why the elderly driver hadn't dropped me off *here* on the day of my arrival instead of the location he had actually chosen. While this path is still pretty far from the home, it's a fraction of the distance that I had been forced to traverse with my immense suitcase.

My instinctual reaction is to curse the elderly driver, but I quickly come to the realization that it was more likely some sort of sadistic initiation tactic; my first of many forms of torture, courtesy of Ms. Pierre.

I approach the driver's side door of the old pick-up truck, flipping through the numerous keys on the ring as I try to find one that matches the tarnished, rusty appearance of the vehicle. As I go through one key after another, I realize that my hands are shaking worse than they had been before, rendering my dexterity virtually non-existent.

Finally, I find a key that looks like it could belong to a beat up clunker like the one in front of me, and I try to insert it into the door's lock a total of four times before it actually finds its way in.

By the time I'm in the driver's seat, I can feel sweat beading on my forehead, along with the continued, intensifying thrums of my tension headache, which has now moved to the back of my skull.

Amidst the pain, my neck and shoulders instinctually cramp up, almost touching the bottom of my earlobes as I try to put the key into the ignition. After a few failed attempts, the key finally finds its home. I pause and take a few calming breaths before turning the engine over.

As I sit there, listening to the angry roar of the archaic engine as it awakens from its slumber, I feel the hairs on my forearms standing on end in response to the intensity of the truck's menacing, low growl.

Placing both of my hands at the top of the dusty steering

wheel, I lean forward and rest my forehead against the backs of my wrists as I try to fight off the tears that are starting to accumulate.

I quietly try to convince myself that I can do this and that no matter how hard it may be, actually going through with this will be far easier than going back into that house and admitting failure to Ms. Pierre.

Taking another deep breath, I gently shift the truck's sticky gears to 'reverse' and start backing out of the shed at about three inches per minute, taking multiple breaks to collect myself amidst the process.

Finally, after the truck has fully emerged from its shelter, I shift the gears to 'drive', before easing my foot off the brake and letting the truck slowly lurch forward, picking up speed as it rolls down the gentle grade of a small hill.

Similar to the path that brought me to the Morgan home, I see a clearing at the bottom of the hill where a crude driveway marked by two tire tracks is barely visible through the tall grass that has grown on either side of the thin, bald strips of dirt and mud.

Contrary to the elderly driver's speedy approach on a similar road at the opposite side of the property, I navigate this path at a crawling pace, terrified of losing control of the vehicle as a result of the failing landscape.

With each bump in the road and every slight jostling of the truck's body, I feel my hands instinctually tighten around the steering wheel. When I glance towards them, I see that my knuckles are bleached white from the constrained blood flow, yet that only makes me grab the wheel harder.

As the barely visible path leads me out of the oak forest towards an intersecting dirt road, I take a moment to sit there, unflexing my hands to let the blood flow freely again.

While the air temperature of the truck's cab is quite cool in actuality, my heightened anxiety, combined with the physical strain in my body makes it feel as though it's one hundred and thirty degrees, and climbing.

I reach down to use the crank to lower the driver's side

window, and then triple check that the truck is in 'park' before I lean towards the passenger side window to do the same.

With both windows down, I feel a gentle breeze pass through the cab of the truck, bringing with it the scents of the surrounding forest. I close my eyes and take some slow, deep breaths, savoring the smells of the outdoors and their naturally grounding abilities.

As I slowly open my eyes again, I glance in the rearview mirror to see two oak trees behind me that are marked with the same three-armed pinwheels with feet at their extremities that I had seen at the entrance of the footpath on the other side of the property.

The images bring back visions of the impenetrable wall of oak trees from my nightmares, but I am quick to shake the negative thoughts from my mind and turn my focus to the road in front of me, looking from left, to right, then left again.

Taking one more deep breath to fuel my confidence, I shift the truck back into 'drive' and pull out, turning left onto the dirt road, heading west towards town.

I carefully increase my speed, ever so slightly as I travel the dirt road. The smoother terrain helps to boost my incrementally growing confidence, yet still, I keep the car moving at a less-than-moderate pace.

Whether it's the time of day, or simply the remote location, there seems to be no other cars on the road, meaning no one to critically honk or yell obscenities in response to my lack of promptness, so I continue to take my time with the drive, growing more and more comfortable by the moment.

As I gently increase my speed a little more, I feel a smile forming on my face in response to the fact that I'm successfully conquering my fear. Despite the nagging presence of my headache and waves of nausea still being present, I feel better than I have in years.

I lean towards the driver's side window, letting my hair dance in the wind. The sensation of the fresh air tickling my scalp creates a sense of joy that I had not expected at the beginning of my journey, so I gather as much air in my lungs as I can and let out a liberating scream in celebration of my victory over my anxieties.

I have done it. I have defeated my fear. I feel invincible. I feel free.

CHAPTER FOURTEEN

Town

Within half an hour I've reached the town's east border. While there is no sign to welcome travelers to this municipality, I start to notice the names of the stores from the bottom of Ms. Pierre's vendor list appearing on old, rotten, wooden signs on either side of me, acting as navigational landmarks.

Adhering to Ms. Pierre's detailed instructions, I continue down the main road, heading towards my first stop, 'Neyman and Son Produce Co.' at the far end of town. As I do so, I can't help but marvel at the decrepit state of the buildings along the way.

It's almost as if the entire town never got out of the Depression era, and now everyone is just waiting for the buildings to fall down around them so they that can reset the town's economy with the insurance payouts.

As I continue to traverse the dirt road, I glance down at Ms. Pierre's list once more. According to her obsessively detailed notations, the drive through town should only take about five minutes; seven if you catch the town's only stop light, which I promptly do.

Staring at the red light in front of me, I find myself baffled by its existence on this barren road. I cynically scoff at the traffic signal in front of me when I suddenly feel my headache start to thrum stronger and stronger, to the point that I can almost hear my brain pushing against the limits of my skull.

Amidst the waves of pain, I can't seem to shake the nagging feeling that I'm being watched. It's then that my attention drifts to the homes on the hill to the left of me. I suddenly become aware of the scowling faces of various townspeople sitting on their porches and staring out their windows, clearly upset by my presence.

Evidently, Ms. Pierre's numerous warnings about the

unwelcoming nature of the townspeople were not exaggerated in the slightest. I turn my head to the right in an attempt to avoid their unrelenting gazes, when I see two men standing on the side of the road looking at me as they whisper to each other with maniacal smirks on their faces.

Judging by the acne scars and the patchy attempts at facial hair, I quickly deduce that these two can't be any older than their late twenties, though their lack of subtlety would suggest a maturity level far below that.

One is wearing a sleeveless t-shirt with the image of a confederate flag displayed across his chest, which on any given day would be considered offensive, to say the least. However, the t-shirt pales in comparison to the countless tattoos of voluptuous cartoon females sporting anti-Semitic symbols and racist slogans that are littered all over his shirtless companion's torso.

I feel another wave of nausea suddenly pick up as I turn my attention back towards the traffic light, silently urging it to change back to green before the two men decide to approach. The longer I sit there though, the more it becomes apparent that this interchange seems to operate with the same functionality as the rest of the town.

In my peripherals, I see the tattooed man step towards the truck, his maniacal grin filling with slime-coated chauvinism as he calls out through the open passenger side window, "You ain't from round here, huh? You want me to, *show you some things*?"

As the shirtless douchebag finishes his painful attempt at a pick up line, his buddy in the confederate t-shirt pontificates the thinly veiled double entendre by grabbing his crotch and biting his lip.

I do my best to hide my eye roll in response, cursing the fact that the truck doesn't have automatic window controls so I could suggestively block them out with a thin layer of glass.

The tattooed man steps forward again as his tone takes on a note of heightened aggression, "Hey! Ain't you gonna say something? I'm talkin' to you, bitch!"

The one in the confederate t-shirt then chimes in, "Yeah. You don't gotta be a *cunt* about it."

I remain silent as I tighten my grip on the steering wheel. The suppression of my anger only intensifies my headache further. With each pulsation of my swelling brain against my skull, I feel my stomach simultaneously churning.

There's nothing that I want more than to lash out at these fucking assholes and teach them about female empowerment by way of knocking their heads in, but I am quick to remind myself how many prying eyes are watching me from up on the hill.

The tattooed prick gets close enough to lean on the passenger side door, allowing him to see my white knuckles on the steering wheel. He slowly slips his head in through the frame of the passenger side window, putting him close enough that I can smell the stale beer on his breath as he venomously whispers, "You know... you'd be a lot sexier if you smiled."

I hear my teeth audibly grind in response, as my stomach and brain continue doing backflips. Finally, as though it was waiting for my anger to reach an echelon before permitting my escape, the light turns green and I slam on the gas pedal.

The hastiness of my departure from the intersection causes the tattooed man-child to awkwardly cartwheel into the dirt. His confederate sidekick feebly attempts to yell after the truck, but almost instantly starts choking on the cloud of dust that the tires have kicked up behind me.

Glancing into the rearview mirror, I see both men giving me the middle finger, so I return the favor and 'salute' them back. Despite the intensity of my headache, I can't help but smile in response to my little victory as I continue speeding away in search of 'Neyman and Son Produce Co.'

Prior to seeing the state of this town, I had imagined some sort of grocery store, or at least a warehouse-style market as my first stop, but soon I find myself staring at a haphazardly constructed fruit stand on the side of the road with crudely painted letters signifying that this is the spot.

I turn the truck around so it's facing east in advance of my backtracking route. As I park, I grab the shopping list and a reusable bag from the passenger seat, before slowly emerging from the vehicle.

Before I've even shut the driver's side door, I can see two

elderly men sitting on the front porch of (presumably) the Neyman home. The two men gently rock in their archaic chairs as they stare at me with deep contempt, from a moderate distance.

Choosing to pay no mind, I approach the younger-looking man who's working the stand. Assuming he's the 'Son' part of the Neyman equation, I greet him with a polite, "Good morning!"

Instead of returning the greeting, he keeps his thumbs hooked under the straps of his denim overalls and spits a copious amount of saliva and chewing tobacco on the ground between us without breaking eye contact.

I awkwardly steer away from the large spot of wet dirt, making my way towards the produce display under a ratty umbrella that's been repeatedly duct-taped to the edge of the cart.

Even as I select my items from the slim pickings of semi-rotten produce, I can feel the eyes of all three Neyman men on me. I try to make haste while appearing to be unfazed by them, putting everything I need into the canvass bag and fishing out some cash before I turn to the younger man and inquire, "How much?"

His eyes slowly move towards my feet, then back up to my face as though he's appraising the price of my purchases based on the quality of my figure. Finally, he spits on the ground again before saying, "Thirty bucks."

I do everything in my power to not scoff at the seemingly arbitrary amount, but the pain in my skull and stomach betray me, causing me to angrily respond, "You can't be serious!"

He looks past me as he says, "You drivin' the Morgan truck, ain't ya?"

While I realize the question is rhetorical in nature, the distraction of the pain in my head and stomach throws me off my game. Like an idiot, I admit, "Yeah, I am. So what?"

The young man visibly squeezes the straps on his overalls in response to my insolence. He locks eyes with me once more, and spits a third time before adjusting his initial quote, "Forty bucks."

Every part of me wants to tell this asshole off for blatantly discriminating against a customer, but another part of me clocks one of the elderly men on the porch standing up from his chair, eager to get involved.

I coldly concede, barking out, "Fine!" before I ball up two twenty dollar bills and purposely throw them towards the mud-puddle of his tobacco spit. He looks up at me, as though he's about to say something else, but before he can, I spit on the ground for good measure.

Quickly pivoting, I storm back towards the truck, muttering every swear word I know on the way, but before I can get back in the truck, the younger man from the produce stand maliciously calls out, "You ain't welcome here!"

I'm so furious I barely even acknowledge hearing him speak. Shifting the truck into gear, I maliciously spin my tires as I peel away, kicking up as much dust as possible in the process to pontificate my exit.

As the truck gently fishtails on the loose dirt road, I notice that the waves of nausea I had been experiencing have now shifted to sharp pains all over my abdomen. My headache also seems to have evolved into a borderline, blinding migraine.

Thankfully, it's not far down the road that I pull into my next stop at the General Store. I make sure to park the truck a few doors over, in the hopes that the shop owner will not be able to pair me with the vehicle.

As I enter the store, I pick up the few items from the list, along with a bottle of water and a small container of ibuprofen. Suppressing the pain as best as I can, I see the shop owner looking me up and down quizzically, so I dismiss his silent inquiry by saying, "Just passing through. Think the heat must be getting to me."

The shop owner says nothing, and continues ringing in my items on his archaic register. As he does so, I notice an old shoebox on the counter with a piece of masking tape on it that says 'chargers'. Based on the thick layer of dust that's collected on both the box and its contents, it's clear that these are not top selling items around these parts.

Nevertheless, I reach over and grab one with a car adapter, ensuring its compatibility with my phone that I had so mindlessly slipped into my pocket when I had gotten dressed this morning.

With a silent, polite nod, I pay for my items and quietly make my way back towards the truck, successfully avoiding any tense conflict that might amplify the pain of my symptoms any further.

As soon as I'm back in the cab of the truck, I pop three ibuprofens and wash them down with nearly half of the bottle of water. As I catch my breath, I pull out my phone and plug it into the truck's cigarette lighter port. Soon, my phone's load screen pops on, so I tuck the device into the glove box to let it reboot while I continue running the rest of my errands.

At each stop, I continue to park a few doors away, maintaining the charade of being someone who's just 'passing through' as I collect the odds and ends from Ms. Pierre's list, as well as some supplies for my upcoming lesson with the children.

Sure enough, my tactics prove somewhat successful as I receive *slightly* warmer greetings and exchanges in relativity to my experience at the produce stand.

However, despite the relative ease of my tasks under this false identity, I still feel the pains in my stomach and head growing with each passing moment, the ibuprofen seemingly having no effect. Nevertheless, I continue forcing myself to push through my tasks until I finally arrive at my last location, the Butcher shop.

Sitting in the cab of the truck, the pain in my stomach makes me double over in the driver's seat. I start pressing on my abdomen in search of any signs of hypersensitivity that would suggest organ rupture, but I find none; just a steady, sharp pain all over.

Forcing myself to exit the truck I slowly drag my feet through the dirt as I make my way towards the Butcher shop and up the small, rickety staircase that leads up to the front door.

As I enter the Butcher shop, a bell above the door announces my presence. I immediately look to my left and see a grizzled, portly man in the back, soaked in sweat as he hacks away at a large, yet unidentifiable piece of animal carcass.

Briefly pausing, the Butcher glances towards me, his blinking eyes comically magnified through the lenses of his coke-bottle glasses. He gives me a polite, yet crooked smile, but says nothing as he goes back to his gruesome work.

Despite the extreme efforts this portly Butcher is putting into each violent hack, the wisps of black hair that thinly veil his sizeable bald spot remain swept to one side, presumably held in place by the beads of sweat on his rouged face.

The white apron that the Butcher is wearing is smeared with the blood of his labor, somewhat of an occupational hazard for his trade I would assume; yet the sheer level of gore of this particular scene feels almost excessive in nature, especially given my bouts of debilitating nausea.

Eventually, the Butcher delivers his final chop, severing a sizeable piece of meat from the carcass. With one hand and an audible grunt, he swings the severed flesh to a nearby table before he buries his cleaver into the large wooded chopping block and takes a moment to catch his breath.

As the Butcher looks back towards me, his magnified eyes shift back and forth as he attempts to focus. I see his face suddenly change as he realizes that I'm not one of his regular customers, prompting him to tentatively approach from the back as he scans my face.

Now that the sound of his hacking cleaver has ceased, I can hear him loudly sucking on a hard candy, which only makes the momentary silence all the more unnerving.

Between audible slurps, the Butcher asks, "Can I help ya?"

I quickly turn my attention towards the list that Ms. Pierre has provided and scan the page for the specific items I'm supposed to pick up, only to find the notation that says, 'ask for the standing order under *Morgan*'.

Desperately searching for a way to word my order without having to admit my connections to the Morgan Family, I start to stutter a response, but before my words can even take form, the Butcher audibly sucks on his hard candy once more as he says, "Lemme guess. You're the new Morgan girl."

I hesitate, saying nothing, but my silence speaks more in response to his inquiry than my words would have anyway.

The Butcher wipes the sweat off his brow with a bloodied hand, incidentally painting his forehead crimson in the process. I silently prepare myself for a bout of prejudicial hatred, similar to what I had experienced at the produce stand, but instead, the Butcher dutifully moves to a large fridge and begins to root around for the order I'm meant to pick up.

Soon, he produces a stack of fresh meats; each cut, wrapped in brown paper and tied with string. As he slams the items onto the counter, the sound of the impact causes the pain in my headache to spike once more.

Despite my attempt to hide the pain, I know that he's seen me wincing because his sideways grin suddenly fades as he asks, "You alright there, girlie?"

Desperately trying to spare myself a lengthy conversation, I dismiss his inquiry with as much patience as my body will allow me, "I'm fine."

He continues sucking on his candy, as he says, "Y'know... I'll never understand why so many pretty little things like you would wanna work for people like them Morgans."

I try to shrug off his statement, but my brow naturally furrows in curiosity towards his choice of wording. I gently attempt to correct him, "I'm sorry, you must be mistaken. I'm the only one they've hired to work in the home."

His smile returns with a patronizing twist as he says, "Right now, sure. But you ain't the first... probably ain't gonna be the last, neither."

I feel the nausea and headache intensify once more, feeding into one another in an endless loop of physical anguish as my mind spins with confusion towards this new information.

Before I've even contemplated his words fully, his smile fades as he adds, "Do yourself a favor, girlie... get away from there. Somethin' ain't right about that family."

Instinctually, I try to gather more information, asking, "What do you-?" but before I can finish my inquiry, the bell over the Butcher's door calls out once more as a middle-aged couple enter the store behind me.

I turn to face them and immediately see their smiles turn to scowls. Clearly they have spotted the truck a few doors over, and have now paired me with it. Another sharp pain in my abdomen kicks in, so I practically throw the money at the Butcher, grab the meats and make my way out of the store towards the truck with haste.

Throwing the meats into the cab of the truck through the open window, I try to focus my blurring vision as I fumble with the keys.

While I'm distracted with my failing dexterity, I suddenly feel myself get pushed up against the driver's side door from behind. My forehead collides with the window's frame, immediately amplifying my headache and stomach pains to an unbearable level.

With my face pressed against the cab of the truck, I look in the side view mirror and see the reflection of someone's forearm with a tattoo of a busty mermaid, winking suggestively as she tips her SS hat.

I feel my adrenaline spike as my natural instincts for self-defense kick in, but before I can turn and strike, I feel the hands of a second man restraining me against the truck as well.

The second man is applying pressure from behind my right shoulder, aggravating the injury from the accident, making me feel as though my arm is going to pop out of its socket at any moment.

Suddenly, my nose fills with the smell of stale beer as the tattooed man presses his nose against my temple and aggressively whispers in my ear, "Well, well... if it ain't the rude *cunt* from earlier. I think it's time you got taught a lesson in manners."

His face is pressed so hard against the side of my head that I'm barely able to respond, but I still manage a mumbled, "Fuck you."

I hear him laugh in response before he whispers in my ear, "That's exactly what I was thinkin' sweetheart."

I then hear his sidekick chime in, "Fuckin' get 'er Clayton! Grab 'er by the pussy!"

By the time I feel Clayton's hand reaching around my waist towards my navel, I'm screaming at the top of my lungs. The force of my screams makes my head pound even harder to the point that it feels like my skull will fracture at any second, but the thought of his unwanted touch motivates me to keep fighting, even if my head explodes as a result.

Between screams, I hear the sound of the bell from the Butcher's door ring out and, through the passenger side window, I see the middle-aged couple as they exit the shop.

I gather as much air as possible, before I scream, "HELP!!!" as loud as I can.

The middle-aged couple jumps at first, shocked by the sound of my fearful panic, but soon they come running towards the source of the noise. I maintain my ground, certain that my aggressors will be scared off by the presence of witnesses, yet Clayton and his friend don't seem to relent.

Soon the middle-aged couple comes around the front of the truck with looks of concern on their faces. I wait for them to intervene, but when they catch a glimpse of me, their faces fill with derision and they promptly turn and walk away, leaving my attackers to continue their assault at will.

Clayton, suddenly presses his palm against my navel, pushing my backside towards him as he rubs himself against me. He makes sure that I can feel the presence of his swollen member as he whispers, "You don't gotta like it. That's what makes it fun."

His hand slowly moves down from my navel, under the waist of my jeans, until I feel the tips of his filthy, nicotine-stained fingers sliding between my legs.

As he begins to grip me, I feel the nausea and headache peaking, causing my whole body to wretch wildly. Clayton must hear my dry heaves because he keeps his lower body pressed against me, but pulls his head away, ever so slightly.

Feeling the pressure against the side of my head removed momentarily, I seize the opportunity and throw the back of my skull into Clayton's face as hard as I can, shattering his nose in the process. I hear him whimper before he stumbles backwards and lands on his ass as the blood starts to flow and the tent in his pants promptly deflates.

Clayton's sidekick steps back in shocked response to the attack, but soon he refocuses and begins his approach in defense of his friend. Before he's able to reach me though, the nausea spikes once more and I unintentionally empty the contents of my stomach into his face.

Frozen in shock and disgust, Clayton's confederate sidekick hesitates long enough that I can kick him in his tiny balls with enough force to send him stumbling backwards, tripping over Clayton who's still on the ground crying and bleeding.

Wiping my mouth clean, I quickly jump into the driver's seat of the truck, start the engine and peel away, making sure to shoot a wave of dirt in their faces as I do so.

As I'm speeding away, the two men scream out names like, 'bitch' and, 'cunt', but contrary to the last time I drove away from these two, I'm too shaken up to even contemplate a response this time.

I continue making haste as I tear out of town, repeatedly checking my rear and side view mirrors to make sure that my two aggressors didn't follow me. Sure enough, the coast appears to be clear, so I let the truck slow to a more comfortable speed.

As the truck's speed decreases, I suddenly feel my emotions begin to pour forward along with a steady stream of tears. Instead of fighting them off, I set them free and allow myself to scream and cry freely in the seclusion of the truck as I continue to slowly travel the open road.

After about ten minutes I feel the tears beginning to slow and I notice that my headache and nausea seem to have faded slightly. Perhaps it was a result of the emotional release that allowed my body to soothe itself, or maybe it was the physical relief gained from regurgitating all over Clayton's sidekick. Either way, with the incremental release of my nagging pain, so too comes a wave of clarity and the echo of the Butcher's words, '*you ain't the first... probably ain't gonna be the last neither.*'

What the hell did he mean by that? As far as I know, I am the only one that Ms. Pierre has hired for this position. Though there have been numerous occasions where she had made sure to mention '*other candidates*' that could replace me, likely as a method of tactful intimidation, she has never once mentioned anyone who might have *preceded* me.

If there *were* other girls, what happened to them? Did Ms. Pierre just simply scare them off with her various forms of emotional torture? If so, I wouldn't be surprised. But what if they didn't just *leave*? What if something worse happened to them? What if something worse is destined to happen to me?

As my mind races through the hypotheticals surrounding the Butcher's words and my ensuing inquiries, I suddenly notice the light from my phone glowing in the glove box of the truck's cab.

I try to keep my eyes on the road as I reach over and fish out my device. Glancing at the screen, I see that it is fully charged, but only has one bar of service due to my remote surroundings.

Trying to find more of a signal, I lift my device up towards the front windshield, but as I do, I suddenly feel the Morgan truck shoot forward as a result of getting rear-ended. The force of the impact causes me to drop my phone as my head whips backwards into the headrest and I scramble to get both hands back on the wheel to maintain control.

My eyes dart towards the rearview mirror, where I see a much larger pick up truck; in far better condition than the one I'm in, pursuing me with haste. I don't even need to see the face of the driver know exactly who's behind me.

As the pursuing truck moves into the left lane, they speed up and match my pace so that Clayton's sidekick can start screaming at me from the passenger-seat of their truck.

Leaning out of the passenger-side window, I see the remnants of my vomit on the sleeveless confederate t-shirt as Clayton's sidekick produces a baseball bat from within the vehicle and swings it close enough to the cab of my truck that he takes the side mirror clean off.

I push the gas pedal to the floor in an attempt to speed away, but the age of the engine only allows my truck to travel so fast. Clayton easily matches my speed as they both continue to yell obscenities at me and the sidekick keeps swinging his bat.

Thankfully, a car coming in the opposite direction spots the two men in the wrong lane and leans on their horn long enough to force the men to slow and fall in behind me for fear of a head-on collision.

As the car in the opposite lane passes us, Clayton gives my rear fender another bump before pulling forward once more so that his sidekick can take a few more menacing swings of his bat.

By some form of miracle, I see the symbol of the three-armed pinwheels on two trees, not too far ahead. Despite the spiking level of fear I am feeling all over my body, I keep my eyes trained on the entrance to the hidden driveway, counting down the seconds to the turn.

Clayton's sidekick takes a few more swings, grazing the driver's side door and putting a pretty sizeable dent in the front hood. He's about to swing again, when I finally reach the entrance and take a sharp right turn, hearing the tires skidding beneath me as the truck fishtails onto the two thin strips that mark the path back to the Morgan home.

I hear the tires of Clayton's truck skid as well, as he slams on the brakes and backs up to the entrance of the hidden driveway. I glance in my rearview mirror, expecting to see them follow me towards the home, but for some reason, they surrender their pursuit at the marked trees, turning their truck around, and driving away.

I gently drop my speed back down as I question the surrender of their pursuit. It wasn't like their truck couldn't handle the terrain. If anything, they would have been far better equipped to do so. They certainly had seemed motivated enough to chase me off the edge of a cliff if they needed to, but something about the edge of the Morgan property seemed to give them pause, *scare* them even.

The curious nature of the whole situation makes me start to wonder what, exactly, it is about the Morgan family that the people of this town dislike so much? Were it simply a hatred towards the family, this place would have likely been burnt down centuries ago. But now, seeing the reaction of Clayton and his friend to the Morgan property, combined with the Butcher's warning about getting away from this house, I can't help but theorize that it must be something much deeper.

As the thoughts continue cycling through my head, I suddenly notice that my headache and nausea are all but gone. It is as if my return to safety has suddenly put my entire body at ease.

Despite the improvement in physical state though, the lasting trauma of the sexual attack, combined with the residual fear of the ensuing road rage, leaves my hands shaking and my heart racing.

I hear Ms. Pierre's words looping through my head as she cautions me against staying in town any longer than I needed to. I think back to the way that she had seemed so concerned about the way I was dressed and the '*dark intentions of men*' that she had so vaguely, yet sincerely referenced in her warnings.

As much as I can't stand her, I can't help but think that I should have heeded Ms. Pierre's warning. Soon I find myself rolling through hypothetical scenarios that would have saved me this feeling of trauma.

Maybe if I hadn't stood there talking to the Butcher, I would have been able to leave town before Clayton and his buddy were able to find me. Maybe if I hadn't aggravated Clayton and his sidekick in the first place, they wouldn't have felt compelled to exact revenge against me like they had. Maybe if I had just gotten over my fear of driving sooner, I wouldn't have taken so long to get to town and possibly could have avoided the whole situation to begin with.

I feel a wave of self-loathing wash over me as I start to blame myself for what happened. I should have known better... I should have listened... I should have just gotten in and gotten out like I was supposed to.

As I park the truck under the crooked shed's awning and turn off the ignition, I remain in the driver's seat for the better part of twenty minutes as I unabashedly cry in the silent solitude of the truck's cab.

CHAPTER FIFTEEN

Through the Keyhole

Still sitting in the cab of the truck, I lift my head and wipe away the last of the tears from my eyes, taking a moment to gather myself before I exit the vehicle. Bag-by-bag, I load the groceries into my arms and start making my way back towards the Morgan home.

Despite my ability to escape my attackers and return safely to the house, I'm still flashing back to the assault with every passing moment. Over and over, I see the image of Clayton's Nazi Mermaid tattoo reflected in the side view mirror as I feel his invasive hand slip down the front of my jeans.

Even now, I can still smell the stale beer on his breath as he encourages me to fight back for the sake of his own vile arousal. I can even taste the dust in the air, lingering with a hint of rusty metal from being pushed up against the truck's cab as it mingles with the saltiness of my tears.

As I finally reach the Morgan home, I pause at the front door, taking a deep breath and putting on a plastic smile in the event that I encounter anyone upon my arrival. Much to my surprise, as I enter the home, I find the place hauntingly quiet.

While the silence is unnerving at first, I soon welcome it amidst my current circumstances. The last thing I want to do right now is talk to someone, especially Ms. Pierre.

I spend the better part of half an hour quietly putting away the groceries, making sure to take my time, so that I can take full advantage of the solitude while trying to quell my emotions.

Repeatedly, I fight off the urge to start crying again and, save for a few tears that slip through here and there; I am somewhat successful in suppressing the instinct to do so.

Sadly, that's more than I can say in regards to my failing dexterity as a result of my shaking hands. So, once I finish with the groceries, I opt to retire to my room to continue to try to get my head straight and steady my nerves.

As I ascend the stairs, I find myself gripping the handrail with white knuckles as I flash back to the middle-aged couple's betrayal. How could they just walk away? How could they just *ignore* a woman in distress in the middle of the morning and out in the open like that? Come to think of it, why didn't anyone *else* intervene?

I feel my teeth gritting with hatred towards every one of those grizzled faces that stared at me with contempt as I had driven through town. A sense of loathing washes over me in response to their very existence, not to mention the shit town that they call home.

My swirling thoughts of anger combined with the eerie silence of the home, creates enough of a distraction that I don't even register the autonomous process of traversing the lengthy hallway.

By the time I come back to reality, I'm standing outside of my bedroom. I instinctually reach for the door handle, but before I'm able to turn it, I hear a sound coming from down the hall that makes me freeze in my tracks.

Something faint, soft even, yet filled with so much sadness... the sound of someone crying.

I pause for a moment, trying to verify what I think I've heard, when the sobbing suddenly becomes louder. Immediately the hairs on my arms simultaneously stand on end as I feel my eyes widen with equal parts intrigue and fear.

Against my better judgment, I start moving down the corridor, following the sound of the crying towards its source. Before long, I find myself standing outside of the mysterious room at the end of the hall, listening to the sounds of gentle whimpers coming from the other side of the locked door.

I glance over my shoulder to verify that the hallway is still empty before I slowly kneel down and lean my head towards the door to peek through the archaic keyhole beneath the doorknob.

The sound of crying continues to ring out, but I see no possible source of it within the empty room. What I do see though, immediately negates Ms. Pierre's story of this room merely being used for 'storage'.

On the right, I see an old desk covered in a thick layer of dust and cobwebs. Sitting on top of the desk, in a dusty glass bottle, is a miniature recreation of a ship similar to the one depicted in the painting in the 'salon'.

I strain my eyes to look just beyond the ship in a bottle and see, what appears to be, a leather-bound book. While the book is closed and nearly impossible to see from this lateral angle there is something about it that keeps my gaze upon it for a few seconds longer than needed.

My focus only breaks away from the book when the sound of crying suddenly returns. I carefully scan over the collection of shelving units covered in as much dust as there are antique books filling them, searching the shadows on either side of each unit for anyone who might be concealed within their midst.

As my eyes continue shifting around, they fall upon what looks like a spiral staircase on the left side of the room, leading up to some sort of second level.

I lean back from the door as I contemplate the location of this staircase. Quickly thinking back to the towering height of the ceiling in Macha and Nemain's bedroom in comparison to the much shorter height of the ceiling in mine, I start to put two and two together.

As my presumptive mind races around the idea of a hidden room above mine, and the answers it must *surely* contain, I quickly lean my head against the door once more to verify everything that I've seen.

Closing one eye and peering through the tiny keyhole with anticipation coursing through my veins, I see that the details of the room remain the same. However the layout of the room quickly becomes the last of my concerns as the source of the crying noise simultaneously reveals itself.

Directly in the center of the room, the cloaked woman holds still, gazing directly at me. I immediately feel my eyes widen with terror as my body freezes with fear.

Like so many other times, I see two amber eyes slowly start to glow from within the cloaked woman's hood. Instinctually, I recoil from the door, falling backwards in the middle of the hallway, and bumping the back of my head on the floor.

As I open my eyes and look up, I see the cloaked woman standing over me, the glowing amber eyes of the large crow shining brightly as the creature slowly emerges from within her dark hood.

Suddenly, my ears are filled with the deafening sound of screeching tires, twisting metal and breaking glass as the crow flies directly towards me with menacing speed from point blank range.

I jolt awake, screaming, and find myself still sitting in the cab of the truck, under the tilted awning of the shed. There are tears in my eyes and my hands are still shaking, but now I can't tell if it's from the trauma of my attack or the residual fear from my apparent nightmare.

Either way, I take a moment to reorient myself, wiping my eyes and taking some deep, cleansing breaths. I grab my phone out of the glove box and pocket it before slowly exiting the truck. Bag-by-bag, I load the groceries into my arms before I start making my way towards the Morgan home.

Traversing the distance between the truck and house, I feel my mind circling in confusion towards not only what had happened in town, but the apparent response I'm having to it by spontaneously falling asleep mere moments after the conclusion of the traumatic event.

I mean sure, I had once read an article in school that claimed ongoing psychological stress could *theoretically* lead to cases of narcolepsy, but it had never been verified. Even if it had been, it was still considered a long-term effect as opposed to an instantaneous response like I had just experienced.

As I continue to roll this mystery over in my head, I see the front door of the Morgan home present itself on the horizon. I quickly shift my focus towards gathering myself both physically and emotionally.

Reaching for the handle on the door, I take a deep breath in preparation for Ms. Pierre to be on the other side, waiting to ask what took me so long.

However, as I enter the house, I can't help but notice the overwhelming silence throughout. I immediately feel the hairs on my arms simultaneously stand on end in response to the echo of my subconscious projection from only moments ago.

I try to shake off the nagging feeling of having experienced this all before, but the blurring of lines between my dream state and my current reality haunts my every thought and movement.

Taking my time to put away the groceries, I try to remind myself of the sheer size of the home as well as each room's ability to trap sound behind their thick wooden doors. With the thought of the doors in the home though, my mind keeps circling back to the image of that mysterious office I saw through the keyhole at the end of the hall.

Soon, I find myself obsessing over whether the images I had seen were merely a fabricated projection, or if they were more clairvoyant in nature. Whether the cloaked woman is awaiting my gaze on the other side of that door, or not, I can't fight the overwhelming compulsion to see if *anything* in that room matches what I had seen sub-consciously.

I finish putting away the last of the groceries, as curiosity finally seizes me in its poisonous talons. Soon, I find myself making my way towards the stairs with haste, my mind racing as I do so.

Along the way, my eyes dart back and forth; desperately searching for anything that would signify if this were reality or just another dream. Alas, nothing presents itself as particularly telling, so I continue up the stairs.

Upon reaching the upstairs hallway, I once again find myself surrounded by eerie silence. I repeatedly tell myself that this is merely coincidence, that there is nothing to fear, that I should keep pressing on and investigate this mysterious room to either verify, or dispel the rumors of my newest inquisitive obsession. Hopefully putting my mind at ease, one way or another.

Quietly tiptoeing down the corridor, I pass by the children's room and hear the faint, muffled sound of Ms. Pierre's voice as she conducts one of the children's afternoon lessons. At first, I let out a quiet sigh of relief in response to the noise as it momentarily grounds me, giving me a sense of certainty that I am in the waking world.

I then mischievously smirk to myself as I realize Ms. Pierre will likely remain occupied for the next while, thus buying me some time to conduct my investigation.

However, just as I'm about to continue down the hall, the tone of Ms. Pierre's voice rises dramatically. While it's difficult to make out the words she is saying, I can't help but think of the thickness of the door and the sheer volume that would be required to be *this* audible from outside of the room.

With this realization, comes a feeling of overwhelming concern for the children. I move closer to the door to see if I can catch any specifics of what has gotten Ms. Pierre so riled up, but one word is barely distinguishable from the next, so I move even closer.

Gently placing my hand on the embossed Triquetra, and pressing my ear up against a flat portion of the door to the right of the symbol, I hear Ms. Pierre's voice suddenly reach an echelon of both volume and anger, as she screams, "I SAID ENOUGH!!!"

Her curt demand is followed by the sound of a sharp impact, causing my eyes to pop open as I realize it was the sound of someone being struck by an open hand.

Suddenly, every defensive feeling I have towards Macha and Nemain take over. Without thinking, I throw the door to the children's room open to interrupt the situation before it can escalate any further.

Upon entry, Ms. Pierre reflexively pivots, with a fire in her eyes as she says, "What!?"

While every part of my instinct wants to launch myself towards Ms. Pierre for even *considering* an act of violence against one of the children, I force myself to remember that my only form of 'proof' is a muffled noise through a large piece of wood.

Besides, were I to attack towards Ms. Pierre verbally or physically, it would likely result in me being fired and banished from the home, thus allowing any abuse of the children to continue. But if I were able to *prove* it somehow, then maybe I could *save* these children from her, just like the cloaked woman wants me to.

I take a breath to calm myself before I craft my response, "I- I just wanted to let you know that I'm back from town and everything has been put away."

Ms. Pierre purses her lips and folds her shaking hands at her waist in response to my pointless interruption. However, the stillness of her stance accents either side of her corset as it rhythmically stretches and contracts, showing that she is out of breath.

To add to the visible evidence of her physical exertion, her normally airtight bun has come loose in places, causing strings of silver hair to fall down either side of her washed out face.

Seeing me critically analyzing her as I stand there, Ms. Pierre quickly, yet subtly collects herself as she calms the tone of her voice and inquires, "Will there be anything else, Miss Woodall?"

I glance over Ms. Pierre's shoulder and see Nemain rubbing her reddened cheek. As she does, I can see the remnants of tears in her eyes before she turns away from me, ashamed that I'm witnessing her moment of weakness.

Feeling my fist clenching at the sight of Nemain's suffering, I contain myself and rhetorically inquire, "Is everything alright in here?"

Ms. Pierre is quick to answer, "Everything is fine, Miss Woodall. Nemain and I were merely having a spirited debate regarding the merits of the Oxford Comma. One must be passionate about grammar if they are to express themselves in a clear manner. Isn't that right, Nemain?"

Nemain says nothing in response. Even if she had verified this obvious falsity, I still wouldn't buy it, so I step further into the room, creating a sense of physical presence as I clarify my inquiry with stern intent, "*Actually* Ms. Pierre, I was asking Macha and Nemain," shifting my look to their averted eyes, I ask, "are you two alright?"

Neither of the children look towards me, let alone answer, but their silence speaks volumes nonetheless.

I turn my attention back towards Ms. Pierre with a fire in my eyes and catch a moment of shame in hers as she realizes that I clearly have heard more than she thought I did. She knows now that the timing of my entry was more than simply coincidence.

Turning towards the children in the hopes of dispelling the situation faster, Ms. Pierre kindly floats a suggestion, "Perhaps… we could all use a break from today's lesson. While it's a tad early in the day's schedule, how would everyone feel about some extended recreational time?"

Macha immediately perks up at the opportunity to go out and play, whereas Nemain remains standing by the window with her back turned to everyone else. While she is hiding her face, the soft shake in her shoulders tells me that she's still crying.

I cut the silence short, by responding in place of the children, "I think that sounds like a great idea, Ms. Pierre. In fact, I think I might join you as well. A little fresh air could do us *all* some good."

Before I've finished speaking, Macha is already halfway out the door and making her way down the hallway. I turn back towards Ms. Pierre to see her sheepishly avoiding my gaze for fear of it inciting more shame than she's already feeling.

Seeing Nemain still standing by the window, I diplomatically excuse Ms. Pierre with enough sternness in my voice to insinuate that it's not a polite suggestion, "Ms. Pierre, why don't you go keep an eye on Macha? Nemain and I will catch up in a moment."

I see Ms. Pierre's hesitance at first, likely driven by the concerned feeling one gets when they know that two people are about to talk about them, the moment they leave the room.

While she is visibly desperate to remain in the power position, Ms. Pierre also knows she doesn't have a leg to stand on in this moment, so she quietly pivots and obliges, following Macha downstairs.

I wait until Ms. Pierre is out of earshot before I turn towards Nemain, who still has her back to me. Slowly approaching, I softly say, "It's okay, she's gone now."

Save for a few sniffles, Nemain does not respond to me, yet I can see the shaking in her shoulders has slowed, signifying that her crying has softened.

I cease my approach at the halfway point between us, exhibiting my understanding for Nemain's need to be alone right now, as I say, "Hey. Take all the time you need, okay? But just know, that if you ever want to talk, I'm here for you. You can always trust me."

I see Nemain's head lift slightly at the sensitivity of the offer, yet she keeps her back turned to me and says nothing.

Understanding how broken her trust towards authority figures currently is, I slowly start to back out of the room as I try to present the option as soothingly as I can, "I'm going to go outside, so that you can have some time to yourself. But please, come and join us at some point. I'm sure Macha would love to have her sister there, and you know what? I'd love to have you out there with us too. But only when *you're* ready, okay?"

Despite my ability to use a calming voice in the moment, my heart breaks for Nemain the second I exit the children's room and softly close the door behind me.

I feel an undying instinct to whisk both her and Macha away from here, to a place where Ms. Pierre could never hurt them again. With that protective desire comes the fire of my anger towards the idea that Ms. Pierre would ever *intentionally* hurt these children.

The intensity of the moment, combined with the events in town, all seem to wash over me like a tidal wave. By the time I reach the top of the stairs at the end of the hallway, I feel the compounded stress come to a head, as my knees suddenly get weak beneath me.

I gently sit on the top step and bury my face in my hands as I start to cry. I cry for Nemain. I cry for Macha. I cry for myself and I even cry for Andy. By the time the first loop of my circling, melancholy thoughts have come and gone, I just let myself continue crying because it starts to feel better than holding it all in.

Moments later, between the sounds of my own sobbing, I hear the door to the children's room slowly open as Nemain quietly makes her way into the hall. I do my best to wipe my eyes and collect myself as she tentatively approaches.

At first, she keeps her eyes trained on the floor as I stand to greet her, but as Nemain slowly looks up to my face, I see a soft empathy in her eyes that I've never seen before. Inquisitively, she tilts her head and says, "You've been crying, too."

I do my best to hold back another wave of tears that are pushing against the gates, as I say, "I think we're all having a bit of a tough day."

With wisdom beyond her years, Nemain nods at my statement, silently understanding that I've been suffering as well, yet lacking the intrusive instinct most people would have to inquire further.

Cutting the silence short, I descend the first step as I turn to Nemain, "What do you say? Shall we go catch up with Macha before she has all the fun without us?"

Nemain says nothing in response, but quietly matches my slowed pace as we descend the stairs silently, side by side, step-by-step.

Once we are nearly two thirds of the way down the stairs, I suddenly feel a small hand quietly wrap itself around mine in both the search of security, and the offering of sympathy.

I say nothing, but gently squeeze her hand in response to the gesture, both as an act of reassurance and a showing of gratitude.

As we continue descending the stairs together, I feel a single tear of joy forming. As it brims the edge of my eyelid, I quietly wipe it away before looking down at Nemain and smiling to myself.

While it may have taken some time, Nemain has finally lowered her guard and let me in.

CHAPTER SIXTEEN

Recreational Time

I smile to myself as I watch Macha and Nemain play in the clearing in front of the Morgan home. Despite the residual anger towards Ms. Pierre, along with the lingering fear from Clayton's attack, I take a deep breath, allowing myself a moment to absorb the calming beauty of my surroundings.

My eyes dance between the branches of the large oak trees that surround the property, the canopy of leaves above us twisting and dancing in the gentle breeze. With the movement of each oak leaf, the light of the afternoon sun seems to sparkle as it sneaks through the impenetrable barrier in tiny, momentary specs of brightness.

Turning my attention back towards the children, I feel a sense of warmth within me, as they become lost in their respective worlds of imagination, enjoying the simple pleasures of childhood as it transports them far from here, if even for the moment.

Macha has taken to a small stick that she is using as a mock crayon as she crouches down and scribbles pictures in the dirt that only she can understand. While the patterns seem detached and nonsensical, her deep level of contemplative focus tells me that she sees her creation as a masterpiece.

Meanwhile, Nemain is in the distance with a small, nylon net in one hand and a large mason jar in the other as she tries to catch butterflies that flutter about. She giggles each time they evade her attempts at capture, showing that she cares more about the playful pursuit than the idea of victory, itself.

Thanks to Ms. Pierre's regime of strict scheduling and advanced lesson plans, I had come to accept the girls as miniature versions of adults over my time within the home. Seeing them now though, I suddenly realize that underneath their rigid exteriors, Macha and Nemain really are just children.

Despite the pleasantness of the scene, I can feel the weight of Ms. Pierre's silence as she sits on a large rock behind me. Whether she is contemplating her impulsive actions, or calculating her next move so as to return to the position of power, remains unknown. Either way, I'm happy that she has opted for silence, as the last thing I want right now is to speak to her, let alone look at her.

As Macha places her stick on the ground, wipes her dirty hands on her clothes and starts gathering pebbles to add to her 'drawing', I hear Ms. Pierre inhale behind me as though she is about to say something. I brace myself, trying to contain my anger in advance of her speaking, yet she says nothing.

A few more tension-filled seconds of contemplative silence pass before she finally finds her words and says, "You must think of me as some kind of monster."

Despite a million combative responses flipping through my mind at once, I opt to say none of them, keeping my back to her as I cross my arms in silent protest.

Sure enough, my silence prompts Ms. Pierre to continue with her attempted justification of her actions, "Miss Woodall, you have to understand that I-"

I keep my back to her, but turn my head sharply to the side so I can cut her off with a hushed, yet cold tone that remains inaudible to the children, "-No. *You* have to understand! There is *no* excuse for assault, of *any* kind!"

Ms. Pierre pauses for a moment. I'm unsure of how she has received my scorn, but soon her tone shifts to one of deep regret as she says, "Believe me, I know that... More so than you could ever imagine."

At first, I assume the regret in Ms. Pierre's voice is in regards to her actions against Nemain, but as I hear a barely audible sniffle behind me, I realize her statement carries a much deeper truth.

Thinking back to when Ms. Pierre had been teaching me 'the routine' of the household, I suddenly remember an odd exchange amidst our conversation. After I had suggested that children should be allowed to select their own hobbies, she had responded by suggesting that such a practice would only result in little boys 'raping and murdering every living thing they see'.

At the time, I had suspected that Ms. Pierre's statement was driven by some kind of personal experience, but had been quick to dismiss it from my mind. But then I suddenly remember that my suspicions had resurfaced as recently as this morning when Ms. Pierre had cautioned me about attracting the 'dark intentions of men' by showing exposing skin.

The passing memory of the warning that I chose not to heed suddenly sends me back to my assault in town, and the ensuing incident on the road as Clayton and his sidekick had chased me all the way back to the edge of the Morgan property.

I feel my fists clenching at the memory of my experience, as a tidal wave of emotion swells within me, forcing me to relive each moment over and over again in a matter of seconds.

Clocking both the physical and emotional reactions that I'm having to the resurgence of these memories, I am suddenly hit by a moment of clarity as I put two and two together and find a context to Ms. Pierre's standoffish nature.

Despite my residual hatred towards Ms. Pierre in the wake of her assault on Nemain, I feel a wave of empathy washing over me. Keeping my back turned to her, I softly inquire, "How long ago were you assaulted?"

Though she says nothing, I hear Ms. Pierre quickly collect herself in response to the precision of my sudden perception. I can hear the threads of the fabrics in her clothes creak as she straightens her back, yet remains silent.

I don't have to see Ms. Pierre's face to know that she is pursing her lips and raising an eyebrow at the very mention of such a thing so, after a long bout of tension-filled silence, I finally relax my posture and turn towards her with soft concern in my eyes.

No matter how cold the expression on Ms. Pierre's face is; all I can see is the pain hidden behind her eyes. It's the anguish of a much younger woman that lives deep within her soul, trapped by her inability to even acknowledge the existence of such agony.

Without flinching, Ms. Pierre suddenly spits venom, "Miss Woodall, I have no idea what you *think* you are referencing, but how *dare* you make such a supposition!"

I'm taken aback by the sudden nature of Ms. Pierre's

emotional escalation. While I understand the propensity to not want to discuss her long-suppressed trauma, I have never witnessed such a visceral response towards the offer of a sympathetic ear.

Ms. Pierre then narrows her eyes as she stares directly into mine with the fires of hatred burning within her, "Even if I *were* to have experienced something like that, simply mentioning it is the equivalent of asking me to relive the entire *vile* experience! I would have thought someone with your supposed '*training*' would understand that!"

I suddenly feel my back straightening as my defensiveness grows in response to her challenging my expertise, "Excuse me?! I was just-"

Before I can explain myself, Ms. Pierre cuts in once more and asks, "-Are you *intentionally* trying to cause me pain, Miss Woodall? Do you really hate me *that* much?"

While part of me wants to launch at her with verbal confirmation of how horrible of a person I think she is, I try to contain myself and slow my anger. Despite her accusations towards the purity of my initial intent, I softly say, "Ms. Pierre, I didn't mean any harm. I was just-"

Ms. Pierre suddenly stands up, stepping towards me, "-I know exactly what you're doing Miss Woodall! You're trying to find my weaknesses so you can get rid of me! You're trying to separate me from these children like I'm some sort of horrible creature that's poisoning them with my very presence!"

I stand and take the verbal assault without a response, primarily because I'm so aghast at her unfounded accusations that I find myself literally speechless.

Seconds later, Ms. Pierre takes a few steps forward and extends her index finger towards me, pontificating the thesis of her attack as she pokes me in my bad shoulder, "Let me make this *abundantly* clear for you, Miss Woodall. *You* will *not* replace me!"

The combination of the intensity in Ms. Pierre's eyes, combined with the aggravated pain in my shoulder, causes the anger inside of me to swell, taking hold of every fiber of my being. I suddenly fire back without thinking, "I'm not trying to replace you! I'm trying to *help* you!"

Ms. Pierre pauses for a moment, slowly retreating back to the rock and sitting down again. As she does, she clears her throat and purses her lips in an attempt to contain herself in the wake of her emotional outburst.

Gently folding her hands in her lap, Ms. Pierre visibly swallows her anger before taking on a much more diplomatic tone, "I apologize, Miss Woodall. I don't know what came over me. I guess I have been so concerned about the *children's* adjustments to a new face in the home, that I appear to have neglected my *own* transition into our new living situation."

While part of me thinks that she is merely avoiding confrontation, I find myself starting to wonder if Ms. Pierre's vulnerable concession could actually carry some form of sincerity within it.

Maybe Ms. Pierre's inability to accept assistance was what pushed away the previous employees that the Butcher had mentioned? Ms. Pierre did say so herself, she has raised Macha and Nemain *since birth*. The more I think about it, the more I realize that her naturally frigid sternness makes much more sense in the context of maternal defensiveness.

Suddenly it becomes clear. The majority of Ms. Pierre's anger has nothing to do with me as an individual, but merely what I *represent*. She is resisting against the acceptance of her inevitable reality. Some day, Macha and Nemain will live on without her, or worse, they will live under the care of someone else, like me.

Ms. Pierre is not afraid I will *take* the children from her, she is afraid that after she's gone, the children will *forget* her.

With this new understanding taken into consideration, I take a moment to calm myself, finding empathy in the moment as I say, "In all fairness, I think the stress of the adjustment period has been getting to all of us."

Ms. Pierre suddenly perks up in response. She says nothing, but her face is washed over with inquisitiveness towards my statement.

I shrug dismissively at her silent inquiry, quickly digging up a scapegoat explanation, "I've been having some trouble sleeping. Just some bad dreams, that's all."

Ms. Pierre says nothing in response, but something about her stillness tells me that she has experienced her fair share of sleepless nights in this home as well.

Amidst the moment of mutual sympathy, I recognize the sudden opportunity to ensure the protection of the girls without seeming overbearing, so I shift gears, asking, "Ms. Pierre, how would you feel about me conducting my first lesson with the children a little earlier than we had planned?"

At first, Ms. Pierre remains physically still, but I can see the wheels turning as she assesses the request from all angles before responding, "How early were you thinking, Miss Woodall?"

Bringing a warm smile to my face, I tactfully answer, "Whenever you feel it's appropriate. I just figured that this way, I could help alleviate some of your duties, along with some of your stress. I know that working with the children will help to alleviate some of mine. Consider it a mutually beneficial proposal that might even help to smooth out this transition for the girls as well."

Taking a moment to consider it, Ms. Pierre hesitantly nods in agreement, saying, "Very well. You may conduct your lesson tomorrow morning. Unless, of course, you feel you need more time to prepare?"

I emphatically respond, "I'll spend all night preparing, if I have to."

Ms. Pierre then pauses for a moment before she follows up by inquiring, "I trust you were able to gather the supplies you require from town this morning?"

The diplomacy of the moment causes me to respond without thinking, as a certain level of knee-jerk familiarity takes over and I casually blurt out, "Even if I didn't, I'd rather make do with what I have, than-" I quickly cut myself off before I mention anything that might suggest my apprehensiveness towards heading back into town.

Ms. Pierre pauses for a moment as her back straightens and she asks, "...Than what?"

Visibly scrambling to find something to fill in the gap, I flounder as I say, "Than... have to postpone this opportunity to a later date."

Scrutinizing me with her eyes, it doesn't take long for Ms.

Pierre to connect the dots and a, "…What happened to you this morning?"

Realizing the roles within our conversation have suddenly flipped, I default to trying to play dumb, "I- I'm not sure what you mean."

Still critically analyzing me, Ms. Pierre can tell that something is off and continues to press her inquiry, "You were late returning to the home. What took you so long?"

I attempt to back-pedal, scrambling for a fictionalized response, "Oh… the locals saw the truck, so they felt compelled to make me wait out of spite. You were right, they are *not* welcoming people."

Ms. Pierre looks at me with dissecting eyes as a single eyebrow rises. She knows I'm not giving her the whole truth on purpose, and while I can't tell what it is, something about my face is betraying me, based on the way she is studying me.

I cut the awkward silence by tactfully adding; "Also, I wasn't feeling so great this morning so I may have been dragging my feet a bit too."

Ms. Pierre's face suddenly shifts from one of intrigue to one of concern towards the mention of my maladies.

Assuming she's worried about a sickness spreading through the household, I quickly follow up with a self-diagnosis, "It was just a bit of a headache and a small bout of nausea. Got a little worse as the day went on, but don't worry, it's passed and I feel much better now."

I watch as Ms. Pierre's face drops at the description of my specific symptoms. For some reason, the mention of my headache and nausea while in town seem to have ignited a sense of anger-fueled jealousy in her eyes.

Quickly going over my words for anything that might have been construed as offensive, I find no reasoning for the simple mention of migraine-like symptoms, to incite such a strong reaction in Ms. Pierre.

As much out of awkwardness as confusion and fear, I choose to not acknowledge the visible emotional shift that I'm witnessing, and opt to casually pivot around to check on Macha and Nemain, instead.

My mind races in response to Ms. Pierre's inexplicably erratic emotional reactions as my eyes scan the entirety of the clearing in front of me.

However, I quickly put aside my distracted thoughts as I suddenly feel my heart skip a beat. My back straightens as my eyes double in speed, scanning back and forth over the clearing a hundred times in half a second while a wave of panic washes over me.

Suddenly, I see Ms. Pierre standing in my peripherals with concern on her face as she too scans the clearing with fear in her eyes.

After a moment, I look to Ms. Pierre and frantically ask, "Where's Nemain?"

CHAPTER SEVENTEEN

Travels

Without hesitation, I turn towards Ms. Pierre with an authoritative tone, "Stay here with Macha. I'll go find her."

Before Ms. Pierre has curtly nodded in response, I've already taken off, bounding towards the clearing in search of Nemain.

Within my first few strides, I see a look of concern wash over Macha's face. She hasn't noticed the absence of her sister, but she can clearly tell that something is wrong based on the sudden nature of my urgency.

As Macha's eyes begin to widen in response to the confusion, suggesting the onset of tears, I feel the instinct to slow my pace so as not to spread worry. However, just as I'm about to do so, Ms. Pierre steps forward and starts verbalizing her admiration towards Macha's drawing in the dirt.

Thankfully, Ms. Pierre's distraction pulls enough focus that I am able to pass by Macha quietly before resuming my pace and sprinting towards the middle of the clearing.

Scanning the edges of the forest, I attempt to minimize the concern in my voice as I start calling out Nemain's name in a soft, almost playful tone, as though it were a game of hide-and-seek.

Underneath my sprightly tone though, I am riddled with panic. My eyes bounce from tree to tree, as I hear nothing but the echo of my own voice in response to my calls. The longer the silence between each attempt lasts, the more I start to hypothesize about all of the horrible scenarios that could have resulted in Nemain's absence.

First, I worry that she may have wandered off and hurt herself, prompting images to flash through my mind of Nemain sitting at the base of a hill with a twisted ankle or a broken leg. Tears begin welling up in my eyes at the mere thought of Nemain being trapped, defenseless, and worse... alone.

It doesn't take long before my imaginings of her potential situation become progressively darker, causing my dread to simultaneously increase.

Soon, I am thinking of the carnivorous predators that must surely be living in these woods, attracted to the smell of Nemain's blood, then upon finding the source of the scent, dragging her helpless body off to their various caves and dens for consumption.

The mere thought of these hungry animals then steers my imagination towards the worst possible scenario with the worst kind of predators, Clayton and his confederate sidekick.

Soon, I'm weaving a hypothetical narrative that after the incident on the road, the two men had snuck onto the Morgan property to exact their revenge on me. Then, after realizing they couldn't get to me without being seen, they took Nemain instead.

The tears start to flow freely at the mere thought of what those fucking monsters could be doing to her, but my anger and determination to save Nemain forces me to wipe my eyes clean and stay focused for her sake.

Frantically, I scan the ground for any signs of what direction she might have gone in. I look for footprints in the dirt, broken leaves, drag marks, *anything* that might give me a clue towards where she has gone.

As the breeze picks up, my heart suddenly sinks, as I spot a small ribbon dangling from a twig that's sticking out of one of the tree trunks; a ribbon that Nemain had been wearing in her hair when I had last seen her.

I immediately run towards the slim piece of fabric as it twists in the breeze, pulling it from the tree and gripping it in my hand. Before I can even contemplate my actions, I run into the woods blindly, praying to every God that I can think of, that I'm going the right way and, more importantly, that Nemain is still alive.

Soon, I find myself surrounded by immense oak trees on all sides. The Morgan home is barely visible between the staggered, immense trunks, causing alarms to go off in the back of my mind as I am reminded of the impenetrable wall of trees from my nightmares.

I am quick to silence my nagging fear, putting aside my own terror so that I can focus on seeking out any other evidence that would steer me towards Nemain's location, yet I find nothing.

Frantically spinning in circles while silently cursing the immensity of the trees, I continue calling out Nemain's name, more panicked now, yet still, I hear no response.

My instincts scream at me to start sprinting, but I have no idea what direction to run in. I try to silence my impulses with logic, telling myself that if I prematurely run in any direction, it could lead me further away from her, potentially resulting in *both* of us getting lost.

I feel my breaths becoming shallower as the panic continues to rise within me. My nagging imagination begins projecting images of all of the horrible things that Clayton and his buddy would do to a defenseless little girl, like Nemain.

Soon, my fists are clenching as my feeling of panic is replaced with vindictive rage. I silently swear to myself that if either of them has laid a *finger* upon Nemain, I will tear their throats out with my bare hands, right then and there.

Before I realize my tone has shifted, I'm screaming Nemain's name at the top of my lungs, no longer able to hide the fear in my voice as the idea of the worst possible outcome drifts through my mind... finding her lifeless, violated body.

Continuing to spin in circles of panic as the tears are now streaming, full force, from my eyes I feel my anger and hatred towards Clayton and his sidekick, suddenly shift to self-imposed guilt and regret towards my own negligence.

Why had I turned my back on the children? Why had I let myself get distracted by my argument with Ms. Pierre? I should have been watching the girls. I should have warned Ms. Pierre about what happened in town. How could I be so stupid and careless? How can I be expected to *save* Macha and Nemain like the cloaked woman wants me to, when I can't even *protect* them to begin with?

Then... like a divine reward for my silent penance... I see it.

About thirty yards away, a monarch butterfly flutters its wings as it clumsily floats between two trees. It's erratic movement is quickly followed by the faint sound of giggling in response to the insect evading yet another attempted capture.

Before the impulse has even left my brain, I'm sprinting in the direction of the sound, weaving around the large oak tree trunks as I continue to call out Nemain's name with newfound hope and purpose.

Finally, I come into a small clearing to find Nemain giggling as she spins in circles, still in pursuit of her prey. I double over, out of breath, thanking every mystical force in the universe for helping me to find her, safe and sound.

As I try to bring saliva back to my mouth while actively willing my heart rate to slow down, I hear Nemain proudly call out in a mocking tone, "Ha! Got you!"

At first, I think she's addressing me, like this was all some sort of practical joke, but when I look up at her, I see that she has finally succeeded in capturing the delicate creature within her net.

Slowly, Nemain pinches the middle of the net to keep the butterfly contained as she methodically holds the jar between her knees and twists off the perforated lid. Ever so carefully, Nemain holds the Mason jar upside down over the net as she gently releases the insect.

Thinking it sees a path to freedom, the butterfly naturally floats upwards into the jar, and before it can figure out what's happened, Nemain is twisting the lid back on, sealing the insect within the container's transparent walls.

As Nemain finishes her meticulous process, I finally catch enough of my breath to speak, "Nemain, you can't just run off like that! Didn't you hear me calling your name?"

Nemain all but shrugs in response, as she plainly says, "I didn't want to scare her away. Isn't she pretty?"

Holding the jar up towards me, Nemain proudly shows me how picturesque her new pet butterfly is. While every part of me wants to launch into a disciplinary speech of how I was 'worried sick', I can't help but give in to my physical and emotional exhaustion.

As I sit on the ground and let my body relax, I can't help but smile at the sight of Nemain's pure state of joy as she continues to study the creature with scrutiny and asks, "What do you think we should we name her?"

The tension in my body slowly releases as I take a moment to glance at the orange, black and white wings of the butterfly. I quietly chuckle to myself before I respond, "How about, *Victoria*?"

Nemain looks at me for a moment, and then glances towards the butterfly as though she's searching for the source of inspiration behind such a preposterous moniker for an insect.

I continue smirking as I explain, "... because she's a *Monarch*?"

Playfully unimpressed, Nemain jokingly rolls her eyes at the suggestion, but smiles as she confirms the name with a gentle nod of approval, "*Queen* Victoria."

Despite my body finally resting for a moment, my breathing and pulse still remain uncomfortably elevated. I can't help but lament how out of shape I feel in this moment, but I'm quick to chalk it up to the lasting effects of my horrific experiences in town, combined with the most recent bout of sheer panic that is only now starting to truly subside.

Nemain comes over and sits near me, visibly concerned by the beading sweat on my forehead. Despite her pride in her successful capture of the butterfly, I see her face shift to one of guilt as she says in a meek voice, "I'm sorry I made you scared, Patty. Are you mad at me?"

I softly pull my knees towards my chest as I assure her, "I'm not mad, I was just... worried. Ms. Pierre was too."

Nemain trains her eyes on the ground, fidgeting with some fallen oak leaves as she says, "No she wasn't. Ms. Pierre doesn't care about me."

My heart breaks to hear her say such a thing, especially having just learned of Ms. Pierre's deep-seeded maternal nature towards the children, so I am quick to correct course, "Well, I don't think that's true. I think Ms. Pierre cares about you more than you'll ever know."

It's only now that I see a single tear fall from Nemain's downcast face as she asks, "Then why does she hurt me?"

I try my best to hide my wave of anger towards Ms. Pierre in the moment, attempting to remain diplomatic and not create camps amidst the household as I try to explain, "Ms. Pierre grew up in a time when... things worked differently. But trust me, she's *very* sorry about what she did."

Nemain pauses for a moment, still staring at the ground as she says, "I don't care. I *hate* her."

While every part of me wants to side with Nemain, I remind myself to remain the peacekeeper, "Now, now. That's not a very nice thing to say about someone, no matter the circumstances. You know, more often than not, when people think they hate someone, it turns out they *actually* love them. Sometimes we just get confused by the shadow that frustration can cast, but when you really think about it, hate and love are the same emotions, just in a different light."

Despite the logic in my words, Nemain still seems resistant to the idea, remaining silent as she continues to pull apart her dried oak leaf, piece-by-piece.

I drop into a whisper as I say, "Look, what Ms. Pierre did this morning... that's not okay. It's never okay. She knows she made a mistake, and she's *very* sorry about it. But I want you to know that, so long as I'm around, I will do *everything* in my power to make sure that it *never* happens to you, or Macha, ever again."

Nemain looks up at me with a light in her eyes, as though she's suddenly discovered her champion was disguised as a peasant this whole time.

Giving her asmile, I continue to offer assurance, "Like I said earlier, if you ever need to talk about *anything*, you can trust me. I'm really good at keeping secrets."

Nemain's face suddenly softens as she looks up at me and says, "I know you are, Patty."

Initially, I'm a little confused by the statement, so I silently furrow my brow in curiosity towards its meaning.

Before I can even inquire further, Nemain turns her focus back to her jar as she explains, "I saw your scars. You're really good at hiding them."

Instinctually, I pull down on the sleeves of my hoodie, shocked that a child her age has noticed the markings, but has not felt the impulse to ask or say anything about them, prior to this moment.

With wisdom beyond her years, Nemain taps the Mason jar

gently as she sympathetically continues, "I'm sorry that you went through whatever it was that made you do that to yourself."

I scramble for a response amidst the shock of the moment. Despite my mind moving a thousand miles a minute, I'm having trouble finding the words to express my gratitude for her sympathetic discretion while simultaneously justifying the poor choices of my past to a child her age.

During my fumbling silence, Nemain thinks for a moment before adding, "Also... I'm sorry I've been so mean to you."

Thankful for the quick change in subject, I try to remain casual as I say, "You don't need to be. I was a new face in your home, and I may have come on a little strong. I think we both just needed a little time to adjust."

Nemain looks back down at the ground as she says, "I still shouldn't have been so cruel."

Despite every fiber of my being wanting to pull Nemain in for a hug, I respect her space and keep my distance as I softly say, "I totally get it. You were just trying to protect your sister. If anything, it shows that you're a strong person."

Though she's still staring at the ground, I see Nemain smile a bit in response to my compliment.

I take a relaxed sigh, enjoying the quiet of the woods for a moment before I turn to Nemain once more and say, "You know, now that we're getting to know each other better, I want you to know that my offer still stands. I'd love to be your friend, if you'll have me."

Taking a moment to consider the offer, Nemain slowly lifts her head and turns to me with a smile as she says, "...Okay."

By the time we're finished speaking, I can't tell if the conversation has served as more of an emotional relief for Nemain, or me. Either way, we both remain sitting for a moment of pleasant silence together, before I finally say, "Alright. How about you, me, and Queen Victoria make our way back to the house, huh?"

Nemain nods, picking up her Mason jar with her new companion inside. As we start to make our way back towards the Morgan home, I feel Nemain's tiny hand slip into mine as she looks up at me, and smiles once more. It takes every ounce of strength for me not to break down and weep joyful tears in response to the gesture.

Reaching the edge of the woods, I see Ms. Pierre still standing where I had left her, still keeping Macha distracted while frantically scanning the landscape, in search of either Nemain or myself.

As we come into the clearing, Ms. Pierre finally spots us and places her hand on her heart before sitting back down on her rock and breathing a visible sigh of relief.

Before we're even halfway back across the clearing, Nemain looks up at me with an excited sparkle in her eye. I give her a silent nod, releasing her hand as she runs ahead to show Ms. Pierre her new pet butterfly.

By the time I've caught up, Ms. Pierre is holding the jar tentatively. It's clear that she's not comfortable being near the insect, but nevertheless, she goes through the motions of appreciation for Nemain's sake, hesitantly saying, "Well... I suppose that *is* a logical name."

Suddenly, Nemain wraps her arms around her elderly matriarch in a beautiful embrace, during which I see a look of pleasant shock on Ms. Pierre's face in response to the unsolicited gesture.

Amidst the hug, Ms. Pierre turns towards me, not in search of an explanation towards Nemain's emotional shift, nor even as a look of thanks, but one of pure wonderment towards this moment that she's clearly wanted for so long.

Despite the brief nature of the embrace, I finally see a sense of relief wash over Ms. Pierre, and for the first time since I've met her, a smile crosses her face. By no means is it a *beaming* smile, but one of peacefulness, showing that nothing else in the world matters, if even for just this moment.

CHAPTER EIGHTEEN

The Locked Room

With the sun down, I return to my room for the night, eager to put the day behind me along with the varied, heightened experiences that came with it.

Be it the fight with Ms. Pierre, the assault in town, the panic of momentarily losing Nemain, or simply all of it combined, I find myself exhausted not only physically and mentally, but above all else, emotionally.

Despite all that has happened though, I still can't help but softly smile in response to how such a chain of negative experiences could have led to a somewhat positive conclusion. While I, myself, am *far* from 'okay', for the first time since my arrival, there's a sense of peace and harmony within the Morgan home.

As I finish changing into a pair of comfortable sweatpants and a long-sleeved t-shirt, I start to dig through a small collection of books that I brought with me, specifically in search of one titled, 'Art Therapy for Children: Mending Homes Through Creativity'.

I start flipping through the various sections that I dog-eared in the days when I was back at school. Scanning the pages, I read up on various approaches to creative projects that will allow children to express parts of their psyche that might, otherwise, remain repressed.

Finding the specific passage regarding suggested subject matter for children dealing with suspected trauma, I open one of my drawers to get some some scrap paper and a pen so I can take notes.

As I open the drawer, I see Macha's drawing that I had found on my bed this morning, still folded into thirds from when I had stashed it away for later study. I bring it to the small table, along with my note-taking materials and slowly unfold the page.

Before I'm able to give the drawing my full attention though,

I hear a knock at my door, crisp and firm, yet somewhat softer than previous nights.

I quickly pull down on my sleeves and throw on my robe to ensure my scars remain hidden. Nemain may have revealed her awareness of them earlier, but I still have to be careful so as to not allow Ms. Pierre to know. Despite the day ending in such a positive manner, I'm still wary of her underlying intentions, especially since I witnessed her uncharacteristically snap during our argument.

As I quietly answer my door, I find Ms. Pierre standing on the other side, holding the tray with my dinner under the same old silver cloche. To my surprise, she has a relatively pleasant smile on her face, despite her wrinkles of sternness naturally dampening any visible forms of happiness.

Politely smiling, I go through the motions, taking the tray from her and giving thanks, already knowing that I probably won't eat anything that's been prepared. Yet, despite the tray being handed off, Ms. Pierre remains standing in place, as though she feels compelled to say something, but can't find the words.

While this has traditionally been a tension-fueled portion of our nightly routine, filled with escalating, combative statements towards one another, I too find myself at a loss for words to fill the void of silence.

Finally, Ms. Pierre glances over my shoulder and breaks the awkward moment by commenting on the textbook and note-taking materials that I have on my small table, "I see you are taking this lesson rather seriously."

Recognizing that my book may be deemed as 'unsuitable material' I try to gently back-pedal, "Oh, I'm just reviewing some of my past studies. Can't let the old knowledge bank grow stagnant."

Ms. Pierre gives a soft nod before completely contradicting everything I've come to learn about her by sincerely saying, "Well, try not to work too hard, *Patricia*."

I'm thrown off by her sudden kindness, not to mention her use of my first name. I can tell by the cadence of her delivery that she feels as unnatural using the informal address as I feel hearing it from her.

We both hover for another moment of pleasant, yet awkward silence. While Ms. Pierre's lips remain sealed, I can tell that there is still something she desperately wants to say to me, but for some reason she's resisting the urge.

I remain standing in my doorway, waiting for words that never come as Ms. Pierre finally gives a quick nod and pivots, heading off towards her room.

Gently nudging my door closed, I consider the experience of past 'dinners' and opt to place the tray off to the side, ignoring the meal as I return to my books and start skimming through a section titled, 'Approaching the Broken Inner Child'.

While I may only be teaching a *strictly* supervised lesson in Arts and Crafts tomorrow, I'm going to make sure to maximize my time with Macha and Nemain, not only to strengthen the bond between us, but to simultaneously try to find out more about this family and what it is that I'm meant to '*save them*' from.

I sit there taking furious notes, flipping pages back and forth for the better part of half an hour when I suddenly catch a welcoming aroma drifting through the air and into my nostrils.

The distraction of curiosity soon gets the better of me and I put my pen down in order to seek out the source of the smell. Much to my surprise, I am led towards the tray, yet even though I've identified the source of the scent, I remain wary of the pleasant aromas emanating from beneath the silver cloche, given the misleading nature of the cuisine from past nights.

I defensively lean back as I grip the top of the cloche and lift it upwards to reveal what kind of malicious manipulation I'm being subjected to this evening. When the steam clears and I look down though, I suddenly feel the onset of tears of relief in response to what lies before me.

Perfectly displayed on the plate are a gooey grilled cheese sandwich, a crisp Caesar salad and a side of homemade French fries. While it may only be simple fare, it's the first meal that has been brought to me that is not only decently prepared, but also possesses some semblance of the comforting familiarity of my old life.

I immediately dive into the sandwich, taking a large bite and giving a moment for the warm cheese and grilled, buttery bread to hug me via my taste buds. It's such a welcome relief from my previous meals, that I'm already taking a second bite before I've swallowed the first.

When it's all said and done, it has taken me about five minutes to wolf down the entire plate. I quickly wash it down with the cool glass of water that has also been provided, feeling both satiated and reinvigorated with energy.

Taking my tray to the hallway, I purposely position the cloche to reveal that the entire plate has been consumed. I can't tell if this was a peace offering after today's events, suggesting the other meals were *purposely* spoiled, or if it's just the simplicity of the cuisine that resulted in a successful preparation. Either way, I want it to be clear that it is a welcomed change.

I gently close my door once more and move back to the small table to continue my studying. Before I know it, two hours have flown by, but without the distraction of an empty stomach or my mind spinning with constant seething anger, I feel as though I have enough energy that I could keep at it for another six.

Despite how energetic I may feel though, the comfort food soon takes its effect; creating a wave of lethargy as my eyelids begin to softly drift closed. I try to shake myself to stay awake and keep working, but my efforts are feeble at best. Soon, I feel my head becoming heavy as the words on the page begin to blur.

What feels like mere seconds later, I wake up with a start to find my head resting on the open textbook. I quickly sit upright, shaking out the momentary disorientation as I get up, close the book, and stretch my back before making my way towards the bed.

Throwing back the covers so as to clear a path for myself to get into bed with the least amount of effort possible, I remove my robe and lazily throw it into the corner. I'm about to climb onto the mattress when I suddenly give pause, hearing something coming from the hallway.

Hovering near my door, I attempt to verify if I *actually* heard something, or simply imagined it amidst my semi-conscious state. As if on cue, I hear the sound of muffled crying coming from the other side of the door, as clear as day.

Despite the instantaneous goose bumps that develop on my arms, I quickly put my robe back on and pull down on its sleeves before slowly opening my bedroom door to investigate.

As the gap between the door and the archway grows, so too does the volume of the crying, yet by the time that I have the door fully open, I can clearly discern that the sound has moved further down the hallway.

I hesitantly exit my room, taking a moment to wait for the next wave of sobbing so that I can verify the direction I think it's coming from.

Within seconds, my initial beliefs are confirmed, so I glance over my shoulder towards Ms. Pierre's room to make sure I'm alone before I start making my way towards the locked room at the end of the hall.

As I approach the room, I still feel a sense of apprehension after seeing the cloaked woman on the other side of the keyhole in my dream. Already knowing that this door is permanently locked, I opt to lean my ear against the door to ensure that this is the source of the noise.

Much to my surprise, as I press my ear against the thick wooden surface of the door, it suddenly moves inwards, opening a crack and allowing me passage into the previously quarantined area. Cautiously, I push the door open a little further to reveal the room in its entirety.

Moments later, without even realizing I've physically moved, I find myself standing in the middle of the forbidden office as a chill goes up my back in response to every aspect of the room. *Everything*, right down to the thickness of the layers of dust, matches what I had seen in my nightmare when I had come back from town.

To my right is the desk, complete with the large glass container on its side, with a miniature recreation of the ship that Pater Morgan had stowed away on, contained within it. With my new proximity to the model, I can now see that it was constructed with such neurotic precision that even the small strings used to simulate the ship's ropes, have been tied off for authenticity as opposed to glued in place.

Also exactly like in my dream, just beyond the miniature ship is a leather-bound notebook, covered in a thick enough layer of dust that it camouflages perfectly amidst the rest of the desk's surface.

Naturally, I move towards the book, standing over it from behind the desk chair where someone used to sit. I slowly pick up the notebook, attempting to blow off decades worth of dust, but I have minimal success due to the sheer amount that has compounded over time.

Running my hand from the top to the bottom of the book's cover to reveal what's beneath, I feel a shiver run up my back as an embossed image passes beneath my fingertips.

Looking down at the book's leather cover, I notice the symbol of the Triquetra placed in the center, surrounded by a perfect circle; exactly like the book that the cloaked woman had handed me as we mourned over Andy's body.

As a wave of shock washes over me, I inadvertently drop the book onto the desk's surface. I immediately freeze in place for fear that someone has heard my momentary stumble, and will come to investigate the noise.

Hearing no movement in the hallways though, I slowly pick up the book once more and place my fingers under the edge of its cover. I am about to open it, when suddenly, the sound of crying returns, only this time it's closer and louder than it had been before.

I lift my head to see the spiral staircase before me on the opposite side of the room, leading up to the partially concealed loft area.

Abandoning my position at the desk, along with the leather bound book, I cross the room and slowly ascend the stairs. I approach each step with extreme caution, fully cognizant of both the age of the structure itself, and its failing integrity as a result of an extended period of disregard.

By the time I've reached the top of the creaking staircase, the sound of the crying has stopped once more, but upon my arrival to the second level of the room, I quickly realize that this loft area stretches much further than I had initially anticipated.

Thinking back to the length of the hallway by comparison, I quickly deduce that this area must extend *at least* as far as my bedroom, if not all the way to Ms. Pierre's.

Looking around the space, it becomes obvious that this was clearly once used as an extension of the office below. However, while the lower area of the room, surrounding the desk, seems to have been orderly and clean prior to the onset of dust and cobwebs, this upper portion of the room is littered with various sketches and papers splayed across a collection of tables as well as the floor.

Based on the sheer number of drawings of Triquetras, pinwheels with three feet, and other mysterious symbols, it quickly becomes evident that whoever was conducting this study had eventually subsided to the madness of their obsession. So much so, that even the sight of the room now, long after its occupant has gone, remains unnerving, to say the least.

Nevertheless, I continue wandering the space when I suddenly notice a stack of something in one of the dark corners. Previously hidden by the complete lack of light, my eyes continue to adjust to the darkness as my proximity to the corner narrows, faintly revealing the shape before me.

Stacked like hastily laid bricks, are a pile of suitcases varying in both style and age, as made evident by the amount of dust gathered upon them in ascending order from the bottom up.

Were one to stumble upon this pile, they would likely assume that this was merely old, outdated luggage that the Morgan family had used through the ages, but given the unsettling nature of my surroundings, something compels me to examine them further.

I reach out towards one of the luggage tags to see whom these bags belong to when I suddenly get the overwhelming feeling that I'm being watched.

Frozen in place, I hold my breath for a moment to listen for any signs of a presence behind me. Much to my relief, I hear nothing except the gentle movement of the cool air as it drifts past either side of my head. Despite the silence though, I still can't shake the nagging feeling that I'm not alone.

After a few moments I surrender to my paranoia and turn around, only to be met by seven individuals staring back at me with looks of sorrow and fear permanently stained on their decaying faces.

While in various stages of deterioration, each woman standing before me appears to be wearing similar tattered clothing that, at one point, might have resembled the uniforms in the cupboard that smells of mothballs. However, contrary to *my* mandatory regalia, each of these women's uniforms is complimented with a pendant draped around their neck.

Each pendant is no more than two inches wide, square in shape, and appears to be woven from straw. From each corner of each square, the ends stick out as though the pendant were left unfinished by design.

Suspended from old, frayed string, the pendants give the impression that they would itch like a burlap shirt collar, yet none of the decaying women seem bothered by them as they keep their gazes trained upon me with surgical scrutiny.

My instincts tell me to run, to scream, to do anything to escape, but cornered in the loft area of a room that I'm not supposed to be in, and surrounded by seven seemingly undead individuals, I find myself frozen in fear, forced to take in the horrific sights before me.

The entities continue to stare at me with piercing precision, slowly raising their left arms, or what remains of them in some cases, and reaching out towards me.

The sheer sight makes my chest begin to burn with dread. Reflexively, I place my palm on my heart, only to feel something in my hand when it gets there. Looking down, I see the same square pendant woven from straw, hanging around my neck as well.

Confused, I try to rip the pendant off, but even though the string is old and frayed, it resists my efforts to the point that it might as well be made of pure steel.

After a few more attempts, resulting in a sharp pain in the back of my neck from where the string refused to snap, I give up on trying to shed the pendant and turn my attention back towards the decaying women.

However, as I lift my head, I discover that they are no longer there.

Instead, standing in the place of the seven undead women who were there only moments ago, is the cloaked woman from my nightmares. She stares directly at me as two glowing amber eyes slowly begin to illuminate within the shadows of her hood, lined by stringy, silver hair.

I suddenly feel my hands become both warm and wet. I look down to see that my scars have broken open and blood is now pouring freely from my wrists, pooling on the floor around my feet.

Desperately trying to remind myself that this is all just a nightmare, I close my eyes in preparation for what I know comes next.

Sure enough, within seconds, I hear the horrible song of screeching tires, breaking glass and twisting metal as the cloaked woman's crow presumably flies towards me with immeasurable speed, causing me to flinch in anticipation of its attack.

My eyes fly open and I find myself gasping for air while lying in bed.

Instinctually, my hand flies up towards my throat to check if the square pendant, woven from straw, is still there. Thankfully, it is not. I then quickly turn my attention towards my wrists and take an audible sigh of relief as I verify that my scars remain intact.

Admittedly, I am unsure of how or when I ended up getting into bed and under the covers, but at this point I quickly dismiss the mystery as low priority and centralize my focus on catching my breath and calming my racing heart.

I silently curse the night. After such a positive end to the day, I foolishly had assumed that I would have been able to enjoy at least *one* night of restful sleep, but clearly my subconscious had different plans.

Lying there, staring up at the silk canopy's mesmerizing dance in the gentle breeze, I find myself thankful that at least *one* thing in my life remains calming.

However, despite the soothing nature of the image before me, I can't seem to silence my mind as it races obsessively over the height of my ceiling and the proximity of my room to the locked office down the hall.

Even though I know my experience within the locked room has merely been subconscious projections, I still can't help but wonder how accurate my visions might be. With a complete lack of reality-based context though, my thoughts endlessly loop with no concrete answer in sight.

My obsession with the mystery of the locked room quickly spirals out of control, and before I even know it, I have spent the better part of the night endlessly rolling through a million unanswered questions, over and over again.

Soon, the light of the morning sun begins to breach the sky outside my window, signaling a new day's beginning. I surrender to the light and slowly get out of bed before I begin to dress myself in my uniform on virtually no sleep.

As I stare at myself in the mirror, I take notice of the evergrowing manifestation of exhaustion on my face, and nature's lovely gift of a few more stress-induced grey hairs that have sprouted in place of the one I had previously plucked.

But even as I stare at the mirror with distaste, lamenting my slowly deteriorating physical state, I still can't let go of my obsession. So I promise myself that *somehow, some way,* I *will* get into that room at the end of the hall.

As I solidify my promise to myself, I start to do up the top button on my blouse, only to feel an odd sensation at the back of my neck. Opening my collar, I lean towards the mirror to inspect further, and my heart immediately skips a beat.

Wrapping around the back of my neck, I find a thin line of bruising... no thicker than an old, frayed string.

CHAPTER NINETEEN

Blurred Line

I stand at my bedroom window; contemplatively spectating as the sun slowly invades the darkened sky.

The looming presence of far-reaching cloud cover implies the threat of rain, but even the collection of bulbous clouds cannot hide the orange and purple hues of the sunrise as they sneak through the weather system, accenting every curvature of the cumulonimbus mass.

With a quivering hand, I gently rub the back of my neck, haunted by the mysterious bruising that seems to have transcended my subconscious state. The sheer thought of *anything* being able to cross such a threshold raises too many questions for my brain to be able to process at this point.

A few weeks ago, when I had awoken to find pieces of bark at the foot of my mattress, I was scared at first, but logic was quick to swoop in, dismissing it as an absentminded coincidence; likely the result of forgetting to wipe my feet before getting into bed.

But now, after finding the undeniable marks on my neck, I am filled with disorienting fear and unsettling confusion. I am no longer sure of whether I am currently in the conscious world or if this is all just another false projection, destined to take a dark left turn at any moment.

Snapping back from my drifting thoughts, I suddenly realize that involuntary tears have been streaming from my emotionless eyes this entire time. I chalk it up to exhaustion and quickly wipe my cheeks dry, taking one last glimpse at my wearied visage in the mirror before making my way downstairs to the kitchen to begin my daily duties.

I barely register the rancid scent of Ms. Pierre's beet porridge until I reach the kitchen door. In past days, I had feebly tried to hold my breath amidst the aroma of rot, but now I find myself apathetically drained by its role in my daily routine.

Silently crossing the kitchen, I forgo my coffee and burnt toast, opting to proceed straight towards my bucket like a dutiful automaton.

Ms. Pierre momentarily ceases her stirring and turns towards me as she rhetorically inquires, "Are you feeling alright, Miss Woodall?"

What a loaded question.

I can't even contemplate a way in which I could truncate my cycling thoughts in the moment, so I dismissively abbreviate my state of being, "Just a bit of a sore neck. Must've slept funny or something."

Ms. Pierre's spoon clanks against the edge of the pot, prompting me to shift my attention towards her. As my gaze falls upon her, I see her hands shaking and a bitter expression washing over her face, evidently in offense to something I said, or did.

For a moment, I'm fearful of the reaction I have triggered, but Ms. Pierre is quick to swallow her odd, unjustified hatred towards me before turning back to the pot and resuming her stirring of the cement-like mixture with as much force as she can muster.

Wary of Ms. Pierre's increasingly imbalanced emotions, I quickly gather the last of my supplies and make my way out of the kitchen without saying anything or even looking at her, for fear of eliciting more anger.

I can't help but think back to living with my Mom. Walking on eggshells every waking moment of every day, for fear of providing her supposed reasoning for continued psychological abuse.

Once upstairs, I fly through the majority of the dusting, only slowing my pace once I reach the locked room at the end of the hall. Simply being this close to the door riddles me with temptation to peek through the keyhole, but before the thought even passes through my mind in full, I hear the echo of movement on the stairs, coming from the opposite end of the hall.

Quickly grabbing my bucket and rag, I run back to my bedroom door to make it appear as though I've just finished washing the windows in my room by the time Ms. Pierre reaches the top step.

I flash a pleasant smile as I pass her in the hallway, making sure to remain silent until she has had a chance to wake the children, but before Ms. Pierre enters the children's room, she seizes me by the arm with surprising, sudden force.

The tightness of her grip is as impressive as it is aggressive, and I can't help but notice the residual hatred in her face as she scowls towards me, and whispers, "Recreational time will be conducted indoors due to the weather. Your lesson will begin *promptly* afterwards. Make sure your duties are completed *prior* to that time, is that understood?"

I politely nod in agreement, trying to subtly pull my arm away from her talon-like grip. Ms. Pierre releases me as suddenly as she had grabbed me, glancing towards her hand as though she was unaware she had seized me to begin with. Looking up at me with a momentary whisper of confusion, sadness and, what looks like, fear in her eyes, Ms. Pierre sheepishly turns towards the children's room and enters, saying nothing by way of an apology or explanation for the violent outburst.

Slowly backing away from the door, I can't help but wonder what has set Ms. Pierre off so early in the day. My mind scrambles as I try to figure what it was that I had said or did, that could have incited such fury, but the only words I have even voiced towards her this morning were in regards to a sore neck.

Perhaps I just deluded myself into believing that Ms. Pierre's pleasantness would remain after yesterday's events. An admittedly foolish assumption, as this version of Ms. Pierre is much closer to her natural state than anything I had seen in the past twelve hours or so.

Even with that considered though, there's something about her growing instability that makes me concerned; not only for her own safety, or even mine for that matter, but for Macha and Nemain's.

By the time the children are in the kitchen for breakfast, I'm nearly done washing the majority of windows on the main floor, bringing me into the sunroom, just off the 'salon'.

Most days, I have found my thoughts drifting while in this room, my eyes getting lost in the gnarled roots of the immense oak tree as I think back to one of my first sleepless nights in this house. But today, with the atmosphere of the pending storm, a certain feeling of darkness is cast upon the room and I can't help but feel as though the tree is *watching* me.

Trying to silence my paranoid mind, I wipe the panes of glass in front of me when I hear the first few drops of rain beginning to fall. Looking up, I watch as they make thumping contact with the panes of glass above me, prompting me to contentedly shrug as nature offers to rinse the outside portions of the windows on my behalf. At least it's saving me some time and effort.

Macha and Nemain suddenly exit the kitchen, making their way up the stairs for the commencement of their morning lessons. I can't help but smirk as the sounds of their footsteps on the stairs fall in rhythm with the sound of raindrops impacting the glass above me.

Taking a moment to watch the rain fall on the dilapidated back portion of the property, I become mesmerized by the odd angles at which the water splashes as it ricochets off the tilted, broken patio stones that the oak tree's roots had so violently shattered during its patient invasion.

The rain continues to increase in both quantity and fury and I lift my head to watch the water pour off the gargantuan oak leaves, towering above. As my eyes dance between the small streams of water, I suddenly notice something moving deep within the branches of the immense oak tree.

The hairs on the back of my neck immediately stand on end as I shift my position and see a large crow staring back at me, its gaze unrelenting, as it shifts back and forth on a partially concealed branch.

I take a few steps in either direction, but the crow remains dialed into me, as though I'm the only thing it sees. Soon, the rain turns borderline torrential, obscuring the distance between the bird and I with a heavy, vertical sheet of water.

Stepping towards the window, I keep my eyes trained on the area where I had seen the crow, but the increasingly severe precipitation prevents me from having a clear view of the tree anymore, let alone the bird itself.

I'm about to give up on trying to spot my aviary stalker when my focus suddenly shifts towards some kind of obscured movement directly in front of me.

Squinting my eyes and trying to focus on the blurred shape through the rain, I take another step towards the window, putting me close enough to feel the coolness emanating off the glass from less than an inch away.

Half of a second later, I jump back as the crow that was perched in the branches flies through the heavy downpour and directly into the windowpane where I had been standing, pugnaciously cracking the glass on impact.

With my back against the wall and my eyes wide with shock, I slowly lower my gaze from the fractured pane of glass where the crow had made its impact, to the ground, where the twisted, wet carcass of the bird now lies; its head at an awkward ninety degree angle to the right, its beak and eyes wide open, yet lifeless.

Horrified, I turn my attention back up to the point of impact where the crow had ended itself but, impossibly, the crack in the glass appears to suddenly be gone. Confused, I frantically glance back down to the ground where the crow's carcass was only moments ago, but find no signs that the bird was ever there to begin with.

In a state of disbelief, I reach out and touch the cool pane of glass to verify that it remains intact, as I perceive it. Sure enough, it remains smooth and flat, with no signs of imperfection or failing integrity.

The rain begins to let up, bringing the immense oak back into view. As the tree reveals itself through the storm, my eyes dart back up to its branches. Still sitting on the very branch it was on when the rain had started, I see a large crow staring at me with laser focus.

Terrified, I slowly back out of the sunroom, into the salon, still trying to process what has just happened. I slowly pivot away from the sunroom and make my way into the kitchen while my mind endlessly back flips as it tries to find some sort of conscious traction.

Contrary to this morning, my zombified arrival in the kitchen goes unaddressed by Ms. Pierre as she moves the last of the breakfast plates from the table to the counter. I empty my bucket in the sink and proceed to silently start doing the morning dishes as I continue circling back to the blurred line of reality from moments ago.

Though I don't look up, I can feel Ms. Pierre's eyes on me the entire time. As to whether she is deriving enjoyment from my clear state of terror, or my mere presence has somehow triggered another wave of unjustified anger from her, remains unsaid. Either way, she opts to maintain her silence before exiting the kitchen and making her way upstairs to commence the children's morning lessons.

For the better part of the next hour or so, I silently do the dishes and the inventory, as instructed. While my body is going through the motions of my daily tasks, my distracted mind has reached an echelon of turmoil, confusion and fear.

While my time in this house has been plagued with an ever-growing pile of unanswered questions, suspicions and dark imaginings, I now find myself sincerely wondering if *I* might be the problem.

Between the hauntingly vivid nightmares blurring the line of consciousness, the perceived conversations with a supposedly mute child, and whatever just happened in the sunroom, the only common thread between all of these occurrences is, *me*.

Maybe I am losing my mind. Maybe this inability to discern my own state of consciousness is entirely self-perpetuated. Maybe it's the result of a psychological break. After all, paranoia is not an uncommon symptom of such a diagnosis, and I'm clearly not experiencing any shortage of that. But if that were the case, would I really be so *aware* of my psychological degradation? Would I really be able to self-analyze with such scrutiny?

Regardless of the state of my own mental health, I can't stop thinking about how it would affect Macha and Nemain, if I were to become suddenly unable to provide care for them.

Whether it is the symptoms of a budding form of compulsive madness or simply my naturally stubborn nature, I can't let go of the sense of protective duty I feel towards them. I *need* to stay here and fight through whatever is happening to me, for *their* sake. I *need* to get myself right in the head, for *their* safety. If I don't find a way to fix *myself*, how can I ever expect to *save them* from Ms. Pierre, or anything else for that matter?

I suddenly realize how much time has passed while I've been contemplatively pacing the kitchen after finishing my duties. Quickly bounding up the stairs, I move towards my room with haste and scan over my notes, hoping that preparation will mask my current instability.

Thankfully last night, before my mind drifted off to the twisted land of my nightmares, I had compiled enough of a strategic lesson plan to maximize my time with the children while not arousing suspicion from Ms. Pierre.

In my lesson plan, I have created a list of suggested drawing assignments that appear as mere simple tasks that will lightly challenge Macha and Nemain's abilities to create artistic representations.

However, beneath the innocuous surface of these simple drawings, I have specifically chosen subject matter that will help me to analyze the children's relationships with Ms. Pierre, their awareness/familiarity of their birth parents, as well as a few disassociated assignments that at best, will provide a glimpse of any hidden behavioral traits, or at the least, will appear random enough to throw Ms. Pierre off my scent, should she become skeptical.

Subversive? Sure. But I silently justify it as a necessary manipulation for the overall sake of my understanding of this home, this family and, most importantly, my own mental health for the sake of the children.

Checking the time on my phone, I shake my head with derision towards the complete lack of cellular signal and quickly fading battery life. It's amazing how a device I used to cherish, has been so effectively depreciated by geographical location, rendering it less valuable than the very materials it's made from.

With just over an hour until my lesson begins I hear the faint sound of Ms. Pierre opening the door to the children's room as she goes to fetch their lunch.

Remembering how stern she was this morning about being on time for my lesson, I lean out of my room and call after her as she makes her way down the hallway, "Ms. Pierre? Would you mind if I started setting up for my lesson now? Or would you prefer that I wait until after the children have finished their lunch?"

Ms. Pierre is slow to stop, let alone turn around to face me. So much so, that I am expecting her to lash out at me at any moment, but as she pivots, I suddenly notice how pale she looks, even from this distance. Her typically stern face is as devoid of color as it is emotion, almost making her look like a ghost.

Reaching out her right hand in an attempt to brace herself against the wall, Ms. Pierre suddenly collapses. I try to sprint towards her as I see her going down, but by the time I'm able to cross the distance between us, she's already down on her hands and knees, visibly shaking and gasping for air as though she's being strangled.

I frantically kneel beside Ms. Pierre, coaxing her to breathe as I try to prop her failing body up against the wall into a sitting position. As her back makes contact with the wall, she suddenly snaps out of her debilitated state as though someone had flicked a light switch, her physical state dramatically improving as a sudden awareness floods into her eyes.

Feeling concern, I gently suggest, "Maybe you should lay down for a bit."

Ms. Pierre is quick to shake off my suggestion, wrapping her gnarled fingers around my hands and pulling them off of her as though she is disgusted by my physical contact.

Standing up with the assistance of the wall, Ms. Pierre adjusts her dress and composes herself as the color returns to her face and her shaking slowly subsides, "Just a dizzy spell, Miss Woodall. Nothing to worry yourself with."

Ms. Pierre then makes her way towards the stairs to continue towards the kitchen as though nothing has happened, but after seeing her stumble like that, I can't let her navigate the staircase on her own with good conscience, so I follow with the intent of assisting her.

Before I am able to even reach out my hands to offer my help, Ms. Pierre quickly turns towards me with a look of fear in her eyes, as she screams, "NO!" Quickly collecting herself from the odd outburst, Ms. Pierre clears her throat before softening her tone, "I'm fine, Miss Woodall. Thank you."

At first, I assume her reaction is driven by embarrassment towards her moment of vulnerability, but it's then that I notice she is gripping the railing so hard that her knuckles are white; almost as though she sincerely thinks that I had the intent of attacking amidst her moment of weakness.

Ms. Pierre slowly makes her way down while I remain at the top of the staircase, confused and offended as to how she could think that I would even be *capable* of such an act.

I spend the better part of ten minutes, pacing the hallway at the top of the stairs, waiting to see if Ms. Pierre will require any assistance coming back up. Listening for any signs that she is approaching the base of the staircase, I hear the kitchen door open a short while later, followed by the sound of sharp footsteps on the hardwood floor.

For fear of seeming like the over-bearing relative of an elderly person who recently 'had a spill', I casually lean against the far wall of the hallway, pretending to direct my attention towards my notes as she begins her climb.

Despite her momentary stumble earlier, Ms. Pierre ascends the stairs with ease while carrying a large tray with two small, silver cloches covering the children's lunch.

I continue staring at my notes, pretending not to occasionally glance towards her, in order to check in on her progress while watching for any signs of 'dizziness'.

By the time Ms. Pierre reaches the top of the steps, she promptly passes me, curtly saying, "I told you, I'm fine."

I try to play it off casually, "Oh, I wasn't-" but before I can even finish my lie, Ms. Pierre shoots me a glance that tells me it's not worth the effort.

I silently concede, following Ms. Pierre towards the children's room and opening the door for her so she is able to keep the tray balanced. I don't even receive so much as a thankful nod in return.

As I'm about to follow her into the room with my notes in hand, Ms. Pierre stops me in the doorframe, turning and blocking my path with the tray as she says, "Why don't we let the children eat first? You may join us closer to the scheduled time of your lesson."

I don't even have time to respond before Ms. Pierre uses her foot to kick the door closed in my face. So much so, that by the time the door finds its frame, my nose is an inch and a half away from the center of the embossed symbol of the Triquetra.

Quietly making my way back to my room, I do my best to suppress the growing frustration towards Ms. Pierre's return to the 'dark side'. She was hard enough to deal with prior to yesterday, but having now learned that she *does* possess the ability to be kind and pleasant, if even for a moment, it only makes her sourness all the more infuriating.

I spend the better part of forty-five minutes frenetically pacing my room as I try to quell my anger towards Ms. Pierre. Though I try to occupy my body in an attempt to silence my mind, I can't help but find my thoughts drifting towards dark theories as to why, exactly, I'm not permitted in the children's room until *after* lunch.

First, I start imagining all of the patronizing lies that Ms. Pierre is likely feeding to Macha and Nemain in advance of my lesson, *"Now children. I realize that you're very smart, but some people, are not. People like Miss Woodall. So let's just be kind and try not to embarrass her while she tries her best, shall we?"*

Next, I find my mind drifting into even darker territory as I start to imagine her lording over the two girls, ensuring they consume their meals in full, under threat of being punished or hit. After all, she's already struck Nemain, and given the general quality of Ms. Pierre's cooking (save for last night's dinner), I would understand if the children had trouble getting lunch down on a daily basis.

Soon my imagination starts to spiral out of control and I find myself clenching my fists and breathing heavily as I imagine Ms. Pierre force-feeding the children, holding them down as she shoves rancid sustenance into their mouths against their will, while tears stream down the sides of their faces.

My heart fills with hatred as I think back to moments ago when Ms. Pierre had collapsed in the hallway and I start to lament my instinct to help her. It's then that an entirely uncharacteristic thought passes through my head...

I should have just let the bitch die.

The moment I hear the thought in my mind I freeze in place, terrified that I would even consider such a thing. This isn't me. These can't be my thoughts. What is wrong with me? Have I really strayed that far from myself so as to wish *death* upon someone? I feel as though there's a dark presence in my mind that I can't see, but I can feel slowly taking over, shattering my psyche like slow-growing roots from a tree pushing up through once-solid patio stones.

I continue contemplating the apparent deterioration of my morality as I resume my frantic pacing. While I had initially tried to busy myself to quiet my anger, I now do it to silence the developing fear of my own thoughts, reminding myself that I need to get right in the head before I face the children or Ms. Pierre.

As if on inconvenient cue, I hear the door to the children's room open as Ms. Pierre calls out from down the hall, "Miss Woodall? It's time."

CHAPTER TWENTY

Arts & Crafts

As I enter the children's room, I see Ms. Pierre clearing the plates from lunch and placing them on her silver tray. Macha is lying on a small cushion, flipping through the pages of an archaic children's book with the insignia of a tree on its cover, in place of a title, whereas Nemain is halfway into the depths of an old trunk at the side of the room, beneath one of the stained glass windows.

Kindly greeting the children, I earn a smile from Macha as she momentarily peeks over the faded, blue hardcover. I smile in return as she shifts her eyes back to the page to finish whatever passage she is currently reading.

Nemain, on the other hand, is quick to close the lid on the large trunk and run towards me with excitement as she inquires, "Is it time? What are we making? Did you bring clay?"

Smiling at her sudden fervor, I pleasantly respond, "Sorry, no clay."

Nemain slightly deflates in response, but still remains excited for the lesson, as she takes her seat at the small table in front of me and patiently folds her hands while bouncing her leg in anticipation. Meanwhile, Macha has put her book away on a shelf and has come over to join us as well, sitting attentively with an expectant smile on her face.

Placing a small stack of paper on the table, I begin my lesson, "I couldn't help but notice that the walls in my room are looking *pretty* empty. So I figured we could spend our first class together, making some drawings so I have something to decorate with."

I catch a glimpse of Ms. Pierre's scowl from the corner, she is clearly already unimpressed with today's lesson plan. Her tightly pursed lips tell me that she's fighting off the instinct to comment on the simplicity of my curriculum; especially after witnessing how much research I had put into my preparation last night.

On one hand, for the sake of my goal to subversively dig for information through the specific assignments, Ms. Pierre's under-estimation of my abilities is a blessing in disguise. After all, the lower her expectations, the less likely it is that she'll suspect I'm up to something.

But on the other hand, this *is* a supervised lesson. If my teaching abilities don't make a good impression today, this may be the only chance I get to work with these children in such a capacity.

All that considered; I straighten my back and attempt to heighten the aptitude of my vernacular by adding, "I will present various concepts to you by way of words or phrases, at which point each of you will create a tangible adaptation of what the prompt inspires."

Glancing towards Ms. Pierre, I see that her scowl has softened and one eyebrow has risen in response to my addendum. I take it as a silent approval to proceed with my lesson, so I turn back towards the girls.

As my focus shifts, I see Nemain patiently waiting with her hand raised, as though we're in a lecture hall. The action is so formal that I feel ridiculous having to call on her so that she may voice her inquiry, especially since the only other student is supposedly mute. Nevertheless, I go through the motions, pointing at her as I say, "Yes, Nemain?"

Lowering her hand, she glances towards Ms. Pierre before turning back to me and sheepishly asking, "Will we be punished for mistakes?"

The mere fact that she asks this sparks the anger within me. I'm flooded with another wave of dark suspicions of the horrible things Ms. Pierre does to these children behind closed doors.

Nevertheless, I force myself to pleasantly smile as I explain loud enough for Ms. Pierre to hear my words, "In *this* class, there is so such thing as a *mistake*. I want you to let your creativity run free on the page without worrying about *getting it right*."

Macha and Nemain glance at each other as though they have never even known such a system to exist. Meanwhile, I see Ms. Pierre begrudgingly purse her lips once more as she turns away from us and pretends to busy herself by tidying the room. While it's a relief to no longer have her scrutinizing gaze upon me, I know that she's still intently listening to my every word.

I instruct Macha and Nemain to each grab one piece of paper. As they do, I make a ceremonious production of placing a large box of crayons that I bought in town between them, as though it was the Holy Grail. This elicits some giggles from the girls, and a pretty hefty eye roll from Ms. Pierre as she glances in my direction before turning away once more.

Once the crayons are down, I crouch so that I'm at eye-level with the children, making them feel like we are conspiring equals, "For your first assignment, I would like the two of you to draw whatever comes to mind when you hear the word... *Home*."

While I have successfully deceived Ms. Pierre and the girls into thinking that this exercise is entirely built around challenging the artist's ability to interpret and adapt, I've got a sizeable checklist of things that I'm *actually* watching for.

My intention is to keep the tone of the lesson, along with the individual assignments, generally light and fun, but as I quietly watch the children's creations, I'm secretly noting things like use of scale, color choices and placement on the page, thus allowing unfiltered creative instincts to speak on the children's behalf.

Nemain is quick to grab a red crayon and go straight to work. It's not much of a surprise as the use of red shades often denotes excitement in children, something she's already exhibited; not to mention, young girls have a natural propensity towards warmer colors.

But when I notice the deep crimson shade that she has chosen, I give momentary pause. The darkness of the shade suggests a sense of dominance that drives her subconscious. Considering that she is the older of two siblings and has clearly displayed a strong sense of self, I'm not shocked, but I still take note nonetheless.

It's then that I notice Macha, has not selected *any* crayon and is simply staring blankly at the empty page with a furrowed brow of contemplation.

Gently crouching beside her, and returning to eye level, I offer encouragement, "You can draw *whatever* comes to mind. There's *no* wrong answer."

Macha slowly turns towards me. There's something about the way she looks at me that's unnerving, as though she is the only one who can see through my simplistic charade.

For a moment, I feel my heart and mind simultaneously begin to race. What if she knows this is all a test? What if she finally decides to break her silence to call me out on my deception?

I try to quiet my paranoid mind, offering a comforting smile to her along with a reassuring nod to mask my internalized panic.

Amidst the tense silence, Macha slowly reaches towards the crayons, blindly grabbing one while watching my face the entire time to see if I react to her selection.

I keep my eyes trained on hers, while maintaining a positive and supportive expression on my face. I hold it for so long that I can't even tell if my smile is still coming off as sincere, or utterly plastic.

Thankfully, before Macha's piercing gaze is able to crack my façade, her face softens and she seemingly shrugs off her suspicion, shifting her focus to the paper and getting to work on her drawing.

I slowly back away, not only to give her space to work, but to also let myself quietly breath out the momentary wave of tension. As I circle the table and come back to Nemain's side, I find myself hyper-aware of my facial expressions and audible tone, wondering if anyone else can see through them like Macha seemed to.

Glancing at Nemain's drawing, I notice that she has depicted both herself and her sister, side by side, holding hands. It's not surprising, as one doesn't typically need a psychology degree to know that children will draw themselves in the proximity of those they feel most emotionally connected to. One thing I do notice though, is how Nemain seems to be positioning all of her images to the lower left portion of the page.

I flashback to my readings from last night, specifically a passage that stated, *'Justification of a child's rendering to the lower-left area of a page typically denotes one of two possibilities: a) a longing for the past, as result of an unacknowledged sense of loss, typically resulting from a death in the family, or b) the need for a nurturing presence to validate and overcome feelings of insecurity and/or inadequacy in the present. This is most commonly found in subjects who have experienced extended periods of psychological abuse, typically from a figure of authority.'*

It's no secret that Ms. Pierre's treatment of both the children and myself, easily qualifies as psychological abuse on a daily basis. Given that I've suffered under her thumb for only a portion of the time that the children have, I naturally assume that the latter diagnosis is the most applicable.

But then my mind circles back to the prior portion of the analysis, '*a longing for the past, as result of an unacknowledged sense of loss, typically resulting from a death in the family'.*

I start to wonder if Nemain, as the oldest child, might actually *remember* her mother. If that's the case, *how much* does she remember? Does she remember her mother's death? Or is it just a blurred image of someone being there one day, and gone the next? What about her father? Does she remember him leaving? Does she know why he left? Would she recall any family stories he had told her prior to that? Moreover, would she be willing to share such memories with me, were I to ask?

I hover around the room, rolling over these thoughts while allowing the girls some time to finish their first drawing assignment. Insentiently, my focus drifts up to the ceiling that towers above me at twice the height of the ceiling in my own room.

My thoughts shift back to my dream from the previous night, and the hidden area above my bedroom where I had seen the seven decaying women reaching towards me before I found the square pendant woven from straw hanging around my neck.

I feel a chill run up my back as I shake the thought from my mind, giving a soft rub to the bruised area on the back of my neck as it rubs against my uniform's collar. I force myself to shift my focus towards tangible objects in the room, using them as footholds to keep my mind in the present moment so as to not get distracted by the dark residual imagery from my blurred sense of conscious reality.

As I scan the room, my eyes fall upon an empty mason jar on the floor, its perforated lid sitting upside down, beside it. I quickly identify it as the jar that Nemain had used to capture her butterfly, yet Queen Victoria is nowhere to be seen.

I glance back towards the girls to see them still working away. Ms. Pierre has shifted closer to them, still maintaining her charade of 'tidying the room' while subtly craning her neck to inspect Macha and Nemain's drawings.

With all three of them distracted, I take a moment to quickly scan the room for any signs of a terrarium or any other kind of habitat to which Nemain could have transferred her pet butterfly into, yet I see no such things.

Starting to make my way back towards the table that the children are working at, I glance up towards the ceiling once more, this time in search of Queen Victoria.

I naturally assume that if Nemain's butterfly isn't in some kind of container at eye level, it must have escaped. If that's the case, it must be fluttering around the top of the room in a fruitless search for a way out. But as my eyes trace the ceiling, I see no signs of the creature anywhere.

Lowering my gaze back towards Macha and Nemain, I catch Ms. Pierre's scrutinizing stare. She has turned her attention away from the girls and is now watching my every move, trying to read me like a card shark at a high-stakes poker table.

I flash a pleasant smile as if to convince her that I merely had gotten lost in admiration of the architecture as the girls finished their assignment, but Ms. Pierre remains dialed into me with laser focus and dissecting intensity.

Returning to the table, I glance over the children's shoulders to glimpse at their progress. Macha has scribbled all over the page; similar to the pencil drawing she had done in my room a few nights ago. While the drawing itself is colorful and utterly abstract, I gently place my hand on her shoulder, giving a smile as I say, "Wow. That's *really* good."

Macha looks up at me, with a smirk. I can see she's still quizzical towards my ultimate intent, but appreciates the positive critique, nonetheless.

Before I can even move towards Nemain, she slams her crayon down on the table's surface and proudly announces, "Done!"

Ms. Pierre quickly snakes in beside me to see Nemain's

creation as she proudly lifts her paper toward us, showing four figures standing outside of the Morgan Home.

Pointing to each of the figures in the drawing, Nemain proceeds to identify the individuals from left to right, "This is Macha. This is me. This is you, Patty. And Ms. Pierre is over there, on the other side."

While my heart melts in response to Nemain drawing me beside her, holding her hand, I am quick to mute my response as I see Ms. Pierre's face noticeably sour.

I can already tell that the distance that has been put between her and everyone else in the picture is acting as salt in the wound, antagonizing her unfounded hatred towards me, based on her supposition that I'm trying to 'replace her'.

Without even noticing the awkward tension that her drawing has created, Nemain continues to identify other objects on the page, "This is our house, that's Queen Victoria, and Daddy is back there."

I pause for a moment. My instincts tell me to glance towards Ms. Pierre to verify that I wasn't the only one that heard the statement, but given the bouts of anger she has exhibited this morning combined with her currently offended state, I opt to forgo any attempts at a silent colloquy between us and keep my focus towards Nemain as I seek clarification, "I'm sorry, *where* is he?"

Nemain looks up at me, disappointed at how I could be confused by something so simple, so she points towards the branches of a tree that are peeking over the roof of the house and says, "He's out back. Where he always is."

I try to mute my response to this, so as not to reveal the fact that I'm actively prying for information, but my face betrays me, and my brow instinctually furrows as I contemplate the gravity of Nemain's words.

Before I am even able to construct further inquiry, Ms. Pierre quickly cuts in, "Perhaps we should move on to the next assignment, Miss Woodall? We only have so much time scheduled for this lesson."

Gently nodding in agreement, I go back to my list of associative words and phrases. Still feeling Ms. Pierre's judgmental gaze upon me, while also wary of Macha's silent suspicions, I opt to lob a few softball phrases like, 'friendship' and 'fun' to throw them off any trail I may have created.

I continue to present the next handful of assignments to the children with as much positive energy as I had with the first, but I consistently find myself drifting back to Nemain's words.

'*He's out back... Where he always is.*'

Going through the motions so as not to arouse Ms. Pierre's prying suspicions, I take the time to inspect every one of the children's drawings, making sure to equally analyze the aspects of each piece to hide the fact that I'm only *actually* focusing on a few.

By the conclusion of my hour-long lesson with the children, I have gathered a series of drawings from both Macha and Nemain. I collect them into a stack as I emphatically state, "You should both be *very* proud of these. I can't wait to put these up in my room."

Both children smile in response to this. Macha, having surrendered her suspicions around the mid-point of the lesson, seemed to actually enjoy herself by the end. Even though most of her drawings are nonsensical scribbles of random shapes and almost every color in the box of crayons, I still intend to take them back to my room, along with Nemain's drawings, for further examination.

Ms. Pierre chimes in firmly and suddenly, "Thank you Miss Woodall. Children? Tidy your work areas. The remainder of your afternoon lessons will commence shortly."

As the children take a moment to put away the crayons, I kneel down to assist them, seizing the opportunity to quietly speak with Nemain, "I noticed Queen Victoria's jar is empty..."

While part of me is expecting that Nemain will become sad with the mention of her escaped pet, her eyes instantly fill with excitement, instead.

Grabbing me by the hand, Nemain pulls me over towards the large trunk that she was digging through at the tail end of her indoor recreation time, and kneels in front of it with an anticipatory smile on her face.

Gently placing her palms on top of the chest, Nemain turns towards me and says, "I was talking with Queen Victoria and she said she never wants to grow old or sick."

I automatically chalk up Nemain's perceived conversation as the fantasies of an overactive imagination, yet still, I remain curious as to how she perceives a creature would be able to avoid aging or becoming ill.

As she slowly opens the lid of the chest, Nemain reaches her arm in to grab a small rectangular box with a piece of silk wrapped around it. With one hand, she guides the trunk's lid back down as she hands me the mysterious object with the other.

Confused, I slowly pull back the fabric to see the corner of a glass case with a couple inches worth of cotton inside. As I continue to remove the silk, I see Queen Victoria lying on top of the cotton, with three-inch pins through her wings and tail, each of which is firmly anchored in a cork liner at the bottom of the box.

Nemain looks up at me with raised eyebrows, as though she's expecting praise, "See? Now she'll be pretty forever."

I stand there holding the glass case with both hands, horrified at Nemain's makeshift crucifixion of her supposedly beloved pet. I don't know what bothers me more, the fact that she has done such a thing to this poor creature, or the fact that she seems unaware that she has taken the insect's life in the process.

Nemain suddenly washes over with sadness as she notices my facial reaction and asks, "What's the matter, Patty? Don't you think she's pretty?"

I desperately search for a way to respond without sounding like I am accusing Nemain of murder, but I can't help feeling shaken by the sight of what's she's done and how proud of it she is.

While torturing animals is one of the most common signs of violent tendencies in children, Nemain's complacent nature makes the entire moment almost fell sociopathic in nature.

Part of me wants to cry, not just for the life of this poor insect, but also for Nemain's complete lack of understanding of what she's done. She can tell this upsets me, prompting her to continue looking at me quizzically, as though she's trying to figure out what's so offensive about the whole thing.

I try to drum up some sort of sensitive, tactical approach to the reality of the moment, but the only words that come to my lips are, "Why would you-?"

Before I can even finish my question, I freeze in horror as I watch Queen Victoria's wings move, ever so slightly. I try to convince myself that I am just imagining things, like the crow that flew into the window, but as I continue to stare at the insect, my eyes widen in terror as the poor creature resumes flicking its wings in an attempt to escape this torture.

Nemain looks at me with an odd sense of softness in her eyes as she continues to explain; "Now she'll be my friend forever... just like all the others."

I glance towards Nemain as I echo her statement with confusion, "...Others?"

Giving a quick nod, Nemain then reaches towards the trunk and opens the lid all the way to reveal countless other glass cases, each containing butterflies that have been haphazardly crucified like Queen Victoria.

While my instinct is to recoil in fear, I can't take my eyes away from the gruesome imagery before me. The sheer sight of these poor creatures, when contextualized against Nemain's soft smile creates a sense of panic and worry that makes my hands start to shake.

My focus continues to dance between Queen Victoria, Nemain and the contents of the trunk, as the sound of soft tapping quietly fills the room, steadily increasing in volume with each passing second. Initially, I chalk up the sound to another wave of rain tapping against the windows and roof.

As my attention drifts back towards the contents of the trunk though, I see the captive butterflies *all* flicking their wings, desperately attempting to break free of their cases, many tearing their appendages in the process as the three-inch pins stubbornly resist their efforts.

The sound of countless wings tapping against glass cases continues to grow in volume, making the room feel like it's vibrating, blurring my vision in the process. I try to ignore the sound, but it quickly reaches a nearly deafening level of intensity, prompting me to visibly grimace in response.

Shifting my focus towards Nemain, I see a look of confused

concern in her eyes in response to my clearly ailing physical and mental states. I snap my attention towards Macha and Ms. Pierre only to realize that they are not even reacting to the noise. It quickly becomes clear that I am the only one who is hearing any of this.

I try to quiet my mind, reminding myself over and over that this is just another hallucination courtesy of my heightened level of exhaustion, but no sooner does the thought pass through my brain than I hear the sound of a soft crack, pulling my focus back towards the trunk.

Frozen with apprehension, I notice that some of the glass cases in the trunk have started to break amidst the vibrations. Slowly, each of the fractures begins to spread, creating a living mosaic of fissures that erratically fork as they spread across the surfaces of each individual box.

As if on command, every single case in the trunk suddenly explodes, blasting a wave of broken fragments of glass in every direction.

Shortly after, a tornado of butterflies emerges from within the trunk, funneling upwards with aggressive force to the towering ceiling above.

The unbearable sound of a million furious, flapping wings echoes throughout the room as the swarm churns within itself like a giant, colorful amoeba. I look up; already dreading what might come next, when the entire swarm suddenly shifts course and dives directly towards me with vicious intent.

I instinctually try to shield myself as they approach, feeling Queen Victoria's case slip from my fingers in the process. Covering my head and bracing for the impending attack, the room suddenly falls silent... save for the sound of a single glass case shattering on the floor at my feet.

It's then that the room is filled with a different noise altogether, the sound of Nemain's soft whimpers set to the rhythm of Ms. Pierre's crisp footsteps as she makes a hurried approach.

I slowly lower my arms to see Nemain kneeling on the ground, crying as she reaches out towards Queen Victoria, who is now lying on the floor amidst a shattered glass case. Sitting a few inches off to the side is a severed butterfly wing, presumably ripped off by the force of the impact.

I snap my attention towards the trunk, expecting to see remnants of glass and cotton, but now it is filled with children's books, stuffed dolls and a few playful knick-knacks, with no signs that butterflies or glass cases were in there to begin with.

Ms. Pierre quickly scoops up Nemain, pulling her away from the collection of sharp edges while looking at me incredulously, as if to ask what the hell would possess me to endanger a child like this.

Desperately, I search for the right phrasing to simultaneously apologize and explain my actions, but my growing fear and confusion leaves me unable to find words in the moment.

Still holding Nemain back, Ms. Pierre sharply states, "I think that's *quite* enough for today."

Riddled with guilt and shame, I scramble to fix the situation, "I'm- I'm so sorry- Let me get a broom and I'll-"

Ms. Pierre cuts me off, "-That *won't* be necessary, Miss Woodall."

I continue to feebly insist, "No, no. It's my fault. I'll just-"

Ms. Pierre interjects once again, this time with a venomous tone and a look of ultimate authority, "-*you* have done *enough!*"

I turn and cross the distance of the room without protest, my shoulders hanging heavy with regret. Despite having my back to her, I can still feel Ms. Pierre's eyes upon me, her hatred towards my existence growing with each passing moment.

I can't say I blame her. With the sound of each sob that comes from Nemain, I too, hate myself more and more.

Though Macha remains at the small table with a shocked expression on her face, I can't even bring myself to give her a comforting look amidst the circumstances. Instead, I gather the stack of the children's drawings and silently make my exit.

As I move into the hallway, closing the children's bedroom door behind me, I feel tears beginning to fill my eyes and spill down my cheeks as the shame washes over me.

I quickly pivot and run to my bedroom, absent-mindedly slamming the door behind me, and tossing the stack of drawings on to my table as I fall to my knees and cry for the better part of half an hour.

Initially, I had intended to use this time to dissect the children's drawings, but as I lay, crumpled on the ground, broken by my blurred sense of reality and riddled with guilt derived from the consequences of my mental instability, critical analysis of children's artwork is the furthest thing from my mind.

I start to wonder if I should just give up. If I should just pack my things and leave this place. Of course, I couldn't go home to my parents in the face of failure, nor would I want to. But even as the thoughts of running away pass through my mind, I hear the cloaked woman's voice reminding me of my objective. I must '*save them*'.

Despite everything that's going on with my deteriorating mental state, I still can't shake my obsessive obligation to protect those children. Yes, I am directly responsible for what just happened with Queen Victoria, and yes, Nemain will likely hate me as a result. While it will take some time to earn her trust back at this point, if I were to cut and run after doing such a thing, she would *never* forgive me.

I slowly get up off the ground, trying to stifle my sobs. While the tears continue to fall down my face, I shift my focus to figuring out how to fix what I have broken.

Moments later, I am back where my day began, staring contemplatively out of my bedroom window. I watch as the light of day fruitlessly continues its battle against the immense clouds that populate the sky. I reflexively scoff at the sun's feeble efforts, knowing that darkness will inevitably resume its reign in only a matter of hours.

Despite all of the scattered thoughts that keep looping through my mind in regards to Nemain, the cloaked woman, and my own ostensive state of consciousness, one phrase keeps cutting through all the noise, obsessively echoing over, and over again...
'*He's out back... Where he always is.*'

CHAPTER TWENTY-ONE

Broken

The faint light of the sun continues waning as I pace back and forth in my room. I attempt to slow my racing heartbeat, control my erratic breathing, and empty my summersaulting mind, but the spectrum of my spastic emotions seems to resist my every effort.

The stack of Macha and Nemain's drawings remains splayed out on my table from when I had so haphazardly tossed them there, hours ago. I can't even bring myself to look at them, for fear of sparking another wave of guilt, regret and mortification from how my lesson with the children ended.

Even just the passing thought of the drawings causes Ms. Pierre's cold voice to echo through my mind, over and over again, "*You* have done *enough!*" As I look back and take inventory of the day, I can't say that I disagree with her.

In the matter of a one-hour lesson I successfully manipulated two children into unknowingly providing insight into their lives, solely for the sake of my own gain. I then lied to their faces about my underlying intent, thus taking advantage of the trust I have fought so hard to build with each of them.

As if that weren't bad enough, I then proceeded to decimate Queen Victoria right in front of Nemain. It was an accident, of course, but it was also completely avoidable. If I had just listened to my better instincts when they screamed at me, saying that I was not in the right frame of mind to be around the children, I could have avoided this whole situation.

Even now, I'm *still* questioning my mental capabilities and the negative effect they could have on the children. My waking hallucinations of crows flying into windows and tornadoes of malicious butterflies are proof enough, but even if I were to put those aside, I would still be facing the struggle of my tangled spider web of emotional instability on the *best* of days.

Maybe Ms. Pierre was right all along. Maybe I'm not cut out for this position.

Amidst my surge of self-loathing, I can't help but find myself thinking back to when I was living at my parent's place and how my bedroom had acted as my self-induced prison; curtains drawn at all times, stale air practically dripping with anguish and remorse amidst the bouts of psychological abuse from both my Mom and myself.

As my eyes scan my current surroundings, I think back to my first day in the Morgan home. When I had initially entered this room, I had been blinded by its grandeur, and the lavish form of comfort that it offered; foolishly assuming that a change of scenery would put the black hole of negativity behind me.

Now, as I continue pacing back and forth, that old familiar feeling has returned, just overlaid upon a different backdrop. I hadn't even considered that this palatial living condition would eventually become a refection of my self-made dungeon, yet I have arrived in this moment, nonetheless.

I scowl at the four walls that surround me, loathing the rubber-like way they bounce my thoughts back at me, every hour of every day. It's as if they've been conspiring with Ms. Pierre, working in tandem to push me towards this inevitable mental collapse.

Then it occurs to me... this is *exactly* what Ms. Pierre wants.

Thinking back over my time in the Morgan home, the majority of the stress and anguish I've suffered has been as a result of *her* actions, not mine. She's been trying to break me from the very moment that I started lugging my suitcase down that endless path.

Ms. Pierre is the one who's run me ragged with stress, leading to sleepless nights and in turn, semi-conscious hallucinations. *Ms. Pierre* is the one who's been serving me *purposely*-spoiled meals, likely as an attempt to weaken me, both physically and emotionally. *Ms. Pierre* is the one who made me get back behind the wheel and drive into town before I was ready to face my fear. *Ms. Pierre* is the reason Clayton and his buddy had the opportunity to attack me.

Everything that's happened, all of it... it's *her* fault.

It's then that a dark thought from the back of my mind rears its ugly head once more... *I should have just let her die.*

As the words pass though my mind, I freeze in place, horrified that I would have the instinct to think such a thing, not once, but *twice* in one day.

Yes, I'm going through a myriad of emotions right now, and yes, they are mostly fueled by hatred and anger towards Ms. Pierre, but that's still no excuse to wish *death* upon her. It's no excuse to imagine myself standing over her as she gasps for her last breath of air; reaching towards me for help that I spitefully refuse to give.

I shake my head free of the dark thought, becoming suddenly cognizant of how many hours have passed.

At some point during my mental turmoil, night has fallen and I now find myself staring blankly out of my window into the abyss of night. The heavy cloud cover from earlier in the day remains, as made evident by the complete absence of stars above and the lack of soft moonlight accenting the edges of the tree outside my window.

Save for a few leaves, mere inches away from the glass that are catching the dim light leaking out of my room, I might as well be staring into the center of a black hole. Oddly, I find comfort in that, along with a feeling of envy towards the emptiness of night. I can't help but wonder what it would be like to void myself of any and all feelings, if even just for a moment.

My drifting thoughts are suddenly interrupted by a sharp knock at the door.

Already dreading tonight's encounter with Ms. Pierre, I take a deep breath and try to suppress my residual anger to go through the motions of pleasantly accepting my dinner with as little conflict as possible. However, as soon as I open the door and see Ms. Pierre's pursed lips and raised eyebrow, I know my efforts have been rendered futile before they've even begun.

Ms. Pierre thrusts the tray into my chest before I'm ready to receive it, so much so that I'm momentarily winded by the impact.

Taking advantage of my temporary breathlessness, Ms. Pierre

crosses her hands at her waist and says, "You think you're clever, don't you, Miss Woodall?"

Still trying to find my breath, I look up at her with an incredulous expression upon my face.

Without hesitation, she continues, "Don't think for *one second* that I don't know what you're up to."

Alarms start going off in my mind. I silently wonder if Ms. Pierre figured out the hidden purpose of my lesson plan on her own, or if Macha finally broke her lifelong silence to implicate me. Either way, the actual accusation remains loosely worded, so I tactfully maintain my charade of ignorance, scrunching my face as I say, "I'm not sure I understa-"

Ms. Pierre sharply cuts back in, "-Your 'lesson'. I know *exactly* what you were trying to achieve in there."

My arms begin to shake as my palms suddenly become sweaty. I can't tell if it's from the weight of the tray, or the shame of being caught. Regardless, Ms. Pierre has found me out and I can no longer hide from the truth.

While I'm unsure of what the consequences will be for such a betrayal, I figure it's best to come clean about my hidden intentions while I still have the opportunity to do so, "I- I was just trying to-"

Thankfully, Ms. Pierre is so fired up that she chimes in before I can fully admit my guilt, "-You prompted those children to subliminally display their hatred for me! Through *crayon drawings*, no less! You should be *ashamed* of yourself, Miss Woodall. Manipulating Macha and Nemain to do your bidding? It's as deplorable as it is disgusting!"

Part of me feels a wave of relief as I realize that Ms. Pierre didn't *actually* figure out the hidden intentions of my lesson plan. Yet still, I feel my anger build in response to the unfounded assumption that she *has* made.

Taking a confident breath, I fire back, "Ms. Pierre, I assure you that your accusations are baseless. I had no goal of hurting you through the children." For the sake of civility, I know that's where I should leave it, but my anger takes hold and I can't help but blurt out a venomous addendum, "If the children's drawings really bother you *that* much, perhaps you should try looking *inward* to find the real problem."

I can't help but recognize the hypocritical nature of my statement as I watch Ms. Pierre's face turn a dark shade of red before she fires back, "You will *not* turn those children against me!"

Fueled by my residual hatred towards the woman in front of me, I maliciously scoff while blurting out, "I don't have to. You're doing that all on your own."

For the first time, I see the true face of Ms. Pierre's rage as her eyes widen and her jaw clenches. She leans in, nearly whispering as she says, "Miss Woodall, I caution you not to forget yourself. I have done *nothing* but provide for these children for as long as they can remember. I have devoted myself to their well-being in ways that you will *never* understand. Yes, I may be stern. Yes, I may have a *particular* way of doing things. But these children are products of *my* upbringing nonetheless. How *dare* you question my methods."

While my instincts tell me to take the hit and walk away, I find myself too deep in the sea of frustrated anger to willingly back down, so instead, I come back with a haymaker, "You're right. Why would I question your methods? It's not like Nemain torturing animals is a textbook warning sign for violent behavior."

Rolling her eyes, Ms. Pierre attempts to dismiss the accusation, "She is a child. She's just trying to understand how the world works. It's an innocent mistake."

I audibly scoff at Ms. Pierre's proclivity to dismiss Nemain's actions, "At her age, with a deceased parent no less, Nemain should at least have a *loose* understanding of the difference between life and death. Didn't you discuss it with her after her mother passed away? Or were you just too busy trying to fill those shoes while they were still warm?"

Ms. Pierre purses her lips once more, "Miss Woodall, you are treading towards a conversation that is not yours to discuss."

I ignore the warning shot and continue charging on, "And what was that about their father? You told me he left, but Nemain seems to think he *lives out back*. That is not healthy, and the longer you lie to her, the more damage it is going to cause in the end."

Ms. Pierre takes another step forward and stares me directly in the eyes with contempt. Despite her meek, elderly frame, something about the intensity in her whispered tone suddenly sends a wave of intimidation washing over me, "Miss Woodall, the history of this family is *none* of your concern. The state of those children is *none* of your concern. You are here to assist *me*. You are here to work for *me*. Is that understood?"

I childishly stand my ground, "So we're just ignoring it then? Great."

Ms. Pierre moves close enough that I can feel the tray push against my mid-section. While her voice becomes even quieter, it somehow grows in intensity, "I understand that you feel as though you know how to raise these children better than I do; that you see yourself as a better mentor, a more positive influence. But I see you, Miss Woodall. I know what you've done. And I assure you... I will *not* allow these children to be raised by an addict whose recklessness killed her *own brother*."

I freeze at the affirmation that Ms. Pierre has known about the accident this whole time. The sheer gravity of such a realization knocks the wind out of me far more than the tray did. My vision immediately starts to blur as tears quickly fill my eyes.

Amidst my moment of vulnerability, Ms. Pierre steps back, smiling contemptuously as she hisses, "Sweet dreams, Miss Woodall" before pivoting and striding away from me.

I remain frozen in place, staring at the spot she held moments ago, as I try to process what the hell just happened. Only once the tears start falling down my face, do I step back into my room, shutting the door behind me and slamming the tray onto the small table.

I frenetically shift back and forth, unsure of what to do in the moment, but filled with anxious energy and the fire of pure rage. I continuously roll over Ms. Pierre's words in my head, while trying to comprehend the implications they carry.

She *knew*. She knew about the accident. She knew that I killed Andy. She knew how the aftermath ruined my life. She knew I was desperate for employment and had no other options on the horizon. She knew I would do anything to hang onto this job, no matter how terrible she was to me. She knew, and she continued to try to break me.

Ms. Pierre never wanted an employee; she wanted someone to torture.

The more it all comes together, the more my anger towards her grows. Tears are now flowing freely as I stare at the tray in front of me with hatred towards the curvature of the cloche as it glows in the flickering light of the propane lamps. It is as though it's offering promises of fine cuisine, but I know it's merely masking the rancid concoction it actually conceals. After all, it's just another one of Ms. Pierre's instruments of torture.

My heart is racing again, my breathing elevated once more. I silently grit my teeth behind tightly sealed lips, and before I make the conscious decision to do so, I seize the tray from either side and I hurl it at my bedroom door with every ounce of strength I have left.

The plate shatters into a collection of sharp fragments, its horrid offerings falling to the floor. The silver cloche lands upside down and settles upon a sizeable dent I've created in its side, an apt punishment for its complicit role in Ms. Pierre's schemes.

Having released the aromas of the horrid food, my nostrils soon fill with what could only be described as the scent of 'acidic fecal matter' as it infiltrates the room with its stench.

In a fit of rage, I scream at the top of my lungs until I run out of air.

I feel my knees suddenly give out from under me and I crumple to the floor, bawling for the better part of an hour as I realize that Ms. Pierre has finally succeeded... she's irrevocably broken me.

Remaining on the floor until my audible sobbing subsides, my sorrow and pain suddenly shift gears, giving way to the return of my anger and vengeful intent. I start plotting my next course of action as I utilize one of the pieces of the broken plate to finish scraping the last of the pungent 'food' off the floor.

As I pile the broken dishes onto the tray, I find my conviction once more and start scheming as to how to get back at Ms. Pierre. I need to send her a message. I need to show her that I'm not going to live under her thumb anymore.

Placing the tray of broken dishes in the hallway, I find myself lamenting all of the rules and stipulations that have been implemented in this house, under the guise of upholding stability... then it hits me.

Ms. Pierre's entire raison d'être is maintaining order. The most effective way to get back at her is to start actively disobeying her.

Childish? Maybe. But she's the one who has pushed me this close to the edge, leaving me with nothing left to lose, so I might as well try to grab her on my way down. But I need to be tactful; start small. I need to find information on her. Something I can use as ammunition as I flip the tables and hurt her like she's hurt me.

It's then that my attention drifts to the end of the hallway... to the locked office.

My mind cycles through every spy movie I've ever seen, as I pop back into my room and grab two bobby pins from the bedside table. Clutching them in my fist, I take a deep breath and return to the hallway, making my way towards the sealed room, each step filled with more determination than the last.

By the time I reach the door to the room, I have straightened out both of the bobby pins, something I've seen countless actors do on the big screen. I slowly kneel, checking over my shoulder to make sure that the coast is clear as the Mission Impossible theme plays quietly in the back of my mind.

Taking a bobby pin in each hand and inserting them into the lock at random angles, I quickly realize that I have no idea what I'm doing. I've never picked a lock before, and the only time I've *seen* it done, was in works of fiction. Regardless, I continue moving each bobby pin erratically, in the hopes of stumbling upon success.

I don't.

After a solid handful of minutes listening to the bobby pins fruitlessly click against one other, I lean back from the keyhole and sigh with derision towards my futile efforts.

However, despite my lack of success, I refuse to leave this door without some semblance of victory by way of truth, so I check down the hallway once more to ensure that I'm alone before closing one eye and leaning towards the keyhole.

While the room is barely lit by the faint moonlight sneaking through the thick clouds, my eyes adjust quickly to the darkness. Though I can't see much, what I can see makes the hairs on the back of my bruised neck instantly stand on end.

To my right I see a desk, exactly where I had seen it in my dreams. Sitting on top of it is a large glass jug, the dust upon its curvature highlighted by the dim light, masking my ability to see the model ship that is undoubtedly within.

The limited amount of light prevents me from being able to see all the way to the far wall, but as my focus drifts across the dark space, I feel my heart nearly jump out of my chest as I see the faint outline of an old spiral staircase on the left side of the room.

I shift my weight, trying to reposition myself to a better perspective, but I am limited by the peripheral boundaries of the keyhole.

I'm about to give up completely when suddenly, I hear a voice beside me whisper, "What are you doing?"

Nearly falling backwards in response, I whip my head around to see Nemain standing next to me in her nightgown.

Beads of guilty sweat instantly form on my forehead as I scramble for a half-assed explanation, "I heard- I *thought* I heard something... But, it was just a draft."

I see a look of suspicion wash over Nemain's face. I can't say I blame her, considering the complete lack of conviction in my lie, especially when combined with her already fleeting trust towards me ever since I dropped Queen Victoria.

Preemptively deflecting her suspicions, I softly ask "What are you doing up so late?"

Nemain's head dips a little as she says, "... I- I can't sleep."

I remain at eye level, placing my hand on her shoulder, "Having bad dreams?"

She shakes her head, but says nothing outside of that. I can't help but see the similar mannerisms between Nemain and her sister in the moment. While my instincts tell me that her restlessness is likely tied to my blunder from earlier, I'm certainly not going to be the one to voice that assumption and potentially bring back the emotions that come with it. So instead, I loosely inquire, "What is it? What's bothering you?"

Nemain hesitates at first, but then finally concedes, "... it's Macha."

Naturally, I assume that Macha is having another sleepless night, based on her previous nightmares about the cloaked woman, so I try to offer a solution, "Well, why don't you tell Macha to come hang out in my room until you've had a chance to fall asleep?"

Nemain shakes her head again, "No... I don't want to wake her up."

Confused, I try to connect the dots as best as I can, "Oh! If she's talking in her sleep, just give her a little nudge. She won't wake up, but she'll come out of her dream enough that she'll at least stop for a little while."

Shaking her head once more, I now see a whisper of fear in Nemain's eyes, along with a quivering lip suggesting the pending onset of tears. I look down, suddenly noticing it's not just her lip that's quivering; it's her *entire* body.

It then becomes clear. Nemain's fear is towards her own sister, and she's not just scared, she's *terrified*.

My concern grows exponentially as goose bumps present themselves on my arms. Tentatively, I inquire, "What exactly is Macha doing?"

A single tear falls from Nemain's eye as she hesitantly says, "I-I told her to stop, but she won't listen to me. No matter how much I say no, she just keeps doing it."

Nemain's single tear is soon joined by a collection of its brethren, streaking down her cheeks and dripping off her chin. Though she's visibly fragile in the moment, I still continue pushing for answers, "Keeps doing what? You can tell me."

Slowly lifting her head, the dim light from the propane lamps in the hallway dances upon Nemain's damp cheekbones. Though hesitant to put it to words, she finally concedes and confesses, "She... she keeps sneaking into my dreams."

CHAPTER TWENTY-TWO

"See"

Even though I know Nemain's belief that Macha has been consciously entering her dreams defies all logic, in the back of my mind I can't help but wonder if such a thing *could* theoretically be feasible.

As my mind drifts back to the late night visits Macha had made to my room, I start to wonder if it's possible that those experiences could have just been dreams as well. After all, that would explain the confusion surrounding the conversations I was *certain* we had, and her *supposed* lifelong diagnosis of Mutism.

It's then that I think back to the drawings that had been left behind on my bed the morning after her most recent visit. As I remember them now, I realize there is an undeniable consistency of style between those drawings and the ones she had created during my Arts and Crafts lesson, meaning she *must* have been there.

Utilizing those tangible aspects as footholds, I am quick to assert my conviction and shake off any passing consideration towards the obtuse, paranormal theory.

Snapping back to the present moment, I see Nemain's fear-fueled expression looking towards me expectantly, so I try to ease her worry by explaining the science behind dreams as simplistically as I can.

Remaining at eye-level with her, I try to abridge my thesis in leman's terms, "You know, dreams are like a broken telephone for our brains. The right side will often use familiar people and places to try to send a message to the left side."

I can already tell that Nemain is not pleased with my attempt to explain away her experience, as her fearful expression shifts to one of disappointment towards my narrow-mindedness.

Aware of her unreceptiveness, I continue with a personal spin,

"I used to have this dream all the time, where I showed up to school with no clothes on. I was so embarrassed every single time it happened, and no matter how much I tried to force myself to double and triple check that I was clothed, the dreams always ended the same way."

Whether it's the mention of my own experience with recurring dreams, or the silly nature of my subconscious embarrassment, I notice Nemain's face soften a bit as she starts to listen more intently.

Quieting my voice even more, so as to make it feel like we're sharing secrets, I continue, "But then a friend of mine, who studies dreams, explained to me that my feeling of embarrassment had nothing to do with my clothes. It was the right side of my brain trying to tell the left side that I was pretending to be someone I wasn't."

Nemain's face drops once again in response to the anti-climactic conclusion of my experience, rolling her eyes at the self-help nature of the underlying message.

While she is clearly not subscribing to the science I'm selling, I can't help but notice the comfort that I'm finding in my own explanation, especially on the tail end of a day filled with waking dreams. In the moment, I can't help but wonder what angry crows and butterfly tornadoes might represent in regards to my *own* conscious mind.

Quickly shifting my focus back to Nemain, I ask, "What is Macha doing when she comes into your dreams?"

Hesitating for a moment, Nemain thinks back to her subconscious projections from moments ago, "She just says the same thing, over and over, 'it's almost time'."

Though I'm actively trying to disprove Nemain's belief that this was all real, I can't help but find myself intrigued by this mysterious tidbit, so I keep pushing, "... Almost time for what?"

Shaking her head, Nemain is quick to say, "She won't tell me."

I can't help but find myself mesmerized by the vague nature of the message, so I keep digging further, "Have you tried asking her? In your dreams, I mean."

Nemain nods silently as tears begin to resurface along with the quivering throughout her body.

Concerned towards her physical and emotional shift, I inquire, "What did she say?"

As she looks up at me, a single tear falls down Nemain's cheek, "Nothing. She just... *changes*."

Something about the inflection in Nemain's voice sends a chill up my spine. It's almost as if I'm experiencing her fear vicariously in the moment, yet still my curiosity gets the better of me, so I continue prying, "... Changes, how?"

Nemain's eyes widen as terrified tears fall in response to the resurgence of the imagery from her nightmare. While I desperately want to know more about what she's seen, I know that I've pushed far enough and now feel compelled to help her find comfort through logic.

Gently placing my hand on her shoulder in an attempt to bring her back into the present, I say, "You know; I've seen how much you try to protect your sister. You must really love her."

Nemain shrugs with affirmation, clearly confused as to where this is going as she says, "Yeah. I guess so."

I can't help but smirk at the nonchalant response, as I begin to theorize, "Well, *maybe* Macha is appearing in your dreams because, *to you*, she represents your protective nature. When she's saying '*it's almost time*', your brain might be trying to help you understand that the older she gets, the more she's going to be able to protect herself. When you think of it that way, it might explain why she's '*changing*', wouldn't it?"

I can still see the residual cynicism in Nemain's eyes as she absorbs my attempt at decoding her subconscious. Something about the way she looks at me, tells me that she's accepting of my theory, but doesn't remotely believe in its merits.

Standing up from my crouched position, I gently turn Nemain around and start walking her back towards her room.

On the way, I attempt to solidify the logic of my argument, in the hopes that it will ease Nemain's mind, "Sometimes dreams *feel* scary or real, because they're rooted in strong emotions from deep inside of us. In this case, your love for Macha." Nemain looks up at me with a slight smile, so I quickly add, "I sure wish I was lucky enough to have a sister like you when I was growing up."

Slightly bashful at the compliment, Nemain turns her face away to hide her smile. As she does so, I see her notice the broken plates piled on the silver tray, sitting outside of my room, prompting her to immediately turn back towards me with a look of concern.

Before she can inquire about it, I sheepishly excuse the mess with a half-hearted lie, "Oh, I dropped my tray earlier. I've always been a little clumsy."

My explanation towards the aftermath of my tantrum is received with as much skepticism as my scientific dismissal of Nemain's dreams. Regardless, I continue leading Nemain back to her room as though nothing is wrong, despite all evidence pointing to the contrary.

Opening the door to the children's room, I usher her through as I say, "Try to go back to sleep, and if Macha comes back, just remember that it's not *really* her. It's your *love* for her," it's clear that Nemain is still reluctant to return to her slumber, so I offer an addendum, "and if that doesn't work... just remember I'm down the hall, and you can come and hang out *anytime* you need to."

Still filled with concern, Nemain gives a diffident nod before disappearing into the darkness. Softly closing the door to the children's room, I gently press my hand against the embossed symbol of the Triquetra in an attempt to mute the sound of the door finding its frame.

As I return to my own room, I remove my robe and slowly crawl under the slightly chilled covers that have been awaiting me all along.

Laying on my back and staring up at the silk canopy above me, I can still feel the tiny flame of hatred towards Ms. Pierre burning deep within me. However, after my failed attempt at picking the lock, and my ensuing conversation with Nemain, my vengeful instincts have been effectively grounded by equal doses of vulnerability and purpose.

Before I know it, exhaustion slips in to fill the emotional void, washing over me like a warm bath.

Amidst my fleeting state of consciousness, I can't help but roll over my conversation with Nemain about dream imagery, only now I consider my words in regards to my *own* subconscious projections.

The cloaked woman, the crow, the impenetrable wall of trees, it all has to mean something, but the more I think about it, the more I realize that none of the imagery possesses any significance to me other than to inspire a heightened sense of fear.

I try to focus my thoughts, hoping to gain some semblance of a clinical perspective, but my eyelids feel as heavy as cinderblocks, and the blankets have grown warm with my body heat, thus distracting my mind with the siren's song of comfort.

Soon, my body feels as though it's sinking into the mattress and my vision begins to blur as I slowly slip from the conscious world.

I am now sitting at the breakfast table in my parent's darkened kitchen. I scan back and forth between the blank stares from Mom, Dad and Andy, as blood pours from their mouths, like the red wax dripping down the stack of Banana pancakes.

As though it were a well-rehearsed play, I knock my chair backwards as I stand from the table, turning towards the kitchen window to see the large crow staring at me, as my hands suddenly feel warm and wet.

Glancing down towards my forearms, I see that my scars have broken open and blood is pouring down my wrists, falling to the kitchen floor and pooling around my feet.

Instinctually backing away from the sight of it all, I trip over the toppled kitchen chair and soon find myself, as I have so many nights before, suspended upside down in the wreckage of my car, in the middle of the highway.

The large crow is now perched beside me, upside down, in the driver's seat. It continues to stare at me menacingly, cocking its head back and forth as it calculates its inevitable attack.

I excruciatingly free myself from the wreckage, only to find myself standing over the white, bloodstained sheet as it billows in the breeze. A strong gust of wind suddenly rips it away, revealing the carnage of Andy's remains as the symbol of the Triquetra is burned into his chest from the inside.

Though I've seen all of this play out in prior nightmares, I still feel compelled to turn away from the morbid sight of my brother's corpse being desecrated before me, thus leading me to realize I'm now encircled by an impenetrable wall of large oak trees, each bearing the symbol of the three-armed pinwheel with feet at its extremities.

I hear the sound of crying behind me, prompting me to turn back towards Andy's body, only to find the cloaked woman now kneeling beside him, softly weeping.

Slowly approaching until I am standing beside the cloaked woman, we share in the moment of mourning before she reaches into her cloak and produces the leather bound book with the symbol of the Triquetra embossed upon its front cover.

I feebly open the book in an attempt to read what's written upon its pages, but before I am able to decipher anything, the words dissipate, as they have in prior dreams.

Slamming the book closed in frustration, I turn to the cloaked woman for further guidance that I know will likely not come.

Her face remains obscured by the shadows of her hood, but I see her wisps of stringy, silver hair shift as she tilts her head towards me and says, *"Save them."*

I try to speak but, yet again, find myself voiceless. Instead of getting more frustrated or fearful though, I move closer to her this time.

Kneeling beside her while giving a cartoonish shrug and a confused look, I attempt to silently insinuate my lack of understanding in the hopes that she might clarify further in this iteration of my nightmare.

Despite reflexively tilting her head away from me, so as to keep her face obscured from view, the cloaked woman seems to sympathize with my voiceless state, and for the first time adds, *"See"*.

I attempt to escalate my conveyance of confusion, in the hopes that the cloaked woman will further clarify her vague message.

In response, she merely repeats herself with more assertion, "*See*".

My frustrated anger towards the ambiguous request from the cloaked woman begins to rise. I am about to fruitlessly attempt to gain clarification once more, when suddenly; the ground beneath me starts to move.

Within seconds, the roots of the surrounding oak trees start to perforate the circular clearing, snaking above and below ground as they reach inwards towards the cloaked woman and I, in the center.

I feel the instinct to run, but soon find the roots binding me by my calves and ankles, restraining me in my kneeling position. With each attempt to wiggle myself free of their grasp, their grip only tightens as they continue to coil up the lower half of my body.

Shifting my focus back towards Andy, I freeze in place as I see similar roots emerge from the area surrounding him, wrapping around his remains.

I watch, horrified, as the ground beneath Andy suddenly falls away and the roots holding his body slowly lower him into the pure darkness of whatever subterranean realm resides below.

Now wrapped around my thighs and waist, the roots continue to suppress me as I try to lean forwards and watch my brother as he descends out of sight. Moments later I find myself thankful for the restraint, because the moment Andy is gone, a large oak tree suddenly emerges from within the cavernous breach at a furious pace.

As the tree shoots upwards, it seems to age rapidly, its trunk growing thicker by the second, its bark withering and turning grey. In a matter of moments, the large oak is towering above the clearing, sheltering the cloaked woman and I beneath its canopy of plumage.

Staring up at the sheer immensity of the tree as it continues to grow, I finally surrender to the will of the roots, relaxing my body into their secure confinement.

As I lower my focus from the branches above, I realize that I am no longer in the circular clearing. I am now at the base of the immense oak tree in the back of the Morgan property.

Turning to my left, I see that the cloaked woman has remained beside me throughout the violent, environmental transition, patient and unflinching all the while. As the tree's rapid, destructive growth finally ceases, the cloaked woman tilts her head towards me yet again.

Anticipating further instructions, I intently lean towards her. However, instead of speaking, she reaches out and seizes me by the arm with immeasurable speed, her gnarled fingers wrapping tightly around my wrist.

My eyes widen with fear as she hisses her message once more, "*SEE*".

I suddenly feel a wave of energy shoot through me like a current of electricity. My head kicks back as I stare into the canopy of the immense oak, and see an evening mist descending rapidly through the branches.

The mist quickly thickens into a light fog, and I start to notice wisps of light moving within the accumulating haze, as though it were some sort of ethereal broadcast, slowly taking form in front of me.

The blurred images slowly find a sense of definition as the fog envelops me, masking me from my surroundings. Suddenly, it feels less like I am being *shown* something; more like my consciousness is being transported so as to *experience* an altered reality.

Before me, I see a man in the hull of a turbulent ship, bracing himself amidst a pile of dead bodies. Based on the only story that Ms. Pierre has shared with me, I immediately assume that this must be the fabled Pater Morgan.

As the scene plays out, I soon notice that Pater is holding hands with one of the bodies beside him. A woman; and she appears to be gripping Pater's hand just as tightly amidst the tossing and turning of the ship as it navigates the stormy waters.

With each sudden shift, their knuckles whiten with fear. The more violent the ship's movements become, the more Pater and the woman brace themselves for the inevitable outcome; as though they *know* they're about to crash.

Pater turns to the woman beside him, muting his own fear and concern so that he can give her a reassuring smile, his eyes filled with love. The woman gives him a soft smile in return before the ship suddenly runs aground, scattering the pile of bodies, along with Pater and the mysterious woman.

The images from the hull of the ship suddenly dissipate, similar to how the words in the cloaked woman's notebook had washed off the page when I had tried to read them. However, just as quickly as the previous scene disappeared, a new one begins to take its place.

This time, Pater is climbing out of the wreckage of the ship, alone.

My heart sinks as I think back to Ms. Pierre's story and how Pater had been the *sole* survivor of the crash. While it had been a sad detail prior to now, it is a heartbreaking factor amidst the new context that he and his love were stowing away together.

However, just as I begin to feel empathetic tears forming in response to his loss, Pater turns around and reaches behind him to assist the woman as she exits the wreckage of the ship, alive.

The two paramours attempt to navigate the rocky shore together, only pausing briefly as Pater stands over the body of one of the deceased crewmembers to bow his head respectfully.

Moments later, they finally reach the top of the rocky embankment. Glancing over their shoulders, Pater and his love take a moment, supporting each other's weight before they proceed to hobble inland, fighting to suppress the pain of their injuries.

Once more, the scene dissipates before jumping forward to show Pater and the mysterious woman putting the finishing touches on the Morgan home.

The two lovers hold each other in an embrace, with beaming smiles on their faces. Slowly kneeling, Pater presses his ear against the woman's slightly protruding belly to listen to the stirring of their unborn child.

I can't help but feel myself smile in response to the pure joy on Pater's face, not to mention the tender pleasantness of the moment as a whole.

The scene dissipates into mist one last time, and I soon find my consciousness transported into an office setting, where Pater is sitting at a desk, writing feverishly into a notebook.

My attention immediately spikes as I take notice of large glass jug on his desk with a model ship inside of it. I quickly deduce that this must be the locked room at the end of the hall.

Pater continues frantically writing in his notebook, shooting occasional glances towards the door of his office as though he is anxiously awaiting someone to arrive.

The sound of knocking suddenly echoes throughout the office, prompting Pater to slam his notebook shut, revealing the symbol of the Triquetra embossed upon its leather cover.

Taking a deep breath, Pater tentatively gets up from his chair to go answer the door. The moment he is out of sight, the room shifts to darkness and the scene before me speeds up.

I watch the rapid onset of dust and cobwebs accumulating upon the desk's surface as though it were elapsed time footage. Within moments, the ship is barely visible within the foggy glass jug, and Pater's notebook is hardly noticeable amidst the inches of grey fluff that seamlessly hide the book's edges.

I quickly realize that this is the exact condition of the locked office that I had seen through the keyhole earlier this evening, as my surroundings then dissipate, bringing me back to the base of the immense oak tree.

Turning to my left, I suddenly realize that the cloaked woman is gone; as are the roots that had held me in place, along with any semblance of the fog I had been enveloped by.

The only evidence of my experience that remains is the leather-bound notebook that the cloaked woman had given to me, still tightly clutched in my hand.

As I stare at the embossed image of the Triquetra, popping out of the notebook's leather cover, I hear the cloaked woman's words echo as if they are dancing upon a gust of wind, *"See"*.

❦　　❦　　❦

My eyes pop open, and I find myself lying in bed, staring up at the silk canopy once more.

Contrary to previous times I have awoken from these dreams, I'm not lying in a pool of my own sweat, nor am I struggling to catch my breath in a state of fear-induced panic. Instead, I find myself renewed, refreshed and reinvigorated by the dream.

I immediately flash back to the guidance I had given Nemain, as I try to decipher the imagery from my *own* dreams, and what they could potentially be trying to communicate to my conscious mind.

My eyes dance back and forth across the silk canopy above me as though my brain is using it as a whiteboard upon which to collect my racing thoughts.

Initially, I had feared the foreboding nature of the cloaked woman, but now I realize that it's entirely possible that she is the personification of all of my unanswered questions, hence the hidden visage.

As for the slightly altered version of Pater's story that had been shown to me, I can't help but feel as though it was intended to represent the half-truths that Ms. Pierre has been feeding me; the variances within the story merely representative of my suspicions towards *her* version of the truth.

I then consider the leather notebook that the cloaked woman had given me, with the Triquetra embossed upon its cover. I have no doubt that it's emblematic of the answers I've been seeking all along, hence my inability to decipher anything on the page when I had tried to read it.

However, the literal nature of Pater's notebook still sitting on the desk at the end of the hall begins to raise questions in regards to how my dreams seem to be acting more like *premonitions* than subliminal messages.

Even after dissecting my own dreams from a quantifiable perspective, I still can't shake the memories of my dreams that seemingly transcended my subconscious state, be it in the form of pieces of bark that I found around my ankles, or more recently, the bruising on the back of my neck.

Then, there are also the unanswered questions surrounding the imagery of the malicious crow, the impenetrable wall of oak trees, and the blood pouring from my own arms as well as my family's mouths.

In fact, the more that I attempt to decode the imagery of my dreams; the more complicated the equation seems to get. While I have no doubt that there is a message in there somewhere, there are far too many variables for me to discern what the ultimate significance may be, thus leaving only one solution.

I *need* to get into that office. I *need* to see what secrets it contains. I *need* to read Pater's journal to get the actual *truth* behind this family.

CHAPTER TWENTY-THREE

Pater's Office

Ever since Ms. Pierre admitted that she had known about my accident, a contemptuous silence between she and I has thickened the air throughout the Morgan home, reminding me of the days when I was living in my parent's house.

Whether it was the venomous way in which she used that information to hurt me in the moment, or her naturally cold, combative nature the rest of the time, I get the distinct sense that she has purposely mined my past for vulnerabilities, solely for the purpose of lording it over me from the very beginning.

I may not possess the same kind of deeply personal ammunition that she has against me, but each passing venomous glare that Ms. Pierre has thrown my way since her vindictive reveal has resulted in further motivation to continue my quest to get into Pater's locked office as an act of vengeful insurgence against her.

Back when I had first arrived at the Morgan home, the regimented schedule that had been dictated to me had initially appeared as a laborious burden. However, since I have started secretly tracking Ms. Pierre's movements over the past few days, the strict routine has proven itself to be an asset, allowing me to accurately predict the timing of her comings and goings, down to the minute.

The consistency of her schedule is so precise that I have started to conceal my phone in my uniform, solely for the purpose of giving myself advance notice of her movements by way of a series of silent alarms.

Thanks to the system I have created, each day has provided a handful of openings for me to sneak in a few attempts at picking the office's lock, none of which have proven efficacious thus far.

During my first few attempts, I successfully broke three hairpins and lost two, one slipping through the keyhole, the other falling from my hand and bouncing under the door. While these failed attempts were frustrating, the lost bobby pins are now evidence of my efforts, thus increasing my need to get into that room exponentially, if even just to cover my tracks.

In my most recent attempts I've made nominal progress, during which I've learned how foolish I was to base my approaches on what I had seen in works of fiction.

Contrary to the methods of various fictional detectives, I know now that the bobby pins are much more effective when bent at ninety-degree angles. Also, while said leading characters will typically poke their tools into a lock, until the door magically opens, I've learned that in actuality the pins need to be used in more of a twisting motion. The similarity of the movement required, to that of using a key, admittedly makes me feel like an idiot for *ever* believing that Hollywood had it right.

However, in the process of discovering the proper method for picking the lock, I've simultaneously come to realize that the bobby pins are not strong enough to withstand the torque that the archaic, rusted lock requires in order to disengage.

As a result, I have spent the majority of today forgoing my windows of opportunity between cleaning duties, in order to search for any objects that might prove durable enough, while curved at the appropriate angle. Sadly, no such object has presented itself thus far.

Wiping the last of the windows in the sunroom, I find myself mesmerized by the immense oak tree in the back portion of the Morgan property, as I have been so many times before.

My thoughts drift back to my dream from a few days ago. Ever since I had watched Andy's body swallowed by the ground, only to replace him with the image of the oak tree that now stands before me, I've found myself wondering if this gargantuan tree might hold more meaning than I had initially perceived.

When combined with Nemain's matter-of-fact comment in regards to her father being 'out back, where he always is', the significance of this tree becomes almost undeniable in the grand scheme of things. Yet without proper context, said meaning remains just as much of a mystery as anything else swirling around in my mind.

My eyes habitually trace through the branches of the tree, when suddenly an epiphany clicks in my mind. With wide eyes of realization, I whip around towards the 'salon', and move towards the polished wooden table with the Morgan family crest embedded within it; more specifically, towards the sculpture of the metal tree that sits *upon* said family crest.

I had briefly clocked this sculpture on my first day, intrigued by the symmetrical nature of how its bald, twisted branches seemed to mirror the visible root system that was embedded in the granite base of the conversation piece. However, since that moment, I had not bothered to pay any mind to it, save for the moments when I've tickled it with the *lateral* flicks of my feather duster each day.

As I stare at the sculpture now though, my eyes scan through the winding maze of bare, metal branches until one, in particular, jumps out at me.

The singular branch I find, has no tangential twigs splicing off its sides, and it bends in the middle to *just* shy of a perfect ninety-degree angle. It presents itself as such an ideal tool that I can't help but wonder if it might have been placed there specifically for this purpose.

Dropping to my knees beside the table, I pinch the branch between my fingers, trying to see if I can wiggle it free. Alas, the metal that it is comprised of remains so solid that even the slightest movement of the branch causes the entire sculpture to shift in response.

Pulling my phone out of my smock, I check to see what my window of time looks like before Ms. Pierre's next departure from the children's room. With just shy of half an hour to play with, I quickly stand and make my way towards the kitchen with haste.

As soon as I'm in the kitchen, I place my bucket of soapy water in the sink and proceed to drop to the floor, opening the cupboard beneath the sink's basin, searching out the small repair kit that is stored at the very back.

Pulling out an old, rusted pair of wire cutters, I open and close the tool to test its functionality. Even with nothing between its jaws, the hinge of the tool still resists my efforts, but at this point, my determination exceeds my frustration, so I quietly mutter, "That'll do" before making my way back towards the sculpture.

I carefully navigate the dull jaws of the wire cutters until they are specifically wrapped around the one branch I'm seeking out. The sheer mass of surrounding branches makes this a nearly impossible task, but I persist for fear of taking a noticeable chunk out of the conversation piece that would incriminate me at a later date.

Squeezing the handles of the wire cutters, I find the thin piece of metal is *still* resisting my efforts, so I use my spare hand to pivot the sculpture's base to give myself more leverage.

By the time I finally feel the branch start to move, I'm standing over the sculpture, knees slightly bent, and both hands shaking as I squeeze the handles of the tool with every ounce of strength I can muster. While the small piece of metal still remains stubbornly attached, I *have* successfully pinched its base enough that I can manipulate the branch on its own.

Twisting my tool back and forth, I continue to weaken the branch's connection to the rest of the sculpture, until suddenly I feel my hands jolt towards me as the small piece of metal finally snaps free, shifting the entire sculpture in the process, causing it to loudly thud against the surface of the table.

I pause for a moment, waiting to hear if there are any reactions to the sound from upstairs. Thankfully, there are none.

Quietly picking up the small piece of metal and tucking it into my waistband, I am about to shift the sculpture back to its original position over the Morgan family crest in the center of the table, when something gives me pause.

When I had initially seen this sculpture sitting in the middle of the table during my tour of the Morgan home, only two letters of the crest were visible, 'M' on the left and 'N' on the right. Naturally, I had assumed that the concealed letters did the rest of the work to spell the name, 'Morgan', but as I look at the name upon the crest in full, I see that it says, *'Morrighan'*.

Assuming that it's merely some kind of traditional Celtic or Gaelic spelling of the contemporary moniker, I don't pay it much mind, but soon my attention drifts to below the name, where I see the edge of a symbol upon the family shield.

Grabbing the metal sculpture, I shift it further away to reveal the symbol of a large Triquetra beneath. Within each of the image's 'petals' of are three smaller glyphs.

Within the top petal is the symbol of the three-armed pinwheel with feet at its extremities, the same one that I had seen at the edges of the Morgan property to signify the entrances to both the driveway and the walking path.

In the bottom left petal, is a similar three-armed pinwheel to the first, but in place of the feet are three spirals, making the symbol feel psychedelically hypnotic in nature.

As my focus drifts to the bottom right petal though, a chill runs through my body as I find myself staring at the symbol of the square pendant, woven from straw, that had been hanging around the necks of each of the seven decayed women from my dream.

Staring at the depiction before me, I desperately try to remember whether or not I had seen this symbol prior, possibly giving logical reasoning to how it had appeared in my dreams. But thinking back, I have never seen this family crest in its entirety until now.

Thankfully, my phone begins to vibrate, shaking me from my trance-like state and allowing enough time for me to place the sculpture back where it was before moving to the kitchen to act as though I've been performing my daily duties all along.

Like clockwork, Ms. Pierre enters the kitchen a few minutes later, remaining silent throughout the process of her lunch preparation. I quietly navigate through the dishes and the daily inventory, attempting to remain invisible, while simultaneously hyper-aware of her every movement.

A short while later, Ms. Pierre exits the kitchen as quietly as she had entered, her sharp footsteps clacking against the hardwood floor as they move towards the staircase.

I wait to hear her making her way upstairs, but suddenly... the footsteps stop.

Immediately my heart begins to race as I picture Ms. Pierre standing in the front hallway, looking at the sculpture of the bare, metal tree and immediately spotting the missing branch from a distance.

The silence lasts a moment too long for my own comfort, and I soon find myself holding my breath while staring at the kitchen door, anticipating Ms. Pierre charging back towards the kitchen with venomous intent, possibly even striking me for my insolence. Much to my surprise though, the footsteps resume moments later, and she makes her way upstairs.

Breathing a sigh of relief, I check my waistband to make sure that the small metal branch hasn't fallen from where I tucked it away. Feeling it against my hipbone, a wave of confidence washes over me, as though I've already gotten away with the perfect crime.

I busy myself in the kitchen for the better part of an hour, to ensure that the children's recreational time has concluded and their afternoon lessons have reconvened. Only then, do I start to make my way upstairs for my next attempt.

As I reach the second floor, I quietly make my way towards the children's room, pressing my ear against the door to hear the muted words of Ms. Pierre as she conducts her afternoon lessons in her signature stern tone.

Confident that everyone is accounted for, I slowly make my way further down the hall, purposely navigating around the creaky spots in the floor that I have mentally mapped over the past few days.

As I reach the locked door, I quietly kneel and look over my shoulder, just to make doubly sure that no one will catch me here like Nemain had a couple of nights ago.

Slowly pulling the small metal branch from my waistband, I gently insert it into the archaic lock, snaking its angle to reach inwards, then down before I tighten my grip around it and twist.

In resistance to my efforts, I hear the various rusted components of the lock grinding against one another, refusing to give way just yet. I am seconds away from surrendering my attempt, when suddenly I hear the lock click as it releases.

My eyes widen with equal amounts of shock towards my success and anxiety towards what lies ahead. Even though I had made continued efforts over the past few days to enter this room,

I hadn't considered my plan of action, should I be successful in my attempts at infiltration.

Checking the time on my phone, I realize that I have the better part of an hour before Ms. Pierre steps out of the room for a brief bathroom break; after all, why wouldn't *that* be scheduled as strictly as anything else?

Glancing down the hallway once more, I slowly stand up, grip the doorknob and gently turn it to hear the latch bolt audibly dislodge from the lip, as the door suddenly begins to move inwards.

In an attempt to minimize the squeaking of the hinges as they experience their first movement in decades, possibly even centuries, I push the door open at a snail's pace, slowly revealing the room within, as my heart rate speeds up.

Once the door is halfway open, my nostrils are inundated with the stench of rot and dust permeating from the long-neglected room. While the scent would be overpowering to many, Ms. Pierre's various interpretations of 'cuisine' seem to have apparently built my tolerance to such horrid aromas over my time here. Another blessing in disguise, I guess.

With my eyes wide, I scan the room; reticent towards the precision with which my dreams have created the layout of a room I have never set foot in, until now. While part of me is enamored by the idea of possessing a subconscious clairvoyance, resulting in such succinct foresight, the momentary feeling of levity is quickly cut short.

Soon, I start to realize that the projections I have seen are almost *too* accurate to have originated from my own subconscious. Everything, down to the old books on the shelves and the layers of dust upon them, proves to be a precise facsimile of the images from my dreams. Even the angle of Pater's desk chair remains *exactly* the way he had left it in the vision that the cloaked woman had shown me.

The more the details hold true to the dreams I have experienced, the more I start to feel terrified and violated by the prospect of some external force inserting its will into my subconscious mind.

As my eyes travel from Pater's chair to the surface of his desk, I feel a chill run up my spine, covering my body with goose bumps, as I stare at a raised portion of dust with a rectangular shape.

Tentatively moving behind the desk, I slowly reach forward, piercing the inches-thick layer of dust with my fingertips to pick up the concealed object beneath.

Gently running my right palm over the object's surface to wipe the dust from it, I feel the embossed symbol of the Triquetra with a perfect circle around it, pass beneath my fingers. Moments later, the leather bound cover of Pater's journal presents itself to me, in full.

Taking a moment to gather myself, I gently place my index finger under the lip of the journal's cover and open it to the first page. Based on prior experiences with this book in my dreams, I'm expecting the words to evaporate off the page the moment I see them, but this time... they remain.

While the handwriting is horrendously sloppy, rendering itself barely legible upon first glance, I take time to allow my eyes to adjust to the crude penmanship and slowly put together the words before me:

It is clear; one's innocence is as relative as the word of one's accusers. While this monarchy claims to be just, they preside over this land with a golden fist, abusing their power in the name of protecting liars who are wrought with corruption, greed and cowardice. They cast pre-determined judgments from an arms length of the truth, vilifying the very citizens that line their purses with tithes.

They see me not as an equal, nor even as a man. All they see is the blood upon my hands, the anger within my heart and the lack of gold lining my pockets as I protest my innocence before their farce of a judicial system.

I have no choice but to flee. Were I to stay, I would merely become another piece of impoverished scrap, destined to satiate the hunger of injustice as they make a spectacle of my death for all to see.

They will undoubtedly mark me as a traitor, and a coward, but their words mean nothing to me. I am guided by a power far more divine than those who place crowns upon their own heads. I have been shown my true purpose.

I shall travel to the coast, in search of a ship setting sail for the Americas. I shall sneak aboard the ship in the dead of night, thus commencing my journey to freedom and a life born anew. I will start over. I will begin again. This, I have been shown. —P.M.

I audibly gasp as the pieces fall into place and I realize I'm not just holding *one* of Pater's journals, I'm holding the journal in which he recorded the story of coming to this land. If I'm going to find any answers towards the mysteries surrounding this house and this family, I will likely find them in here.

Reminding myself of the finite nature of my time in this room, I quickly close the journal, keeping it in my hand as I move towards the archaic spiral staircase leading up to the loft area of Pater's office.

Tentatively placing my foot on the first step, I slowly begin my ascension. Within a few moments, my right hand begins to ache from how hard I'm gripping the dusty railing as the entire structure wobbles beneath my every movement. I even try holding my breath so as to minimize any amplification of the already terrifying, swaying movements with each step, *certain* that the entire staircase will detach from the wall at any moment, taking me with it, to certain death.

Much to my surprise, I reach the top step safely, prompting me to take a deep breath of relief for having survived the journey.

Still holding Pater's journal in my left hand, I scan the loft area, finding countless sketches of Triquetras and other symbols that I had seen on the family crest, splayed everywhere, as though a tornado had recently passed through this space.

As I continue wandering the loft space, the severity of Pater's obsession with these symbols becomes abundantly clear. I start wondering if his anxious behavior from my vision was actually substantiated, or if it was an unfortunate side effect of what appears to be obsessive behavioral patterns, leading to mental collapse.

My eyes dance from one piece of paper to the next, trying to decipher the randomly skewed drawings and scribbled notes as I pass them. When my focus lifts though, I freeze in place as my brow furrows with curiosity.

The only object in this room that I had not previously seen in my dreams stands before me in the form of an easel with a canvas upon it, facing away from my current position.

As I come around the edge of the easel to inspect the front of the canvas, I feel goose bumps form all over my body as a half-finished portrait of a large crow sitting in the branches of an oak tree is revealed.

While the majority of the crow's lower half remains unfinished, its head is fully completed and stares back at me with orange eyes that seem to glow, even in their current, oil-based form.

I immediately feel tears form in my eyes, as a myriad of emotions begin to overwhelm me.

Part of me feels a sense of relief that I'm not the only one who has been haunted by this creature, especially judging by the accuracy of the rendering. However, another part of me feels fear towards the idea that my subconscious attacker has not only transcended the barriers of my own consciousness but someone else's as well.

Despite the terror I feel towards the re-creation of the bird's gaze though, I still feel myself pulled towards it, as if I were caught in some sort of masochistic tractor beam, leading me towards assured self-destruction.

Only once I hear the sound of a floorboard creak under my foot, am I able to cease my approach, pulling my attention from the entrancing image. As I instinctually shift my focus towards the source of the noise, I catch something in my peripheral view, barely visible amidst the shadows in the corner of the room.

Similar to what I had found in my dream, I see a stack of suitcases, piled as though it were a collection of luggage obtained through the ages. The variance in generational styles seem to work in tandem with the incremental differences in the amount of dust gathered upon them, in ascending order.

Examining the stack, I count out eight bags in total, resulting in the top of the stack reaching just above eye-level.

For fear of disturbing the precarious pile, I keep my distance at first, pivoting around the stack of bags as I look for any evidence of whom they may belong to.

Sliding around the left side of the stack, I notice that the suitcase at the top of the pile has a small leather strap looped around its handle, with the other end tucked into the bag itself. Recognizing this as a luggage tag, my eyes widen in anticipation.

Despite my instincts screaming against it, curiosity gets the better of me and I slowly start unzipping the suitcase to find the other end of the tag, ideally with the name of its owner upon it.

I unzip the bag no more than a fraction of an inch before I suddenly feel my phone vibrating from within my smock, signifying that I only have a few minutes before Ms. Pierre exits the children's room.

While part of me wants to risk it and stay in this room to find more answers, I quickly concede to logic, promising myself that I will come back at a later time.

Quickly zipping the suitcase back up, I turn and navigate my way down the spiral staircase with equal parts caution and haste.

Before making my exit, I tuck Pater's journal into the back of my waistband, freeing up both of my hands to pick up the two bobby pins I had lost during my prior attempts at breaking into this room.

Quietly pulling the door closed behind me with virtually no sound, I once again pull the small metal branch from my waistband and attempt to re-lock it. Only then do I realize that I had not accounted for the time it would take to reverse engineer the process of breaking into this room.

With each failed attempt at locking the door, my hands shake more and my breath continues to quicken, only making the task immeasurably harder by the second. I continue twisting with the small metal branch inside the lock, counting down the moments until Ms. Pierre emerges into the hallway, when suddenly, I feel my tool catch, and the bolt slides into place.

Knowing I have mere seconds left, I palm my lock-pick and pull the journal from my waistband before sprinting, full tilt, down the hallway towards my room.

Just as I cross the threshold into my bedroom, I hear the children's door opening behind me, so I quickly move to my bed, tucking both the metal branch and Pater's journal under my pillow, before Ms. Pierre is able to emerge.

Seeing me sitting on my bed in the middle of the afternoon, Ms. Pierre pokes her head into my room with a suspicious look in her scowling eyes.

Muting my breathlessness in the moment, I look up at her with my eyebrows raised expectantly as if to silently, yet rhetorically inquire, 'Can I help you?'

With her lips pursed, Ms. Pierre scans me up and down with surgical dissection before asking, "Why are you *sweating*?"

Scrambling, I quickly attempt to evade her questioning, "I'm not feeling so great. I think I might be coming down with something."

Ms. Pierre's focus suddenly turns to the mattress beside me, where she sees my phone laying on top of the blanket. I hadn't realized until now, but in my haste to hide the lock-pick and notebook under my pillow, my phone had fallen from my smock.

Lazily picking up the phone as though it was meant to be there, I attempt to justify its presence while further substantiating my story, "I might just lay down for a bit. I'll set an alarm so I don't oversleep."

Visibly rolling her eyes at the idea of something as uncouth as an afternoon nap, Ms. Pierre purses her lips even tighter as she shakes her head disapprovingly and says, "Twelve minutes, Miss Woodall. There is still much to be done today."

Feigning concession, I nod weakly before pivoting to lie down and further sell my lie. Ms. Pierre coldly slams my door, before making her way down the upstairs corridor, her sharp footsteps echoing as she descends the stairs.

Breathing a sigh of relief, I slip my hand under my pillow to feel the leather cover of Pater's journal against my fingertips, verifying that this wasn't all just another hallucination.

Smiling to myself, I feel the stress in my body already beginning to ease off, ever so slightly, as I silently celebrate my victory over the wretched woman who rules this house.

Though I want nothing more than to read Pater's journal right now, I force myself to wait until later tonight, when I'll have a chance to read through it, in full, and finally get some answers.

CHAPTER TWENTY-FOUR

The Woman on the Ship

Even though I've been so *graciously* allowed twelve minutes to myself, I'm back on my feet within eight and exiting my room, unable to stave off the anticipation of getting back to Pater's journal, come the end of the day.

As I make my way downstairs, I can't help but notice the bounce in my step, so I take a moment to mute the prominence of my positivity, in order to maintain the façade of not feeling well just a short while ago.

When I enter the kitchen, Ms. Pierre silently hands me a secondary list of duties with the heading, '*To Be Completed by End of Day*'. While I know this list of jobs is clearly a malicious form of penance for my unsanctioned mid-afternoon rest, I opt to receive it warmly, prompting Ms. Pierre's eyebrow to rise with scrutiny.

Choosing to ignore her suspicious scowl, I proceed to sail through the duties with a pleasant smile upon my face, happy to occupy myself, physically, as I attempt to waste away the remaining hours until the sun begins to set.

Over the course of those few hours, there are a few moments where Ms. Pierre and I cross paths, during which it's glaringly evident that she's put off by my seemingly impenetrable bravado. With each glare she throws my way, I can feel her picking me apart, piece-by-piece, questioning my sudden emotional shift, *knowing* that I must be up to something.

While her suspicions are not incorrect, I welcome her periodic surgical stares with an unaffected smile upon my face, partly to keep her distrustful focus on me instead of what might be hidden in my room, but mostly out of spite towards her and her repeated attempts to break me.

By the time that the sun is setting, I have completed my new list of tasks in full, promptly returning to my room. Once there, I take my time changing out of my uniform and into my sleepwear, repeatedly glancing towards my pillows, eagerly anticipating diving into Pater's journal to uncover the answers it might hold.

It takes every fiber of my being to fight off the urge to start reading the journal right now, but I am quick to remind myself that I must remain patient, at least until Ms. Pierre has dropped off my 'dinner'. Only then, will I avoid the risk of being interrupted, or worse, caught with the stolen book in my hand.

Like clockwork, I hear a sharp rapping at my bedroom door signifying that the moment has finally come. I practically dance towards it in anticipation of my solitude, but I am quick to stop myself when I realize that one of my bathrobe's sleeves has ridden up.

Taking a moment to put myself in check, I subdue my shining confidence once more, reminding myself that I still must remain vigilant in the face of Ms. Pierre.

As I pull down the rogue sleeve and hear an impatient, second knock, I finally open the door to find Ms. Pierre's resting, frigid scowl staring back at me. She thrusts the tray in my direction with force, but this time I am quick to seize the tray before it has a chance to connect with my sternum and wind me like it has before.

After successfully blocking her attack, I give Ms. Pierre a silent nod of insincere thanks so as to minimize our exchange before I nudge the door closed with my foot.

Much to my surprise, Ms. Pierre suddenly snaps her left arm out, stopping the door in its path before it eclipses her scowling visage. I can't help but find myself frozen in place, confused by the aggressive gesture as Ms. Pierre attempts to invasively step through the threshold of my room.

Similar to how she had blocked me at the door to the children's room, I remain in place, using the large tray to obstruct her path from further entry as I rhetorically inquire, "Is there something I can help you with?"

Saying nothing, Ms. Pierre subtly cranes her neck, glancing around the room for any clues towards what I might be up to. Finding nothing, she quickly returns her focus towards me, squinting her eyes as though she's trying to get a read on my mannerisms before she reluctantly steps back into the hallway, her unwavering gaze remaining upon me until the door has found its frame once more.

Unsure of whether she is still standing on the other side of the door or not, I remain frozen for a moment, listening for any creaks in the floor that might signify the movement of her departure.

The longer the silence lasts, the more my hands begin to shake, equally caused by the weight of the tray and the anxiety triggered by Ms. Pierre's admittedly valid, yet increasingly intense suspicions. After a minute or so, I finally turn and place the silver tray on the table, before moving back towards the door.

Opening it just a crack, I find the hallway leading in the direction of Ms. Pierre's room empty, yet still, I can't silence my paranoia. Slowly and quietly, I open the door a little further in order to check the other direction, thankfully finding it devoid of her stern presence.

Confident that the coast is clear, I close my door as silently as I can, ignoring my 'meal' by leaving the cloche in place so as to contain any pungent aromas that might distract from this moment of victory.

Moving to the bed, I prop myself upright, leaning back against my pillows as I pull the journal from its hiding place, and slowly open it to the second entry.

Similar to the first page of the journal, which I had read in the previously locked office, Pater's handwriting remains sloppy at best, and the more passionately he weaves his tale, the more erratic the narratives become.

It takes a short while to bounce back and forth through his first few entries in order to truly decipher the chain of events, but after a second pass on a handful of his musings, I start to get a handle on the timeline.

In the first few entries, Pater briefly describes how he successfully boarded the ship, concealing himself within a stack of large crates, as they were loaded into the ship's hull. Over the days in which Pater is awaiting the departure of the ship though, he goes into a fervent account of how he had come to this point in his life.

From what I gather amidst the scattered thoughts and emotional tangents, Pater had been an architect while living in Ireland. During that time, his poverty-stricken town had been ruled over by a man named, Fynbar O'Doherty, described by Pater as, '*a flamboyant man whose soul is as stained with corruption, as his over-sized belly is filled with mutton and mead.*'

Pater then goes on to describe how a handful of disenfranchised citizens had taken part in a small uprising, revolting against the unruly tithes that had been placed upon them, resulting in one wing of the O'Doherty Estate being set ablaze.

After it was all said and done, the Royal Guards had killed the majority of the rebels, but even in the wake of victory over his attackers, Fynbar still felt compelled to make an example of everyone else, in order to ward off any future acts of insurgence.

The citizens had all been summoned to the Town Square under the guise of a public address, however once there, Fynbar's Royal Guards proceeded to drag out two young men by the names of Seamus and Coplen Finnigan, falsely labeling them as the 'traitorous ring leaders'.

According to Pater's account, the two men had been offered a chance to admit their guilt publicly, as Fynbar made a show of loudly pronouncing how kindly he would ease their respective sentences, should they 'choose the path of truthfulness'.

Being the proud young men that Seamus and Coplen were, they declined the opportunity to falsely incriminate themselves, arousing cheers from some of the more emboldened citizens that had gathered.

Clearly having predicted this response, Fynbar then instructed his Royal Guards to bring out 'the third traitor'; Patrick Finnigan... Seamus and Coplen's little eight-year-old brother.

The Royal Guards proceeded to tie off Patrick's tiny arms and legs, each to their own outward-facing horse, providing extra motivation for the confessions that Fynbar had initially requested.

Within a matter of seconds, Seamus and Coplen had confessed to every crime under the sun, welcoming any and all penalties for their insolence on the condition that Fynbar would release their little brother.

Having finally gotten the confessions he sought, Fynbar smirked darkly before turning to his Royal Guards and giving a nod, forcing Seamus and Coplen to watch as little Patrick Finnigan was drawn and quartered right in front of them.

Pater then describes that there was a horrified silence afterwards, just long enough that the townspeople could hear the two brothers audibly sobbing. It was only once Fynbar felt that his message had been made clear, that he finally gave the signal for the two brothers to be relieved of their heads by way of the axe.

In the days following the execution of the Finnigan brothers, silence continued to plague the town. Pater describes it feeling as though everyone was afraid to utter even a single word, for fear of being chosen as Fynbar O'Doherty's next 'example'. As if by the twisted will of fate, it was around that time that Pater was contracted by the Royal Guard to assist in the rebuilding of Fynbar's home.

Pater begrudgingly accepted the job, fearful of what would happen if he were to say no. Little did he realize that decision would be the catalyst towards a very dark turn in his life.

Amidst his descriptions of the endless days of backbreaking labor while working in the O'Doherty Estate, Pater also mentions how each day had been set to the horrific soundtrack of Fynbar repeatedly abusing, raping and imprisoning his already pregnant, young mistress.

While Pater portrays these days as being hard enough on his body and even more so on his conscience, he then begins to describe how his nights became exponentially torturous, as he was haunted by increasingly vivid, recurring nightmares:

While the circumstances that lead there differ from one night to the next, I inevitably find myself before a large door.

Despite my efforts to resist the urge, I open it and immediately find Fynbar staring at me, as though he has been eagerly awaiting my arrival all the while, so that I may witness his sadistic, vile acts.

As I am frozen in the archway, Fynbar relentlessly stares at me, the Devil's grin upon his face, his cheeks reddened, as if to exhibit the strain on his failing heart as he continues to have his way with the poor, young girl's motionless body.

Ignoring her lifelessness, the fire of rage burns within his eyes as he squeezes her throat with one hand and repeatedly strikes her with the other, as if to pontificate each of his violent thrusts.

In past dreams I have tried to stop him, only to find my body rendered motionless. I have tried to call for help, but I find myself voiceless. I have even tried averting my horrified gaze, but that only brings my attention to the body of little Patrick Finnigan, bleeding out on the floor. No arms. No legs. The Triquetra burned into his little chest.

My eyes pop in response to the mention of the Triquetra branding and its similarity to the one I had seen on Andy's chest. Despite the shiver that runs up my spine, my eyes continue to feverishly dance over the words on the page, soon discovering that's not the only commonality:

As though it were penance for the inadvertent, complicit inaction of my dream-self, a large, dark bird, forces its way through the young boy's chest each night, presenting itself, while draped in the gore it has been birthed from.

The dark bird then turns to me, calculating its attack before maliciously flying at me with haste, mimicking the sound of Patrick Finnigan's screams, as he was torn apart.

It's then, that I return to my waking life, destined for yet another day of physical torture, eventually leading to the inevitable reprise of the very same dream, once more.

While I find a modicum of comfort in the fact that I am not the only one to have experienced these vivid nightmares involving the large crow, there is also a wave of fear that washes over me as I consider the possibility that my subconscious may have already been infected by whatever it was that drove Pater to his eventual madness.

Nevertheless, I force myself to continue reading as Pater moves on to describe how he was working late in the O'Doherty Estate one night, listening to yet another round of violent perversions echoing from down the hall.

Whether it was the torture of being endlessly haunted by his inaction, or simply his conscience finally hitting an echelon of tolerance, thus superseding logic... Pater had finally heard enough.

Though he had never been a violent man prior to that moment, Pater Morgan armed himself with a hammer and made his way towards the Mistress' room, intent on taking Fynbar's life.

However, by the time that Pater was halfway down the corridor, the sounds of violence suddenly ceased, giving way to the echoes of hurried, yet heavy footfalls disappearing around the corner.

Finally reaching the Mistress' room, Pater found the young woman slumped over in the corner, limp and lifeless, just like in his dream. Running over to assist her, he describes her quickly pooling blood gathering as much from her head wounds as from between her legs.

Fueled by both shame and regret, Pater attempted everything he could to revive the woman, incidentally getting her blood all over him in the process.

It was then that Pater heard footsteps approaching from the hallway behind him.

Holding the lifeless body of Fynbar's mistress in his arms, covered in her blood, Pater turned around to find himself surrounded by Royal Guards with their weapons drawn.

From behind the small army, he could hear Fynbar instructing the soldiers to arrest Pater and prepare him for public execution, not for the murder of the young woman in his arms, but for the assassination of the heir within her belly.

Later that night, Pater was curled up in his cell, praying for salvation from penance for a crime that was not his. As exhaustion took its hold, Pater could feel himself drifting towards the certain tortures of sleep, only this time, his dreams had permutated to a much more comforting setting as Pater was, in his own words, 'shown his destiny':

> On this night, instead of being forced to witness the horrors I had been shown countless times before, I found myself upon a ship, journeying across the vastness of the Ocean.
>
> Though I am unsure of how I came to my certainty, I somehow knew I had arrived in the Americas. It was then, that I was shown, in quick succession, a life of happiness, freedom, love and prosperity.
>
> While I have never experienced such feelings, I somehow knew that this was the life I was meant to live. This was the life I would live.

Pater then goes on to point out the odd presence of symbols that he refers to as 'Triskellions' upon the trees that surrounded his projected destiny. Despite the euphoric nature of his dream life, he describes becoming wary of these glyphs, unsettled by the mystery that shrouds their mysterious manifestation within the future he was being shown.

Pater then concludes this entry by writing:

> As if by the will of some higher power unbeknownst to me, I awoke in my cell to find the door ajar; the Guard stationed outside, was now slumped in the corner, as lifeless as that poor girl had been, only this Guard's head was facing in the wrong direction.
>
> While suspicious of the convenient nature of my freedom, I welcomed it nonetheless, allowing me to not only escape my imprisonment, but to return home for what few items I could carry before fleeing to the coast, in order to fulfill the destiny I had been shown.
>
> So now here I sit, free of my false accuser, free of the

injustice of my scheduled execution, yet even though I am certain I am en route to my destiny, I am still haunted by the same dreams, night in, night out.

By the time I reach the end of Pater's account of his journey to the coast, I come to realize that I haven't found a single mention of the woman that had been accompanying him in the vision that the cloaked woman had shown me.

I go back and re-read Pater's first few entries a second time, and then a third, certain that I must have missed a page, or skipped a passage, but still I find no reference of any woman with which he made his escape.

Moving on to the next entry, I read Pater's account of the ship's departure from the coast, setting sail for the Americas, unknowingly carrying Pater towards his freedom, and the crew towards their inevitable deaths upon the rocky shores.

Pater's first few entries after setting sail focuses primarily on his constant battle with both seasickness, and the continuance of his nightmares.

Amidst Pater's circumventing about his own journey, he begins to document details of conversations he overhears amidst the ship's crew. At first, the entries mostly consist of idle gossip and the occasional account of sexual relations between shipmates who had assumed they were innocuously hidden in the seclusion of the ship's hull.

But then after two weeks at sea, Pater's journey, once again, takes a dark turn.

Pater describes hearing talk of crewmembers falling ill with a mysterious *'sickness of the mind'*. At first, he chalks it up as the effects of cabin fever amidst such an extensive journey at sea, but soon he takes notice of a growing sense of angered paranoia spreading throughout the ship, affecting the entire crew, and even the Captain.

When Ms. Pierre had told me her abridged version of Pater's story, she had mentioned that the Captain had been 'obsessed' with reaching the Americas, no matter the cost. However, through Pater's next few entries, I learn that it was much more sinister than that.

Pater begins to recount the details as the bodies of crewmembers accumulate in a matter of days. At first, a few were found in various secluded areas of the ship, frozen in rigid states of fear, their skin ghost white, yet no discernable signs to suggest the cause of their deaths.

Soon after, another handful of crewmembers were found at sunrise, having hung themselves from the mast of the ship overnight. According to a conversation Pater had overheard, it was only after they were cut down that the crew realized each of the corpses had smiles upon their faces.

However, despite the unnerving nature of these deaths, one in specific stands out above the rest as *particularly* disturbing.

According to Pater's account, a young man had apparently taken position at the bow of the ship in the middle of the night, sitting cross-legged and singing to himself while meticulously flaying off his own flesh, tossing each chunk into the ocean as though it were chum from a fishing boat.

His corpse was found the next morning, still sitting upright, missing the entire outer layer of his body, his bloodstained knife sitting beside him, gently rocking back and forth on the symbol of the Triquetra that he had carved into the ship's deck.

Amidst the horrific circumstances of the quickly declining crew, Pater also describes how the Captain had begun pacing the deck each night, muttering nonsensical gibberish as though he was having a conversation with someone who wasn't there.

During the Captain's descent into madness, he demanded that the bodies of the dead be stored within the bowels of the ship, as opposed to the traditional burial at sea, providing no reasoning for the decision, nor explanation towards its purpose.

One man had been bold enough to question the choice, so the Captain answered his concerns by stabbing him through the throat. As the obstinate crewmember had bled out, the Captain instructed the others to add his body to the pile.

While I am taken aback by the level of graphic detail that Pater has written, I still find myself distracted by the fact that I can't find any information about any woman that Pater is travelling with, let alone any mention of a woman being present on the ship at all, crew or otherwise.

I feel my eyelids starting to get heavy as the hours pass. While I am fully aware that the likelihood of reading Pater's entire journal in one night is next to zero, the amount of anticipation I have experienced in the face of finally finding answers to my endless questions has already shifted sleep to a secondary priority in the grand scheme of things.

So, I force myself to strain my eyes at each page and continue reading as much as I am physically able to, silently promising my fading consciousness that I will submit once I find mention of this mysterious woman and how she weaves into Pater's story.

As I rub my eyes and move on to the next entry, Pater describes waking one night to hear a mysterious sound, coming from somewhere within the hull of the ship... the sound of a woman softly crying.

My hands immediately begin to shake with anticipation and fear as Pater describes how he made his way towards the stern of the hull, to find the aforementioned pile of crewmember's bodies, before saying:

My eyes danced over the heap of death before me, and that's when I saw her, off to the side, kneeling at the base of the pile. Though her face was hidden beneath the hood of her dark cloak, I could hear her as she wept for the dead.

I feel as though I'm about to jump out of my skin, when I am suddenly interrupted by the sound of soft knocking. Based on the tentative nature of the sound and its low placement on the door, I immediately deduce that it must be Macha.

While part of me wants to ignore the sound so that I can keep reading, the mere thought of neglecting Macha when she *needs* me compels me to put the journal down.

I mark my place with the small metal branch that I used as a lock pick, before stashing the journal beneath my pillow and springing up from the bed to put on my robe.

As I reach towards the door handle though, I suddenly take

notice of my phone sitting on the bedside table, giving me pause. My eyes dart back and forth between my phone and my bed as I think back to all of the times that Ms. Pierre had been so *certain* to correct me on the subject of Macha's mutism.

While the scribbled drawings that Macha had left in my room during her prior visit were proof enough to me that we *had*, in fact, spoken, I also realize that from an outside perspective they are entirely subjective pieces of evidence that don't necessarily support my case.

Tilting my phone against the base of a small gas lamp, I flip my camera to the video setting and hit record before I turn to open the door and find Macha standing before me, her head dipped in shame towards the residual fear of yet another nightmare involving the cloaked woman.

As I invite her in, Macha promptly runs past me and jumps up onto the mattress, seemingly paying no mind to my oddly positioned phone on the nightstand.

Quietly closing my door, I take a seat beside Macha, forcing myself to not even glance towards the phone for fear of revealing that I'm secretly recording our entire visit.

I do it, not only for the sake of proving my own sanity, but also to begin stockpiling my own emotional ammunition against Ms. Pierre, should it ever come to that.

CHAPTER TWENTY-FIVE

Macha

I begin by gently asking Macha, "Did you have another dream about the crying woman?"

Despite how excitedly she had run into my room and jumped up on the mattress, Macha remains reluctant to verbalize her answer and simply nods in response.

While I completely sympathize with her desire to not want to relive the details of her vivid nightmare involving the 'crying woman', I feel compelled to elicit a verbal response from Macha in one form or another, solely for the purpose of selfishly capturing it on my phone.

I proceed to follow up my initial inquiry with a few more softball questions about her current emotional state, even attempting to elicit laughter from her as I revisit my previous anecdote regarding spiders and their butts.

Despite my best efforts, Macha remains non-verbal in her responses, offering only soft nods, occasional shrugs, and one discernably disheartening blank stare in response to the 'spider butt routine'.

Just as I am about to give up on finally gathering proof to negate Ms. Pierre's unfounded diagnosis of Mutism, I suddenly notice Macha staring at the pictures that she had drawn during our Arts and Crafts lesson a few days back.

In the days following my time with the children, I had made a point of prominently hanging Macha and Nemain's drawings on the wall above my small table, partly for sentimental reasons, but mostly to maintain the false façade of purpose behind my lesson plan in case Ms. Pierre were to ever grow suspicious... as she now has.

As Macha continues staring at the pictures, I try to seize the opportunity to win her over with warmness, "They look pretty good up there, don't you think?"

Much to my surprise, Macha scrunches her face with distaste towards the display, turning to me with a look of derision in her eyes as she finally speaks, "You hung them wrong."

While part of me jumps at the fact that I have finally gotten the verbal response I was seeking, I am also somewhat unsettled by the level of vehemence in her reply.

Gently getting up from the bed, I walk over to the pictures, slowly pulling them off the wall as I softly concede, "Okay, how would you like me to hang them?"

I turn to her awaiting instructions that never come. Instead, clearly annoyed by my ignorance towards her artistic creations, Macha hops off the mattress and crosses to me, seizing the papers from my hand before kneeling on the floor and proceeding to stack her drawings in a pile, one on top of another, before handing them back to me with a look on her face that says, 'There.'

Though I'm a little confused at first, I'm not about to challenge her creative vision, so I proceed to clumsily tape all of the pages to the wall, keeping them stacked in a pile as she has requested.

By the time I turn back around, Macha is already sitting back on the mattress with her head dipped, the sullen look on her face having returned.

I secretly glance towards my phone, and then back towards Macha. Gently approaching, I sit beside her once more as I empathetically tilt my head and say, "Nightmares can be pretty scary, huh?"

Macha once again defaults to non-verbal responses, as she softly nods her head and a single tear falls from her eye.

Seeing her in this state of pain, I suddenly feel an overwhelming wave of empathy wash over me. I begin to recognize parts of my self in her, the emotional fragility, the physical exhaustion; the overriding tension caused by a perpetual state of fear and confusion.

I want so much just to reach out and embrace Macha so that we can cry together. Were I able to, I would take her pain away in a heartbeat, even if it meant doubling my own suffering in the process. The sheer inability to do such a thing brings helpless tears to my eyes and even though I attempt to stifle them, my lower lip betrays me, quivering ever so slightly in the process.

In that moment, Macha looks up at me, catching the temporary crack in my supportive veneer. With a quizzical look in her eyes, she innocently asks, "Are you sad, Patty?"

The compassionate curiosity she displays is enough to push me over the edge, causing the first few tears to fall. I try to mask them with a smile as I wipe my eyes and unconvincingly say, "I'm fine."

Macha continues looking at me, confused by my seemingly mixed emotions as she questions the validity of my answer, "...But you're crying. People only cry when they're sad."

I softly correct her as I continue to try to stifle my own emotions, "Well, people can also cry when they're happy."

Scrunching her face as she studies mine, Macha then says, "You don't *look* happy."

Another wave of tears begin to fall in response to Macha's inadvertent wrenching of my heart with her inherent earnestness.

Before I can even try to reply, she gently places her little hand on my knee as her tone takes on a wisdom far beyond her years, "It's okay to be sad, Patty. Feelings are what make us people."

Despite the simplicity of her statement, I can't argue with her logic, so I nod and sincerely smile, "You're absolutely right, Macha. You know, you're very smart. Especially for a girl your age."

I see a momentary smile on Macha's face before the levity dissipates and she tentatively turns her head towards the window, anxiously staring at the leaves of the immense oak tree as they carelessly brush against the windowpanes while gently dancing in the evening breeze.

Seeing the deep concern in Macha's eyes, I naturally assume that her thoughts have drifted back to the 'crying woman' from her dreams, thus creating an unsubstantiated fear that she could be right outside the window, waiting.

While still seated on the bed, I take Macha's hand in mine as I propose an idea, "I'll tell you what. I'm going to go over to the window, just to make sure that it's safe. When you feel like it, you can come over and join me and you'll see that there's nothing to be scared of."

Macha's head snaps towards me with fearful eyes in response to my bold proposal.

I try to soften my pitch, "You don't have to come right away, but I promise that when you do, I'll be right there with you the whole time."

The look of concerned fear remains on Macha's face, even after I get off the bed and subtly pull down on the sleeves of my robe.

As I take the first few steps towards the window, I offer reassurance along the way, "I promise you, there's *nothing* to be scared of."

Though Macha does not get up to follow me as I pass, I can feel her eyes on me the entire way across the room. Around the halfway point, I turn back to her, giving a reassuring smile as I continue my slow approach.

The closer I get to the window though, the more I start to feel my own silent paranoid thoughts churning within my mind. I can't help but begin to wonder if Macha might be justifiably concerned about what may be waiting in the darkness.

In a matter of seconds, I roll through a series of terrifying hypothetical scenarios. What if the cloaked woman *is* back there? What if she's staring up at me, standing beside Andy's mangled corpse? What if the seven decaying women are there instead, reaching out towards me like they had before? What if this panic I'm feeling right now, incites another hallucination like it did with the butterflies in the children's room, or the crow in the sunroom? How would I ever explain something like that to Macha? How would I even explain that to myself?

I slowly let my eyes pan across the obscured view of the back portion of the property. Through the leaves that continue dancing outside my window, I see faint slivers of the immense oak's gnarled roots along with a collection of shattered patio stones glowing in the moonlight. Thankfully, I see nothing else.

Even after my own fears begin to subside though, I still take a moment to do a secondary scan with laser-like scrutiny, still finding no signs of anything out of the ordinary.

Pivoting around with a confident smile on my face, I say, "See?

Nothing there."

Despite my reassurances, Macha remains in place. I am about to try to coerce her towards me when suddenly, her focus shifts to just over my left shoulder as her facial expression morphs from one of concern, to one of pure terror.

Confused, I glance over my shoulder to see what she's looking at and notice something faintly shifting in the darkness. Pivoting the rest of my body towards it, I move closer to the window as I squint my eyes in an attempt to narrow my focus.

As I stand an inch away from the windowpanes, feeling the coolness emanating off the glass, a large crow suddenly flies out of the darkness, directly into the window where I'm standing.

I stumble backwards in response to the impact, almost tripping over my own feet in the process. Once I find my footing again, my eyes are drawn back to the cracked pane of glass and the bloodstain on the other side of the window, marking the point of impact.

Slowly, a drop of the crow's blood begins to trickle downwards. As it reaches the base of the fractured pane of glass though, I feel a shiver move up my spine as it somehow drips off the *inside* of the frame and lands on the floor.

My mind spins in confusion, so much so, that I barely even hear Macha's soft, fearful voice behind me tremble as she says, "...Patty?"

I turn around to see Macha's eyes wide with terror as she points towards the small table at the side of the room, more specifically, the silver tray that holds the dinner that I had opted to neglect.

At first, I'm confused towards what could have possibly scared Macha more than a bird hitting the window in the dead of night, but soon I feel my heart fill with the same dread that Macha is experiencing as the sound of soft tapping coming from within the dented cloche begins to fill the room.

Similar to the window, I feel compelled to move towards it, despite my fearful instincts telling me otherwise. As I slowly approach the table, I hear Macha shift her position on the bed, hugging her knees towards her, fearful of what may ensue.

I can't say that I blame her.

Attempting to find reassurance in logic, I tell myself that it's likely just a rodent of some kind that tried to take advantage of a free meal when no one was looking, only to find itself trapped in a dome of putrid stench with no way out.

Even though my logical brain continues to weave this semi-plausible narrative, I still can't seem to pull my mind away from the feeling that something much more sinister is at play.

Reaching out for the cloche's handle, I suddenly notice how much my hand is trembling with anticipatory fear. But as I'm half a moment away from seizing the cloche by its handle, the tapping suddenly stops.

I remain frozen in place as the room fills with the tension of eerie silence. My logical mind chimes in once more as I rethink my approach, pulling my hand back and opting to crouch down to place my ear against the side of the cloche instead.

Facing Macha as I do so, I listen for any sounds that would signify what kind of animal might be trapped within, but even after a good handful of seconds, I hear nothing.

Standing back up, I shake my head and shrug as I say, "I don't hear anyth-"

My attempted absolution of the moment is cut short when there is a sudden hard impact from within the cloche, denting it outwards at a sharp angle as the sound of the collision resonates off the walls.

I defensively stumble backwards in shock when there is suddenly another loud impact, creating a second spike-shaped imperfection in the metal dome.

Continuing to back away from the cloche, the impacts become increasingly faster and more forceful, until the cloche begins to look less like its intended bell shape, and more like a slowly forming, silver sea urchin.

Little do I realize that the entire time I've been backing away, I've been moving towards the window. By the time I'm within a few feet of the multiple panes of glass, the impacts from within the silver cloche fall silent, giving way to another faint, yet familiar noise.

As though it were being fashioned from a whisper, the room

slowly fills with a cacophony of screeching tires, breaking glass and twisting metal, all riding an endless crescendo until they have reached a deafening decibel.

Macha and I both instinctually cover our ears in response. Soon, I have trouble telling if the room is shaking under the sheer magnitude of the sound, or if it's just my eyes vibrating within my skull.

Without warning, every pane of glass in the large window behind me simultaneously explodes inwards, showering the room with countless glass pebbles. Half a second later, a thousand crows invade the room, flowing through the breach as though they were birthed from the darkness of night.

Running towards Macha, I do my best to cover her with my own body as the murder of crows begins viciously pecking and clawing at my back.

At first, I assume they are merely attacking anything that moves, but soon I notice that one or two of them have perched themselves upon me and are trying to force their heads through the small breaches of my human shield in order to get to Macha.

My defensive strength kicks in and I force myself to withstand the excruciating pain in order to protect her. Tightening my grip on Macha, I scream in resistance to the unrelenting nature of the attack, refusing to submit to the excruciating pain.

Whether it is the progressive weakening of my body, or the persistence of the crows shifting my limbs, I suddenly feel Macha move within my arms. It almost feels as though her body has instantaneously become lighter and cold to the touch.

Only once I shift my focus towards her, do I realize that it is no longer Macha that I am holding in my arms, but the body of Patrick Finnigan instead, his eyes lifeless, his skin pale from blood loss. Where Patrick's arms and legs used to be, there are semi-dried bloody stumps and upon his pale chest, I see the prominent branding of the Triquetra.

I try to release him and run away, but the murder of crows continues their attack, forcing me to watch as a black beak pierces through little Patrick Finnigan's sternum from the inside.

Slowly, the large crow with glowing amber eyes emerges from within the young boy's chest, stretching its wings as they drip with gore, cocking its head as it plans its inevitable attack.

Then, like so many times before, the large crow opens its beak, only adding to the already deafening sounds before it flies towards me with immeasurable speed and malicious intent.

I bolt upright in my bed to find myself alone, the light of the sunrise beginning to illuminate the start of a new day.

Looking down to my right, I see Pater's journal lying on the bed beside me.

I sigh with derision, not only towards the immediate realization that the details from Pater's entries had carried over into my own dreams, but equally towards the realization that Macha's visit was likely a sub-conscious projection as well.

Grabbing the small metal branch that I had utilized as a lock pick; I place it between two pages as a bookmark, before slipping Pater's journal back beneath my pillows. In the process of doing so, I take notice of my phone on the nightstand, still propped up against the base of the small gas lamp.

Quickly glancing under the covers, I realize that I'm also still wearing my robe. I quickly think back over the chain of events from last night, realizing that I had only propped up my phone and put my robe back on *after* Macha had knocked at my door.

I tell myself that she *must* have been in my room last night, and I *must* have recorded the conversation, otherwise, why would my phone still be positioned like that?

Reaching for the device so quickly that I nearly knock over the lamp that it's leaning against, I attempt to activate the home screen, only to realize that the battery has been exhausted as a result of recording through the night.

With a frustrated sigh, I put my phone back down on the nightstand and begin scanning the room for any further proof that might suggest that Macha's visit had *actually* happened.

It's then that I take notice of the drawings on my wall, immediately spotting that Macha's pictures are clumsily taped up in a single stack, as she had requested.

Even though the stack of drawings acts as further proof of her visit, I feel a whisper of fear as I try to figure out where the memories ended and the nightmare began.

My attention snaps towards the silver cloche, still sitting on the small table beneath the drawings. Much to my relief, it remains in a bell-shape, save for the single concave dent from my tantrum a few nights back.

I then turn towards the large window, studying each pane of glass to ensure that they all remain intact with no signs of cracks, chips or drops of blood upon them. Sure enough, they remain as integral and spotless as I had left them yesterday afternoon.

Taking a deep sigh of relief, I come to realize that I must have drifted off at some point *after* I had re-hung Macha's artwork.

The more I think about it, the more it makes sense that I don't remember when I had fallen asleep. After all, I was already dancing the line of consciousness before Macha had even knocked on my door.

Shaking my head, I dismiss the residual fear from my nightmare as I get out of bed and make my way towards the cabinet to start getting into my uniform for the day.

As I cross the room, the tape that I had so clumsily used to hang Macha's stack of drawings suddenly gives way, causing the papers to dance towards the floor, splaying outwards as they land.

Instinctually, I kneel to collect the papers and put them back up on the wall, but as I lower myself, I suddenly notice something about the drawings that sends a chill up my spine.

Individually, Macha's drawings had merely appeared as random scribbles with nonsensical form, emblematic of the chaotic nature of a child's imaginative mind. However, despite the fact that the papers have seemingly fallen at random, they have landed in such a way that they have arranged themselves to collectively reveal a larger image.

Taking a moment to adjust the papers so there are no gaps between them, I stand in shock as I suddenly find myself staring at a perfect rendering of the square pendant, woven from straw that had been hanging around the necks of the seven decaying women.

My mind races as I find myself trying to figure out how Macha would have known that these papers would fall in such a way. Surely it would be impossible to predict such a thing, wouldn't it?

Even though my rational mind attempts to dismiss the image before me as mere coincidence, the level of precision with which the symbol has been rendered seems to negate all logic.

Macha *must* be trying to tell me something.

CHAPTER TWENTY-SIX

Back To Town

I am still in an equal state of shock and confusion, as I remain standing over the macro-image of the square pendant woven from straw that appeared from within Macha's drawings.

I stare at the near-perfect depiction of the symbol, as my mind continues spinning, contemplating not only the probability of such an occurrence, but also what its underlying purpose may be.

My trance-like state is soon broken by the sound of sharp rapping upon my door.

Snapping back into the present moment, I quickly gather the drawings from the floor, putting them into a pile and placing them beside the silver tray on my small table.

I hear a second round of firm knocking as I quickly pull down on the sleeves of my robe and move towards the door to answer. As I do, I grab my phone off of the nightstand and slip it under my pillow, simultaneously scanning the room for any other evidence of Macha's visit.

By the time Ms. Pierre knocks a third time, I finally open the door to see her standing before me, her lips already pursed and her eyebrow raised judgmentally in response to my visible frenetic energy, despite my attempts to mute it.

Naturally straightening my back in response to the frigid nature of her presence, I expectantly raise both of my eyebrows, awaiting either the assignment of some menial task or a fresh batch of inciting slander.

Before she even speaks, I can feel Ms. Pierre dissecting me with her eyes, her face soured in response to my wild-eyed state this early in the morning, especially after it took three rounds of knocking before I finally answered the door. Yet still, she says nothing.

It's as though she is waiting for me to dig my own hole with clumsily phrased verbosity, but I resist the urge to explain myself and remain just as silent as she does in the moment, making a point of trying to continue to mute my erratic mannerisms in the process.

Finally, Ms. Pierre breaks the awkward silence, crossing her hands at her waist as she asks, "Is everything alright, Miss Woodall?"

I try to remain natural, but soon find myself over-analyzing my every movement, curious as to what 'casual' ever looked like as I fumble through my curt response, "Y-Yeah. Why?"

Ms. Pierre looks me over with disparaging curiosity before she finally takes a contemptuous sigh and says; "I will require you to go into town today. I trust this won't be a problem?"

The mere mention of returning to town immediately sends my mind reeling. I suddenly flash through images of Clayton's pugnacious tattoos reflected in the truck's side view mirror as he and his sidekick attack me in broad daylight. The dread towards these memories and potentially having to relive them grows within me, as my palms start to anxiously sweat.

Part of me is certain that she is only asking this of me as continued punishment for my insolence as of late, but the fact that she would ask such a thing the *day* after she had revealed that she knew about the accident the whole time, relights the vengeful fires within me.

A thousand combative responses fly through my head in a matter of seconds, some consisting of verbal outbursts, most comprising of actual physical attacks against the withered old woman in front of me. I try to contain my impulses, but soon feel my own lips starting to purse, as I try to restrain my racing mind.

Despite my attempts to mute the myriad of emotions, my facial expression betrays me and I see a slight smirk growing on Ms. Pierre's face in response to my tense silence. It's obvious that she is, once again, deriving pleasure from my visible turmoil.

I can't tell in the moment if she is purposely antagonizing me towards a physical response, or if she simply just can't pass up basking in the power that she lords over me. Either way, she is only further fueling my vindictive plot against her.

Even though no part of me wants to *ever* go back to that dust bowl of a town, I also recognize that time in the truck will buy me the opportunity to charge my phone and view the video of Macha's visit from last night.

With any luck, the proof that I've gathered of Macha's ability to speak, will be the key to breaking Ms. Pierre the same way she has continuously attempted to break me.

Cutting through the tense silence, Ms. Pierre clears her throat before pushing her inquiry once more, "*Will* that be a problem?"

Not wanting to give her the satisfaction of any semblance of victory, I mute my emotional reaction and internalized debate as I mimic her body language, gently folding my hands at my waist as I fuel my confidence with spite towards Ms. Pierre and say, "No. No problem at all."

Even though she has gotten her answer, Ms. Pierre remains suspiciously hovering in my doorway, as though there's something else that she's waiting for.

Furrowing my brow in response, I suggestively say, "Well... I guess I should start getting ready, then."

I attempt to close the door, but Ms. Pierre suddenly shoots out her arm as she had last night, stopping it in its path. My attention snaps back towards her, as a sudden overwhelming feeling of wariness towards her intent washes over me.

Defensively hovering near the door, I block her intended entry as I coldly ask, "Is there anything else, Ms. Pierre?"

Her cold eyes turn towards me like lasers, only further complimenting her scowl as she raises a crooked index finger and points towards the small table at the side of my room.

I feel a wave of panic grow within me, as I am certain that she is staring at the stack of Macha's drawings that have seemingly been removed from the wall. As I turn my attention towards them, I realize that they are stacked almost *too* neatly on the desk, making it appear as though I've been studying them throughout the night.

Remaining silent, I turn towards Ms. Pierre while feigning ignorance, so as not to inadvertently tip my hand amidst the lack of context.

With a roll of her eyes, Ms. Pierre clarifies her intent, "Your tray, Miss Woodall."

I feel a secret relief ease the tension in my shoulders as I quickly cross to the small table, grab the silver tray with the cloche upon it and bring it back to the doorway.

All the while, Ms. Pierre remains in the frame of the door as she coldly points out, "I believe I told you to leave the tray *outside* your room when you were finished. Were my instructions not clear?"

In the moment, I feel the instinct to shove the tray towards Ms. Pierre in the same way she has done to me over the past few nights, likely cracking a few of the old bag's ribs in the process. Nevertheless, I fight off the impulse and hand the tray over gently and shift my tone so it drips with insincerity, "...oops. Must've forgotten."

As Ms. Pierre receives the tray, she seems to be able to tell that I haven't touched the meal, purely based on weight. Based on her facial expression, it's clear that this offends her, so I remain non-responsive and as unsympathetic to her feelings as she is to mine.

With a single eyebrow raised, and her lips pursed in response to my transgression, Ms. Pierre makes sure to give a cold reminder, "There is reasoning behind the routine I have set forth, Miss Woodall. While simply *forgetting* to adhere to my requests may not *seem* like much to you, the time that is wasted in the wake of negligence will inherently affect the rest of the day's structure."

Even though I know I should keep my mouth shut in the moment, I can't fight off my instincts and sarcastically blurt out, "But then we wouldn't get to have our lovely little chats."

With fury in her eyes, Ms. Pierre opts to leave my comment unacknowledged as she quickly says, "*Don't* let it happen again" before pivoting away from my room and stomping down the corridor towards the stairs.

Somewhat satisfied with my minor victory I close my door and start grabbing casual clothes for my trip into town, this time opting for a pair of less-comfortable, baggier jeans, and an even looser hoodie, so that I may hide both my phone and the charger that I had bought last time I was in town.

As I am about to leave my room I pause for a moment, catching a glimpse of my exhausted visage in the standing mirror. I quickly realize that even in these baggy, form-concealing clothes, Clayton and his sidekick could still recognize my face, so I turn and grab an old, tattered baseball cap and throw it on my head.

Pulling the brim down towards my eyebrows, I successfully hide most of my face, along with the ever-increasing number of grey hairs that seem to be spreading across my scalp like a virus of age.

Looking towards the mirror once more, I can't help but notice that the shadows cast by the hat seem to accentuate the already prominent bags under my eyes, making me look nearly twice my actual age. Sighing with derision, I try to focus on the task at hand, as opposed to dwelling on my slowly deteriorating physical appearance.

By the time I get downstairs and enter the kitchen, Ms. Pierre has clearly opted for the silent treatment, likely in response to my vindictive sarcasm from earlier. I pay it no mind and make my way to the kitchen table, where she has set out my shopping list and the keys to the truck.

Grabbing them both, I quickly turn and make my way back across the kitchen, but before I've exited the room, Ms. Pierre finally gets her shot in as her voice takes on an almost sinister, sarcastic tone, "*Drive Safe.*"

I naturally clench my jaw and my fists in response, fighting off the urge to turn around and drown her in her rancid batch of beet porridge. Instead, I remain silent and proceed towards the front door, putting on my shoes and exiting the Morgan home.

Only once I'm outside and beyond earshot do I start quietly swearing under my breath, calling Ms. Pierre every horrifically offensive name that I can think of, even creating a few new ones in the process.

By the time I'm in driver's seat of the truck, I find myself feeling far more comfortable than I had last time. While I'm still nervous about operating the vehicle, the anxiety is not nearly as debilitating as my previous experience behind the wheel, likely because my mind is more occupied by the anticipation of seeing the video and the dread of heading back towards the domain of my attackers.

I quickly fish the car adapter out of my hoodie and scan the edge of the hill to make sure that Ms. Pierre isn't secretly watching me. Certain that the coast is clear, I plug my phone into the cigarette lighter port and watch as the outline of a battery with a single red line appears on my home screen, signifying that the device is finally being satiated with a charge.

Knowing that I have at least a few minutes before the load screen even presents itself, and then a good handful of minutes after that before I can even log in to the device, I slip the phone into one of the cup-holders and let it gather its strength as I put the truck into gear.

Pulling out from under the makeshift carport, and slowly rolling down the hill towards the winding path marked by two tire-treads, I still remain apprehensive about my speed, making sure that I take my time and maintain control, especially while traversing the winding path to the edge of the Morgan property.

As I reach the base of what one *might* call a driveway, I check in both directions for any other vehicles as my paranoid mind concocts a story of Clayton and his sidekick having waited out here in their truck the entire time.

Seeing no other vehicles though, I am quick to silence my fear, pulling out of the hidden driveway and onto the dirt road leading into town.

However, the moment the tires grip the new terrain, I feel my head start to throb with the beginnings of a spontaneous headache. Similar to before, a wave of light nausea almost immediately follows. I quickly chalk it up as the return of my anxiety symptoms and take a deep breath, as I try to calm myself.

A little ways down the road, I feel beads of sweat beginning to form on my forehead in response to my sudden wave of malaise, so I reach over and crack the driver's side window open, letting the truck's cab fill with the fresh air of the outdoors.

Despite the breeze cooling my face, I still feel the physical strain within me growing as I subconsciously echo my resistance to the pain by tightening my grip on the steering wheel until my knuckles turn white.

By the time I reach the edge of town, the pain in my head and stomach has seemingly spread; infecting every muscle in my body and making them ache with tension. Nevertheless, I force myself to continue pressing on towards the far side of town first, so as to perform my requested duties in backtracking order.

As I traverse the town's main road, I try to keep my facial expressions as emotionless as possible. All the while, under the brim of my hat, my eyes are frantically scanning both sides of the road for any signs of Clayton or his douchebag sidekick.

I pretend not to take notice of the judgmental stares from everyone else as they glare towards the truck with anger and hatred towards my mere presence. In the moment, I can't help but wonder what the Morgans could have *possibly* done to elicit such a residual level of vehement spite from these people.

While my headache, nausea and aching body continue to mount their respective attacks, I try to distract myself from the pain by theorizing about the history between the Morgans and this town.

Perhaps it's in response to the luxurious nature of the Morgan home when compared to the general state of this dilapidated town? After all, it's the only property I've seen in this area that doesn't look like it'll fall over by the will of the next strong breeze.

But then I think back to how Clayton and his friend ceased their pursuit at the edge of the Morgan property, almost as if they were afraid to cross onto it. If that's the general attitude of the townspeople, then no one would even know what the Morgan home looks like, thanks to the shelter of the lush oak forest that surrounds it.

I then wonder if perhaps it's misplaced anger, handed down by countless generations, as a result of jealousy towards Pater being the first settler in the region and claiming the only visibly fertile piece of land. If that were the case, then exaggerated folklore about the Morgans was likely woven by natural progression.

But even in that case, I find it hard to believe that the ancestral envy could create such a unified level of animosity against one family, especially when the only two surviving members of the bloodline are merely *children*.

I start to feel my anger mounting in defense of Macha and Nemain, as the vengeful glares continue to bear down upon me from windows and porches on either side of the road. If these ignorant assholes would just take the time to consider their bigotry, they would realize that they are directing their hatred towards two little girls who likely have no awareness of their family's *supposed* wrongdoings.

Thankfully, the town's only traffic light remains green this time, allowing me to expedite my journey and reach my first stop earlier than expected. I take a moment to collect myself, trying to suppress my growing rage towards the people of this town before I exit the truck. In that moment, I pull my phone from the cup holder to check on its progress.

The screen lights up, displaying the image of a keypad, signifying that the phone has finished loading. Upon entering my passcode though, I attempt to load up the video from last night, only to realize that the small percentage charged battery is unable to fully load the massive video as a result of recording through the night.

With a sigh of impatient frustration, I put the phone back in the cup holder so that it may continue loading while I exit the vehicle and go about my errands.

Partly based on my past experiences with the people of this town, and partly in an attempt to keep my growing animosity towards them muted, I make sure to keep each of my verbal and financial transactions as short as possible.

Soon, I'm thankful for deciding to do so, as by the time I reach the third destination on my list, my nausea, headache and tense muscles continue to near an echelon of pain that is beginning to exceed my physical abilities of tolerance.

By the time I return to the town's only traffic light, I watch as it spitefully turns red, forcing me to begrudgingly adhere to its command. As if by kismet, the moment the truck is stopped, I feel the minimal contents of my stomach rising and I lean out the driver's side window to vomit.

After wiping my mouth clean and spitting out any residual contents, I sheepishly try to ignore the continued stares from the various onlookers as I attempt to *will* the light back to green so I may escape this embarrassing display.

Impatiently sitting in the cab of the truck, I breathe through the excruciating pain. Desperate for a distraction, I check my phone once more to see that it's halfway charged so I press play on the video, only to watch the loading bar drop back to zero percent.

Silently cursing the device's inability to efficiently gather power or perform its basic functions, I immediately start to project my anger towards any and all tech companies for purposely rendering their own products obsolete so as to perpetuate the endless cycle of upgrades.

Practically throwing the phone back into the cup holder, I scan the intersection to once again verify that Clayton and his sidekick are nowhere to be seen. Thankfully, there are no signs of them, but it's then that I notice something that I had not seen on my prior trip.

Off to the right, and slightly obscured by surrounding buildings, I see the edge of a dilapidated sign on a large building with only, '-BRARY' visible.

Having faced the other direction the last time I was stopped at this intersection, I had not taken notice of the sign behind me, but seeing it now I quickly deduce that the town's library is likely the only location with any 'town archives' that might explain the contentious history between the Morgans and the people who live here.

I quickly throw on my turn signal, not that there are any cars around me to alert of my decision anyway, and turn down the road that leads towards the large building, my foot pushing the gas a little harder in anticipation of finding more answers. Soon, I round another corner and see the structure revealed, in full.

The library's façade is *slightly* more maintained than the rest of the buildings in this town, though not by much. Above the steps leading up to the entrance, mounted upon a tilted archway, is the face of an old clock that remains relatively intact, save for a few missing digits around its perimeter and its complete lack of function, made evident by the hands frozen at five and eleven.

Despite my borderline-debilitating physical condition, my

mental fervor is quick to silence my pain as I continue towards the building with equal parts intrigue and exhilaration.

Pulling into the small parking lot, I opt for a spot outside of the line of sight of the front doors, just in case any staff glances outside to see what vehicle I arrived in. Before exiting the truck though, I check my phone to see how much time I can justifiably buy for myself.

Quickly calculating, I figure that if I leave from here in an hour and increase my speed on the road back to the Morgan property, I *should* be able to return within a reasonable enough window of time that would not arouse suspicion from Ms. Pierre.

I tuck my phone under the passenger seat so that it can continue simultaneously charging and loading, while not tempting any passing thieves.

Getting out of the truck I make haste towards the entrance, jogging up the stone steps, two at a time, as I try to ignore the searing pain in my leg muscles that scream for me to stop.

Entering the archaic building, my nostrils are immediately inundated with the smell of aging books and thick dust, similar to how Pater's office had smelled after I had successfully picked the lock and opened the door.

As my eyes adjust to the dim lighting within the building, I see a small, elderly woman with short-cropped, silver hair look up at me from the front desk. The scowl on her face in response to my interruption of her otherwise empty day is so stern that it would possibly even challenge the coldness of Ms. Pierre's firm glare.

I immediately thank my instincts for telling me to park far enough away from the door so as not to immediately give myself away as the 'new Morgan girl'. At least now, I can maintain the false identity of a wayward outsider passing through town.

With a polite nod of greeting, but no words exchanged, I make my way towards an area in the library marked as 'Archives' by way of a dust-ridden, rectangular sign suspended from the ceiling by a rusted chain.

While there are no signs of any computers anywhere in the building, I do see a microfiche reader sitting upon an old wooden table beneath the hanging sign in the middle of the room, so I take a seat in one of the two wooden chairs provided.

At first glance, I wonder if the ancient machine will even work, as it appears to be one of the first of its kind, but much to my surprise when I flick the large power switch, the screen lights up and the sound of the coolant fan loudly hums to life.

I pivot in my chair with the intent of gathering materials from which to source my information, but as I do, I suddenly find the Librarian standing inches away from me, her scowl still prominently displayed upon her face as she begrudgingly asks, "Can I help you?"

Remaining in the wooden chair, I scramble for a response amidst the residual shock of her unexpected presence, "I, um- I was just looking for some information-"

The elderly Librarian visibly rolls her eyes as she plainly states, "You're going to have to be more specific hun, or this is going to take a while."

I sheepishly let out an awkward chuckle in response, but quickly pull it back when I see the sincerity upon her face. Uncomfortably clearing my throat, I attempt to clarify, "I'm looking for some information on the history of this region."

Rolling her eyes once more, the Librarian crosses her arms as if to silently repeat her request for specificity so as to truncate the usage of her time.

Picking up on her not-so-subtle prompt, I go a little deeper while drumming up false reasoning, "I'm just passing through, but someone mentioned something about a family on the edge of town that kind of... caught my interest."

The elderly Librarian furrows her brow in response, remaining in place and studying me as though she's trying to assess my level of truthfulness as she asks, "Who?"

Raising my eyebrows in feigned ignorance, I seek clarification, "I- I'm sorry?"

She continues, "Who told you that?"

Taking a moment, I lean back in the chair, hearing its creak echo into the depths of the otherwise abandoned building. I portray a failing memory as I desperately scramble for a plausible source until finally, I blurt out, "The Butcher. I popped in there to ask for directions and he warned me to avoid that end of town."

The Librarian remains in place, still staring at me with scrutiny. Finally she breaks her silence to say, "...Goddamn it Francis! That son of a bitch don't know how to keep his trap shut. You listen to me, them folks ain't none of your concern."

While I've been all but dismissed from the library, I try to stand my ground and keep pushing for any information the Librarian is willing to give, so I try a different approach, "It's just... I'm a Writer, you see. A Journalist actually, and I'm writing an editorial piece on the unknown stories of undiscovered towns."

The elderly Librarian remains unimpressed by my falsified credentials as she coldly says, "So?"

I continue trying to push, "It's just, a mention of your town *could* result in tourism."

The elderly Librarian shakes her head with disdain as she plainly states, "Hun, do we *look* like a tourist town? Folks round here don't care for outsiders, 'cept *Francis* of course. That man would talk his lips off to a clock, so long as it gave him the time of day."

Attempting to drum up as much charisma as I can amidst my ailing physical state, I flash a plastic smile as I say, "Let's be honest, *no one* likes tourists. But they *do* spend money... even in a town like this."

My proposal is met with an audible scoff as the Librarian proceeds to say, "They still gotta get here first, and ain't *no one* coming to this shit-hole."

I confidently raise my eyebrows as I say, "They would if they had a reason to. Have you ever heard of Estes Park?"

The Librarian remains silent, insinuating that she has not.

I continue, digging up a niche reference from my teen years, "It's okay, nobody had. That is, until Stephen King wrote a little book called, *The Shining*, inspired by a hotel there."

The Librarian uncrosses her arms as she contemplates this information. Her face softens as she takes the bait, "No shit?"

I nod in silent affirmation, mostly because I am trying to silence my internalized screams under the continued assault of my headache, nausea and muscle aches.

Within a matter of seconds, the Librarian says, "Well, since

Francis has already gone and opened his pie-hole, I guess there ain't no harm in giving you the basics."

I feel my body instinctually leaning towards the Librarian, eager to hear her words as she steps away momentarily to open a drawer and produce a scrapbook of newspaper clippings, before returning to the table and pulling over the second wooden chair.

Placing the book on the table and folding her hands in her lap, the elderly Librarian leans towards me ever so slightly, speaking in a whisper as though she's afraid that someone will hear her, "See, as long as there's been people living in this town, we've been under this jinx. Folks round here call it, *'The Curse of the Morgans'*..."

CHAPTER TWENTY-SEVEN

The Curse of the Morgans

The Librarian begins by showing me a couple of newspaper articles that she *claims* will explain 'The Curse of the Morgans', but as she walks me through the details I quickly come to realize that they are *clearly* heavily biased editorials, disguised as news.

The first of such 'articles' starts out as a critical analysis of the town's failing infrastructure as a result of their perpetually crumbling economy. Given the assumed education level of the community as a whole, I have to admit that the article is written with an impressive level of verbosity.

Most of the piece is dedicated to the writer floating a convincing theory that attributes the town's economic woes to the infertility of the land, thus barring any hopes of an agricultural sector. However, in his closing argument, he then takes a hard left turn by making a completely unsubstantiated claim, that the catalyst behind this poor soil condition is the presence of the Morgan Family upon it.

By the time she finishes reading, I can actually hear my teeth grinding together in suppressed offense towards this supposed 'proof', yet still, I remain silent.

The next editorial that the Librarian shows me was written in the eighties by the then local Reverend, Jed Saccharine. She preambles the article by explaining that 'Reverend Jed' had a recurring spot on page three where he would publish his weekly 'fire and brimstone' piece, often lambasting specific members of the community for their lack of purity and faith.

However, the Librarian then taps the news clipping with her index finger and says, "But *this* one though... this was Reverend Jed's last, before he up and left one day, without so much as a goodbye. Some say he grew a conscience, but most of us think he got *scared* away."

I begin reading the article for myself, skimming through the Reverend's description of the crumbling morality that plagues the townspeople, detaching them from God's plan. But suddenly, mid-way through, his tone shifts to one of absolution as he writes:

... I have come to learn the truth of sin. God has shown me that there <u>are</u> times when culpability for one's transgressions do not fall upon the impurity of one's soul, but from the influence of external forces.

By God's divine will, I have been shown that you people are <u>not</u> to blame for your sins, for there is a dark force among us and it poisons our souls without our knowledge.

It tempts us with waking falsities that masquerade as a part of this world. It manipulates us with its lies that we assume to be truth.

None are safe from its blasphemous effect, and so our only hope is to pray, for ourselves, and one another. We are the damned, cursed by darkness... and Morgan be thy name.

As I finish reading, I have to actively fight off the urge to throw the scrapbook across the room in a fit of rage towards the decades of ignorance these people have not only displayed, but also perpetuated by maintaining their unjustified beliefs.

The harder I fight against my impulses though, the more I feel my head throb while my entire body screams in agony. The pain has become so acute that I can feel beads of sweat dripping down my forehead and over the small creases in my face where my emotions are sneaking through.

Nevertheless, I am able to restrain myself from voicing any negative commentary, solely for the purpose of maintaining my charade of journalistic intrigue towards this 'mysterious family from the edge of town' in the hopes that it will eventually uncover something.

The Librarian continues to show me archived articles from the town's newspaper, dating all the way back to the inception of the paper itself, in the 1500's. The more that she shows me, the more I start to realize that this supposed curse has been the town's scapegoat the entire time.

Despite the repeated mentions of the curse though, I can't help but notice the lack of specifics surrounding the nature of it. I begin to wonder if there has *ever* been any proof to substantiate this belief, or if it is merely a myth, that somehow drifted into the realm of perceived truth over time.

Against my better instincts, I bluntly blurt out, "How do you know the curse is real though? None of this really *proves* anything." My intrigue stirs up a stern, offended look from the Librarian, so I quickly add, "It's just- tourists are more inclined to visit, when they believe that they'll *see* or *experience* something."

Taking a moment to contemplate, the Librarian raises one eyebrow as she asks, "So what? You want some kind of story about dead livestock? Weird sicknesses? People seeing things in the night?"

Nodding emphatically, I say, "Yeah, anything along those lines."

The Librarian scoffs before clarifying, "Hun, those *are* the lines." Seeing my furrowed brow of confusion, she continues, "Ain't no healthy livestock around here for miles. Sure, we get produce shipped in by way of the Neymans, but even that spoils in a day or so. Then, of course, there's the sickness. People round here ain't never healthy... I mean *never*. Only Doctor we had, left town six years ago. Said he couldn't keep up with the demand."

I feel my eyes widen at the first semblance of potential evidence to support the claim of the curse, so I proceed to ask, "When did all of this start?"

The Librarian sighs in response, turning to me with a deep sincerity in her eyes as she says, "Depends on who ya ask. Some of the more God-fearin' folk believe this land was cursed since the beginning, and them Morgans was born from the depths of the Devil's soil. Others, myself included, think the curse is something they brought here *with* them, like how Columbus made all them Injuns sick way back when."

I opt to say nothing in response, as I squint my eyes with expectant intrigue, absorbing the Librarian's information with as much attentiveness as I can muster through the sustained physical pain.

She continues, "See, the first settlers in this area found that no matter what they put in the ground, nothin' grew, 'cept oak trees. So... tryin' to make the best of it, they turned to lumber. Didn't take long to learn those damned trees were nearly indestructible, broke almost every tool they had in the process."

As she continues to weave her tale, I think back and suddenly realize that I can't remember seeing *any* other natural vegetation in this entire region except for oak trees, most notably, surrounding the Morgan home.

The Librarian crosses her arms with the confidence of a sage, "I remember when I was just a kid, the people round here called in a couple of Holy Men to bless the land, like God was somehow the problem."

She chuckles, so I mirror her levity before rhetorically inquiring, "I'm assuming that didn't work?"

Shaking her head, the Librarian proceeds to say, "Those men up and fled faster than a Catholic feels guilt. Told us this place was 'tainted by dark forces', like the folks round here didn't already know that."

I continue to fight through the excruciating pain throughout my body, feigning camaraderie in the moment, but soon, the Librarian's sense of revelry ceases, as her face turns sorrowful.

Quieting her tone, she says, "But those holy men, they done pissed *something* off when they was here, 'cause it was just after that the girls started going missing."

I feel a chill run up my back as I seek clarification, "I'm sorry, what?"

The Librarian then proceeds to dip her head a little, her tone continuing to sadden as she says, "First one was a local girl, named Dorothy McNabb; beautiful as the summer sunshine, and stubborn as a mule. Like any teenager, she was dead-set on proving everybody wrong. She *insisted* that the Morgans couldn't be such bad people."

Captivated, I lean forward, "What happened to her?"

Raising her eyebrows, the Librarian continues, "Well, against the advice of her parents, and pretty much everyone else, she walked right up the front door of that Morgan home and offered to work for them. Thing is... she never came back."

I feel about a hundred questions fly through my head in a matter of seconds, but instead of voicing them, I remain silent so as to allow the elderly woman in front of me to continue weaving her tale.

Taking a deep breath, the Librarian looks me deep in the eyes, "'Couple of weeks later, her parents ventured up that way lookin' for her. Some old lady answered the door and told 'em she had never even *heard* of a Dorothy McNabb." Shifting in her seat, the Librarian then says, "Dorothy's parents were rightly suspicious though, insisted on taking a look around the place themselves, but the old lady wouldn't let them in. She said that if they didn't leave the property right then and there, they would suffer the consequences."

I can't help but float an alternate theory, "Well, maybe Dorothy never went there? Maybe she just ran away, and used the Morgans as an excuse?"

The Librarian nods, accepting the theory, "Sure. Some people thought she had just run off with some boy that her Daddy didn't care for, or maybe she went on her own, only to get mauled by a bear or drown in a river somewhere. But deep down, we all knew something darker had happened."

I keep pressing for more info, "Did her parents ever go back to the Morgan home?"

The Librarian shakes her head, "That's the thing, couple days later her parents up and died in their sleep. Rumor is, they was frozen in fear, arms and legs all bent at weird angles, like someone had scared the souls outta them. 'Cept there were no signs anyone else had been there."

Captivated by the dark turn in the story, I then ask, "What about the *other* girls? You said there were more than just Dorothy?"

Shrugging complacently, the Librarian looks me directly in the eyes, "Not much to tell. Handful of girls got hired to work in that home over the next few decades. Some local, others from out of town; but none of 'em, not one, ever came back."

Frozen in shock, I suddenly think back to the Butcher's words, when he had said *'you ain't the first... probably ain't gonna be the last neither.'* At the time, his words had seemed off, but I hadn't understood the weight of them until now.

Suddenly I feel my mind doing backflips as context begins to set in. I think back to the loft area of Pater's office, where I had seen the stack of suitcases in the corner, piled in ascending order of generational style, as made evident by the differing amounts of dust that had gathered upon them.

Every part of my logical mind tries to negate the onset of a theory that those suitcases could belong to the missing women, but there are far too many coincidences lining up to not start speculating about the dark things that might have happened to them.

My thoughts naturally drift towards Ms. Pierre's naturally combative nature and paranoia of 'being replaced' as the children's primary caregiver. In the moment, I can't help but wonder how far she would be willing to go, to avoid losing such a title.

Memories of all of the rotten meals and verbal jabs from my own experiences with her begin to morph into dark theoretical circumstances in which Ms. Pierre has violently murdered these women and disposed of the bodies.

As my hypothetical narratives continue to escalate, logic swoops in once more, reminding me of Ms. Pierre's collapse in the hallway nearly a week ago. I quickly realize that amidst her advanced age and frail state, there's no way that she would be able to perform such a feat, let alone move a body afterwards.

Yet still, even with all of that considered, something in the back of my mind won't let go of my suspicions as my thoughts continue to race.

The dark debate within my mind continues to dance back and forth with increasing speed, until soon, the pain in my head and stomach simultaneously spike without warning, doubling me over in pain as I audibly groan under the assault.

The Librarian recoils at the sudden wave of malady, asking, "Y'alright?"

Fighting off the searing pain, I struggle to take in a few cleansing breaths as I silently nod. With the few breaths I'm able to take, comes a sudden wave of clarity, prompting me to snap my focus towards the clock at the end of the room.

I quickly realize that I've been in this library for *long* past the hour I had allowed myself, lost in the stories of the town, completely forgetting I was on a strict timeline.

Panicked, I bolt up from my wooden chair, knocking it backwards in the process, as I sharply announce, "I have to go!"

I don't have to see the Librarian to know that she watches my exit. I can't really blame her, after the odd nature of my severe pain followed by my suspicious departure; anyone would be captivated to see how it played out.

Hastily making my way towards the truck, I jump into the driver's seat, pausing briefly to projectile vomit out the side of the truck before closing the door and starting the engine.

I roll down the driver's side window in anticipation of a second wave of nausea, but when it doesn't come to fruition, I confidently shift the truck into gear and peel out of the Library's parking lot, fishtailing onto the road towards the town's only traffic light as I try to make up for lost time.

I try to fight through the immeasurable pain in my skull and drum up the beginnings of an excuse in advance of the guaranteed inquisition I'll undoubtedly receive from Ms. Pierre upon my return.

As I reach the intersection, the traffic light stubbornly turns red as though it's trying to further antagonize my already agitated state. In spite of it, I recklessly take the corner at full speed, skidding across the entirety of the road as I continue to floor it back towards the Morgan home.

The moment the truck regains its traction though; something compels me to glance in the rearview mirror.

My heart rate instantly doubles as I notice a large black pickup truck behind me, suddenly gaining speed. I don't need to see the faces that belong to the two silhouettes in the front seat to already know it's Clayton and his sidekick.

Instinctively, I push the gas pedal down to the floor in a feeble attempt to outrun my attackers on the way out of town, all the while, desperately trying to focus amidst the unending pain throughout my body as it continues its assault.

Similar to last time, Clayton's far superior vehicle catches up with my archaic rust-bucket with ease, pulling up along my left side so his friend can yell obscenities at me.

This time though, I wait until their front tires are lined up with the cab of my truck before I crank the wheel to the left, slamming into them with enough force to dent my driver's side door and knock Clayton's sidekick back into his seat.

Clayton's truck skids onto the shoulder, forcing him to slow down and regain control before continuing his pursuit. Within seconds though, he is once again gaining on me as we cross the east border of town, heading towards the seclusion of the long dirt road back towards the Morgan property.

Once more, Clayton speeds up to pass me on the left side and once more I line up my contact to maximize the impact, this time nearly sending his truck into a ditch.

On his third approach though, Clayton remains behind me, tactfully ramming my back bumper in an attempt to make me lose control. I purposely start swerving my vehicle so he is unable to line up for solid contact, and in a fit of frustration, Clayton finally tries to overtake me once more, this time from the right side.

Speeding his truck forward he quickly steals the angular advantage from me, so I secretly watch his hands upon the steering wheel with laser focus, waiting for my moment.

Within seconds I see his grip tighten in advance of cranking his wheel towards me, so I quickly slam on the brakes and watch as Clayton and his sidekick sail across the road in front of me and directly into the trunk of a large oak tree.

On impact, I see Clayton's sidekick smash through the windshield of the truck and skid along the dirt, leaving a trail of bloody mud behind him. Based on the sound of a sustained horn, I can tell that Clayton is still in the driver's seat, either unconscious or dead upon his own steering wheel.

As I sit in my truck, unmoving, I expect my hands to be trembling or for my emotions to be welling up inside of me in response to the residual fear of the attack, or in regret towards potentially killing two men. However, I experience none of these things.

In fact, after Clayton's truck has been incapacitated, I suddenly feel slight alleviation of the soreness throughout my body, my headache eases ever so slightly and I feel my nausea gently ride a smooth denouement.

Rolling my shoulders in relief, I take a deep sigh before stealing one more glance at the wreckage of Clayton's truck. Still seeing no movement from either man, a smirk of justice crosses my face and I slam down the gas pedal, peeling away from the site of the accident.

I keep my eyes focused on the road in front of me for the next few minutes, but soon find myself distracted by a light coming from near my feet. Glancing down, I see that my phone has slid out from under my seat and moved towards the pedals, likely from the sudden stop moments ago.

Slowing my pace ever so slightly, I hook my index finger around the charging cord that's still plugged into the cigarette lighter port, and pull my device towards me.

Splitting my focus between the phone and the road, I enter my passcode to see that my device has now fully charged, and more importantly, the video of Macha's visit from last night has fully loaded as well.

Glancing back towards the road momentarily, I see nothing but an empty straightaway in front of me, so I give in to temptation and press play, immediately hearing my own voice from off screen as I greet Macha at my door and invite her into my room to talk.

Keeping my eyes on the road, I listen to the audio of the recording as I make multiple failed attempts at eliciting a verbal reaction out of a supposedly mute child.

I can't help but roll my eyes as I hear my poorly delivered 'spider butt routine', prompting me to empathize with the blank stare that Macha had given me in response.

A few moments later, I finally hear the cue that had earned a verbal response from Macha, *"They look pretty good up there, don't you think?"* Only, instead of hearing her critique of how I've hung her pictures wrong... I hear nothing.

Glancing towards my phone with a look of confusion, I turn the volume up as high as it will go as I clumsily rewind the video back a few minutes to listen for it again.

Sure enough, the video progresses and I hear, *"They look pretty good up there, don't you think?"* followed by silence once more, until I hear my voice again, *"Okay, how would you like me to hang them?"*

Confused, I rewind the video again, this time ignoring the road in front of me, in order to watch my phone so I can at least catch a glimpse of Macha's lips moving to insinuate that she had responded.

Frozen in shock, I watch myself in the video, sitting on my bed, alone, talking to an empty space on the mattress beside me.

With one hand gripping the steering wheel, I fast-forward the video under the assumption that Macha is simply out of frame, but the more I watch, the more I feel goose bumps covering my arms as I seemingly continue a conversation with no one.

Part of me still tries to dismiss it as a combination of bad framing and poor audio, but even amidst that rationale, I still can't help but start questioning my own sanity. Soon after, my thoughts begin to spiral.

If Macha wasn't there, then had I imagined *all* of her visits? If so, who had left those drawings on my bed? What else had I imagined as real, and how could my subconscious manipulate my perception of reality so convincingly?

I try to quiet my racing thoughts in the moment, but the more I consider the video evidence of my instability, the more I start to identify symptoms of paranoid schizophrenia in my own behavior.

Desperate for any proof of my sanity to negate such considerations, I train my eyes on the screen of my phone, *completely* neglecting the road in front of me as I search the frame for *any* signs of Macha, be they shadows, reflections, *anything* that would signify she was there. Yet still... I see nothing.

Tears soon begin welling up in my eyes as I watch myself screaming under the attack of a murder of crows that isn't there, all while trying to protect a child who was never there either. I can't help but shudder at how far I've fallen off the deep end.

Unable to watch anymore, I toss my phone into the cup holder and shift my focus back towards the road as I wipe the streaming tears out of my eyes.

Without warning, the residual throbbing in my head suddenly

shifts to a piercing pain in the front of my brain, causing everything within my field of vision to temporarily blur.

Soon after, my upper lip begins to feel warm and wet, so I touch the space beneath my nose, pulling my hand away to see fresh blood on my fingertips.

As I stare at my bloodied fingers in disbelief, I suddenly catch a blurred glimpse of something in the distance, approaching the truck with incredible speed.

Squinting my eyes in an attempt to focus through the borderline blindness and pain, I still can't tell what the moving object is, but I remain mesmerized as its proximity to me narrows with each passing moment.

Seconds later, my vision suddenly clears just in time to see a large black crow fly into the truck's windshield, launching pebbles of safety glass towards me.

I naturally flinch at the shock of the impact, inadvertently taking the truck into a skid, which then progresses into an uncontrolled spin before the tires suddenly catch lateral traction, sending the vehicle rolling over itself.

As the world around me spins into a streak of colors, my ears begin stinging under the deafening chorus of screeching tires, shattering glass and twisting metal.

The truck's violent movements finally cease and I find myself suspended, upside down, in the driver's seat, craning my neck as I try to get my bearings.

As I turn my head back and forth though, I feel my eyelids start to get heavy as my body weakens with the slow departure of my consciousness.

Soon, the familiar taste of warm, coppery blood fills my mouth as everything around me slowly dissipates into darkness.

CHAPTER TWENTY-EIGHT

A Single Tear of Purpose

Gasping for air, I suddenly launch back into consciousness to find myself still suspended, upside down, in the driver's seat of the Morgan truck.

As blood pours from my open mouth, it trickles up my cheeks, intermingling with the accumulated sweat; invading my already swollen eyes and making them sting as my vision is blurred.

I try to wipe my eyes, but just by touching them I feel the sudden onset of a sharp, piercing pain in my skull. Soon after, a heightened bout of nausea and the sensation of fresh, searing pain all over my body begins to quickly amplify, as though my nervous system is waking up, seconds behind my consciousness.

Disoriented by the pain and distracted by my clouded memory of the moments leading up to the accident, I instinctually undo my seatbelt, sending my entire body crashing down to the twisted roof of the truck's cab. On impact, I immediately feel the familiar sting of tiny pieces of glass piercing my scalp, only antagonizing the pain in my skull further.

Working my way out of my crumpled position until I'm lying on my stomach, I try to shake my vision into focus in order to scan my surroundings, only once I do, I find that night has enveloped the world around me, cloaking the area in darkness.

I proceed to slowly, and painfully, pull myself out of the vehicle by way of the crumpled driver's side window. Once I've fully exited the wreckage, I attempt to stand, but by the time I get to one knee, the nausea takes control, forcing me to double over and empty my stomach, along with a considerable amount of blood from internal injuries, onto the loose dirt below.

A wave of disorientation and dizziness then sets in as I look back and forth at the road. Even now that I'm out of the truck, I still can't seem to tell which direction is which, leaving me stumbling in circles as I try to discern my location through the one eye that hasn't fully swollen shut yet.

Continuing to frantically pace back and forth, I suddenly feel my right foot slip out from under me, sending me sprawling onto the dirt, narrowly missing the puddle of sludge that had come out of me moments ago.

Looking towards where I had lost my footing, I see the cracked screen of my phone sitting on the ground amidst the remnants of groceries that had been obliterated in the crash.

Still unbearably dizzy, I opt to crawl towards my phone as opposed to walking, and by the time I have the device in my hand I quickly realize that, it too, has been damaged beyond repair in the accident.

Amidst the haziness of a certain concussion, I habitually pocket the now-useless device in my bloodied and torn jeans as I try to get to my feet once more.

Despite the persistence of my nausea, I am able to successfully get into a standing position, but as I do, I suddenly take notice of someone in the distance, standing at the side of the road, facing towards me.

Squinting my swollen eyes, I try to focus on the figure, and soon make out the silhouette of a woman wearing a dark, hooded cloak.

Initially, I feel a chill run up my spine under the assumption that the cloaked woman has returned. My knees begin to weaken and I waver back and forth as I await the inevitable illumination of softly glowing amber eyes to become visible within the woman's hood before the crow launches its attack, like it has so many times before.

However, the longer I stare at her, the more I feel an inexplicable sense of comfort washing over me, in place of my fear.

The woman in the cloak slowly pulls back her hood to reveal a young woman's visage, with pale skin that seems to glow in the darkness. Either side of her face is framed with gently cascading raven hair, as dark as night, that glimmers like a calm lake in the light of the moon.

She looks to me with an expression of tender concern upon

her face, as I continue to try to shake the residual dizziness from my head and center my focus upon her. It's then that I notice that she is waving me towards her, silently signaling me to follow as she slowly turns and begins walking further down the road.

Compelled to maintain the odd sense of security that her presence brings, I fight off the immeasurable pain and force myself to stumble along behind her, occasionally stopping as a result of my failing legs taking me down to my knees, or my escalating nausea forcing another bout of vomiting.

Each time I am forced to pause though, I look up to see that the woman has stopped and is patiently waiting for me to resume the journey, her kindness alone seeming to give me the strength to continue pushing forward.

Before long, I see two trees at the side of the road with the familiar symbols of three-armed pinwheels with feet at their extremities carved into their trunks.

The young woman proceeds to turn off the road and cross through the marked entrance, into the thick population of trees, thus causing me to lose sight of her, so I double my pace in order to catch up.

As I reach the entrance to the Morgan property, I see my silent guide in the distance, waiting for me as she had before. However, the moment I pass between the marked trees, I suddenly notice the rapidly brightening sky above me.

Traversing the winding path marked with two bald tire tracks, I start to wonder exactly how long I had been unconscious in order for the sun to be rising on a new day. But the further I walk, the more I become distracted with the unusual speed with which morning is approaching.

As I marvel at the unnaturally quick-rising sun, I soon feel the pain throughout my body beginning to ease away, along with my nausea and other concussion symptoms. Soon, I look down and notice that all of my wounds have miraculously healed, leaving a feeling of levity and rejuvenation coursing through my veins.

By the time I approach the edge of the clearing in front of the Morgan home, the mid-day sun lights the entire area. Soon, I hear the faint sounds of construction, softly echoing throughout the forest.

Tentatively stepping out from the collection of oak trees, I see the Morgan home standing before me in its infancy, the finishing touches yet to be put upon it.

In front of the home, amidst the various tools and supplies, I see Pater Morgan on one knee, gently pressing his ear against the pregnant belly of the woman from the ship, as I had been shown in a prior vision.

A group of butterflies float by, accenting the beauty of the moment and I can't help but feel a sense of warmth wash over me as I see the glowing smile upon Pater's face, and the look of deep love that the woman gives him in return.

Standing just beyond them, my cloaked guide turns with a soft, welcoming smile upon her face and continues to urge me towards the home. I follow her, but soon notice that as I do, the scene before me begins to permeate ever so slightly, as though I am walking through a living cross-fade.

Within a few steps, the construction of the Morgan home has not only been finished, but the wood paneling has aged with centuries worth of time. While the two individuals before me remain in the exact same position, I quickly notice that their clothes, hairstyles and faces are no longer the same.

The two strangers seemingly take no notice of me as I approach, and as a result, I overhear the man asking, "What should we name her?"

Despite my apparent invisibility, I still try to pass by their conversation as quietly as I can, but I freeze in my tracks as I hear the woman respond by saying, "What about... *Nemain*?"

Whipping around with wild eyes, I turn my attention towards the pregnant woman who has just spoken, and soon find myself staring into the face of the same, pale, raven-haired woman who had guided me here.

Turning towards the cloaked woman in the doorway of the Morgan home, I see her smile at me, softly nodding, as if to verify my assumption that she *is* Macha and Nemain's mother.

As this new understanding sets in, I glance back towards the projection of the happy couple to see that they are no longer there, so I snap my focus back towards my cloaked guide to see her turn and enter the Morgan home, prompting me to pick up my pace once more.

Upon crossing the threshold of the front door, I immediately hear a conversation coming from the 'salon'. I turn to see Mr. and Mrs. Morgan sitting around the wooden table with the sculpture upon it, while holding a newborn Nemain.

They are speaking with someone who has their back to me, but despite not being able to see the woman's face, I know exactly who it is as soon as I hear the stern Irish lilt in her voice.

The woman leans forward to hand her resume to the Morgans, revealing a slightly younger version of Ms. Pierre with alien warmth in her smile and the light of youthful exuberance in her eyes that must have died out long before I had met her.

In the moment, I feel like I am the only one who can see through the false façade she is putting on, as she proceeds to assure the Morgans in a kind, professional manner that she is, "*Excellent* with children."

I feel compelled to warn them, to scream at the top of my lungs to not trust their children with this monster, but before I can even attempt to voice my caution, I feel a hand upon my forearm.

Turning towards my cloaked guide, she silently places her index finger upon her lips before guiding me further into the home, towards the kitchen doorway.

The cloaked version of Mrs. Morgan and I stand side-by-side as we watch the ethereal projection of the day that Mr. and Mrs. Morgan informed a young Nemain that she was about to become a big sister.

A single tear of joy falls down my face as I watch the young version of Nemain jump up from her seat at the kitchen table and press her ear against her mother's belly, as her father had, with her.

My heart aches with pained love for Nemain, not only for the pure joy of the moment, but in longing for a time in her life where she had been innocent, happy and safe from Ms. Pierre's toxic, tyrannical rule.

As the thought of Ms. Pierre passes through my mind, I catch a glimpse of her washing a windowpane at the back of the home, her cold stare directed towards the Morgans with deep contempt.

I then hear a creak behind me, pulling my focus around to see the cloaked Mrs. Morgan summoning me towards the bottom of the staircase. As I cross the vestibule a projection materializes before me of Nemain singing to a young Macha, as she crawls back and forth.

By the time I have reached the bottom step, I turn back around and see the image of Mr. and Mrs. Morgan happily watching their two girls as they embrace one another in the kitchen doorway, where I had been standing only moments ago.

With a smile upon her face, the projected Mrs. Morgan turns to whisper something into Mr. Morgan's ear. Based on his sudden wave of emphatic joy and his gentle caressing of her mid-section, I can tell she has just informed him that a third child is on the way.

At first, I feel myself beaming at the news that she is pregnant again, but the levity washes out of my face as reality sets in and I remember the fact that Mrs. Morgan had died during childbirth.

I suddenly hear another creak, this time at the top of the stairs, and turn see an all-too-familiar silhouette of Ms. Pierre standing with a stern expression upon her face, as she watches the Morgan family with a look of revulsion towards their happiness.

Despite the dark image of Ms. Pierre looming above, the cloaked version of Mrs. Morgan leads me up the stairs and around the corner into the upstairs hallway, where I see slightly older versions of Macha and Nemain chasing one another in endless circles as they giggle with amusement.

Though I feel the urge to sit and watch the girls play for a while, I continue to follow Mrs. Morgan past the laughing children, down the lengthy hallway, towards my bedroom.

As we reach the door to the room, the cloaked version of Mrs. Morgan suddenly gives pause, dipping her head before turning towards me to reveal that her warm smile has faded, and a look of sadness has now washed over her visage.

Looking down, I see that she is gently caressing her suddenly protruding belly. I feel my brow furrow in concern as the bedroom door slowly opens, releasing the deafening screams of her excruciating labor.

Turning back towards the cloaked version of Mrs. Morgan, I see a single tear fall from her eye as she reaches out and gently guides my hand towards her belly. As she softly places my hand upon her womb, my consciousness is suddenly transported into her body on the day she was in labor.

Within seconds, I feel every ounce of pain that Mrs. Morgan did on that day, I experience every wave of emotion that washed through her, all while remaining simultaneously conscious of my own thoughts and feelings, as though I have become some sort of empathetic spectator.

Despite having never gone through labor myself, I immediately recognize that something is going horribly wrong with this delivery. Looking to my left, I see Mr. Morgan pacing back and forth, with a worried look upon his face, shaking his head in disbelief as he tries to cover his ears and mute his wife's painful screams.

Glancing down towards the end of the bed, I suddenly feel my overwhelming sense of dread double as I see Ms. Pierre's head poke up from between Mrs. Morgan's legs, revealing not only that *she* is delivering the baby, but that her arms are coated with Mrs. Morgan's blood up to the elbows.

Despite the gruesome scene, I feel Mrs. Morgan make her final push and with that, comes an unbearable agony, far worse than anything I had experienced in *either* car accident.

Though I am unable to see the child, I already know what's happened, based on Mr. Morgan and Ms. Pierre's speechless expressions. The baby is stillborn.

While I am already aware of the state of the child, I still experience Mrs. Morgan's waves of confusion and sadness as the reality of the situation slowly sets in.

She turns towards Mr. Morgan in the hopes of finding some form of solace, but in place of comfort and reassurance, he covers his mouth in horror as his eyes fill with tears and he runs out of the room.

As the door slams shut behind her husband, Mrs. Morgan shifts her focus back towards Ms. Pierre to see that she is wrapping the deceased child with a blood-soaked white sheet.

Tears quickly come to Mrs. Morgan's eyes and begin flowing down her cheeks. Soon, I am unable to decipher whether the overwhelming sadness that I'm feeling is Mrs. Morgan's or my own, but either way, the tears continue to fall freely.

Ms. Pierre then approaches the side of the bed. While she has a comforting expression upon her face, I can see the dark intent that hides behind her eyes, yet I remain unable to do anything about it, outside of witnessing the events as they unfold before me.

Sitting gently on the mattress, Ms. Pierre produces a small needle from behind her back and begins flicking the side of the syringe as she explains, "It's just a small sedative, dear. To help you sleep."

I feel Mrs. Morgan's desire to resist; yet due to the exhaustion of childbirth combined with the severe blood loss, she is unable to reject the needle, physically or verbally.

Soon, I feel the sting in Mrs. Morgan's arm as Ms. Pierre gives the injection. As the pain begins to dissipate, I simultaneously experience the fleeting moments of Mrs. Morgan's fear and panic as the sedative takes hold.

While Mrs. Morgan's consciousness has faded, mine still remains, and soon I find myself helplessly watching as Ms. Pierre's tender façade sloughs away and is replaced with a dark smirk.

Slowly, Ms. Pierre grabs a pillow from the bed and proceeds to hold it over Mrs. Morgan's face, pressing down with as much force as she can.

Even with the sedative in her system, Mrs. Morgan's body instinctually twitches and convulses as it tries to regain its oxygen supply. With each attempt her body makes to get free, I too, experience the shortness of breath as though it were my own.

Ms. Pierre remains leaning on the pillow with all of her weight, until the twitching in Mrs. Morgan's body finally slows to a halt. Soon after, I actually *feel* Mrs. Morgan's life leave her body, surrounding me with what feels like, a cold, empty darkness as I continue to bear witness, trapped within her corpse.

Ms. Pierre slowly lifts the pillow away, revealing her sinister grin once more. Gently fluffing the pillow, she proceeds to place it back on the bed, before moving towards the standing mirror and straightening her smock as though nothing had happened.

As she continues adjusting her uniform, Ms. Pierre strains her face until she is able to produce a wave of false tears. By the time a convincing amount have accumulated, she proceeds to run out of the room to inform Mr. Morgan that his wife has passed away as a result of 'complications from birth'.

Moments later, I hear Mr. Morgan wail from somewhere in the house as my consciousness is finally transported out of Mrs. Morgan's lifeless body.

I now find myself standing at my bedroom window, staring down towards the gnarled roots of the immense oak tree, as the light of day begins to fade as unnaturally fast as it had come.

In the amber glow of the dusk, I watch as Mr. Morgan drunkenly stumbles towards the roots of the old oak, with a half-full bottle of whiskey in his hand.

Crying over the loss of both his wife and child in the same day, I watch as he proceeds to lie down on the tree's roots and reach into to his pocket to pull something out. It's only once the object catches the light of the fading sun, that I realize it's a small pocketknife.

Before I even have a chance to react, Mr. Morgan quickly slits his wrists, spilling his blood onto the roots of the tree. As his blood pools around him, the faint light of dusk gives way to the darkness of night, creating a noticeable chill in the air.

I glance back towards the bed and see that both Mrs. Morgan's body and the bloodied sheets are no longer upon the mattress, leaving the room feeling cold and lifeless.

Turning my attention back down towards the base of the tree, I see two bodies now lying side by side, each wrapped tightly in the missing, bloodied linens. It doesn't take long to figure out that they are the bodies of Mr. and Mrs. Morgan.

Seconds later, Ms. Pierre approaches and gently places the wrapped body of the deceased child upon them, as though she is putting their corpses on display.

As Ms. Pierre steps back though, the roots of the immense oak tree begin to move. Slowly, they wrap themselves around the three bodies and pull them into the ground in a dark, yet poetic method of burial, prompting tears to well up in my eyes.

After the Morgans have disappeared into the depths of the Earth, I lift my gaze and audibly sob at the loss. It's then that I catch a glimpse of two softly glowing amber eyes staring back at me from within the branches of the immense oak tree.

Amidst the circumstances, I am far to overcome with sorrow to fear the crow's impending attack so, out of spite towards it, I remain unflinching as it flies towards me, screaming its song of screeching tires, breaking glass and twisting metal, until it has crashed through the window, showering me with pebbles of glass.

Reflexively blinking in response to the impact, I suddenly find myself kneeling at the base of the immense oak at the back of the Morgan property.

Turning to my left, I see the cloaked woman, now in the aged form that I had originally seen her in; face obscured, with stringy, silver hair sneaking out from the edges of her hood.

With this new understanding of her story, I feel tears continue to stream down my face towards her life being unfairly cut short. It doesn't take long though for the sorrow in my heart to shift into pure rage towards Ms. Pierre.

Though I've always hated the old bag, the abhorrence I feel now is far beyond anything I have *ever* experienced before. The simple idea that Ms. Pierre had stolen Macha and Nemain's time with their parents leaves me *seething* with fury.

With my teeth gritting in vengeance and my fists clenched to the point that they hurt, I turn towards the cloaked woman confidently, simultaneously discovering that I now have my voice back, as I say, "I *See* now. I will *Save Them.*"

Upon making my promise, my hands suddenly feel warm, and wet. Looking down, I see that the scars on my wrists have broken open and my blood is pouring onto the ground like Mr. Morgan's had, however this time I resist the urge to panic.

The tips of the tree's roots start lifting upwards, reaching towards the source of blood as though they are thirsting for it. Despite the unnerving nature of the tree satiating itself in such a way, I allow the roots to wrap themselves around my arms and the rest of my body, as they continue to feed off of me.

Soon, the roots of the old oak tree begin to lift me in the air, rotating my body so that I am lying on my back as they carry me towards the immense trunk, like a fallen messiah.

As the tree roots slowly lower me towards the ground, I notice that the cloaked woman has vanished, and standing in her place at the base of the tree are Macha and Nemain, both with prideful smiles upon their faces, as though they have finally discovered their champion.

Nemain takes a small step forward as she says, "Thank you, Patty. We love you."

In response to her gratitude, I feel a single tear of purpose fall from my eye, hitting the ground beneath me. As it makes contact, the soil audibly shifts, preparing to receive my body as sacrifice.

The last thing I see is the canopy of oak leaves far above me as the ground slowly seals its own breach and surrounds me with darkness.

My eyes slowly flutter open as I feel the familiar sensation of a seatbelt pressing against my chest, resisting my body's weight.

Suddenly snapping back into consciousness, I gasp for air, only this time I taste no coppery blood in my mouth, nor do I feel the aches and pains throughout my body from the accident.

Snapping my head from one side to the other, I soon realizing that I am sitting in the cab of the Morgan truck, parked under the tilted shed, having seemingly fallen asleep upon the steering wheel.

Disoriented, I scan my surroundings, noticing that the angle of the sun suggests it is approaching mid-day. I start to wonder if I had absent-mindedly fallen asleep prior to making my trip into town, but when I pivot around in my seat, I see the bags of groceries behind me, still fully intact.

My mind races as I come to the realization that I have not only made the trip, but I have returned safely without being cognizant of it. My mind whirs as I try to ascertain what parts of my journey actually happened and which ones were merely projections of my subconscious.

Quickly undoing my seatbelt, I scramble to jump out of the truck's cab, unnerved by my increasingly blurred sense of reality. Slamming the truck door behind me, I immediately scan the side paneling for any signs of scratches or dents from my battle with Clayton's truck... yet I see nothing.

I move to the truck's side mirrors to check my face for any cuts or bruises from the accident, but all I see staring back at me is my exhausted visage, and a few rogue grey hairs that have snuck their way out from under my hat.

As I tuck my hair back under the cap, I notice how much my hands are shaking; however contrary to past dreams involving the cloaked woman, I am not shaking from residual fear, but my rage towards Ms. Pierre amidst this newfound truth.

Gathering the bags from the truck, I start making my way towards the Morgan home. My pace quickens and my fists clench at my sides as I continue to roll over this new information that I've been shown, contemplating how I will use it against Ms. Pierre.

While I am fully aware that the circumstances surrounding the deaths of Mr. and Mrs. Morgan that I've been shown were simply projections within a dream, I still can't help but embrace it as the truth.

After all, my dreams have proven to be one of the few sources of information that I am able to trust as of late, showing me the accurate images of Pater's office, his journal and the stack of suitcases prior to seeing them in real life. Why should this be any different?

Still, I remain aware of the fact that I must try to suppress my new heightened level of hatred towards Ms. Pierre, at least until I have found the proof to substantiate my suppositions well enough to justify taking action.

But try as I might to remain civil and logical, the Morgan home soon becomes visible on the horizon and I see Ms. Pierre standing in the doorway with her arms crossed and a single disapproving eyebrow raised, as she launches into her scolding tone, "What part of *quick trip* did you fail to understand, Miss Woodall? Need I remind you of the importance of structure, and punctuality?"

While countless combative responses fly through my head, I

simply shrug in place of a verbal response.

Passing by Ms. Pierre I enter the home, I feel my jaw clenching as I play out multiple hypothetical scenarios of how I will eventually avenge the lives of Mr. and Mrs. Morgan.

While images of said scenarios are graphic in both nature and intent, what scares me most is when I catch a glimpse of my reflection and realize that amidst these dark, gruesome fantasies of murder... I'm smiling ear to ear.

CHAPTER TWENTY-NINE

Dark Reflections

The moment I catch the dark reflection of my sadistic smile in the glass of the cupboard door, I suddenly feel an overwhelming sense of dread growing within me.

I barely recognize the face that is staring back as being my own. Sure, the features remain the same, save for the effects of extreme exhaustion and stress, but the expression upon it is one I've never seen, nor felt before.

The mere image of this foreign emotional state frightens me at my core and with that fear comes a feeling of shame towards the dark thoughts that had led towards this evil smirk.

Yet, despite these emotions churning within me, the reflection of my face remains the same, powered by anger, filled with dark intent, and worst of all, enjoying every moment of it.

Thankfully, my proximity to the kitchen counter is close enough that when I drop the groceries out of shock towards my unrecognizable visage, nothing falls to the floor.

Already infuriated by my apathetic response to her harsh greeting, Ms. Pierre comes flying towards me with as much fire in her eyes as there is fury in her tone.

As she sidles in beside me, I can hear her take a moment to mute her anger so the children don't overhear, "Miss Woodall, I asked you a question. What part of *quick trip* did you fail to understand? Need I remind you that this household runs on a *strict* schedule?"

Still detached from the current moment, I remain staring at the pane of glass in front of me, lost in the reflection of the darker version of myself. My lack of acknowledgement towards Ms. Pierre's question only perpetuates her anger further.

Continuing her attack, Ms. Pierre surrenders her decorum and barks, "Just who do you think you are?!"

I'm unsure as to whether it's my anger or my exhaustion that tempts me to fire back, but I'm quick to mute my intended assault as I quietly try to explain, "I'm sorry, I just-"

Scoffing at my half-hearted apology, Ms. Pierre leans in even closer to my ear as she says, "Your apologies mean *nothing* to me. Time and time again, you have *purposely* disregarded the rules that I have so *clearly* set out for this household. You have consistently *proven* that you are unfit to be around the children. You are rude, you are obstinate, and worst of all, you are unappreciative of the leniency that I have so graciously provided."

I know I should keep my mouth shut. At this point, I can't trust my self-control enough to unleash my free thought. I don't know if I still have the ability to hold myself back from the atrocious fantasies that are still swirling through my head. But as I fight to contain myself and remain civil in the moment, I feel my emotions slipping.

Against my better judgment, I suddenly blurt out, "*Leniency?* I have done *everything* that you have asked me to, without question. All you've given me in return is criticism, judgment and comments that have *specifically* been intended to hurt me. You have *no* idea how much I've sacrificed, since I've been here!"

Stifling a full laugh, Ms. Pierre leans her head back incredulously, "What exactly have you sacrificed, Miss Woodall? It's not like you were turning down another job to be here, or walking away from a loving family. By giving you this job, I *saved* you, I gave you *purpose*. You had *nothing* until you came here."

Though I know she's just trying to hurt me again, it doesn't make the veracity of her words cut me any less deep. I haven't lost *anything* by disappearing from my old life, because there was nothing left to lose.

Regardless of the truth of the situation though, I still feel my defensive anger swelling. I feel my instincts telling me to fire back at the haggard old woman in front of me, to throw something at her, to smash her withered face through one of the glass cabinet doors, but I am quick to silence these thoughts, gripping the edge of the counter until my knuckles turn white.

My internalized battle renders a complete lack of verbal

response that Ms. Pierre seems to assume is the result of her words hurting me beyond the point of having a clever response. With a satiated smirk on her face, she says, "That's what I thought" before confidently stomping towards the kitchen door, content with her victory and satisfied with, what was intended as, the last word.

Despite feeling defeated and exhausted, I still feel compelled to respond, so I quietly mutter, "If you hate me so much, why don't you just fire me?"

Though she does not turn to face me, I see Ms. Pierre's back straighten as she pauses at the kitchen door. Quietly, she responds, "There are far worse things than being fired, Miss Woodall..."

After dropping her hanging statement, Ms. Pierre exits the kitchen, leaving my mind spinning as I contemplate her words while gripping the counter's edge so firmly that the wood audibly creaks.

So badly, I want to throw these groceries through a window, or chase after the old bitch and pull her down the stairs by her airtight bun as she kicks and screams in resistance and fear, knowing the whole time that she brought this upon herself.

I try to calm myself with some deep breaths as I shift my energy towards putting the groceries away in silence. I'm so distracted by my circling thoughts and my attempts to suppress them, that I barely even register the activity as I complete it, making it feel as though the task only required a handful of seconds.

Still stewing, and with nothing else to do in the moment, I opt to make my way to my bedroom so that I can at least try to deal with these swirling emotions in private.

By the time I reach the upstairs portion of the house, I can hear Ms. Pierre sternly talking to the children, through the thick wooden bedroom door. Even the muted sound of her tone makes me want to spit venom right then and there.

Nevertheless, I continue past the children's room, towards my own door. Upon entering my room, I immediately flop down, laterally across the mattress. My eyes naturally drift up to the silk canopy above my bed, as it performs its gentle rhythmic dance amidst the seemingly perpetual draft in my room.

Even with the calming image of the canopy before me, I still can't stop rolling over Ms. Pierre's words, '*Far worse things than being fired*'.

What the hell does that even mean? Was that some kind of threat? Of course it was. But does she really think that she'd be able to get the upper hand on me? The mere thought makes me scoff with incredulity.

Let her try. Let her put me in my place. Let her try to break me more than she already has. The joke's on her, because there's nothing left to break.

My body already aches from the symptoms of extreme exhaustion and physical strain. My mental state is beyond exhausted from the endless swirling thoughts for weeks on end. Based on the combination of my dreams and the blurred sense of reality as of late, it has also become glaringly evident that my psychological state deteriorated long before I even took notice.

Put shortly, I've got nothing left to lose. I'm ready for whatever she has in store for me. I'm ready to defend myself and fight back. In fact, at this point... I'm practically *begging* for an excuse.

I spend the better part of fifteen minutes rolling over the possible insinuations of Ms. Pierre's threat with so much anger that I soon find myself welcoming it. Something about this newfound level of hatred almost seems to surpass the stress-headaches and tense muscles until it almost tickles me on the inside.

Whether it's the physical sensation, my level of emotional imbalance, or simply my failing mind, my anger soon uncovers the humor of the threat, and I soon find myself giggling at the thought of it.

Soon, my laughter becomes uncontrollable, giving way to a full-blown maniacal belly laugh that is as raucous as it is unsettling. The further I spiral into this hysterical state, the more I realize how far I've drifted from anything resembling sanity.

It's then that the laughter gives way to tears, and then soon after that, full-blown weeping. Before I know it, I've spent the better part of half an hour audibly sobbing, while lying on my back.

By the time I've run out of energy to cry anymore, I force

myself to sit up, and in the process, I catch a glimpse of my reflection from across the room in the standing mirror by the window.

Thankfully, the dark reflection that had stared back at me in the kitchen appears to be gone now, however thanks to the lasting effects of a good hard cry, I now appear twice as exhausted as I had before.

But it's then that something else catches my eye.

Standing up from the bed and crossing towards the mirror, I start to notice deep wrinkles at the edges of my eyes and mouth that had not been there before, and worse, the closer I seem to get to the mirror, the more that I notice visible signs of rapid aging.

My eyes widen with both fear and concern as I slowly pull the baseball cap off my head and I see a full head of stringy, grey hair fall down either side of my face. As the wiry follicles finish their descent, a wave of time seems to be sent through my body and soon, I am staring at a withered, elderly version of myself.

A single tear falls down my face as I remain staring at my reflection in shock, but while I can feel my own jaw slackened in horror, the elderly version of my self that I see in the mirror begins to grin back at me as though it were a sentient being, independent of my presence.

My reflection's smirk continues to stretch into a maniacal smile, far beyond the limits of any human's facial capabilities. Instinctually, I reach out and touch the mirror's surface, watching as my replication's hand does the same. As I feel my fingertips make contact with the mirror's surface, I see the eyes staring back at me beginning to faintly glow with amber light.

As my own eyes widen with fear, the dark, elderly likeness reaches through the glass with lightning speed, and seizes me by the arm, pulling me towards the mirror and cracking the glass with the impact of my face against it.

I awake with a start, to find myself still lying on my bed, below the silk canopy as it billows amidst the moving air.

Bolting upright, I immediately shift my focus towards the

standing mirror, thankfully seeing my own, unaltered reflection staring back at me with no visible signs of aging, no evil smile, and most importantly, no glowing eyes.

Still feeling uncertain as to what state of consciousness I may currently be in, I slowly get up and approach the mirror, staring at every part of the reflection of my face, with surgical scrutiny, to make sure that nothing is altering upon my approach.

By the time I get close enough to fill the frame of the mirror, I am frozen in place, staring at myself with a look of deep concern. While I should be finding comfort in the fact that my unchanging reflection insinuates the solidity of reality, I can't help but break into another wave of tears as I realize how quickly I am losing myself.

It's then that I hear sharp knocking at my door. I quickly wipe my eyes and take a deep breath in preparation for, what undoubtedly will be, my next bout with Ms. Pierre.

As I approach the door, she knocks a second time, so I quickly turn the handle, pulling the door open with an already exhausted expression on my face.

I see Ms. Pierre standing on the other side of the doorway in her signature pose, hands crossed at her waist and a single eyebrow elevated in scrutiny. In place of a verbal response, I simply stand there in an expectant manner, waiting to hear what she could possible have to say at this point.

Taking a short breath, Ms. Pierre immediately launches into a thinly veiled criticism; "Oh. I had assumed you would be back in uniform by now."

Visibly rolling my eyes, I respond with heavy sarcasm, "I was just getting to that."

Pursing her lips in response, Ms. Pierre then says, "I would suggest you do. You have already lost half the day, and your duties will *not* complete themselves."

With that, Ms. Pierre pivots and storms off down the hallway. While the exchange had remained somewhat non-combative in a relative sense, I feel an old sensation returning, reminding me of the fights I used to have with my Mom.

Whenever our initial dust-ups had settled, there had always

been an eerie, quiet calmness that seemed to hover within my parents' home before things inevitably got worse on an exponential level.

Whether it's my lack of energy to fight Ms. Pierre in the moment, or simply my need to occupy my body and mind with anything other than the consideration of my dissipating sanity, I quickly pull off my jeans and hoodie and start getting into my uniform, intent on completing my duties for the day, despite only half of the allotted time to do so.

While the pace of my work is quickened, I barely notice the strain on my body over the remainder of the day as I spend most of the time bouncing between my internalized thoughts of hatred towards Ms. Pierre, and trying to subdue my endless feeling of disorientation as I question the validity of my supposedly conscious state.

By the time night has rolled around, I'm emotionally, physically, and psychologically exhausted, yet I still remain quietly pacing back and forth in my room, awaiting the sound of Ms. Pierre's sharp knocking to signify the commencement of our next battle.

Like clockwork, she arrives at my door and knocks sharply, presumably under the guise of dropping off whatever sludge she has concocted in place of a decent meal.

Spitefully waiting for her to knock a second time, I go to the door and throw it open with the intent of yanking the tray out of her hands before she can consider thrusting it at me. Much to my surprise though, Ms. Pierre is empty handed.

Despite the countless versions of this hypothetical exchange I had imagined over the course of the day, I come out of the gates far hotter than expected, stepping towards her with impatience as I sharply blurt out, "What?!"

Cocking her head in a slightly offended response to my curtness, Ms. Pierre raises both eyebrows in shock, before saying, "Well, I was hoping we would be able to discuss our exchange from earlier today with some *semblance* of civility, but clearly *you* are not prepared to do so."

I cross my arms as I feel my own eyebrows rising, "So *I'm* the problem?"

Ms. Pierre's back straightens at the insinuation, "What exactly are you trying to say, Miss Woodall?"

Even though my instincts tell me to pump the brakes and remain tactful, my emotions take control in the moment, sacrificing my diplomacy and replacing it with juvenile insubordination, "How *dare* you say that I'm 'unfit' to be around the children! I'm the best hope they have! You think you're so infallible when it comes those girls because you *claim* that you raised them, but there's a big difference between *raising* and *ruling*! They don't love you. They *fear* you."

I watch as pure hatred washes over Ms. Pierre's face in response to my attack, yet she remains unnervingly civil as she responds, "Miss Woodall, I realize that you do not like me. You have every right not to. But do *not* question my place in the lives of those children. They *need* me in ways you could *never* understand."

Scoffing at her sense of self-importance, I fire back, "What they *need,* is to be free from you. You are *toxic* and you are harming those girls in ways that you can't even fathom."

I can see that I've hurt her, and as much as I hate to admit it, it feels good. I do my best to mute my pleasure towards her pain, however I can't help but realize that this is how Ms. Pierre must have felt all those times she hurt me.

Slowly, Ms. Pierre swallows her pain and calmly attempts to dismiss my statements, "I can tell that you are exhausted and perhaps this isn't the best time for us to have this conversation. Why don't you get some rest and we can discuss this in the morning?"

In the face of her attempted retreat, I suddenly feel myself brimming with confidence. However this confidence quickly shifts to hubris as I blurt out, "You'd love that wouldn't you? For me to drop my guard, so you can murder me, like you did with Mrs. Morgan?"

As soon as I finish speaking, I freeze in place, realizing that I've tipped my hand far beyond where I had intended to at this point in the exchange. I soon notice that Ms. Pierre is also catatonic with shock towards my accusation. However, where I had expected to see guilt and fear upon her face towards my knowledge of her secrets, I see deep offense and sincere concern in its place.

Taking a step into my room, I see tears beginning to well up in Ms. Pierre's eyes as she furrows her brow and inquires, "What would make you think I could even be *capable* of doing something like that?"

I remain silent, fully cognizant of the fact that my only evidence of her crime had come to me through a projected vision, within a dream. I desperately try to drum up a logical answer, but nothing seems to come to my lips.

Breaking the silence, Ms. Pierre takes another step into the room as the concern on her face grows, "Miss Woodall, I don't know what has led you to believe that I would do such a thing, but I assure you that is *not* the case."

Crossing my arms defensively, I ask, "So what *is* the case then? What *really* happened to the Morgans? No more lies."

Ms. Pierre softly crosses her hands at her waist once more as she tries to remain patient, "As I told you before, Miss Woodall, Mrs. Morgan passed away during the birth of her third child. Unfortunately, the child also succumbed during the delivery. As for Mr. Morgan... he is no longer present."

Despite the consistency in her story, I can't help but be overwhelmed with cynicism towards the seemingly rehearsed nature of her vague dismissal, so I bark back, "What does that mean? *No longer present*?"

Ms. Pierre immediately defaults to her standard spin, "That's really not my place to discu-"

The anger swells within me, as I cut her off by coldly, "-Bullshit."

Dipping her head in disappointment, Ms. Pierre then calculates her attack before asking, "Miss Woodall, have you ever considered that your paranoia towards the intent of others might be a reflection of your *own* lies and betrayals?"

I furrow my brow in frustrated confusion towards her inquiry, "What the hell are you talking about?"

Ms. Pierre sharply follows up, "I found your *hidden treasure*."

My mind races as I try to figure out what she's talking about. Within seconds, I feel the blood drain from my face as alarm bells start going off in my mind and I glance towards my pillows, suddenly noticing they've shifted since the last time I was in my room.

Coldly, Ms. Pierre rhetorically spells it out for me, "Pater's journal? The one that you *stole* from the room at the end of the hall? The *very* room that I had specifically mentioned that you had *no* business in?"

Even though my instinctual defensiveness makes me feel fury towards Ms. Pierre's invasive act, I also recognize that I don't have a leg to stand on in regards to refuting her accusation.

Taking a moment to purse her lips once more, Ms. Pierre quiets her tone; making her words somehow sound sharper, "Let me make myself *abundantly* clear, Miss Woodall. You are *not to* enter that room. You are *not* to go into *any* part of this house that I do not assign to you. Should you find that you are unable to follow these simple rules, I assure you, that you will *suffer the consequences*. Is that understood?"

Feeling completely deflated, I softly nod. Any confidence that I had moments ago has now escaped me as I remain speechlessly dumbfounded.

Ms. Pierre slowly backs away until she has returned to the doorframe of my room. The sternness in her face remains as she says, "I shall give you some time to reflect upon our little chat. It would be my hope that we will be able to discuss these matters with a little more consideration towards one another in the future. If not for the sake of one another, then *at least* for the sake of the children."

As Ms. Pierre slowly exits, the sound of the door latching closed seems to echo through the room amidst the awkward, contemplation-fueled silence.

I take a moment to weigh the consequences of Ms. Pierre's reveal, realizing that I'll never see Pater's journal again, let alone the lock pick that I had been using as a bookmark.

As my mind continues to roll over the implications of being caught red-handed, the sound of an additional 'click' suddenly slices through my focus, pulling me towards my door with curiosity as I reach out and attempt to turn the door handle.

It's then that I realize Ms. Pierre has imprisoned me by locking my bedroom door from the outside.

CHAPTER THIRTY

Consequences

Upon discovering that Ms. Pierre has locked me in my room, I start knocking on the door from the inside, in the hopes of at least appealing to *some* sense of reason, yet there is no response.

As I start to feel my anger mounting along with a bout of claustrophobia, I start thumping and pounding on the door with closed fists. Before I know it, I'm slamming on the door hard enough that I can feel the bruises forming on the outside edges of my hands as I scream out Ms. Pierre's name with fury.

By the time that the pain in my fists becomes too much to bare, I slow myself and drop to one knee so I can try to see if Ms. Pierre is even still present in the hallway to hear my tantrum. Sure enough, as I peer through the keyhole, I see nothing but an empty corridor on the other side.

My mind begins to race through my inventory of belongings that I had brought to this house, desperately trying to remember if I have anything that could be used as a lock pick, in place of the one that Ms. Pierre had inadvertently confiscated when she took Pater's journal.

I start rummaging through my drawers, but I quickly realize that there is nothing of use, prompting me to flop back onto the floor in frustration. Amidst my moment of defeated silence though, I hear the sound of faint, rhythmic creaking coming from the hallway.

Crawling towards my door and listening as intently as I can, I quickly identify it as the sound of a rocking chair, off to the side so as not to be seen through the keyhole, but close enough to my room to hear any attempts at escape.

It becomes clear that Ms. Pierre has been planning my imprisonment in advance, having enough foresight to provide herself a 'guard's chair' so as to stave off any fatigue she may suffer during her 'watch'.

My stomach begins to gurgle in response to the panic induced by my containment, combined with the complete lack of sustenance prior to now. Between the meal I had neglected last night, forgoing breakfast before my trip into town today, and the complete absence of food this evening, I can't remember the last time I ate something.

Placing my hand upon my pained stomach, I try to appeal to my captor through the locked door, "Ms. Pierre? I was wrong, okay? I shouldn't have said the things I did. I wasn't in my right mind. I-I'm sorry."

The only reply I receive is another soft creak of the rocking chair as Ms. Pierre presumably shifts her weight for the sake of her own comfort amidst my desperate apology.

The non-responsive nature of her punishment fills me with frustration. My tone suddenly becomes angrier as I continue to call out to her, "You can't do this! This is false imprisonment! That's one step down from kidnapping!"

Though I predicted her continued silence before I even spoke, it doesn't make it any less infuriating. The longer that I hear nothing from Ms. Pierre's side of the door, the more my stomach continues to digest itself and the more I start to grit my teeth and clench my aching fists in both fury and panic as I start to feel the room closing in around me.

I start pacing the room to try to occupy my body and distract my mind from the growing pain in my gut, but it only makes me more agitated. Hypothetical images of Ms. Pierre smiling to herself as she rocks back and forth in the hallway soon begin flooding my mind, making me seethe with anger towards my captor.

Soon, I feel myself lose all control as I rush at the door with all my strength, pounding upon the thick wood in spite of my aching fists while screaming, "LET ME OUT OF HERE, YOU BITCH!!!!"

The sudden nature of my attack on the door combined with the sheer level of hatred in my voice even surprises me. However, my efforts remain futile, as all I hear in response to my emotional explosion is another series of soft, rhythmic creaks from the rocking chair.

My hopelessness soon gets the better of me and I crumple onto the floor, bawling for the better part of an hour. While I try to keep my crying as quiet as possible, for fear of giving Ms. Pierre any further sense of victory over me, I still can't help but occasionally release an audible whimper as my spirit continues to shatter.

By the time I run out of both energy and tears, I find myself lying on my back, staring up at the ceiling of my room. I begin to think back towards how I had gotten myself into this mess in the first place.

I had been so *desperate* for any sense of worth that I didn't even question the letter when it came to my parents' house. I had been so blinded by the contentious relationship with my Mom that I hadn't even *considered* that things could get so much worse.

Even once I had arrived here and sensed that something was *off* within the Morgan home, I still remained so *damned* stubborn to prove that I could serve a purpose, even in the face of Ms. Pierre's frigid attitude and horrific treatment.

The more that I think about it, the more I realize how many times I should have just quit and left this place, but my overwhelming sense of obligation towards Macha and Nemain kept me here, and for what? All to adhere to the request of a mysterious cloaked woman who remains a fictional projection from my *goddamned dreams*.

I shake my head in derision towards my foolishness as I come back to the present moment and start rolling over my options of how the hell I'm going to get out of this prison.

On one hand, I could resume pounding on my door in the hopes that Ms. Pierre will eventually come around, if not out of common decency, then at least to shut me up before the noise wakes the children.

However, I then remember the near-soundproof nature of the children's room, not to mention that the likelihood of Ms. Pierre folding in the face of compassion is about as probable as having a snowball fight in the seventh ring of hell.

Pivoting around, I begin to consider the large window on the other side of my room. As I approach the multiple panes of glass, I try to estimate the distance from the window frame to the closest branch that looks thick enough to support my weight.

The closer I get though, the more I realize that even if I could, somehow, maintain my momentum and trajectory through both the window and the thick plumage of leaves, there would still be the issue of blindly grasping the branch in the process.

Even if I were to somehow find success in that, I would still have to figure out how to get down the near story-and-a-half drop to the uneven ground below. Best-case scenario, I would sprain my ankle in the process; worst-case, I could break my neck.

Surrendering to my lack of options, I make my way to the bed and flop down upon the mattress, helplessly staring up at the silk canopy above me as I feel my thoughts beginning to drift beyond the moving fabric.

I think back to when I was in the loft area of Pater's office, directly above this room, where I had seen countless, obsessive drawings of Triquetras and other symbols that I had also seen in both my dreams and upon the Morgan Family crest.

Suddenly, my mind shifts to the dark corner of the loft that had concealed the stack of suitcases within its shadows. Unable to let go of the image of those bags, I start thinking about the *way* in which they were stacked, in ascending order of modernity, the oldest of which at the bottom, covered in the thickest layer of dust, almost as if they had been individually placed upon one another, over a series of decades.

Soon, I find myself suddenly thinking back to the Librarian's tale of the various women who had allegedly gone missing after working in the Morgan home. In the moment, I had wondered if there was a connection between the suitcases and those women, but amidst the physical suffering I was experiencing at the time, I had been quick to push the thought aside.

As I re-consider the potential coincidence now though, I soon hear the Butcher's words echoing through my mind, '*ain't the first... probably ain't gonna be the last, neither*'.

The mere thought of it all causes my mind to drift, and soon I am reflecting upon the myriad of exchanges I've had with Ms. Pierre over my time in the Morgan home.

Thoughts of her various methods of torture flood through my

memory in quick succession. Rancid meals, verbal assaults, purposeful misinformation, endless lists, impossible rules, the exhausting workload and, of course, my pre-meditated imprisonment.

While they have all been effective techniques in breaking my mind, body and spirit, I can't help but begin to wonder if these other women had suffered these same tactics. If so, then how much does my experience so far, pale in comparison to what is yet to come?

I start to realize my foolishness in assuming that Ms. Pierre's form of attack would come as some sort of vicious flagrant act. I had spent most of the day preparing myself with hyper-awareness so as to physically defend myself from her attempts at an assault, but as I feel the mental and physical fatigue washing over me as it has so many times before, I suddenly recognize the error of my ways.

Only now do I understand that Ms. Pierre has been playing a long game that began before I even arrived at the Morgan home. Moment, by moment, she's been weakening me, making me doubt my own body and mind, until I have become a shell of my former self.

It's then that I remember her words from our exchange in the kitchen, earlier in the day. She claimed that she had *saved* me by offering this position before citing, not only my lack of employment, but also the broken nature of my family life.

When I had found out that Ms. Pierre knew about the accident that had taken Andy's life, it came as a bit of a surprise, but it wasn't all that shocking due to the public nature of the event. However the unnerving familiarity with which she had commented on the private matters of my family life scares me, and I begin to wonder how she would even go about gaining access to such information.

Suddenly, something clicks into place... she's been *targeting* me from the beginning. She knew that my destitute existence would make me an easy mark. Like a hungry lion, she was weeding out the weakest member of the herd so as to yield maximum results from as little effort as possible.

But even if that were true, why? To what end? Is it all to just satiate some sort of dark, murderous thirst hidden beneath her cold veneer? To find a victim that no one will miss? Or is it something bigger? Something I'm not seeing? Perhaps it's some sort of penance for my past transgressions?

As I continue my internalized debate, I admittedly have trouble even *picturing* Ms. Pierre overpowering someone, thus creating a substantial wave of doubt that washes over my theories. So I try to step back and re-organize my thoughts from a logical perspective, only considering what I *know* to be true.

I *did* walk into the children's room moments after Ms. Pierre had struck Nemain, and when I had discussed this with Nemain in the forest afterwards she *had* mentioned that this was not the first time that Ms. Pierre had hit her, either. Put shortly, Ms. Pierre is *absolutely* capable of acts of violence.

Combining that with her repeated vehement accusations that I am 'trying to replace her', it is also clear that Ms. Pierre would go *any* distance to retain her role as the children's matriarchal figure.

Based on her multiple displays of emotional imbalance and heightened defensiveness when it comes to Macha and Nemain's upbringing, it is pretty safe to assume that her perception of me as a threat to her way of life *could* serve as a plausible motive.

And so, with the presence of a potential motive and evidence of the instincts to act upon it with violence, the only question left is if Ms. Pierre would have the physical *ability* to claim a victim half her age, let alone a series of them.

Thinking back to when she had grabbed my arm a few days ago, it was clear that she possesses more strength than her fragile frame would naturally suggest. But as convincing as that moment may have been, I also remember when she had collapsed in the hallway from 'standing up too fast'.

While every fiber of my being only wants to focus on the facts that will support my theory, I have to admit that the image of her fraily crumpling on the floor negates any realistic consideration towards Ms. Pierre possessing the stamina to commit multiple murders, let alone dispose of multiple bodies.

But in the face of my consideration towards Ms. Pierre's

physical limitations, I can't help but think back to the sedative that I had seen her inject into Mrs. Morgan, prior to suffocating her with the pillow. I start to wonder if this could be Ms. Pierre's modus operandi, thus eliminating any need for physical supremacy over her victims.

While I feel my adrenaline beginning to surge at the possibility of figuring it all out, I am quick to remind myself that any details of Mrs. Morgan's murder came from a vision within a dream. No matter how convincing it may have seemed, I can't consider these details as facts, because I have no proof that they ever even happened.

In fact, when I had accidently let it slip that I was aware of this *alleged* act; Ms. Pierre had denied it with such convincing vehemence that I'm still questioning her culpability now. Yet for some reason I still can't shake the nagging feeling that the truth lies somewhere in the middle, despite how implausible it may all seem.

Suddenly, a memory creeps up in the back of mind of something that Ms. Pierre had said moments before she locked me in my room. She had warned me that if I didn't adhere to her rules, I would '*suffer the consequences*'.

As I weigh her words with more clarity now, I soon realize that those were the exact words that the Librarian had used when telling me the story of the first missing girl, Dorothy McNabb.

The details of the tale slowly start coming back to me.

Dorothy's parents had gone to the Morgan home, where an old lady had greeted them at the door. When the McNabb's had *insisted* that they search the home themselves for any signs of their daughter, the old woman had told them to leave, before warning them that if they didn't, they would '*suffer the consequences*'.

I feel goose bumps on my arms, as my mind begins to race in consideration of the gravity of such a coincidence, but my logical brain is quick to shake off the thought, reminding me that there's no way to prove *any* part of my conversation with the Librarian ever actually happened.

In fact, the more that I think about it, the less certain I become of *any* of my experiences in town, be they at the Library, any of the shops, or even my battles on the road with Clayton and his sidekick. All of those experiences, along with my second accident, were washed away the moment that I woke up with my forehead on the steering wheel of the Morgan truck, safely parked under the tilted shed.

Like so many times before, I find my mind filled with more questions than answers, more theories than evidence, and more unsubstantiated emotions than logic.

While I have minimal certainty of the answers I seek, something within me, be it the guidance of the cloaked woman in my dreams, or simply my ever-growing obsession, *something* tells me that I'll find my answers in Pater's office at the end of the hall.

Unsure of how many hours of my imprisonment have passed, I suddenly snap back into focus when I hear Ms. Pierre speak from the other side of my door, "Miss Woodall?"

I remain spitefully hesitant to respond.

With no verbal reply, Ms. Pierre continues, "In the event that you are not asleep, I want you to know that I will return in the morning. It is my sincere hope that you will be able to see beyond your animosity at that point so as to function as a member of this household with *some* semblance of civility."

I can't help but roll my eyes at her supposition. How could she possibly believe that holding me prisoner will somehow make me *more* compliant? If anything, it's fueled my fire of resistance, giving me more purpose than was already there to be *purposely* insubordinate towards her.

Ms. Pierre finally gives up on her attempt to elicit a response from me, and simply says, "Do try to remember that I'm doing this for your *own* good."

In place of a response, I silently flip my middle finger towards the door with a scowl of hatred on my face, not just towards Ms. Pierre, but also towards what she clearly perceives as being 'just another lesson'.

After she finishes speaking, I hear sharp footsteps making their way down the corridor, followed by the faint sound of Ms. Pierre's door slamming shut in the distance.

Even though I'm fairly certain she has departed from the hallway, I move to my door and press my ear against it to make sure there are no sounds that would signify that this is just another ruse, intent on catching me in an attempted escape.

Sure enough, I hear nothing. No creaks of the chair beside my door, no soft-trodden footsteps signifying her sneaking return, not even the sound of muted breathing. Yet even though I'm sure that Ms. Pierre has departed for the night, there's still the matter of my locked door.

Fruitlessly, I go through my drawers a second time, still turning up no potential tools that could be used to pick the lock. As I scan the room, I can't help but think back to the old logic puzzles they would give us in grade school.

'Angelica is trapped in a room. In that room is a wooden table and a saw. How does she escape?'

Back in the setting of my elementary school, the students would pitch their various ridiculous solutions until they were all inevitably proven wrong when the teacher finally piped up to say, "She saws the table in half, then puts it back together, because *two halves* make a *whole*, then she climbs out through the hole."

If only it were that easy.

As I stand here now, actually *living* the conundrum, I start to realize why such a solution would never occur to 'Angelica', because the one detail that was never included in the original equation is that 'Angelica' is scared as shit and feels like the walls are closing in on her with every passing second.

In actual fact, 'Angelica' would be less likely to attempt this cute, little solution for the sake of family friendly humor, and far more likely to use the saw to slit her own throat in a state of panic.

I shake the dark image from my mind, and soon find myself wishing that the cloaked woman were here with some sort of divine guidance that could lead me to freedom from this imprisonment. If not her, than perhaps whatever entity it was that set Pater free from his cell.

I start remembering the details he had written about his false imprisonment; how he had succumbed to his exhaustion after praying to every deity he could think of for his freedom. Moments later he awoke to find that his cell door was open and the guard that was on duty, was slumped in the corner with his head turned backwards.

The growing darkness inside of me brings a smirk to my face at the idea of a similar fate falling unto me. I envision myself turning around to find my door is unlocked, and then moving to the upstairs hallway to find Ms. Pierre slumped in the corner like Pater's guard had been.

Quickly shaking the thought from my head, I find myself unnerved by the pleasure I'm deriving from these dark imaginings. While I realize that my hatred for Ms. Pierre is on a seemingly unending crescendo, it's still no excuse to consider such circumstances as positives.

Yet even after suppressing these dark urges, I still can't help but hear a tiny voice in the back of mind whispering, '*Would it <u>really</u> be that bad if she was gone? Who would miss her? Who would even know?*'

I pace my room, trying to silence my malicious thoughts, unable to tell if the unwelcome voice in my mind is my own, or if it is some sort of dark influence pushing me towards some sort of inevitable conclusion. Either way, I remain intent on maintaining my values, and standing by my morals as I try to retain my sense of who I am... or at least, who I used to be.

As I continue pacing my room, I suddenly freeze in place as I catch a glimpse of myself in the standing mirror by the window. As I stare at the reflective surface, I see a dark figure standing behind me, in the shadows by my bedroom door. It doesn't take long to identify her as the cloaked woman.

Paralyzed by the idea that my wishful thinking may have summoned her presence, I keep my back to her while staring at her reflection with wide eyes. I try to discern whether she is here peacefully, or if I'm just awaiting the inevitable illumination of the crow's glowing amber eyes to light up within the shadows of her hood.

However, it's then that I suddenly hear a familiar, '*click*'.

Whipping around to face her, I see an empty space where the cloaked woman had been standing half a second ago with no clear signs that she was ever actually there.

Naturally, I feel the immediate return of my fear towards my waking hallucinations and their ability to blur the lines of reality. However, my fear quickly subsides as my focus suddenly shifts towards a new sound as it quietly calls out across the room.

The archaic hinges whisper the strain of their movement; cutting through the tense silence like a song, as I watch my bedroom door slowly, and inexplicably, creak open.

CHAPTER THIRTY-ONE

The Bag

I reach out, grabbing the edge of my bedroom door. Yet, even though I feel the solidity of the wood within my grasp, I still find myself questioning if this is all just another illusion.

Based on the sighting of the cloaked woman that led to my sudden freedom, I'm tempted to believe that this is all just another dream, however the temptation to escape my imprisonment is too appealing to pass up, even if it is merely another fiction of my subconscious.

Standing before the open doorway, I become wary of yet another possibility. If this *isn't* a dream, then it's entirely plausible that it could be some sort of malicious trial from Ms. Pierre to test my loyalty by way of challenging my compliance.

I slowly peek my head out of my room, scanning from one end of the hall to the other, sure that I'll spot Ms. Pierre standing somewhere within the vicinity of my room with her signature scowl upon her face. Shockingly though, I soon discover that the upstairs corridor is devoid of anyone else's presence but my own.

Relieved, yet suspicious, I take a step into the hallway as I continue to scan the lengthy passage. While the coast remains clear, I still feel alarm bells going off in the back of my mind. Even though I know there is nowhere anyone *could* hide, even if they wanted to, I can't shake the feeling that I'm being watched.

I cross to the far side of the hallway, turning my attention towards Ms. Pierre's room to make sure she isn't secretly surveying my movements from the edge of her doorframe. Thankfully, her door appears to remain closed.

As I take a sigh of relief, I suddenly hear the familiar sound of a woman faintly crying at the opposite end of the hall. Pivoting around, I see the cloaked woman standing at the door to Pater's office, the shadows of her hood still hiding her face, despite my recent knowledge that she is the spirit of Mrs. Morgan.

I begin to make my way towards her, still tentative towards her underlying intent. Even though the cloaked woman has proven herself to be an ally, I remain wary, based on my previous experiences with her and how quickly said visions had turned against me.

By the time I have traversed half of the distance between us, I suddenly hear the soft echo of a 'click' come from Pater's office door, followed by the gentle creak of the archaic hinges announcing access to the room.

As I continue my approach, I can't help but question the simplicity of the moment. After all of the painstaking efforts I had to put into gaining admittance to Pater's office the first time, it almost seems *too* easy that it's presenting itself to me now.

Silencing my suspicions, I try to tell myself that it must have all been a method of testing my resolve, a way of *proving* that I would keep true to the promise I had made to the cloaked woman.

After all, I know she wants me to expose Ms. Pierre for her crimes, otherwise why else would she have shown me those visions? She is guiding me towards the truth, no matter how abstract the method may be. She *needs* me to succeed. She *needs* me to protect her children. She *needs* me, to *save them*.

Slowly crossing the threshold into Pater's Office, I quickly turn my focus towards the treacherous spiral staircase on my left that leads to the upper level of the room. While the idea of ascending this shoddy structure scares the hell out of me, I remain determined to find whatever evidence awaits me at the top.

If I can just prove Ms. Pierre's culpability in even *one* of the disappearances of the women who have previously worked in this home, then I'll be able to easily report her to the authorities and get her locked up for the remainder of her miserable life.

Should Ms. Pierre find out about my intent and try to stop me, I'll be ready to defend those children myself, no matter the cost. Regardless of however it plays out, only *one* thing matters at the end of the day... I *will* free these children from Ms. Pierre's tyrannical rule.

Slowly approaching the base of the spiral staircase, I look up to the top and see the cloaked woman now standing on the upper level, awaiting my arrival, so I commence my ascension, step-by-step, feeling the entire column shift under each of my movements.

In an attempt to distract my fear, I momentarily glance down to the lower level of the office, seeing the faint rectangular space upon Pater's desk, devoid of dust, where his journal had once been.

I silently lament my reckless confidence that resulted in Ms. Pierre's discovery of the stolen item, underneath my pillow. If I had just tucked it into the back of a drawer, or even between the mattresses, I'm sure I would have gotten away with it. Though, realistically, what does it matter now? Snapping back into focus, I suddenly realize that amidst my absent-minded thoughts, I've already reached the top step.

My eyes try to adjust to the darkness, as I scan the loft area. Slowly, soft accents of the strewn papers that litter the room begin to present themselves, along with the easel at the far end of the room, highlighted by a single strip of moonlight.

Standing just beyond the canvas that's been placed upon the easel, I see the barely visible outline of the cloaked woman, pointing towards the shadowy corner in which the stack of suitcases is hidden from view.

As I cross towards her, I glance at the barely visible sketches of various Celtic symbols on the floor. I begin wondering how long Pater had lived in this home before his madness had taken its hold.

Was he aware of his slowly crumbling mental state, like I am? Was his perception of reality as blurred as mine? If so, what had it all inevitably led to? Full-blown madness? Suicide? Had Pater's fate been so unmentionable that the family refused to acknowledge its history? Is *that* why there are no photographs or paintings of family members to speak of?

By the time I lift my eyes towards the easel, the cloaked woman has once again disappeared, yet regardless of her absence I continue my path, knowing exactly where she is guiding me.

Slowly coming around the edge of the canvas, I glance towards the image upon it and soon find myself lost in the amber eyes of the half-painted crow. Even now, as an unfinished depiction of the bird, I still can't help but feel as though its lifelike eyes are staring directly into my soul.

Thankfully, my determination to find evidence supersedes my inexplicable, subconscious urge to get lost in the painting as I had before. I quickly force myself to avert my stare and pivot towards the shadow-filled corner where the bags are piled.

As I stare at the faint outline of the precarious stack, I marvel at how it seems to have defied the laws of physics by remaining standing for as long as it has. The bags, themselves, seem to have been haphazardly tossed upon one another with zero regard for structural integrity or safety for anyone within the vicinity of the pile.

Naturally, my eyes drift to the bag that sits on top; a larger suitcase with charcoal grey, nylon fabric on the outside, and seemingly the most logical place to start.

I move to the zippers on the side of the bag where I had previously seen a small strip of leather that looked like the strap of a luggage tag. As I attempt to find the other end though, I quickly realize that the tag has been removed from the strap long ago.

While my instincts tell me to not to disturb the precarious pile, my curiosity and determination quickly overturn the debate in my head, and soon I find myself wrapping my arms around the large suitcase like some sort of disgruntled baggage handler.

I attempt to laboriously lift the bag and pull it towards me, but it proves to be heavier than I had anticipated and I immediately recognize the error of my ways as the stack topples towards me, knocking me over in the process.

As the bags fall around me, I freeze in place, certain that I will hear the faint sound of Ms. Pierre's door flying open followed by her sharp footsteps charging down the hall. Much to my surprise though, I hear nothing.

Giving a few extra silent seconds to make sure that the coast is clear, I slowly lift my head and begin to get back to my feet, however it's then that something catches my attention from the corner of my eye.

Slowly pivoting back towards the canvas, I notice that the

image of the crow with glowing amber eyes is now inexplicably missing from the painting, as though the sound of the luggage impacting the floor had spooked it off its branch.

I feel my heart fill with fear as I begin to wonder if the creature has somehow transitioned from its oil-based existence, and transcended into reality in order to stalk me from some dark corner of the room.

Even as I stare at the blank space on the canvas now, I'm unable to silence the feeling that I'm being watched, that there are eyes cast upon me from somewhere within the dimly lit room.

I tentatively lean my body to the left, peeking out from behind the imagined safety of the canvas. It's then that my gaze is met by the stares of the seven decaying women standing around the room, each in their various states of rot, each with a square pendant woven from straw hanging around their necks.

I quickly move my hand to the nape of my own neck, certain that I will once again find myself burdened by a similar pendant, however this time, I feel nothing there.

Turning my attention back towards the decaying women, I watch as they slowly raise a single arm to each point at a different suitcase. As they do so, the pendants around their necks begin to softly glow, providing a cool white light that illuminates the room in full.

The more my eyes dance back and forth between each decaying woman and the bags that they are pointing at, the more I feel foolish for not having recognized the underlying connection prior to now.

These are the spirits of Ms. Pierre's victims, and they want justice in the afterlife, just as much as I do. They too are guiding me towards the truth.

My eyes immediately drift towards the bag that was at the bottom of the pile. I quickly deduce that this must be the oldest of the suitcases, based not only on its style, but also the level of deterioration of the woman who's pointing at it.

I shift the suitcase towards me, noticing that despite the firm structure of its clunky wooden frame, the bag itself is surprisingly lightweight.

Running my hands over the tan-colored burlap that coats the

outside of the suitcase, I soon reach the edges where the material disappears under a dark brown leather border that is naturally distressed from decades of neglect.

At the top of the bag are two small strips of leather that look like the ends of two miniature belts. I make quick work of releasing each of them and opening the top of the suitcase to find it filled with a small collection of archaic clothing that reminds me of my uniform.

Shifting a few cotton blouses to the side, I soon uncover a stack of old black and white photographs. Carefully removing them from the suitcase, I bring the tattered pictures towards me, studying each image with surgical scrutiny for any evidence they may conceal.

The first photograph is of a man with a mustache that is as full, as his expression is stern. The sheer size of his facial hair would almost appear comedic, were it not for the intensity of his dark eyes that would elicit a confession from an innocent man.

Flipping the photograph over, I see a single word written in the top left corner, '*Father*'. While the photo itself has presented no insight towards the identity of the owner of this bag, I can't help but feel empathy towards whoever was raised by this man as his spiteful glare hauntingly reminds me of my Mom's.

In the next photo, I find the image of an equally stern woman, only in place of the intense stare that 'Father' had, her eyes tell the tale of a world that has broken her at her core, forcing her to endure her laborious existence in a time when she is neither seen, nor heard.

Flipping the photo over, I see the same handwriting in the top left corner, this time presenting the word, '*Mother*'.

Based on the age and condition of the photographs, I figure that it is unlikely that I'll find any form of official documentation that would identify the decaying woman before me, so I continue flipping through the photos, checking the backs of each of them until I find something that presents itself as a clue.

About mid-way through the stack of photographs, I suddenly feel my heart skip a beat as I find the image of a young woman standing in front of the Library from town, only the building is still under construction.

Holding my breath in anticipation, I slowly flip the photo over and move my eyes towards the top left corner, where I see the same handwriting spell out, '*Dorothy at the Library*'.

My focus whips upwards towards the decaying woman as I realize that Dorothy McNabb *had* come to work in the Morgan home after all.

A sudden wave of clarity washes over me as I slowly rise to my feet. My eyes dance between the various decaying women and the suitcases splayed out on the floor before me. Within seconds, I identify that there are *seven* women, but *eight* suitcases.

It's then that I spot the one bag that is not paired with an owner... a large bag with a charcoal grey, nylon fabric exterior; the bag that had previously been sitting at the top of the stack.

Flipping it over, I proceed to open the suitcase, revealing a much more plentiful collection of somewhat modern clothing within. Judging by the multiple pairs of ripped jeans and a 'Pixies' t-shirt that sits on top, it's safe to assume that this bag likely dates back to the mid-to-late nineties.

Grabbing a pile of t-shirts with names of bands that I've never heard of, I move them to the side before doing the same with a stack of boxer shorts and a couple pairs of wool socks until I finally come across an old pair of black, ankle-high Doc Martin boots, sitting on their side with something sticking out of the left one.

Removing the item, I find myself holding a worn down black leather wallet with some sort of deteriorated sticker upon it and a chain coming from its fold.

Opening the wallet, I audibly gasp when I see a driver's license in the plastic inlay that says, '*Name: Rosalie Pierre. Birthdate: 1973.*'

Disbelieving of what I'm holding in my hands, I stare at the driver's license for upwards of a minute, reading and re-reading the name and birthdate over, and over again. While I'm vexed with confusion towards what this could all mean, it doesn't take long for logic to catch up and fill in the blanks.

Ms. Pierre is burying her crimes by shrouding her true identity and hiding behind the names of her victims.

I feel a smirk of victory slowly cross my face as I wrap my mind around the fact that I *finally* have the proof I've been seeking. Now I'll be able to confront Ms. Pierre, or whoever she is, and get the truth out of her by threatening to expose her on multiple charges of kidnapping and murder.

Hell, after I'm done with her, she'll *wish* I had just reported her for child abuse. At least the penalty for that would have paled in comparison to the shit-storm she's going to face now.

I quickly remove the *real* Rosalie Pierre's driver's license from the wallet and grip it in my left hand as I stand back up. As I do, I notice that the seven decaying women have vanished and the image of the crow has returned to the canvas, as well.

Normally I would find myself in a state of disoriented confusion as I try to wrap my mind around what I'm certain is reality, and what couldn't possibly be. However now, I simply dismiss the debate amidst the far more important thoughts of how I will best utilize the evidence that I've found.

Glancing at the mess of suitcases before me, I momentarily consider re-stacking them to cover my tracks, but I am quick to remind myself of the noise that the pile had made when it toppled over.

I opt to leave the bags as they are, allowing myself the ability to plead ignorance in the event that Ms. Pierre *had* heard them fall. In fact, part of me *hopes* that she heard the noise and that she will investigate in the morning. Maybe, when she finds the open bags and missing driver's license, she'll experience the same kind of fearful dread that she's incited in me so many times.

Content with my momentary victory and the one that's yet to come, I practically skip towards the top of the spiral staircase as I exit the loft area of the room. I'm so lost in my sense of triumph that I foolishly neglect to pay mind to the treacherous nature of the stairs, and begin making my descent as I would with any staircase.

Carelessly bouncing my weight back and forth with each step, I immediately recognize my error the moment that I hear metal frame of the structure begin to audibly groan.

I already know it's too late, yet still, I try to race down the remainder of the archaic staircase before it fully detaches from the wall. I'm about halfway down when it finally begins to list forwards, tumbling towards Pater's desk, smashing it into splinters on impact.

Moments later, my eyes pop open and I find myself pinned underneath the twisted metal scraps of what used to be the spiral staircase. Unable to move under its weight, I try to spit out the taste of blood and dust that has settled in my mouth, but it merely dribbles down my chin in spite of my efforts.

Turning my eyes towards the loft area of Pater's office, I see the cloaked woman staring at me from where the stairs had previously been attached. Slowly, two glowing amber eyes begin to illuminate within her shadowy hood, and within seconds I am deafened by the sound of screeching tires, breaking glass and twisting metal as the large crow emerges and flies directly towards me with immeasurable speed, and malicious intent.

I jolt awake to find myself standing in the middle of the upstairs hallway, just outside my bedroom.

Momentarily disoriented, and still suffering from the residual fear of yet another waking dream, I tighten my fists in an attempt to quell my overwhelming anxiety. It's then that I realize there's something in my left hand.

Glancing down towards it, I see the face of the real Rosalie Pierre staring back at me from the photo upon her driver's license that I'm still, somehow, in possession of.

My eyes dance back and forth over the laminate card, knowing I should feel confused and fearful towards the presence of the item, yet still I can't help but feel a sense of calm growing within me to find that I've retained my evidence.

Continuing to stare at the driver's license, I push my door open and enter my bedroom as I shift my thoughts towards the only things that matters... strategizing the manner in which I will tactfully use this evidence to take down this imposter who *claims* to be Rosalie Pierre.

However, I quickly come to realize that time is *not* on my side when I suddenly hear the sound of someone clearing their throat.

Looking up, I see the woman who is masquerading as 'Ms. Pierre', standing in the middle of my bedroom, awaiting my return with hands crossed at her waist.

With a single eyebrow raised in judgment towards my insubordination, she coldly says, "Miss Woodall, we need to talk."

I quickly pocket the driver's license, and nod sheepishly as I take a deep breath in preparation for her verbal assault.

In doing so though, I soon find that for the first time since I've entered the Morgan home, I am *not* fearful of her attack, but in fact *welcoming* of it.

Little does she know, I've already got the upper hand.

CHAPTER THIRTY-TWO

Not What I Wanted

In the face of my pending battle with Ms. Pierre, my back immediately straightens as my pulse quickens and the fires of rage swell within me like a rising tide, fueled by my over-riding sense of confidence.

At first, I say nothing in response to her invasive presence within my room. Partly because I'm so shocked by it, but mainly because I'm scrambling through my scattered thoughts to try to find the ideal launching pad from which I will mount my attack.

As I continue calculating my approach, Ms. Pierre is the first to break the silence, "Before you begin weaving your lies and excuses, Miss Woodall, know that my patience is wearing thin."

Squinting my eyes with thinly veiled hatred, I respond through gritted teeth, "Is it?"

Pursing her lips and raising an eyebrow, Ms. Pierre launches into her attack, "Time, and time again you have *purposely* disobeyed the *very* clear instructions you have been given, and *insist* on sticking your nose where it doesn't belong. You do not respect the rules of this household, you do not respect the privacy of this family, and you *certainly* do not respect *me*."

I audibly scoff before barking back at her, "*Respect*?! You *imprisoned* me!"

Ms. Pierre's face tightens even further as she drops her tone to a sharp whisper, "Miss Woodall, lower your voice. The children will hear you."

Begrudgingly, I step further into the room and quietly close the door behind me, rolling my eyes in the process.

Before I've even turned back around, Ms. Pierre continues her attempts to tear me down, "I must ask, *why* are you still here?"

I remain incredulously silent, unsure of how, exactly, to word my response.

Before I have a chance to answer, Ms. Pierre cuts back in once more, "You clearly don't *want* to be here, so why is it that you remain?"

I can't help but audibly scoff once more at her attempt to rid me from this household. She sincerely believes that she still holds the power in this argument, but she has no idea that I'm merely lying in wait for the opportunity to expose her false identity.

Getting visibly frustrated by my cynical expression and lack of verbal responses, Ms. Pierre's tone grows a little harsher as she asks, "What happened to the *eager, capable* version of you that I met on your first day? Or was that a lie as well?"

As her inquiry lands, I feel a smile begin to form on my face as I quietly and flatly say, "Well, we've all told our fair share of lies, haven't we... *Rosalie Pierre*?"

Ms. Pierre's brow furrows in the face of my vague insinuation as she tilts her head to the side in confusion. Were it not for her sociopathic tendencies, I might even believe the sincerity of her facial expression, but I am quick to remind myself that it's likely just another lie.

I feel my heart fill with venomous rage as I slowly slip my hand into my pocket and pinch my fingers around the corner of the laminate identification card, preparing for my reveal while harshly inquiring, "How many were there?"

Shaking her head incredulously, Ms. Pierre responds, "I don't know what you-"

I cut her off, impatiently, "-How many others came before me?"

Shaking her head in response, Ms. Pierre tries to contest my accusation, "I assure you, Miss Woodall, I have no idea what you are talking about."

Taking a step closer, I jab my index finger towards her, "*Seven!* You have baited *seven* women into this household! At least, those are the ones that I know of."

I see a legitimate look of fear beginning to develop on Ms. Pierre's face in response to the intensity of my indictments. The mere sight of it causes my confidence to swell and my voice to continue intensifying.

Taking another step towards her as I tighten my grip on the driver's license in my pocket, I continue my verbal assault, "I'll admit, I lied to you on occasion, but it was always in the name of self-preservation. But *your* lies are a whole other kind of evil. I *know* you're not who you say you are! I *know* about the things you did to those women, because I have *proof*!"

I see tears beginning to form in Ms. Pierre's eyes. In the moment, I'm so fired up that I can't tell if they are fearful in nature, as a result of my aggression, or guilt-ridden as a result of finally being found out. Either way, I pull the driver's license from my pocket, thrusting the laminate card towards her so my evidence can do the talking for me.

Upon seeing the license, Ms. Pierre freezes as her eyes widen and her lip begins to quiver ever so slightly, before she asks, "...Where did you find that?"

I pull the laminate card away from her as I confidently punch out, "The *very same* room that I found the belongings of all of the other girls you murdered. Pater's Office. I guess that's why you tried to keep me out of there, what with all of the evidence of your crimes stashed away so carelessly."

Ms. Pierre's lip continues quivering as she scrambles to find her words, "-That —It's not what it looks like. Please... you need to understand-"

I jump in, cutting her off mid-sentence, "-Understand what, exactly?

Taking a breath, she launches into her spiel, "...Miss Woodall, there are forces at work here that are far beyond either of our control, let alone our understanding-"

Crossing my arms in disdain, my anger takes on a mocking tone, "-Seriously!? I've caught you red-handed, and you're just going to blame some *outside influence*?"

"That's not what I'm trying to-"

"-Then what? Please enlighten me with more of your lies!"

"I'm not lying to you, I swear, I-"

Holding up the laminate card once more, I fire back, "-*This* is Rosalie Pierre, so who the fuck are *you*!?"

Ms. Pierre begins floundering, "I- If you would just let me explain, there is a perfectly reasonable-"

"-BULLSHIT!"

Ms. Pierre's frustration kicks in full force, as she finally musters the confidence to combat my accusations, "Miss Woodall! I am not *pretending* to be the woman in that photo, because I *AM* her!!!"

Shaking my head in skepticism, I desperately don't want to believe the words coming out of her mouth, however something about the earnestness in her voice gives me pause. I glance towards the license incredulously as I say, "No. Th- That's impossible."

Despite the conviction in my belief that this is just another lie, I suddenly take notice of the similarity between the eyes of the young woman in the photo and those of the elderly woman standing before me.

My focus drifts over Ms. Pierre's shoulder, where I catch a glimpse of myself in the mirror and think back to all the times I had stood in that very spot, lamenting how progressively tired I have looked since I've moved into this house.

I think of the bags under my eyes, the deepening wrinkles around my mouth and the sudden population of sporadic grey hairs upon my head. In the moment, I can't help but wonder if those were all symptoms of prolonged exhaustion and depression, as I had assumed them to be, or if there might be an implausible truth to Ms. Pierre's words.

Shifting my focus back towards Ms. Pierre, whispers of doubt begin sneaking into my angered expression, prompting her to continue explaining, "Despite my outward appearance, I assure you that I *am* the woman in that photo. *This* is what I was trying to tell you, Miss Woodall. This house it... it *changes* you."

Despite her preposterous rationalization, my logical brain soon finds that the oddly shaped pieces somehow line up with my personal experiences. Shaking the thought from my head, I quickly remind myself that the woman in front of me is a career manipulator and I can't allow myself to take a single word she says for face value.

Clenching my fists in an attempt to retain my feeling of authority, I fire back, "If you're attempting to convince me of your innocence, you may want to try something a little more plausible."

A wave of tears form in Ms. Pierre's eyes as she tries to appeal to my reasonable side, "I know it makes no sense, but I promise you, it *is* the truth. This home... it bends the conventional laws of reality to its will."

Even though she's putting up a convincing façade, I still see Ms. Pierre's scattered explanations for the falsities they must be. Just like a wounded animal that's been backed into a corner, she's employing every self-preservation tactic she can think of in order to distract from the truth, even if it includes fantastical paranormal theories that seem to be pulled from some B-Horror movie.

The tears in Ms. Pierre's eyes begin to fall, as she attempts to echo her claims of innocence, "I promise you- I did not do the things you think I have. You must believe me. *Please.*"

I feel my heartbeat elevating as I tighten my face and land my next blow, "No. What I *must* do is protect Macha and Nemain! I have to *save them,* from you!"

Ms. Pierre's face suddenly loses all expression as she quietly inquires, "...What did you just say?"

Confused by her odd tactic, I naturally lose all power in my statement through repetition; "I have to *save them,* from you."

I watch as, what looks like pity, washes over Ms. Pierre's face, "You're having the dreams."

A chill runs up my back in response to her statement, however I still remain on the defensive, shielding any form of vulnerability from her, so I mute my fearful reaction with feigned confusion.

Clearly not buying my manufactured brand of ignorance, Ms. Pierre clarifies, "The woman in the hood has come to you, hasn't she?"

Despite my best efforts to subdue my reaction, my eyes pop at the accuracy of Ms. Pierre's analysis, yet still, I remain silent for fear of revealing too much and tipping the scales in her favor.

In response to my sustained silence, Ms. Pierre continues, "She used to come to me in my dreams as well. When I first got here, she would visit me nightly. She showed me wonderful, yet *terrifying* things that I foolishly assumed to be truthful. In the end though, it only amplified the madness that this house projects upon those within it. It *infects* people like you and me with confusion and paranoia, until we no longer know what's real anymore."

While I don't want to believe the words coming out of Ms. Pierre's mouth, I can't help but identify with every symptom she describes. When combined with the glaring sincerity in her tone, I find myself frozen in place, mesmerized by the details of her story, similar to when she had told me the tale of Pater's journey on my first day.

Ms. Pierre glances down at the floor with a look of softness that I've never seen upon her face, as she woefully says, "I see those very changes happening in you, Miss Woodall. It had been my hope that you would have come to your senses by now and left this place on your own volition. *That* is why I have been treating you so dreadfully. *That* is why I have been so horrible to you." A single tear falls down Ms. Pierre's cheek, as if to amplify the dramatic impact of the moment as she adds, "But now... now, I fear it is too late."

I furrow my brow at the odd statement as I ask, "Too late for what?"

Ms. Pierre lifts her gaze towards me once more, as she says, "The woman in the hood, she is a *liar*. She deceives for the purpose of her *own* agenda. She manipulates, and misleads with false truths. She is *not* who she appears to be, Miss Woodall."

Even though Ms. Pierre's scattered statements are somehow giving me pause, I still feel my hatred towards her continuing to build as the dark instincts in the back of mind begin to take over.

The more Ms. Pierre attempts to excuse her horrid behavior, the more I feel my teeth gritting in fury towards her intended justifications. How *dare* she stand in front of me trying to validate her abusive behavior as an attempt to 'help me'! How *dare* she even think *any* of her actions were excusable, regardless of the circumstances!

My dark instincts continue nagging at me from the back of my mind, urging me to just get it over with, to launch myself at the old bag, shatter her body, fracture her mind, obliterate her spirit... I want to *break* her.

As the evil thoughts continue to dance through my brain, I feel fear towards them. I shake my head in an attempt to physically dismiss the sinister instincts from creeping any further into the forefront of my conscious mind, but my face soon betrays me.

Ms. Pierre clearly sees the amplification of my sub-conscious aggression kicking in, so she tries to go one step further, "When you traveled into town, you felt the sickness, didn't you?"

I feel my face continuing to tighten, but still, I remain silent as I continue to try to control my vehement rage amidst my growing fear.

Taking on a pleading tone, Ms. Pierre continues her attempt to convince me of her lies, "That's what she does. She *binds* you here. She makes it so that you can't physically leave this place."

Shaking my head, I downplay the symptoms I had experienced as I say, "The only thing that's kept me here is the need to protect those children!"

Tears begin streaming down Ms. Pierre's face. Amidst her audible sobs, she is barely able to utter, "That's just what she *wants* you to believe, but they... they're not children."

Even though Ms. Pierre's argument has become increasingly convincing despite its complete lack of its grounding in reality, the moment she involves the children in her justifications is the moment I feel myself lose all control, "-Stop! Don't you *DARE* involve them in this!"

Ms. Pierre suddenly drops to her knees as tears continue streaming down her face, "Please, you have to believe me, they are not what they seem to-"

I take a vengeful step towards her as I scream out, "-I said *STOP!*"

The sheer decibel level of my voice in the moment almost seems to make the entire room shake. At first I wonder if it is merely my own perception being thrown off as I become increasingly blinded with anger, but I can tell by Ms. Pierre's sudden look of terror that I'm not the only one who experienced the sensation.

Visibly shaking, Ms. Pierre seems to make a sudden realization, as she mutters, "No. Please. Not yet."

Annoyed by her increasingly pathetic tactics, I bark out,

"What the hell are you talking about!?"

In place of a response, Ms. Pierre inexplicably resorts to negotiation tactics, "Please, I'll do anything! You can have Pater's journal back! Read it cover to cover if you want, just please, not yet... I'm not ready to die."

My mind and body both freeze in response to Ms. Pierre's assumption towards my intentions. I naturally soften my voice as I explain, "Jesus, I'm not going to *kill* you!"

Ms. Pierre continues sobbing as she softly nods her head, "Yes. You will. She has shown me. I just didn't know it would be this soon."

Confused and frightened by this sudden pivot, I keep my distance from Ms. Pierre as I soften my verbal approach and try to explain, "Look, I have no intentions of-"

Ms. Pierre snaps her focus towards me, "-*You* may not intend it, but this is what I'm trying to tell you... *neither* of us are in control of our fate anymore."

A million questions swirl through my head at once as I gently step towards Ms. Pierre in order to help her up. Though my motivations are not malicious in nature, she springs to her feet in response, flinching as she backs away from me with a look of sheer terror in her eyes.

I cease my approach with my hand still outstretched as I calmly say, "It's okay. I'm not going to hurt you."

Despite my assurance, Ms. Pierre continues backing away from me as she shakes her head, "You don't get it. *You* are not in control anymore. *They* are."

I feel my frustration continuing to build, "Who!?"

Ms. Pierre hesitates for a moment, as though she already knows I'm not going to believe her, "...Macha and Nemain. They are manipulating you."

Pursing my lips in offence, I once again yell at her, "I said, leave them out of this!"

Lifting her hands in a pathetic attempt to keep me at bay, Ms. Pierre says, "I know you don't want to believe me, but *they* are the ones who are-"

I subconsciously take another step towards her with a

furrowed brow, "-I'm warning you for the last time! Don't you *DARE* try to implicate those children!"

Ms. Pierre mirrors my movement once more, by taking another step backwards as she screams, "Stay back!"

Heeding her request, I once again hold my distance as I attempt to reassure her with soft words. However, in doing so, I can hear my tone taking on the very aggression I'm trying to suppress, "For the last time, I'm *not* trying to *hurt* you! Just *talk* to me!"

The growing vehemence of my tone incites even more fear in Ms. Pierre's eyes. She softly shakes her head as her lower lip begins to quiver once more, "It's too late. You can't stop them."

My jaw tightens as I feel literal warmth growing inside of me, fueling my already furious state. How dare this horrible woman attempt to place culpability upon the children that she has victimized with abuse! How dare she think that I would even consider subscribing to such a notion!

I step forward once more, this time in defense of the children as I yell out, "You can blame *me* for anything you want! You can even blame whatever bullshit *forces* you *claim* are at work! But I am warning you for the *last* time, leave those girls alone! They have *NOTHING* to do with this!"

Shaking her head in equal parts disagreement and fear, Ms. Pierre tries to push her position once last time, "But they are-"

I cut in, fueled by the fire that's coursing through my veins, "-You have repeatedly abused those children. You have broken them down, time and time again. Yet still, *somehow*, you have the audacity to claim that *they* are at fault for *your* actions!? You disgust me!"

Raising her quivering hands in protest, Ms. Pierre says, "That's not what I-"

Pursing my lips in anger, I continue my approach, as I yell, "-No! I've had *enough* of your lies! You can try to convince me of whatever bullshit you want, but I see you for the monster you really are! You are a *cancer* on this household, and I have had *enough* of your lies!"

Ms. Pierre continues retreating from me until her back is pressing against my bedroom window as she pleads, "Please. Stop.

I don't-"

I suddenly feel the warmth within me shift into a foreign strength, pushing my voice with a power I've never experienced before, as I scream, "-I said, *ENOUGH!!!*"

Whether it is a result of Ms. Pierre's shifting bodyweight, or the reprisal of my voice's newfound decibel level, every pane of glass in the immense window before me simultaneously shatters outwards.

I'm so lost in the spectacle of the moment that by the time I lower my gaze, Ms. Pierre is already falling backwards. I scramble to try to grab her hand before she falls, but miss her flailing arm by mere inches, leaving me standing over her as she plummets downward.

Ms. Pierre stares directly into my eyes with a look of terror that almost makes her descent seem to play out in a slow-motion ballet of thrashing limbs and shards of glass, falling in beautiful, yet tragic harmony.

However captivating the moment may be though, it is cut short when Ms. Pierre makes her sharp, violent impact on the crooked patio stones below. Based on the contorted position she lands in and her quickly pooling blood, it's abundantly clear that she's dead on impact.

As I stand in the open window frame, I feel the expressions of shock and horror upon my face. Yet, somewhere within the back of my mind, an inexplicable pang of satisfaction begins to fill my heart in reaction to the sight of Ms. Pierre's lifeless body and the fulfillment of my promise to the cloaked woman.

I try to shake any sense of victory from my body, but the more I try to fight it, the more it seems to amplify my sinister pleasure. I force myself to avert my gaze from the twisted corpse of my adversary, lifting my focus to the branches of the tree directly in front of me, but when I do, I find myself frozen in place.

Amidst the darkness of night, I see two glowing amber eyes staring back at me from within the shadowy branches of the immense oak tree. However, instead of experiencing the inherent fear that the crow's presence has typically incited in me, I feel warmed by its company.

Soon, I feel my facial muscles involuntarily shift, as my mouth curls into a dark smirk. Despite fighting the urge to find enjoyment in the moment, I soon find myself closing my eyes, raising my arms and taking a deep satisfied breath, bathing in the victory of the moment as though I were a gladiator at the Coliseum.

I feel dark arrogance coursing through my mind and body and am truly unable to tell if it is genuinely mine. Similar to when my consciousness had been trapped in Mrs. Morgan's body while giving birth, I am now being forced to play the role of unwilling spectator, only this time it is to the horrific egotism within my *own* body.

Slowly reopening my eyes, I suddenly find myself standing at the base of the immense oak tree, unsure of how I have gotten here.

At first, I almost feel thankful for this sudden shift of location, as it *must* mean that this is all just a dream. As I look down though, I see the sobering reality of tiny shards of glass, strewn all over the ground like miniature icebergs in the quickly forming red ocean of Ms. Pierre's blood as it continues to pool.

Looking to my left, I see the cloaked woman kneeling at the perimeter of the oak tree's root system, as she has done so many times before. Though her face remains hidden within the shadows of her hood, I can tell that her attention is directed towards something behind me, so I follow her gaze.

Pivoting around, I see Ms. Pierre's contorted body still lying on the crooked patio stones, her empty gaze still directed towards my bedroom's window frame, despite the odd angle of her neck.

Regardless of how badly I want to avert my eyes from the horrific imagery before me, I still find myself unable to control my physical form, and so my body forces me to take in the graphic sight.

However, it's then that something catches my eye.

The odd angle of Ms. Pierre's neck, as result of the harsh impact, has forced the top two buttons of her blouse to pop off, revealing the nape of her neck for the first time since I've known her.

Seeing it now, I feel a chill run up my spine as I notice something hanging there; a square pendant woven from straw, exactly like the ones that had been around the necks of the seven decaying women.

The simple sight of the pendant sends a wave of emotion washing over me as I suddenly realize that Ms. Pierre, the owner of the eighth, unclaimed bag, is now condemned to the same fate as her seven predecessors. She *was* telling the truth. She *is* Rosalie Pierre, and *I* have now trapped her within this home, for an eternity.

As the gravity of my actions begins to set in, I suddenly regain control of my body's functions. Dropping to my knees beside Ms. Pierre's body, I frantically check for a pulse that I already know isn't there.

Fruitlessly attempting to adjust her head so I can begin to administer CPR, I hear whatever part of her spinal cord that had remained connected, audibly snap, thus rendering any further attempts at resuscitation useless.

A mixture of emotion begins swirling through me as the clarity of the moment continues to reveal itself. Feelings of guilt, anger, sorrow, fear, regret and confusion flood through every fiber of my being as I turn to the cloaked woman and try to explain, "This is *not* what I wanted! This was an accident! I didn't mean to-"

The cloaked woman silences me by putting a single finger up towards her shadow-cast face. I heed her request, falling silent as she turns her focus towards the roots of the tree.

Following her gaze, I see the overgrown root system beginning to shift. Slowly, the tree extends its gnarled digits, coiling them around Ms. Pierre's body and gently lifting into the air as her square pendant begins to glow with a soft, white light, almost as though her spirit were now trapped within it.

Similar to my dreams, Ms. Pierre's body is gently carried by the roots, towards the base of the tree, where the ground opens to receive her. As she is lowered into the darkened depths of the Earth, the root system closes above her, extinguishing any signs of the light from her glowing pendant.

The accuracy of the imagery to what I had seen in my dream is haunting, to say the least. But when combined with the verification of Ms. Pierre's words in regards to 'the dreams' fore-telling her fate, I feel myself quivering in confused terror.

I turn back towards the cloaked woman, fearful of what might come next, but as my focus shifts to her, she simply mirrors my movement, returning my gaze in silence.

Despite my growing sense of dread, I hold my ground, certain that the glowing amber eyes from within the shadows of the cloaked woman's hood will begin to illuminate at any moment. However this time, that is not the case.

Instead, the cloaked woman slowly dips her head and moves her gnarled hands to either side of her hood, taking hold of the fabric so that she may slowly reveal herself to me.

At first, all I see is the thin patches of stringy silver hair atop her head as they are released from the confinement of the large hood, but soon, she lifts her face towards me.

Based on my previous dream, I naturally assume that an aged version of the spirit of Mrs. Morgan is beneath the darkened hood, but I soon feel the terror within my heart double, as the cloaked woman reveals her *true* face to me.

Despite age withering her visage, my sense of recognition im-mediately sets in, causing tears to form in my eyes along with a feeling of utter breathlessness in the face of this newfound dark truth.

The cloaked woman... is *me.*

CHAPTER THIRTY-THREE

Brigid's Cross

I jolt awake, gasping for air, only to find myself sitting in bed, the sun having already risen.

Temporarily blinded by the brightness of morning, I instinctually raise my arm to shield my eyes from the piercing beams of light as I try to gather my thoughts amidst the cloud of disorientation.

Unsure of how, or when, I had returned to my room, I soon feel the onset of a slight pounding in my head. The soft thrums slowly increase in severity as the images of my withered face upon the cloaked woman's body flash through my mind, along with the memory of Ms. Pierre slowly plummeting to her death.

Amidst the vivid, cycling images, I feel the guilt and fear return to me, anew. I try pushing away my memories of the horrific events, but it seems that the harder I try, the more visceral my emotions become and soon, the tears begin to flow.

I climb out of bed and move away from the distraction of the debilitating brightness, but as I do so, something catches my attention from the other side of the room.

Having been blinded by the sun's rays when I had first awoken, and then by my tears shortly after, I had not noticed until now that *somehow* my bedroom window appears to be fully intact; as though it had never been blown out by my inhuman scream. My mind races as I quickly realize that if that *is* the case, then Ms. Pierre never fell to her death either.

Skeptically, I move across the room, extending my hand so I can verify that the presence of the panes of glass is not just another false projection, courtesy of my failing mind. Sure enough, I soon feel the smooth surface; warmed by the light of the sun, press against my palm.

On any other day, the sensation would likely spawn a sense of blissful comfort; however in *this* moment all I feel is fear and confusion towards its existence.

Is it possible? Had I dreamt the whole thing? That can't possibly be true. Everything felt so visceral, so *real*.

Admittedly, this wouldn't be the first time my dreams had convincingly mislead me to believe they were true. Then again, it also wouldn't be the first time that, what I perceived to be conscious reality, fell victim to the incursion of hallucinations, driven by my subconscious mind.

How can I even try to discern whether *anything* is real or not, when I can't even tell what reality *is* anymore?

Stepping closer to the glass, I shade my eyes from the light of the sun so I can scan the broken patio stones below. Scrutinizing every inch of the back part of the property that is visible through the large oak's plumage, I can see no signs of dried bloodstains or circular impacts that would suggest someone had landed beneath my window.

My mind spins as it tries to process whether or not Ms. Pierre's death had actually occurred. While, emotionally, it still feels as though I had witnessed her demise only moments ago, logic seems to negate that theory by way of the substantive, contradictory reality I currently find myself in.

Thinking back over my memories of last night, I can't help but begin to wonder if *any* of it actually happened. Had I gone back to Pater's office? Had I finally called Ms. Pierre out on her crimes? Had I actually found Rosalie Pierre's driver's license?

Something in my mind clicks. I race towards the discarded jeans that I had been wearing last night, sitting in a pile of dirty clothes in the corner, and dig through the pockets to see if the driver's license is still there.

With each empty pocket I rifle through, the storm cloud of guilt within me dissipates further. I start to embrace the fact that Ms. Pierre's death *was* just another dream and immediately feel my heart beginning to swell with relief.

By the time I find the final pocket empty, I proceed to dig through the rest of the clothes, before releasing a liberating sigh as the absence of the license quickly dispels the destructive feelings and images that had been churning within me.

However, the moment of levity is short-lived.

I suddenly feel a wave of panic as I realize that *if* Ms. Pierre is still alive, she's likely downstairs, preparing breakfast for the children while simultaneously chomping at the bit to criticize how late I've slept in... again.

Quickly throwing on my uniform, I bound down the lengthy hallway with as much speed as I can, but as I reach the top of the staircase I suddenly freeze in place.

Cocking my head as I sniff the air, I can't help but notice the absence of the familiar stench of Ms. Pierre's beet porridge, a smell that had *consistently* haunted my olfactory senses every morning I had spent in this home.

While part of me wants to simply dismiss this alteration to the morning routine as a blessing in disguise, I can't help but feel the alarm bells of doubt going off in the back of my mind.

Hovering at the top of the stairs, I consider the infuriatingly consistent nature of Ms. Pierre's 'routine' and her undying aversion towards any deviations from it. I assure myself that she *must* be in the kitchen by this point of the day... unless something *did* happen to her.

The longer I remain in place, the more I become hyper-aware of the profoundly haunting silence throughout the household. I hear no sounds of clanking pots or knives clicking against a chopping board. No sounds of sharp footsteps on hardwood floors, or firm discipline being handed down to the children. Not even the sounds of a spoon occasionally grazing the side of a ceramic bowl amidst an uncomfortably silent meal.

As the feelings of fear and guilt begin building once more, I pivot around, hastily making my way back down the hall towards Ms. Pierre's room. As I do, I try to stave off my negative suspicions with moments of fleeting hope, telling myself there must be *some* sort of reasoning behind her absence, other than falling to her death.

By the time I reach her door, I find myself silently praying to every higher power I can name, that she has simply slept through the morning, like I did. However, deep in my heart, I know something *bad* must have happened, whatever that may be.

I adjust my smock, double-checking that my sleeves are pulled down to hide my scars before I gently knock on Ms. Pierre's door.

Waiting for a response, I can't help but feel a sense of nervous anticipation accelerating my heart. Were I even able to catch a *glimpse* of her signature scowl right now, it would alleviate immeasurable amounts of guilt, fear and regret.

A few seconds pass without an answer, so I knock a second time, telling myself that she's simply making me wait, as I had done each time she had knocked on my door.

Another handful of seconds passes by, still with no answer, and soon a sense of dread returns to the forefront of my mind.

Despite my better judgment, I reach out and grab the doorknob, twisting it before pushing the door open a crack and gently calling out, "Ms. Pierre?"

Hearing no answer, I continue to open the door, scanning the room as I do so, yet still, I see no signs of her.

Suddenly, the vivid images of Ms. Pierre falling from my window return to my mind, but I am quick to shake them from my head and convince myself that she's probably just collapsed somewhere that's out of my current line of sight.

Stepping further into the room with heightening urgency, I check the far side of the bed, and behind a chaise lounge near her window, but still, I see no signs of her; yet despite any evidence to back it up, I continue to coerce myself into believing that she *must* be alive, *somewhere*.

I'm about to leave Ms. Pierre's room to continue my fruitless search downstairs, when something suddenly steals my attention from the corner of the room.

Sitting on a small table, at the top of a pile of old books, I notice a familiar leather-bound cover, with the insignia of the Triquetra inside of a perfect circle, embossed upon it.

Whether it is my subconsciously driven opportunistic desires, or simply my mindlessness in the moment, I pick up Pater's journal and take it with me as I exit the room and make my way downstairs.

By the time I reach the main floor of the house, I realize that I am still surrounded by an uncomfortable level of silence, suggesting Ms. Pierre is nowhere near. Still, I play it safe by tucking Pater's journal into the back of my waistband before slowly pushing the kitchen door open and softly calling out, "Ms. Pierre?"

As predicted, I receive no response.

By the time the door is all the way open I find the kitchen empty, with no signs that *anyone* has been in there recently, let alone Ms. Pierre or the girls.

My eyes dance back and forth, disbelievingly, while my mind continues to churn in a tornado of thought. Desperately, I try to process my perceived reality against the tangible one that I am facing in the moment, hoping I can find *some* semblance of truth.

Opening one of the deeper drawers, I remove Pater's journal from my waistband and conceal it under a stack of dishtowels before moving to one of the kitchen windows. I scan the back portion of the Morgan property in the hopes of seeing Ms. Pierre attending to some yard work, but again, there are no signs of her.

Slowly, my eyes drift towards the roots of the immense oak tree. While they remain still, I can't help but feel like the gnarled roots at its base are silently mocking me amidst my struggle to decipher what's real.

Images of the tree consuming Ms. Pierre's body flash through my mind, but I quickly push them away, reminding myself that it *must* have all been a dream and there's bound to be a logical, grounded explanation for her absence.

My eyes suddenly widen as I consider the inevitable effects of old age. Frantically, I scan the back of the property once more, still finding it devoid of any signs of Ms. Pierre, so I bolt from the kitchen and sprint to the front door as fast as my frumpy uniform will allow.

Throwing the door open, I fully expect to find Ms. Pierre lying face down, in front of the Morgan home, gasping for air while in the midst of a heart-attack, or stroke.

However, as I run a few steps out into the clearing, frantically scanning the perimeter of the Morgan property, I see no signs of her anywhere.

After stubbornly scanning the entirety of the clearing a second, and third time, I finally surrender to my sense of defeat and head back inside.

Closing the front door behind me, I contemplatively make my way back to the kitchen as I consider where to look next. No matter how hard I try to focus on my search though, I can't help but feel distracted by tangential thoughts of Pater's Journal, almost as if it's *calling* to me.

Whether it's my morbid curiosity, or simply my need to distract my mind from the growing frustration, I proceed to open the drawer, push the dishtowels aside, and pull Pater's journal out, placing it on the counter.

Staring at the symbol of the Triquetra on the cover, I take a deep breath before picking up the book and fishing my index finger over the top edge to find the gap where I had left my lock pick as a bookmark.

Within half a second, I feel the small space between pages and flip the journal open, only when I do, it is not the lock pick that I see holding my place. Instead, I see the face of a young Rosalie Pierre looking up at me from her driver's license.

My fear quickly mounts its return as I realize that it *wasn't* a dream after all. With that fear, comes the pangs of guilt, not only in regards to what I've done, but towards all of the times that I had even *considered* the end of Ms. Pierre's life.

While my actions may not have been pre-meditated, the intent surely was. I had silently wished death upon Ms. Pierre countless times leading up to her actual demise. Even after she had fallen, I remember feeling myself *smile* at the sight of her twisted body.

Tears quickly well up in my eyes and I begin to audibly sob as I relive the whole experience in a matter of seconds. All the while, my logical brain spins its wheels as it tries to dissect the facts and negate what, my heart tells me, is the truth.

I slam my palms down on the counter in a fit of frustration towards my internal debate, and in the process, glance down to the page that had been marked in Pater's journal.

There, I see a familiar image staring back at me... the symbol of the square pendant, woven from straw; the one that I had seen on each of the decaying women... and Ms. Pierre's corpse.

I frantically scan over the passage beside the image in the hopes it will reveal anything grounded in fact, but instead, Pater rambles on about the glyph's 'true meaning'.

Pater refers to the image as, '*Brigid's Cross*', noting it is, '*commonly known as the Celtic symbol of motherhood*'. However, he then goes on to mention that its deeper significance may insinuate a much more literal take on, '*the giver of life*'.

Just as I am about to flip the page and continue reading, I hear the sounds of small footsteps in the upstairs hallway, moving towards the stairs. I quickly place Rosalie Pierre's laminate ID card back in Pater's journal before concealing it in the dishtowel drawer once more.

Wiping my eyes, I do my best to collect myself both emotionally and physically before turning towards the kitchen door to greet Macha and Nemain.

Both of the girls enter the kitchen tentatively, with looks of concern on their faces. Though I am desperately trying to suppress my own overwhelming sense of worry, I feel my face betray me, splaying my truth in spite of my efforts.

A few steps into the kitchen, Nemain asks, "Why didn't anyone wake us?"

Trying to keep my emotions in check, I drum up a gentle lie, "I'm sorry. I lost track of time. I was *just* coming to do that."

Nemain noticeably scowls at my response, as she looks me up and down scrutinizing the visible nervous tension that riddles every inch of my body before she asks, "Where's Ms. Pierre?"

I suddenly realize I have been so caught up in trying to answer that question for my own sake, that I hadn't even considered the children as part of the equation. What will I tell them? *How* will I tell them?

Frantically, I draw at the first available straw that comes into my mind, "She- uh- Ms. Pierre had to leave... Family emergency. She left me in charge."

I can tell that Nemain isn't buying my lie, but she says nothing to refute it in the moment.

Shifting gears, I move into a more nurturing tone, "Why don't you and Macha grab a seat at the table, and I'll get started on breakfast?"

Both Macha and Nemain apprehensively comply with my request, though Nemain keeps her eyes trained on me the whole way over to the table, and continues to do so, even after she's sat down.

Feeling her dissecting gaze upon me, I quietly make my way to the pantry and take a sigh of relief for having gotten through the initial round of explaining away Ms. Pierre's absence. While I am fully aware that the truth will eventually come out, at least now I've bought myself some time.

I quickly search the pantry for anything that might result in a suitable breakfast before making my way back to the kitchen and whipping up a batch of oatmeal with maple syrup, brown sugar and cinnamon, as well as two side plates of fruit; cut up and arranged to look like happy faces.

While it is, admittedly, a transparent attempt at appeasing the girls, I hope that providing a slight switch-up to 'the routine' will elicit enough distraction for them not to want to ask further questions about their missing matriarch; at least for now.

Despite the horrific images and memories that continue swirling in my mind, I swallow my fear in order to dramatically present breakfast, placing the dishes in front of each of the girls as I proclaim, "Today, we're doing breakfast *my* way."

In the moment, I expect that my efforts will result in reactions of surprised smiles from the girls, but instead, I receive the polar opposite.

Macha stares at her bowl of oatmeal quizzically, as though she's trying to understand what it is that she's looking at and why it has been placed in front of her. Nemain, on the other hand, is a little less tactful and proceeds to push both the bowl and plate away as she coldly says, "I don't want this."

I attempt a classic negotiation tactic, "How do you know? You haven't even tried it?"

Nemain takes a contemptuous sigh before reaching for the bowl, rolling her eyes with disdain, and shoving a spoonful of oatmeal into her mouth.

I wait for her eyes light up, as any child's would at the presence of sweetness. Instead, she gags, spitting out the contents of her mouth, before turning to me with venom in her eyes, as though I were attempting to poison her.

I try my best to win her back, "Okay, not a fan of the oatmeal. What about the fruit?"

Crossing her arms, she angrily repeats herself, "I. Don't. Want. This."

Still thinking I can win her over, I playfully make another attempt, "Just try it."

Without a moment's hesitation, Nemain screams, "I said, NO!!!"

As if to pontificate her stance, Nemain swipes her bowl away, sending it across the room with immeasurable force, causing it to explode against the far wall, leaving only a small glob of oatmeal to mark the point of impact.

While part of me instinctually wants to condemn such an action, I find myself frozen in shock at the sheer *force* of it.

Amidst my confusion, Nemain rises to her feet angrily and takes on a vehement tone as she repeats her previous inquiry, "*WHERE* is Ms. Pierre!?"

The firm tone of her question throws me further off balance, especially in the wake of the exploding bowl, so I try to maintain my original falsehood with a touch of patient authority in my voice, "I told you, Nemain. Ms. Pierre had a family emer-"

Before I even finish speaking, Nemain launches back at me, "-LIAR!"

Something about the growing power in her voice shifts my fearfulness from the confusing circumstances of last night's events, to the present moment. While I've seen my fair share of children with anger problems and habitual tantrums, I've never seen a child filled with *pure rage*, until now.

Unsure of how to even approach a response, I opt to forgo addressing Nemain's anger in the hopes of deflating it with inaction.

Carefully shifting my focus, I take a knee beside Macha and ask, "How would you feel about ditching classes today, and going outside to play instead?"

Macha's eyes light up at the idea before Nemain chimes in, "That's *not* what we're supposed to be doing! We're *supposed* to be learning! *Ms. Pierre* says-"

Doing my best to swallow my growing frustration and offense to her tone, I curtly answer, "-Ms. Pierre isn't here right now, Nemain! *I* have been left in charge! So we're trying something *different*, because *I* said so!"

My temporarily combative tone catches me off guard, and I immediately feel the guilt set in for having talked to a child in such a manner. As I turn towards Nemain, I see her frozen in a look of contemptuously shocked silence.

I feel the impetus to apologize, but find myself speechless in the wake of my emotional outburst. Only then do I notice how much my hands are quivering from adrenaline, in the wake of a temporary release from my swirling emotions.

Thankfully, Macha gently tugs on the cuff of my sleeve, breaking the tense silence and shifting my attention towards her.

Looking up at me with doe-like green eyes, she produces a small brown box from behind her back and silently presents it to me.

Confused, but welcoming of the gesture I take the box from her and say, "Is this for me?" off her nod, I make a point of emphatically saying, "Thank you, Macha."

With a smile on my face, I lift the box closer to me before slowly removing the top and looking inside. My eyes widen with terror when I see the box contains Brigid's Cross... a square pendant, woven from straw, and hung from a frayed string.

Reflexively recoiling at the sight of the necklace, I incidentally pitch the box across the table and onto the ground. The moment it makes contact with the floor, I realize what I've done and turn to see Macha's green eyes filled with anger and sadness in response to my fervent rejection.

Nemain charges towards the pendant, picking it up by its string and shaking it at me with anger, "Macha made this for *you*! You *have* to wear it!"

I desperately search for plausible reasoning to object to the idea, but my vocabulary fails me, leaving me stuttering a series of half words.

Seeing my struggle, Nemain seizes the opportunity to call me out on my apprehension, "Why don't you want to wear it, Patty?"

I scramble to come up with an answer, "It's not that I don't want to, I just-"

Nemain ignores my attempt at an explanation, taking on a sinister, all-knowing tone in the face of my discomfort, "-*Ms. Pierre* always wears hers. Why won't *you*?"

The more that Nemain's dark intent grows, the more I can feel panic and fear growing within me. Desperately I search for the words to express my feelings, but it seems as though the harder I try, the less I am able to verbalize any reasoning.

Finally, Nemain asks again, in an almost rhetorical tone, "*Where* is Ms. Pierre, Patty?"

Trying to hide my growing sense of trepidation, I attempt the same response I had used before, "For the last time, Nemain, Ms. Pierre had to leave for a fam-"

Nemain tightens her fists in response to my lie, as her face falls into a hardened scowl and she screams, "-TELL US THE TRUTH!!!"

The volume of Nemain's voice shakes the entire house with its power and I soon find myself flashing back to when my own scream had blasted out my bedroom window. In the moment, I had not only been confused by the sheer spectacle of the moment, but, more so, by the mysterious source of such power, as though some outside influence had momentarily taken control of my body.

Suddenly, my mind is flooded with memories of Ms. Pierre's outrageous claims, leading up to her demise. As I hear them now, I begin to wonder if they were the lies and false accusations that I had perceived them to be, or if they had, in fact, been truthful.

Ms. Pierre had *warned* me about the children, she claimed that they were not what they seemed to be, that they were *manipulating* me; that *they* were in control.

As I weigh the gravity of Ms. Pierre's words, I snap back into the present moment and suddenly notice that Macha has adopted the same scowl as her sister and is now standing at her side.

Amidst my exponentially growing panic, I try to find a way to shift the topic of conversation away from anything that will anger the girls further, "How about a little fresh air? We could go outside and-"

Before I can even finish the thought, I suddenly notice something shift in the composition of both Nemain and Macha's eyes. Where light green irises had once surrounded their pupils; there are now amber ones instead.

My body fills with terror as I try pleading for the children to calm down, but as I retreat from them, I soon feel my back make contact with the edge of the kitchen island, forcing me to freeze in place.

Slowly, Macha and Nemain approach, their eyes no longer simply taking on an amber hue, but *glowing*, in spite of the light of day.

As the intensity of the light in their eyes continues to grow, Nemain suddenly speaks in a voice that carries far too much power and authority to belong to a child her size, "*We know what you did. We know you killed Ms. Pierre.*"

While her indictment is jarring enough, the foreign properties of her voice are even more terrifying. It's almost as if she has suddenly become possessed by a spirit intent on utilizing her meek body as a vessel from which to launch its judgment of my transgressions.

Nemain continues, "*You need not lie, Patricia. We just want to hear you say it.*"

Something about the certainty in her tone fills me with shame, not only towards the act itself, but also towards my horrific attempt to pretend nothing was wrong. Soon my eyes fill with tears as I desperately profess, "I- I didn't mean to! It was an accident!"

Ceasing their approach, the brightness in both Macha and Nemain's eyes continues to intensify, masking their pupils and eye sockets with blinding light. I avert my gaze, trying to shield my eyes from them, but soon I hear a familiar sound that sends a shiver up my spine... a soft tapping at the kitchen window.

I suddenly take notice of a large crow that has perched itself on the outside ledge so as to spectate upon the events unfolding within the Morgan home. However, as the creature cocks its head, I feel my fear double as I notice that its eyes are *also* glowing with the same amber light.

Turning back towards the girls, I see Nemain tilt her head

patronizingly as she asks, "*You thought about it, didn't you, Patricia? You <u>wanted</u> her dead. You <u>enjoyed</u> killing her, just admit it. It's not the first life you've taken. Nor will it be the last.*"

I shake my head to negate her statement, but deep down I know she's at least *partially* right. I *did* think about it. I *did* want it. I *did* cause Andy's death, and yes, I *did* find momentary enjoyment in Ms. Pierre's. But I would never *dream* of taking another life, no matter the circumstances.

Macha slowly raises her hand and I hear the sound of a drawer opening behind me. Within seconds, I watch with confusion as Pater's Journal sails across the room to be received by her open palm.

Nemain's sinister grin grows as she says, "*Did you sincerely think you would find the answers you seek in <u>there</u>? Pater was a fool. He had no understanding of his place in all of this. Don't worry though… soon you shall learn yours.*"

My mind scrambles, as it tries to find an explanation to the gravity of Nemain's words but despite my efforts, all I keep coming back to is Ms. Pierre's echoing claim, '*they are not children*'.

Feeling an overwhelming sense of panic wash over me, I pivot and try to run from the kitchen, but before I can reach the door, my body suddenly pitches backwards.

Summersaulting through the air, I land on the kitchen table with enough force that all of its legs simultaneously give way beneath me, knocking out what little wind was left in my lungs from the first impact.

Disoriented and dizzied, I open my eyes with an upside down perspective of both Macha and Nemain approaching from across the room as the crow outside the window shifts to a closer ledge.

My brain thumps within my skull as my vision begins to blur. I try to retain what little consciousness I still possess in order to fight off, what I fear, might be the end.

Amidst my fleeting consciousness, I see the faded image of Macha taking a knee beside me to gently hang Brigid's Cross around my neck. Within seconds, I see the glow of soft white light emitting from the pendant as something shifts inside of me.

Soon, I notice my wakefulness melting away much more rapidly, almost as though some outside influence is *guiding* me towards a subconscious state.

My vision continues to fade as I look up at the glowing amber eyes of the girls standing over me. With what little energy I have left, I ask, "What *are* you?" but before I am able to receive an answer, everything fades to black and I feel my body concede.

From somewhere within the void of nothingness though, one word echoes through my mind... '*Morrighan*'.

CHAPTER THIRTY-FOUR

Pater and The Morrighan

Wisps of ethereal light emerge from the darkness, slowly filling my field of vision as the imagery before me begins to take form.

My nostrils are invaded with the smell of salt and rot, followed by the sounds of rhythmically creaking wood, and the methodical pounding of turbulent waters.

Before the vision even finishes taking form, I realize that I am in the hull of the ship that Pater Morgan had stowed away upon, while making his journey to the New World.

I try to sit up, but similar to my vision within Mrs. Morgan's body, I find myself trapped as an unwilling spectator to this tale.

As my projected reality comes into focus, the body I am encapsulated within suddenly jolts awake, gasping for air. I experience every moment of their breathlessness as if it were my own.

My host quickly scans their surroundings, revealing a tight little niche amidst a stack of crates, fully concealed from any wandering eyes.

Only once I notice the leather bound book, with an embossed Triquetra inside a perfect circle upon its cover, do I realize that I am seeing this vision through Pater Morgan's eyes.

Confused, Pater rises to his feet and feels a soft thrumming in his head, which I share the sensation of. Despite the sudden onset of the painful distraction though, a much softer sound seems to cut through all of the noise and steal his attention... the sound of a woman crying, somewhere within the hull of the ship.

I try to will Pater to not follow it, but once again I find myself forced to helplessly watch as he navigates through the darkness, foolishly seeking out the source of the sorrowful sound.

Finally, Pater comes across a pile of corpses carelessly discarded atop one another. I experience his bafflement towards the gruesome sight, while simultaneously identifying them, in my own mind, as the bodies that will eventually save his life.

On the far side of the pile, faintly lit by a kerosene torch, is a young woman kneeling, crying into her hands, her face hidden from view.

While my previous vision had shown Pater surviving this trip with a woman he had met upon the ship, I find myself wary towards the uncomfortably familiar nature of her mannerisms.

Despite my continued attempts to fight against Pater's instincts, he continues to approach the young woman, kindly asking her if there is, 'anything he can do' while warning her that, 'a ship at sea is not a safe way for a woman to travel alone'.

Though she keeps her head downcast, the young woman stifles her tears, as if to silently acknowledge Pater's presence.

Taking it as an invitation, Pater kneels beside her and asks, "Did you know them?"

The young woman remains silent, but gently tilts her head, insinuating that she heard the question, but doesn't want to answer.

Sharing in her moment of mourning, Pater softly asks, "What happened to them?"

The young woman whispers, in a barely audible tone, "...*see*".

Panic washes over me as I realize that this is the cloaked woman in disguise. I try to warn Pater from within his own head, but he is either impervious to my influence, or purposely ignoring the voice in the back of his mind.

The young woman repeats herself, increasing her volume and hissing, "*See.*"

I experience Pater's growing confusion as though it were my own. I try to focus all of my energy on willing him to run away, but before he is able to, the young woman quickly seizes his arm with the gnarled digits of a much older woman's hand.

Pater glances at her withered and blistered fingers with fearful bafflement before turning back towards her face to see it has been replaced with the shadowy hood of a dark cloak.

The cloaked woman's grip tightens as she repeats herself once more, "*SEE!*"

Suddenly, Pater's and my shared lungs unwillingly empty

themselves, leaving us gasping for air but unable to draw a single breath.

Pater's head snaps upwards to see a thick fog churning over itself as it quickly descends, surrounding us with a storm cloud of imagery as our shared mind is filled with a cacophony of dark visions, flashing by in jarringly off-tempo successions.

At first, I see flashes of the ship's crew, quickly losing their grips on sanity. En masse, they begin to exhibit the onset of several schizophrenic symptoms with growing severity.

Some maniacally laugh themselves into catatonic states, while others exhibit paranoid hallucinatory symptoms, the majority though develop compulsive ticks that result in the methodical removal of their own hair, teeth and eventually, skin.

As their acts of self-harm amplify exponentially over a matter of seconds, Pater and I begin experiencing the waves of unjustified paranoia, disorienting confusion, horrific fear and pure rage that the crewmembers are enduring.

For a moment, it feels as though the swirling emotions within us are echoing the turbulence of the sea we're sailing upon, but it's then that the vision takes an even darker turn.

Amidst the plague of madness I watch, as the crewmembers begin turning on one another, not only resorting to acts of violence and murder, but mutilation, cannibalism and necrophilia as well.

In one such projection, I watch four crewmembers surround a much smaller man, beating him within half an inch of his life. Once he is subdued, they strap him to the deck of the ship and purposely keep him conscious as they take turns feasting on the upper portion of his body while satisfying themselves with his lower half.

All the while, the pungent smell of disease and septic rot continues to intensify, stinging Pater's nostrils with its unwelcomed presence as our ears begin ringing with the endless chorus of screams from the collective mental collapse of the crew.

Just as it all becomes too much to bare, the vision jumps forward, now showing us images of the tempestuous waters, and the fast approaching rocky shore.

The Captain holds position at the helm, intent on wrecking the ship, seemingly with no regard for his own life, let alone those of his skeleton crew that remains upon it.

Laughing in the face of death, the Captain's eyes become wild with destructive intent, but seconds before the ship meets its demise, the vision fades to darkness.

The feeling of terror towards the inevitable fills both Pater and I to our core as we hear the deafening sound of the ship running aground, being torn to pieces by the serrated shoreline in the process.

In the wake of the impact, we share the horrific sensation of our limbs being torn from our body, accented by the smell of fire and thick smoke filling our lungs, and choking us before we can scream.

We simultaneously gasp for air between coughing fits, when I suddenly notice the taste of bitter, salty water in Pater's mouth. Seconds later, his throat fills with seawater from within and we begin drowning.

As my panic reaches its echelon, I am suddenly released from the vision and brought back to the hull of the ship, free of Pater's body. While my concern for my own survival begins to subside, I notice that Pater is still on his knees, still drowning.

I feel the instinct to beg the cloaked woman to free him, but before I am able to utter a word, Pater suddenly snaps out of the vision, falling forwards and coughing up a throat full of seawater as he fights to breathe.

Watching the pool of saltwater trickle to the left, I suddenly realize that the pile of crewmembers' bodies has somehow disappeared; seemingly with no trace they were ever there to begin with.

It's then that I hear Pater begin unabashedly bawling on the ground. I turn back towards him to see that he is curled up in a fetal position and begging, as he had in his cell, "Please. Help me escape this horrid fate."

The cloaked woman says nothing in response to Pater's request, and amidst the strained silence, he begins slowing his sobs.

With a tone full of regret and shame, Pater reluctantly pleads, "Promise to spare my life, and it shall forever be pledged to thee...

Morrighan."

My heart skips a beat as I think back to the table in the 'salon' and realize that the word was *not* an archaic spelling of the Morgan name, as I had assumed it to be, but in fact, the *name* of the cloaked woman.

The Morrighan slowly reaches out with her spindly fingers and rests her hand upon Pater's shoulder, bringing him into an upright position. Leaning towards him, she exhales her wishes into his ear.

I watch as Pater's eyes widen with terror in response to her inaudible request. New tears begin streaming from his eyes as he gently shakes his head, while looking at the empty space where the pile of dead bodies had been, only moments ago.

The Morrighan pulls away from Pater's ear and proceeds to point upwards, to the deck of the ship, as she hisses, "*Save them.*"

For a moment, I feel confusion, for when I had received the same instructions, I had assumed it was in reference to Macha and Nemain, but under this new context, I begin to understand the much darker nature of the Morrighan's request.

She is instructing Pater to '*save*' the crew from their suffering form of mortality, to trade *their* lives for his own.

Pater's face shifts, already regretting the words he is about to say as he quietly mutters through his tears, "...I pledge my life to thee."

The vision of Pater and the Morrighan then dissipates, and within seconds, a new one materializes before my eyes, this time, an outside perspective of the rocky shore, hours after the ship's crash.

Smells of thick smoke and saltwater fill the air as I hear the sounds of the few surviving crewmembers screaming in excruciating pain, their lungs slowly filling with seawater as their bodies are repeatedly smashed against the jagged rocks.

From a distance I see Pater crawling out of the ship's wreckage with barely a scratch upon him. While he seems to be in good physical standing, something about his erratic mannerisms suggest that, between the prior vision and now, he has fallen deep into the void of his own mental collapse.

As he gets himself free of the wreckage, Pater turns around

and offers his hand to someone, only this time... there is no one there.

Slowly navigating his way up the rocky shore, Pater keeps his hand curled in a manner that would suggest he is holding someone else's; all the while he gently coaxes his invisible companion up the embankment of jagged rocks with words of care and encouragement.

In the moment, I feel empathy towards his hallucinatory state. I can't help but think back to Macha's visits and how I had been so *certain* she was speaking to me, only to learn from the video I had captured that she wasn't even there to begin with.

Shaking the thought from my mind, I try to at least find solace in the fact that Pater is seemingly blissful in his madness, but I am immediately proven wrong.

Halfway up the rocks, Pater stops to look down at a member of the crew who is splayed out awkwardly, bleeding into the salty waters of the ocean.

In my previous vision I had assumed that Pater was mourning the loss of this man. But in *this* version, I hear the crewmember's voice, pleading with Pater to show him mercy and end his suffering.

For a moment, it appears as if Pater is going to oblige the man's request, but as he reaches his hands out to do so, he hesitates, suddenly cocking his head to the left.

There, the Morrighan appears over Pater's shoulder, whispering in his ear as she had in the hull of the ship.

Upon her request, Pater's face shifts into a cold stare as he looks back down at the man who is suffering at his feet and stomps on his wounded leg, amplifying the poor man's agony exponentially.

The injured crewmember releases a bloodcurdling scream, and with it comes ethereal fumes of softly glowing white light that float up from the crewmember's body and drift into the shadowy hood of the Morrighan.

As the vision of the rocky shore fades away, I learn the Morrighan's true intent. She feeds off of *suffering*. *That's* why the crew fell into violent madness. *That's* why she enlisted Pater's help to '*save them*' from mortality. She was *satiating* herself in order to survive the journey to a new land.

A new vision begins to take form, this time displaying the image of the Morgan home in its infancy, and Pater feverishly working away in front of it.

Contrary to the environment of solely oak trees that I have come to know, the clearing surrounding the house is now lush with a wide variation of plant life. While I find the deviation puzzling, to say the least, I soon notice something different in Pater as well.

As if to contradict the pleasant nature of when I had seen him with his pregnant bride, Pater's eyes are now wild with compulsive obsession. Endlessly, he toils away, seemingly paying no mind to the blood-soaked bandages that cover his hands, let alone his need for sustenance or sleep.

Time elapses and I watch as, in a matter of seconds, Pater becomes increasingly emaciated and littered with wounds from his endless laboring while the Morgan home evolves into completion behind him.

Only once the house is finished, does Pater finally subside to his exhaustion and collapse into a heap. Only then is he finally allowed to rest. Only then does the Morrighan appear at his side, lifting him into the air and carrying him into the monument he has constructed for her.

As the front door closes behind them, the vision fades once more, shifting to an overhead view of Pater sitting at his desk. Based on his healed wounds and the length of his hair, it is clear that a good amount of time has passed.

Feverishly, Pater scrawls notes into his journal, surrounded by countless sketches of various Celtic symbols, including the Triquetra, and Brigid's Cross. As he does so, he continuously glances towards his office door with paranoid anxiety as though he is expecting someone to arrive at any moment.

Suddenly, a faint noise causes Pater to perk up, freezing in place. After a second of consideration, he quickly rises from his desk, slamming the journal closed, before making his way out of the office with a heightened sense of purpose.

My perspective instinctually follows Pater down the long

upstairs hallway, floating behind him as he bounds down the stairs and throws the front door open.

From just over Pater's shoulder, I see countless amber dots surrounding the moonlit clearing in front of the Morgan home. I feel a wave of panic as I initially assume they are the eyes of hundreds of malicious crows, but that panic soon dissipates when I realize the lights are not glowing, but *flickering*.

My sense of relief is short-lived though, and it is quickly replaced with overwhelming concern as I recognize that the lights are coming from countless torches, quickly approaching the Morgan home.

Nearly a hundred people, presumably settlers from the surrounding area, march through the forest and into the clearing with a unified thirst for vengeance in their eyes as they viciously call Pater's name.

The townspeople encircle the house as Pater steps through the front door making a feeble attempt to calm the angry mob. Before he can speak though, an older man near the front of the crowd, presumably the leader, steps forward to yell, "Where are they, Pater!?"

Lifting his hands in a peacekeeping manner, Pater says, "I don't have your children!"

Suddenly an older woman from the mob steps forward, her rage only slightly stifled by her tears as she screams, "Yes you do! I saw it! We *all* saw it!"

Pater makes a futile attempt to negate the accusation, "I know you *think* you did, but it is not the *truth*, I-"

Before Pater can finish his explanation, his voice is drowned out by the countless others yelling back at him.

The leader lifts his hand, silencing the mob before turning back to Pater, with a warning, "If you do not return our children, we will *burn* this home to the ground, along with *you* and that damned *witch* you serve!"

Pater begins to flounder, frantically pleading with the mob, "Please! She is tricking you! She is making you *think* they are missing, but I promise you, your children are *safe*! It's *you* that she's after!"

The leader of the mob takes a deep breath to prepare a response, but before he is able to verbalize his retort, a younger man from the back of the crowd calls out, "LIAR!!!" before launching his torch towards the home.

Both Pater and I watch as the orange flame cartwheels through the air, smashing through one of the front windows. Moments later, it is joined by countless others that begin coming in from all angles.

Pater desperately pleads with the mob, "Please! Stop! You don't understand what you're doing!"

The flames in and around the Morgan home grow, illuminating the faces of the mob as they exhibit vindictive smiles in the warm, orange glow of the destructive inferno.

While I see a look of fear upon Pater's face, his stillness tells me that it is not directed towards the state of the home he had worked so hard to build, but instead towards what he knows is coming in retaliation to this attack.

The light of the fire enveloping the Morgan home slowly begins to dim as the flames inexplicably extinguish themselves. In the fading light of the dwindling inferno, I see a look of confusion wash over the faces of the mob as they look to one another with bafflement.

Seconds after the last of the flames go out, the entire perimeter of the clearing suddenly sets ablaze, encircling the angry mob with the very fires they had cast upon the home.

A few of the townspeople instinctually attempt retreat, only to be vaporized by the intensity of the flames, cutting their screams of excruciating pain short.

As though they are fueled by fear, the fire begins encroaching upon the mob, forcing them into an uncomfortably tight grouping.

Pater's expression then shifts to sadness as he drops to his knees and pleads into the air, "You don't have to do this! They are *innocent* people!"

From behind Pater, the Morrighan suddenly appears in the front doorway of the home. Slowly and methodically, she moves towards the townspeople, crossing through the flames, unscathed, drawing the attention of the mob, and causing them to fall silent with terror.

Pater tries begging with her once more, "Please! There *must* be another way!"

Turning her head to the side, the Morrighan silences Pater with a single glance, making him sag with regretful subservience.

Snapping her attention back to the townspeople, the Morrighan spreads her arms and tilts her shadowy hood upwards. I immediately recognize it as the same position my body took after Ms. Pierre fell from my window.

By the will of the Morrighan, the angry mob suddenly turns on one another with blinding rage. Savagely, they attack each other, severing limbs, and tearing the flesh off the bodies of their comrades.

Unbeknownst to them, their acts of violence release countless ethereal waves of softly glowing white light, floating from the mutilated bodies of the dead, towards the Morrighan's hood to strengthen her with their suffering.

The mob's leader remains frozen in place, untouched by the others, but forced to witness his people's demise for his enemy's gain. As the last body falls, he stands amongst the pile of gore that was once his compatriots, his face filled with fury.

However, instead of launching himself at his enemy, the leader inexplicably turns towards the Morrighan and begins brazenly laughing in her face.

Pater shakes his head, trying to tell the man to stop, but the leader continues his act of defiance as he produces a silver blade from within his robes and suddenly holds it to his own throat, saying, "This is one soul you shall *not* claim."

As a final act of protest, the leader of the mob attempts to take his own life, but before his blade can break skin, the Morrighan raises her hand, stopping him in the act as she slowly steps towards him and his eyes widen with fear.

Pater calls out once more from behind her, "Spare him! I beg you!"

Ignoring Pater's plea, the Morrighan reaches out with a gnarled finger, and touches the mob leader's forehead.

I watch in horror as his face contorts into a state of paralyzed, twisted fear. Within seconds, his life drains from him, turning his skin ghost pale and immortalizing the terrified expression with which he perished.

As the Morrighan turns away from her victim, the fires move inwards, swallowing the mob's remains before extinguishing themselves, leaving only a pile of ash where they had been.

Pater slowly approaches the edge of the burnt circle, dropping to his knees with a sense of defeat as he places his right hand on the pile of ashes where the mob's leader had stood, only moments ago.

With his head bowed, Pater's breathing becomes audibly heavier. Though I am no longer witnessing these events from his perspective, I can feel his growing rage, as though it were my own.

Suddenly, Pater gets to his feet, turning to the Morrighan to scream, "No more!!!"

The Morrighan's back straightens in response to Pater's disobedience, prompting her to pivot around to face him.

Standing his ground, Pater yells, "I refuse to do your bidding any longer!"

The Morrighan approaches him, saying nothing, merely intimidating her servant by way of her presence, but instead of backing down from the dark spirit that controls him, Pater defiantly remains in place.

Reaching out, the Morrighan places her gnarled hand upon Pater's shoulder, causing him to fall to his knees once more, seemingly powerless against her influence. While it is a convincing act of subservience, Pater's charade is short lived.

Grabbing the Morrighan's wrist with his left hand, Pater then seizes the silver blade from beneath the ashes with his right, driving it into the Morrighan's heart.

In response to his betrayal, Pater is suddenly launched into the air, over the roof of the immense house and out of sight, as the Morrighan releases a relentless, piercing cry that makes my ears ring.

I watch as she tries to remove the blade from her chest, but with each attempt at grasping it, her gnarled hands seem to burn on contact with the silver that the weapon is comprised of.

Before long, a blinding white light begins to emit from the Morrighan's wound, seemingly tearing her apart from the inside as she falls to her knees. The weaker she gets, the more unbearable the white light becomes, along with her steadily intensifying painful cries.

Shielding my eyes from the blinding light, I hear one final deafening scream before a shockwave of energy shoots outwards from the Morrighan's location.

Lowering my arm, I slowly turn towards where the Morrighan had perished to see three small amber orbs hovering in her place.

In the light of their faint glow, I see that the vegetation that had once surrounded the Morgan home has now all withered and died, as though the shockwave of energy that the Morrighan had released was comprised of pure poison.

The three glowing orbs begin slowly circling one another. As I watch their movements, I come to realize that it is a result of their sentient resistance against an invisible force that is trying to pull them apart.

Despite their efforts, one of the orbs suddenly breaks free and is propelled away from the clearing, momentarily illuminating the desecrated branches of the dead forest as it disappears into the distance.

The other two orbs remain successful in their defiance though, and begin to slow their circling movements as their light begins to dissipate. Soon, they are replaced by the image of two young girls standing in the middle of the clearing.

Taking each other's hand, the two girls proceed to skip towards the Morgan home, and while I am unable to see their faces, I know they are Macha and Nemain.

My perspective instinctually follows them, drifting in the wake of their path all the way to the sunroom at the back of the house, just off the salon.

There, I find myself frozen, standing mere inches from the panes of glass, as I have so many times before. Only now, where the immense oak tree *should* be, I see Pater's lifeless body.

Scanning the patio stones around him, I soon notice that they are cracked and dilapidated as a result of the immeasurable force of his impact, negating my initial suspicion that the oak tree had done this damage over time.

I feel the natural instinct to mourn Pater, but before I am able to, the sight of Macha and Nemain approaching his body, and kneeling at his side, distracts me.

The girls gently place their hands upon Pater's body as the ground begins to violently shake. I watch as the earth beneath Pater opens up, swallowing his body and from the void into which he disappears, an immense oak tree suddenly sprouts up, aging as rapidly as it is emerging from the ground.

My eyes follow the quickly developing plumage of the oak's canopy, and I see, what looks like, millions of tiny glowing seeds being cast outwards over the landscape.

As the miniature glowing lights descend to the ground, countless other small oak trees instantly begin to sprout up, replacing any and all plant life that had once dwelled in the area.

While I marvel at the oak tree colonization, I soon feel my focus pulled towards the faint sound of someone knocking on a door behind me. I pivot towards the source of the noise, causing my perspective to naturally drift towards the front of the Morgan home.

When the door opens, I am temporarily blinded by the light of day, but as my eyes adjust I see a young woman standing in the archway, holding an old suitcase, coated in tan burlap with a brown leather trim.

Based on the young woman's attire, I can tell that a good handful of decades have passed between the story of Pater's demise and the one I'm currently seeing.

The young woman politely introduces herself, "Good morning. My name is Dorothy. I received your letter."

Dorothy holds up a discolored envelope, and I immediately recognize the flawless penmanship upon it, used to write, '*Miss Dorothy McNabb*'.

My perspective slowly pulls back, to reveal Macha and Nemain standing at either side of the door, welcoming her into the home.

Similar to what I had done on my first day, Dorothy marvels at the grandeur of the estate as she enters the vestibule, clearly taken aback by the palatial nature of the home.

However, I find myself more focused on Macha and Nemain in the moment, as they share a sinister smile with one another behind Dorothy's back.

Soon, the girls follow Dorothy further into the home as Macha produces a necklace from behind her back with Brigid's Cross hanging from it.

As the door slowly closes behind them, the vision fades to darkness and I realize *this* is how it all began.

CHAPTER THIRTY-FIVE

The Ninth

My eyes slowly drift open to reveal my bed's silk canopy, gently billowing above me. I remain on my back, watching its gentle movements as I roll over the visions I have just been shown, evaluating the gravity of this new truth.

Thoughts of Pater's willful subservience in the name of self-preservation fills me with pity at first. However, as I weigh the consequences of my own actions, I soon feel that pity replaced by shame, realizing I wouldn't even be here, were it not for my decision to flee my parents' home, the first chance I saw.

At the time, it had seemed like the most volatile environment I could have possibly been surrounded by, but little did I realize I would sacrifice everything in the process of trying to save myself from it.

I feel a wave of hatred towards myself as I think back to Ms. Pierre's *repeated* attempts at coercing me to leave, and how I had stubbornly remained against her wishes, as though I were trying to prove that my, otherwise, empty life was worth something.

As I think of it now, I lament how foolish I was to have finally found a sense of purpose through a dream. I had *fully* subscribed to the falsified idea that I was *destined* to save Macha and Nemain from Ms. Pierre's abusive tendencies.

Never in my wildest dreams would I have guessed that Ms. Pierre was the *victim* all along.

With abhorrence, I reflect on each of my miniature revolts against the only woman who was trying to save me. I had let her avoidance of the truth cloud my perception with suspicions of the buried history of a family that never existed. I had become fixated on finding answers when there were none to be found, all the while fueled by morsels of fictional evidence created in the depths of my subconscious.

I had become *obsessed*… the same way that Pater had *obsessed* over his journal and drawings. *That's* what Ms. Pierre was talking about when she said this house '*changes people*'.

Pater had been bound to the Morrighan by the blood oath he made in the hull of the ship, and in the wake of his betrayal, he had inadvertently cursed this land. Anyone who had dared to enter this home would fall under the Morrighan's binding spell, as countless others had, prior to Ms. Pierre.

That's why she was so obstinate towards the idea of being replaced. *That's* why she refused to leave Macha and Nemain's side. Ms. Pierre *had* to be near them. Not only for the sake of her *own* survival, but *theirs* as well. They were feeding off her life energy, sapping it through the Brigid's Cross pendant, hanging from her neck.

I suddenly move my hand to the nape of my own neck and feel my heart skip a beat as my fingertips immediately feel the rough texture of woven straw. As soon as I feel the pendant there, my memories of what happened in the kitchen come flooding back to me with force.

Bolting upright, I see Macha and Nemain standing at the foot of my bed, their eyes still softly glowing with amber light as they await my return to consciousness.

Seeing my sudden movement, Nemain begins to speak in the same formidable tone she had used in the kitchen, carrying ages of wisdom and dark intent, "*We have awaited your arrival for some time, Patricia. Though, admittedly, we had not expected you to dispose of Ms. Pierre so promptly.*"

I remain frozen, unsure of how to respond as tears begin welling up in my eyes.

Noticing my apprehensive silence, Nemain continues, "*Shhh… you needn't worry about Rosalie, nor anyone that came before her. They were merely expendable rations, sustaining us until the time of your arrival. You are the one we've been waiting for.*"

My voice trembles as I ask, "Why me?"

Grinning to herself, Nemain explains as she approaches the right side of the bed, "*I should clarify. This has nothing to do with you as an individual… rather it is your timing that makes you special,*" *for you are the <u>Ninth</u>.”*

At first I feel confused, but then Ms. Pierre’s explanation of the Triquetra flashes through my mind, prompting me to echo her words, “The power of three.”

Nemain nods in agreement, *“There is an inherent strength in the number, upon which <u>all</u> of existence is built by deities such as ourselves. Pater foolishly assumed he could undo our existence with a mortal weapon, but he merely delayed the inevitable by fracturing us into these... <u>terse</u> forms. It was merely a matter of time before we gathered enough power to unify once more.”*

As it all comes together, tears stream from my eyes, “Three souls for three pieces.”

Seemingly impressed with my correct assumption, Nemain turns to me before she continues, *“As the ninth, <u>you</u> are our final piece. <u>You</u> shall be the entity that makes us whole again. <u>You</u> shall be the vessel of true power.”*

I feel my jaw instinctually clench in both resistance and fear. I gather a feigned sense of courage, and even though I feel like I’m trying to stare down the Devil himself, I obstinately ask, “And what if I refuse?”

Nemain’s face washes of all kindness. For a moment, I assume she is going to psychokinetically hurl me across the room as she had before, but then I hear another voice say, *“The only choice you have is whether or not you will give yourself to us willingly.”*

My eyes widen with shock and confusion as I realize the second voice has come from Macha. The mere contrast of her petite physique against such a darkly powerful voice causes my fear to double as her words send a shiver down my spine.

With a smirk of dark confidence, Macha continues while moving to the left side of the bed, her glowing eyes trained upon me, *“The moment you entered this home, you were bound to us. You silently pledged your mind, body and soul to our re-unification. Now you bare the mark of the Life Giver, making the circle complete.”*

Instinctually, I shake my head in response to the idea that I have been unconsciously subscribed to a fate I was unaware of, but as I consider Macha’s declaration, I begin to realize that all of the signs had been right in front of me all along. My quickly aging visage, the over protectiveness of children I barely knew, and of course, the drastic shift in the imagery of my dreams.

For years prior to coming here, I had experienced the same recurring nightmare about Andy and the accident. While those dreams had haunted me nightly with horrifically vivid images, they were merely memories, amplified by guilt, playing on loop.

It was only once I had come to the Morgan home that the recurring nature of my dream had finally deviated, pushing me away from my past, and pulling me towards a fixation upon the new visions that were being shown to me each night.

As the imagery of those dreams became exponentially more vivid over time, they blurred the line between reality and fiction. Naturally, I had assumed that it was my own mind that was breaking, but now I see the truth.

Macha and Nemain have been inside my head from the moment I arrived, witnessing my memories, altering my thoughts, *manipulating* me, just like Ms. Pierre had said.

As if to verify my suspicion of their abilities, Macha takes my hand in hers as she says, *"We showed you what you needed to see, in order to arrive at this moment."*

Nemain then takes my other hand as she mirrors her sister's comforting tone, *"We know you felt as though you were being plagued with confusion and fear, but that was not the case. They were becoming a <u>part</u> of you, weaving themselves into the very fiber of your being. Soon, you shall learn their true power."*

Still resistant to their grand scheme, I try to pull my hands away from Macha and Nemain, but quickly feel their grip tighten.

Incredulously, I turn to them with anger in my voice, "Let me GO!"

The light in Macha's eyes intensifies as she announces, *"Misperception shall be your shield. Terror, your sword."*

Nemain's eyes then intensify as well, *"We shall make you a <u>God</u>. Give yourself to us, Patricia."*

I try to pull my hands free once more, but Macha and Nemain keep me pinned to the mattress from either side with minimal effort, as though I'm being crucified with ease.

The light in Nemain's eyes continues to intensify as she lifts her free hand to reveal that it is now the gnarled, twisted hand of the Morrighan. Gently, she places a single talon-like fingernail upon my wrist, dancing it over my scar, as she says, "*Come now. You were close to ending it all once. What more do you have to live for?*"

As the sun quickly fades outside my window, the room begins to shake amidst the sudden onset of night. I turn towards Macha and see that she too, has developed one of the Morrighan's twisted hands.

Macha's grip on my wrist tightens so hard that I can feel my bones bending as she continues the appeal to my weaker instincts, "*You have been kind to us, Patricia. Let us return the favor. Give yourself willingly, and we shall show mercy in your final days.*"

Futilely, I fight them with every ounce of energy I have left, "Why should I? You're just going kill me anyway!"

The shaking of the room continues to strengthen as Macha leans in towards me to darkly whisper, "*Yes... But we can make you suffer first.*"

Suddenly, I feel a pain in my wrist and I turn to see Nemain dragging her jagged, talon-like nail over my scar, slicing open the wound. Soon, the palm of my hand feels warm and wet as my blood flows over it, spilling onto the floor.

Squeezing my arm so as to amplify the blood flow, Nemain's voice grows louder, "*You shall be the personification of our singular existence!*"

I then feel a pain in my other wrist and turn to see Macha mirroring her sister's actions as she proclaims, "*You shall make the world bend their knee in subservience to our will! You shall be the Queen of Nightmares! The Harbinger of Fear!*"

Screaming in excruciating pain and immeasurable terror, I continue trying to fight against the inhuman strength of Macha and Nemain's grip, but with each failed effort, I find myself thinking back to Pater, bawling in the fetal position, in the hull of the ship.

Whether it is the extreme blood loss or simply recognizing that I'm at my breaking point, as Pater had been, I soon feel overwhelmed with the urge to surrender, but against my better judgment I fight off the instinct, *willing* myself to resist until my very last breath.

As though the room senses my momentary consideration of submission, it suddenly stops shaking and I feel Macha and Nemain loosen their grip on my wrists, ever so slightly.

Confused, I lift my head as I hear a faint sound coming from across the room, the sound of a fracture slowly spreading across glass.

Turning my attention towards my bedroom window, I watch as each pane of glass simultaneously explodes inward, showering me with tiny pebbles of shrapnel as I hear the familiar sound of hundreds of crows flapping their wings.

Frozen in horror, I watch the endless murder churn upon itself, like a quickly approaching storm cloud. Suddenly, the center of the malicious mass parts, and a much larger crow, with glowing amber eyes emerges, perching itself at the foot of my bed, cocking its head to calculate its next move, as it had so many times in my dreams.

Nemain turns towards the large crow and says, "*Welcome, sister.*"

Seeing the incredulous look in my eye, Macha explains, "*Badb. The Crow Goddess. We had lost her, but you guided her home.*"

Badb suddenly flaps her wings, repositioning herself to the center of my chest. The moment she lands, I feel all of the air pushed out of my lungs under her immense weight.

Despite my breathlessness, I become transfixed as Badb then begins to unfold from within herself, shifting from the crow that had haunted so many of my dreams to a the form of a small feral child.

She remains perched upon me, studying my face with glowing eyes as tears of blood stream from them, leaving crimson lines down either side of her face that perfectly frame her curled lips and jagged, toothy smile.

I look down at her hands as she slowly pushes her talon-like fingers into my chest, piercing the spots between my ribs as though she is reaching for my organs through a chain-link fence.

All the while, I can smell my flesh burning and I watch as the symbol of the Triquetra is branded into my chest from the inside. The pain is unbearable. I try to scream, but with no air in my lungs, I am left with no voice.

In place of my cries of pain though, ethereal fumes of glowing white light begin floating from the pendant around my neck, dancing towards Badb's widening serrated mouth to feed her with my suffering.

With each wisp of light that escapes, I feel my life not only draining from me, but being *drawn* from my body, weakening me with each passing second.

My heart rate slows as my vision begins to blur. I feel my bones becoming weaker by the second as my skin starts to feel like it's sagging. Soon after, I feel a few of my teeth coming loose, falling into the back of my throat and choking me as I fruitlessly continue trying to scream.

In spite of the pain, I maintain my struggle, but my increasingly frail ribcage soon begins to give out under Badb's weight. At first, I only hear a few audible cracks, but moments later three of the ribs on my right side snap, piercing my empty lungs.

My physical suffering reaches an echelon as my mind and spirit simultaneously break. With tears in my eyes, I finally find my voice to scream, "Okay!!!"

Badb ceases her consumption for a moment, cocking her head as if to verify my concession.

With tears streaming from my eyes, I fight through my audible sobs to shamefully mutter, "Okay... I- I pledge my life to thee."

Macha and Nemain smile as they release me. They reach out to join hands with Badb as the amber light in each of their eyes intensifies to the point it stings mine, forcing me to shield myself from the brightness.

Moments later, the three children disappear into the blinding light, reverting back into the form of three glowing amber orbs that begin circling each other with dizzying speed as their light continues to intensify, warming my skin with its presence.

As the movement of the orbs turns to a blur, a shockwave of energy suddenly explodes outwards, knocking me out cold.

I awake with a start, gasping for air, to find myself sitting in bed.

Frantically, I move my hand to the nape of my neck, expecting to find Brigid's Cross hanging there, but instead, I feel nothing.

I quickly shift my attention towards my wrists and my chest to find them intact; the only signs of wounds being the old scars that have been there for years.

Scanning the room, lit by the morning sun, I notice that my window remains intact and there are no signs of Macha, Nemain, or Badb anywhere.

Taking an exhausted sigh of relief, I try to slow my racing heart and center myself in reality before throwing the sweat soaked blankets off of me and getting out of bed.

Instinctually, I turn towards the standing mirror by the window, expecting to see my slowly withering visage staring back at me... only now, I appear to look as healthy as I did on my first day in the Morgan home.

I slowly approach the mirror, noticing that the bags that were under my eyes seem to have vanished, along with the wrinkles at the edges of my mouth. In their place, there is a warm rosiness in my cheeks and brightness in my eyes that I can't remember ever seeing before.

Tilting my head down, ever so slightly, I soon notice that the quickly growing population of grey hairs on top of my head seems to not only have been eradicated over night, but it has also left my hair with more volume and sheen than it has ever possessed prior.

In the moment, I can't help but wonder if it had *all* been a dream, but as I run my hand through my hair, I suddenly freeze in place.

A chill runs up my spine as I lower my hand and see wrinkles on the back of it, with faint signs of age spots popping up between the distended veins and swollen knuckles.

My eyes become wide with shock and terror as I look at my other hand to see that it is gnarled and withered with age as well.

Turning my attention back towards the standing mirror in front of me, I watch my face rapidly mature, until it becomes the aged version of myself that the cloaked woman had revealed herself to be.

Tears begin forming in my eyes, and I can feel them running down my cheeks, but the reflection in the mirror seems to negate that sensation as it smiles back at me with dark intent and sinister power.

Refusing to believe the vision before me, I lift my hand to gently wipe away the tears that I feel falling down my cheek, but as my fingertips make contact with my face, I feel only dry, wrinkled skin, and the edge of the smile that I see in my reflection.

Suddenly, something in the lower part of the mirror moves, pulling my attention towards it. I watch in the mirror as Nemain and Macha step out from behind me, reaching up to hold each of my hands while Badb, back in her crow form, perches herself on my shoulder.

I feel terror in my heart, but my reflection does not show it. Instead, it continues smiling back at me, as though it is trying to remind me that any semblance of control I retain, is merely temporary.

Even though my consciousness remains within my body, I no longer possess authority over its actions or intent. I no longer have a jurisdiction over my eventual purpose, or the effect that my existence will have on this world.

Similar to so many of the visions I have seen, I am now just an unwilling spectator within my own body, unsure of how much longer the Morrighan will allow me to remain.

CHAPTER THIRTY-SIX

Every Day Is The Same

Every day is the same...

I wander the Morgan home in silence, as the end of my time on this Earth draws near.

Now that the children are gone, there is no need to go through the motions of any 'routine' anymore, but as a small compensation for my willful compliance, the Morrighan has allowed me to live my few remaining days in peace, free of her dark influence.

I pour myself a cup of coffee and shuffle my aching, aged bones to the sunroom, just off the salon. There, I sit and talk to the immense oak tree for hours, under the belief that Pater is still consciously present amidst the eternal form he has been trapped within.

Regaling the stories of my past, I tell Pater about Andy, my parents, and as many good memories as I am able to recall, before I lose them forever. While it does little to comfort me, it acts as a distraction from the present moment that I am trapped in, and all of the horrible things that are yet to come, after I am gone.

This home is my prison, this quickly failing body, my death sentence. Soon, I shall perish within the very walls that have condemned me to this fate.

My strength continues to grow as the moment of my resurgence draws closer.

The veil has been lifted; there is no need to hide anymore. Now I simply lie in wait, feeding off of this mortal shell's suffering from the recesses of her mind.

I spend her remaining days gathering my power and calculating my approach, strengthening my dark influence as my hatred towards humanity continues to grow.

Disgusted by the pathetic weakness of mankind, I listen with loathing as they whine over their perceived hardships; all under the foolish belief that their paltry forms of tribulations are somehow the echelon of their suffering. Soon, I shall show them how wrong they truly are.

Amidst their insignificant squabbles, I can feel their hatred growing, along with their perpetual frustration as a result of their self-induced versions of pain. While I salivate at the thought of amplifying their suffering, I eagerly await the enjoyment I will gather from magnifying the very anguish they inflict upon one another.

This Earth shall be my playground, the people my toys. Soon, their minds shall become the penitentiaries in which I will endlessly torture them for my own gain.

My knees have become old and weak, rendering the stairs a nearly impossible task. As a result, I now retire each night to the couch in the salon, where I reflect on my time within the Morgan home.

While I know that my experiences within this house were all an elaborate fiction, I still can't help but relive the relationships I had developed with each of the children over time and wonder if any part of it had been true.

My will is strengthening as it slowly erases the remnants of my host. As I continue to focus my energy through the power of this home, I can feel my inevitability fast approaching.

While it is merely a matter of patience, I cannot deny my eager anticipation towards the methods by which this world shall be torn apart over time, by way of my triplicate form, now unified as one.

I think back to Macha's vulnerability when she had visited me in the midst of the night. So badly, I wanted to protect her and provide the love and support she needed in order to build courage to conquer the fear incited by her nightmares.

Macha, the Goddess of Fertility and Sovereignty, shall be my left hand. She shall reap the land of all animals and vegetation, poisoning all potable water with her touch. Those who rely upon the Earth's bounty for survival shall be deprived of her gifts as she starves them into embracing me as their new God.

Then there was Nemain, who had been *so* resistant to my presence at first, but as we built our bond over time, it had made it so much more meaningful that she would willingly lower her barriers to me, embracing our budding companionship.

Nemain, the Goddess of Havoc and War, shall be my right hand. Through her, I shall incite fury into the hearts of those who <u>dare</u> to oppose me. The blinding anger she perpetuates shall motivate them to destroy one another, ridding the world of my enemies by way of their own distrustful hand.

I get so lost in the memories that I have to actively remind myself that they were *all* methods of manipulation. The girls had identified my subconscious need for a purpose, and had *exploited* it by appealing to my maternal instincts with lies.

Those who remain shall be subjugated to the power of Badb, the crow Goddess, as she blankets the land with endless fear and confusion, slowly tearing apart humanity's minds with her deceitful apparitions and altered truths.

My body creaks with each subtle movement as my mind continues to churn and my eyes sting with exhaustion. I lay flat on my back in the darkness, staring at the ceiling while pleading for sleep that refuses to come. Amid my restless state, I silently pray for my life to finally extinguish, to free me from this horrific curse.

My power shall become immeasurable as I bleed this land dry before moving to the next one, and the one after that. Each soul shall desperately plead for mercy, which I will refuse to give. Their suffering shall act as dishes in my feast of cruelty, until the Earth is finally cleansed, freeing it from the scourge of humanity.

My head aches as I fight to organize my tangentially fleeting thoughts amidst my failing memory. My spirit continues to fracture until it has become mere dust particles of what I used to recognize as my sense of self.

My anticipation grows as I carefully calculate my plans for this world. This mortal vessel shall soon be mine, no longer weakened by the failing mind of its inhabitant, no longer plagued by the burden of its pathetic mortality.

I lie in wait; comforted by the belief that this will all be over soon.

I lie in wait, anticipating satiation from the suffering that will inevitably come.

My mind is broken. I can't tell what is real anymore. I have nothing left to give.

My influence grows. I shall bend reality as I see fit. I will take everything.

I am losing myself.

I am eternal.

I am no one, and I will soon perish from this world.

I am the Morrighan, the Queen of Nightmares, and I will lay waste to this world.

Every day is the same...

...No day shall ever be the same again.

ABOUT THE AUTHOR

Born and raised in Toronto, Canada, Paul Kingston (aka. "PK") found his love for Horror at a very young age, often sneaking off with his Cousins to watch 80's and 90's Horror Films that he was far too young to be watching.

His parents would often try to dismiss the ensuing nightmares and fears by reminding him that it was 'all pretend', and that those movies were created by a bunch of 'sick people who sit around tables, scheming to scare kids'.

While their efforts to dismiss the genre were valiant, they inadvertently planted a seed that would soon blossom into PK's obsession with becoming one of those 'sick people'.

When he's not working on his Novels, PK is also an Actor/Writer and Sketch Comedy Instructor, living in Los Angeles with his lovely and talented wife, Leslie and his adorable kitty, Lili.